D1269718

The House

on the Mound

Books by August Derleth

NOVELS

Still Is the Summer Night · Wind over Wisconsin · Bright Journey · Restless Is the River · Sweet Genevieve · Evening in Spring · The Shield of the Valiant · The Moon-Tenders

SHORT STORIES

Place of Hawks · Any Day Now · Country Growth · Sac Prairie People · The House of Moonlight

POETRY

Hawk on the Wind · Man Track Here · Wind in the Elms · Here on a Darkling Plain · Rind of Earth · And You, Thoreau! · Selected Poems · The Edge of Night · Habitant of Dusk · Psyche · Rendezvous in a Landscape · Country Poems

MISCELLANEOUS PROSE

Village Year · Still Small Voice: The Biography of Zona Gale · Atmosphere of Houses · The Milwaukee Road · The Wisconsin: River of a Thousand Isles · Village Daybook · H. P. L.: A Memoir

JUVENILES

The Country of the Hawk · The Captive Island . Empire of Fur · Oliver, the Wayward Owl · A Boy's Way · Land of Gray Gold · It's a Boy's World · Land of Sky-Blue Waters · Father Marquette and the Great Rivers · St. Ignatius and the Company of Jesus · Columbus and the New World

AUGUST DERLETH

The House on the Mound

DUELL, SLOAN AND PEARCE

NEW YORK

Library of Congress Catalogue Card Number: 58-5563

First edition

Manufactured in the United States of America

for Florence, Martha, and Anne—
and all the other girls at the
Villa Louis

Contents

Prologue: The Mound

Always the land was there—the rising mound between the great river on the west and the long, sluggish water on the east—sometimes an island; sometimes, in high water, when the thaws came down, only the mass of treetops above the flood. Trees covered it—cottonwoods, soft maples, quaking aspens, birches, the hushing poplars whose leaves talked even on windless days; and animals roamed it—lynx and bear and buffalo, mink, raccoon, busy muskrats who built lesser mounds in the long water, and beavers, who felled the trees that others might grow in their place.

The Indians came—the builders of mounds, those who marked their presence by the raising of land in the shapes of totems: the bear, the serpent, the thunderbird—the proud Sioux and their cousins, the Winnebago, who, drawing westward, gave place to the Algonquins: the Fox, the Sauk, the Pottawatomi, the Menominee, each in turn who loved this land . . .

Beyond the river to the west rose tall, wooded bluffs, and east of the long water a prairie reached to another ridge of hills, green, too, with trees. To the prairie at this place came the Indians of all the nations nearby to sit in council. South, the land swept down to make the valley of the great river, and in the north, winding among the wooded hills, came another river to lose itself in the greater, to flow south to the vast blue water which was the sea.

The river above the mound reached into the north, almost touching another which flowed northward to the lakes, and these in turn reached to country which the white men had already found, beyond which they sought eagerly and tenaciously for a way to the western sea, a passage into the northwest, coming always closer, up the St. Lawrence, through the lakes, to Mackinac, to La Baye, and at last down the river north of the mound, which the Indians called Ouisconsin.

The black robe was the first of the white men to see the meeting place of the rivers—the Ouisconsin and that greater which the Indians named Father of Waters—and he, Marquette, with his companion, Joliet, gave thanks to God, and went into the south without seeing the mound. After them came others —the French voyageurs *and* coureurs de bois, *who, in honor of a Fox chieftain named Akim, signifying "dog," named the place of the mound the Prairie du Chien. The traders came next . . .*

First there were the French, for almost a hundred years. Then came the English, and after them the Americans. Soldiers came up the great river and saw the mound, invaded it, cut down many of the trees on the highest part, and built a fort named Shelby. Scarcely a year later the British came down from the north, with traders and Indians, besieged Fort Shelby, and forced its surrender, changing its name to Fort McKay. The British held it for a year, then with the peace, abandoned it. The heavens fell upon it; a falling meteor fired it, and flames ate it greedily to its foundations. Then the Americans built Fort Crawford there, and held it for a decade and a half, before deserting it in favor of a newer fort to the south. The face of the mound had changed.

Then for almost three decades more it lay in ruin. Beside the long water rude houses rose to shelter the traders and their families, named Brisbois, Mercier, Courtois, Aird, Gagnier, Cadotte, Rolette, Jandron, Hebert, Vertefeuille, Chanfourt, Campbell, McNair, La Chapelle, Creti, Gardepi . . . Beside the river, a warehouse rose for the American Fur Company, and at last the richest and most powerful of the traders looked upon the mound and thought it fair where it lay along the great river, bought it, and had built upon it the finest house along the upper reaches of that river, a house of two high-ceilinged stories, with great cellars on three levels, and a spacious attic, with proud chimneys, four of them rising at the gables, a house embraced by a wide, gracious veranda, a house with a great kitchen facing north and west, a handsome dining room adjoining a library separated by a wide hall from a drawing room, a morning room, and a conservatory on the south, a house with great double doors on the east and west, and broad stairs to the upper floor, with leaded windows of stained glass initialed H. L. D. to face the sunset on the landing, a house to command the river and the bluffs to the west, and the prairie of the dog to the east . . .

And to the house on the mound Hercules Dousman brought his wife, Jane Fisher, widow of "King" Joe Rolette, and there, in the year that the mound became part of the new state of Wisconsin, their son was born . . .

1. To Temper Clay

Spring, 1848

With one eye on the well-lit veranda, Hercules was only half aware of what Bernard Brisbois was saying. Beyond the threshold of the drawing room guests were crowded about Jane, who reclined on a sofa close to the baby; now and then Hercules caught a glimpse of her dancing eyes, her proud smile. In the spacious hall, other guests stood in little groups, talking animatedly. Only one guest had yet to arrive, and he was late, understandably—since Dr. Foote could hardly call his time his own.

The tall, broad-shouldered figure of Bernard Brisbois shut off Hercules' view from time to time, as he shifted position and gesticulated. Brisbois' pale, almost hypnotic eyes under his high, arched brows and his domelike forehead were fixed unwaveringly on Hercules, and his voice, although it was almost lost in the hum of conversation, nevertheless carried clearly to Hercules.

"If what the latest dispatches from abroad about widespread unrest in Italy and the German countries say is true," he was saying, "I foresee a great increase in immigrants. Metternich is said to have written Count Apponyi that the general condition of Europe is dangerous—coming from him, that would seem to be conclusive. They say he's been forced to resign and has fled Austria. Italy's in revolt, and the February revolution in Paris has spread through the German states into Hungary and the neighboring countries. Now that we're at peace with Mexico once more and California's open to us—there's a rumor they've found gold out there, but I put little stock in that—this country will be the natural place to which those who are tired of unsettled conditions abroad will want to come. You know what that'll mean to Wisconsin Territory, Dousman—more and more people coming in across the lakes, up the Mississippi, even overland. We'll have to be prepared for them; I look to a great advance in steamboating on the Upper Mississippi; we'll need railroads, we'll need . . ."

"Excuse me, Brisbois," said Hercules, seeing Dr. Foote mounting the veranda.

He slipped away and met the doctor at the door.

"You're late," he said, smiling.

"If the ladies of Prairie du Chien will have babies without concern for my previous engagements, Hercules, I can't be depended on," answered the doctor. "However, I couldn't very well stay away from here on this occasion. But whatever possessed you to let Jane do this—only five days after the boy was born?

"You know Jane as well as I. How successful were you in keeping her from taking care of the smallpox cases in the pesthouse not so many years ago?" Hercules shook his head. "She has a mind of her own; she wanted this party; I couldn't stop her. Besides, she's stronger than you think."

At this moment Jane Dousman called from the drawing room. "Is that Doctaire Foote at las'? Come in, Doctaire!"

"We're coming," answered Hercules.

He propelled Dr. Foote across the threshold into the drawing room. The crowd separated to let them through. The doctor recognized almost everyone present; he walked past nodding and smiling until at last they came up to an elaborately decorated cradle. Beyond the cradle stood Jane's maid, Eugenie, a dark, impassive woman of middle age. On the sofa near the cradle Jane half-lay, half-sat; she was radiant in a beautiful evening gown that Hercules had had sent out from New York. Her neckline was cut daringly low, and a pearl necklace lay against her skin. Her blue eyes flashed with excitement.

"Well, here's the reason for all this glitter, Doctor—my son and heir—Hercules Louis Dousman II—"

"I shall call him Dédé," interrupted Jane. "It seems to me enough to have one Hercules Louis, but Mistaire Dousman, he do not think so."

"If you can see the boy under all those covers," continued Hercules imperturbably.

"I see him. The poor child's half-smothered. Don't you know babies can be kept too warm?" Dr. Foote reached down and twitched two of the blankets back, folding them over the bottom of the cradle. "There, that's better." He raised his eyes, narrowed against the blue smoke rising from many cigars, to the woman behind the cradle. "Eugenie!"

Eugenie bent forward anxiously. "Yes, sair?"

"Take these blankets away and let the child have a little more air."

Jane's eyes widened, and her mouth grew stubborn. Hercules thought, as always, How striking she is when she's disturbed or angry!

"What are you do, Eugenie?" she cried. "He will take chill—pairhaps the lung fevair."

"The doctaire say . . ."

"Nonsense, Jane!" said the doctor. "You know better. I'll wager you didn't smother any of your children by Rolette. It's time to take the child out of this smoky room, anyway."

Jane's anger died; she sighed. "Always there is some man who tell me what to do," she complained. "Firs' it was Papa, then it was M'sieu' Rolette . . . Now, come," she took his arm, "walk with me," and drew herself up beside him. "You see how strong I am—pairhaps there is Indian blood in me, too!"

Hercules watched them walk away, glanced fleetingly at his son, who lay calmly asleep in the midst of the tumult of conversation, then edged away. He followed the wall, avoiding the knots of men and women, though here and there he was stopped momentarily by a comment directed at him. He reached the hall; Brisbois had gone elsewhere. He crossed it and passed into the study. There he paused once more to answer some badinage from other guests—all old friends from Prairie du Chien, but presently he got past into the dining room, and out into the kitchen, past the cook and the young women from the village here to help with the party, and out the back door of the house.

He breathed a sigh of relief. He stood alone, savoring his cigar. The early April night was warm, and a sense of well-being filled him. The sickle of the moon, not far from new, was lowering over the dark hills in the west, not far from Jupiter, the evening star; its wan light lay at the foot of the steps, spreading outward. As he stood gazing out from the house—to the Mississippi's east channel, so tranquil on the west, just across the long slope of lawn where Jane's grape arbors were ready to be uncovered; to the tree-girt islands beyond and the western hills beyond them; to the mainland town of Prairie du Chien on the east and the island part of town immediately nearby—his town now for more than twenty years, he felt that he had reached the apex of all his desires. Behind him rose the muted sounds of talk and laughter, of glasses clinking, of movement in the house; from all around him in the dark rose the sounds of the night—herons called out from time to time at fishing along the Mississippi; owls called eerily out of the islands; voices rose from the Marais de St. Feriole, where someone was on the water of that slough which divided the island of the mound from the village, and dogs barked all up and down the river.

Hercules stood thinking of the years gone by. He had come a long way since that day in 1826 when he had left Mackinac for Prairie du Chien, as the agent of Astor's Fur Company, joining Joe Rolette at the Company's post. Now Joe was gone, and Joe's widow had become his own wife. Joe dead six years now, and the days of the great brigades of *voyageurs* dead almost before him. In those twenty years other changes had come so fast as to bewilder a man; time had pushed the fur traders westward, scattered the Indians, brought ever more and more people into the Territory of Wisconsin that was so soon to join the ranks of the states.

A soft wind made a hushing sound in the flowering limbs of a maple planted not many years before at the back door, disseminating a delicate perfume. Over to Hercules' right, just off to the northeast from the back door of the house, loomed the icehouse and dairy; beyond it, a little more to the northeast, stood the small dark rectangle of the Company office, surmounting the wine cellar. Looking at it, Hercules' thoughts came swiftly back to the present and Byron Kilbourn's letter about the proposed railroad from Milwaukee to Prairieville—to Waukesha, he corrected himself in his thoughts, still accustomed to think of the town by its old name. He had meant to read it again, to discover if he could all that lurked between Kilbourn's lines.

He crossed to the office and let himself in. Walking in the darkness without touching anything, he crossed to the far end where his desk stood. He lit the lamp and sat down. He put his cigar on a tray. The letter was still where he had left it, face down, under a ledger, meant for his sight first thing in the morning. He pushed the ledger aside and turned over the letter.

Dear Dousman,

Things have moved very rapidly since you were last in Milwaukee concerning matters of our mutual interest. I need hardly tell you, since you foresaw it, that the Rock River Canal project is as good as done for, and the gentlemen of the Company are now interesting themselves in the railroad. Now that the legislature has given the Milwaukee & Waukesha Company a charter, we are planning a formal organization probably early next year—there are a lot of details to be seen to first—and possibly a change of name to the Milwaukee & Mississippi Company, because, pursuant to our discussion, the goal of Prairie du Chien as western terminus of the road is still very much before us, even though we've made no decision as yet, could not, in fact, until we have the engineers' estimates on alternate routes . . .

A step creaked behind Hercules.

He flipped over the letter, slid the ledger back upon it, and turned.

A man in late middle age, indistinct in the darkness there, stood on the threshold. Hercules had expected one of the guests to have made his way to the office, drawn by the light. But it was someone from the village. His eyes grew accustomed to the darkness; the dim light took on strength now that he no longer gazed at the white paper.

"Why, it's Souligne!" he exclaimed, recognizing the onetime *voyageur*. "Come in, Souligne. How many months is it since I've seen you? Almost a year."

Souligne came in, wearing that same apologetic air which had always been in such contrast to the gusto of his old partner, Lapiage. The two men had traveled the fur routes between Mackinac and Green Bay, Green Bay and the Portage, down the Wisconsin to Prairie du Chien for many years; Lapiage was still at it, but Souligne had retired, although he was not as old as he looked.

"Sit down, Souligne," Hercules went on. "I was thinking just the other day—I was going over one of the old ledgers—how long ago it seems that the trade kept us busy morning and night."

Souligne sat down on the chair Hercules had pulled up to the desk with one foot as he talked. Still he said nothing. He looked troubled. Had he come for money? But it could hardly be that. Souligne would have no need to come for money by night, and the very fact that he came so in the dark, obviously hoping to find him in the office, unaware that a party was in progress in the house, was an indication that the matter was of greater gravity. Something serious bothered him. Hercules tried to think what it might be. He bent toward him, his eyes solicitous.

"You're all right, Souligne?"

Souligne nodded. "I think a long time to see Mr. Dousman." His old habit of laying a finger against his fine, thin nose recurred. He, too, bent forward and sat there, oddly birdlike. He seemed uncertain about how to proceed; his watery eyes looked earnestly into Dousman's, as if to fathom what lay behind them; his uncertain lips trembled. "And now tonight I say to myself,

'Souligne,' I say, 'Souligne, it is better that you go before something perhaps happens to you.' So I am here."

Hercules waited, saying nothing; he was mystified.

From his pocket Souligne, feeling encouraged by Hercules' silence, took two folded papers. Hercules glanced at them. Unlined, he noticed, and rough, like drawing paper. As Souligne unfolded them with trembling hands, Hercules saw that there were crude drawings on them. His eyes made sure they were neither plans nor maps.

"I want to show you something, Mr. Dousman," Souligne said quietly. "Just to show you."

He pushed the drawings over to Hercules.

They were of a boy's head—a full view, a profile. Hercules looked at them in wonder. What was in Souligne's mind? Hercules flashed a glance at the old *voyageur;* Souligne's face was impassive. Hercules peered more closely at the drawings.

He saw a fresh-faced boy, with a quirky smile and deep-set eyes. He had long dark hair swept away from a high forehead. His nose was strong. In profile, the boy reminded Hercules of his brother George. George had looked a little like this as a boy. And John something like the drawing in full face. The boy could not be more than ten, if that old. He looked up.

"Who is this boy?" he asked.

"He belongs to Jean and Julia Brunet. They call him George."

"George Brunet," repeated Hercules. Then he said thoughtfully, "But Julia was that sister of Joe Rolette who had no children."

"He was adopted, Mr. Dousman."

"Adopted—so! A half-breed's child?"

"He doesn't look like it. I'm damned if I can see much half-breed in him. Maybe a quarter—if his mother was a half-breed. I wanted you to see these drawings."

"Where did you get them?"

"I had them made. It was after something came to me—oh, quite a few years ago. Now I'm not well. I didn't want to go without saying this to you."

Hercules was more perplexed than before. He waited on Souligne's words.

"Doesn't he remind you of somebody, Mr. Dousman?"

"Why, yes, I thought he looked a little like my brother George. And he's named George, too. A coincidence."

Souligne said nothing, only looked at him out of eyes weighted with meaning.

Hercules grew impatient, but at the same time he was profoundly puzzled by Souligne's attitude. The old *voyageur* had always been a reserved though hearty fellow, not much given to idle talk, always letting his partner, Lapiage, speak for him, as if reluctant to speak himself. Souligne could swear as lustily as any of the men, and, with a little whisky in him, he could sing and dance as spiritedly as any. He sat here now like a stranger to himself.

But Hercules saw that he had said what Souligne meant him to say. How could that have meaning? George Dousman had not been in Prairie du Chien for years.

"How old is this boy?" he asked abruptly.

"I believe he's eight years old."

Hercules could not take his eyes off the drawings, save only to glance at Souligne now and then. He was still aware of the distant music from the house, he knew he should return to the party, and he swiveled on his chair in irritation.

"What do you know of this boy?" he demanded.

"Julia Brunet wanted him because she had no son of her own. But perhaps—I think this is true—perhaps there was another reason." He paused, a little diffidently. Then he said gently, "Mr. Dousman—you remember Cecile Gardepi?"

The name struck Hercules like a blow. He remembered her—a pretty, dark-eyed girl. Two years after the death of his first wife, Margaret—at a time when troubles in business and worry over Joe Rolette's drinking were besetting him—he had been depressed, too—he had met Cecile Gardepi, and for one memorable week . . . But Souligne was talking, faster and more confidently now.

"That was in 1840, Mr. Dousman. It wasn't long after that time she was with you—maybe six or seven weeks—something like that, she went away."

"Yes, I know. I looked for her."

"But only here, Mr. Dousman. She went to Green Bay. A sister of hers lived there. She stayed there many months—almost a year. She had this boy there. Who knew this but Julia Brunet? She took him into her home—Father Van Brock baptized him—and she's kept him ever since. You know what Mrs. Brunet says of you, Mr. Dousman? She's always said Joe Rolette told her one day when he was bitter against you this thing—'He's got my business; he's got my lands. Maybe next he'll get my wife.' Just as it happened. So she kept this boy perhaps because she remembered what her brother said."

At last Hercules knew what Souligne was getting at. He could not believe it. Yet here were the drawings to show. And it was true—Cecile had gone away, come back for only a little while, then gone for good. She was beyond reach now, drowned in the Mississippi near St. Louis six years ago in a steamboat accident.

"What are you trying to tell me, Souligne?" he asked bluntly.

"I try to say, Mr. Dousman, I think this boy, George Brunet, is your son."

A confusion of emotions boiled up in Hercules. He tried not to show by any signs that Souligne's words troubled him. "This will bear looking into," he said quietly, struggling to keep his voice under control, so that Souligne might not know by any inflection how much he had stirred him. "How many people, do you think, suspect this?"

"Julia Brunet knows. Perhaps no one else—I don't know. I only guessed when I saw this boy, who lives near me. Day after day I saw him, and I thought how much he looks like you. Could this be? I asked myself. One day George Catlin came through on his way up the river—you remember him, Mr. Dousman?—the man who painted the pictures of the Indians—that was quite a time ago, a long spell—I went along for a way to guide him when he went west of Fort Snelling—and I asked him to make these drawings, to show you. That was a month ago."

"Why did you wait till now to show them to me?"

"I didn't want to come when others were here. You were always busy, never alone. Since the boy was born in the big house there have been so many people here . . ."

"That's so," agreed Hercules.

"So I came by night on the chance—and here I find you alone, and the house full."

Hercules looked at the drawings again. How like his brother the boy looked! And by the same token, how like himself! He could not take his eyes from the rough but strong lines Catlin had drawn.

"Leave these with me, Souligne."

"I expected to, Mr. Dousman."

"I'll do a little investigating. In the meantime, keep your ears open, too, Souligne. I don't forget a favor."

"You may want to see the boy for yourself, Mr. Dousman," said Souligne. "If you do—you can call on me—you can see him from the window easy if he's outside."

"I'll see."

He stood up. Souligne followed his example.

"I've got to get back to the house," said Hercules.

He put out the hurricane lamp.

They walked to the door of the office together. Souligne slipped out first, bade Hercules a soft good night, and stepped down into the darkness. For a few moments he remained a vague wraith; then he reached the brick walk that led up from the front gate to the house, and was lost to sight.

Hercules made no move toward the house. The last thing he wanted to do was to rejoin the party in his present frame of mind. He wanted to be alone to think of what Souligne had brought to him. He stood there until he was sure Souligne had gone beyond sight of the office, then he turned and slipped back into the building.

He sat down at his desk without lighting the lamp, trying to think what he must do. In those few moments with Souligne, it seemed to him, a little cloud had come up to shadow his private landscape, to temper, as it were, that satisfaction with his life which had seemed to him, with the birth of their son, his right.

He did not want to light the lamp for fear that its glow would draw someone seeking him from the house. Just the same, he had to have another glance at Catlin's drawings; so he lit the lamp again and looked carefully at them.

It was certainly true: the boy was a Dousman. He could even see something of his mother in him. He leaned over and looked at the pale spectral reflection of his own face in the dark pane of the window, his face lit by the light of the lamp: the dark, thinning hair, still worn long, the intense eyes under the dome-like brow, the long, broad nose, the wide mouth, the long, big-boned face cupped by his high, open white collar and the black tie knotted at his neck. The boy's face was more delicate, but the resemblance between the reflection in the glass and the face on the papers was too strong to be denied.

He put out the lamp again. He lit another cigar and sat to think. What troubled him was not alone the boy's existence, but what it was that lay in Mrs. Brunet's mind to keep him secret from his father. Julia had had little use for him ever since his marriage to Joe's widow; it did not matter that he had paid Joe's debts and helped take care of his children—indeed, he was even now sending money to young Joe, up in Selkirk's settlement, in Pembina, and writing constantly for money over and above what he earned there.

If he *is* mine! he reminded himself.

But he dared not take refuge in this. Of course not. He must decide what to do. That decision could not come easily. He sat in the darkness turning the problem over and over in his mind, and his thoughts presently went astray, from the boy to Cecile. How pleasant she had been for that week! He had not forgotten her. Far from it. But if he had to, how could he explain her to Jane? Would she understand that a man could love one woman and yet take another? Would the mitigating circumstances of Jane's being Rolette's wife, and Hercules' own wife having died two years before, alter the view she might be expected to take conventionally?

How could he say to Jane, "Yes, Jane, I loved you all that time—you knew I did—but Cecile comforted me, and I supposed I loved her, too—a comfort you couldn't have given me, short of adultery, which would have left us both unhappy?" Now this boy would remind him forever of Cecile—and after he had almost put her safely under lock in a far recess of his memory. He saw her again in his mind's eye—the merry gray eyes, the voluptuous body, the laughing mouth; he almost felt her hands and her dark, windy hair on his face. At the moment the memory of Cecile Gardepi pushed even Jane from his thoughts.

Eight years ago! How time flew! It seemed only yesterday that he had come to Prairie du Chien. Yet it was twenty-two years ago. And all the events of those years made a kaleidoscope there in the darkened office—the first meeting with "King" Joe Rolette—that great, powerful man, who had been brought to his end at last by debt and drink; his own gradual assumption of control in Astor's American Fur Company office; his joint purchase of the Company in the end; the duel with Captain John Marsh, friend of the Sioux and provocateur of troubles between whites and Indians and among the tribes, too; the capture and death of Red Bird; the end of the Black Hawk War; the growth of Prairie du Chien, and his own increasing wealth out of furs, and his investments in land throughout the Territory of Wisconsin, in shipping, in grain.

His cigar had gone out. He lit it again, and puffed on it, savoring its flavor. There was nothing to be gained by looking too deeply into the past. Those had been good years, although he had waited a long time for Jane. Now the future promised to be even brighter than old Drew, his father's *engagé,* had predicted for him when Hercules was a boy, embattled against the British in possession of Mackinac in the War of 1812. The future lay in Jane and Hercules Louis II and their life together in the house on the mound.

And the boy—George Brunet?

The first thing, of course, he must see the boy for himself. Quietly, arousing no suspicion. It would not do to give anyone else grounds for thinking what Souligne thought. Souligne at least was an old friend, incapable of betrayal. Julia Brunet might be biding her time. But for what? He could pay her anything she asked, and he would not miss it. His investments in land alone had been returned to him tenfold. But he knew even as he thought it that Julia Brunet was not after money, whatever she had in mind.

After seeing the boy, he must decide what to do. But what could be done, other than wait upon Julia Brunet's move? Had he been alone, Hercules knew what he would do without hesitation—claim the boy, establish him publicly as his own. But he was no longer alone. He must now consider Jane, their son, even the various businesses for which he was responsible, to say nothing of certain delicate negotiations which were always in progress here and there throughout the entire Mississippi Valley, from St. Louis—even New Orleans—to the headwaters of the great river on the one side and to New York on the other.

One thing at a time, he thought. There was no good in trying to examine all possible avenues of action at once, without being certain of the boy's identity. He would have to learn how he had been baptized. He supposed "Gardepi"; he could not be sure. And whether in Green Bay or in Prairie du Chien. And what if he had been baptized with the Brunet name? Hercules snorted with irritation. He disliked any mystery, and there was some mystery in this. He could understand Cecile Gardepi's not wanting him to know. It had been the same with Margaret Campbell—she would have said nothing; it had been left to her father to come to Hercules. So they had been married, and Emily's birth had been too much for Margaret. Perhaps he would have married Cecile, too, if he had known. There was no telling now what he would have done eight years ago, when Rolette's health was already such that he knew Jane would not be married long any more before death widowed her.

A burst of music from the house awakened him anew to his responsibilities as host. He must go back. Nevertheless, he must have another look at the drawings. He lit the lamp once more —just enough to see the boy's face in Catlin's strong lines— then he blew it out. He glanced at the face, and a kind of shudder went through him, as if he had seen a ghost.

His cigar had gone out. He pushed it aside, groped for another in his desk, lit it, and walked out of the office. He descended the steps and crossed to the back of the house. He was reluctant to go in, so he stood there, puffing at his cigar.

The night seemed subtly changed. The wind had gone down; nothing but silence came from the trees where before there had been the susurrus of windy leaves. The air seemed charged with impending events. The sounds from the house seemed louder, because the herons and owls no longer called, and only the voice of the Mississippi rose from the far side of the lawn which swept down the mound from the house to the water's edge. Once forts had stood on this mound—the British soldiers, then the Americans at the last. The British had been here at the same time as Hercules and Drew and Hercules' father had been aligned against the British in possession of their home on Mackinac. He thought of this now, consciously, in an effort to take his mind off the drawings he had seen and the implications for the future implicit in them.

But he could not put off forever going back to the party. Already well over an hour had gone by; the moon had set; the evening star had vanished from the heavens; clouds were up patching the stars out of sight. He turned and went in to walk through the kitchen and back the way he had come, among people who, he was sure, had never missed him.

But Jane had noticed that he had gone. Seeing him reach the threshold of the drawing room, she excused herself and left the little group where she had been standing, crossed the room, and came up to him, taking him affectionately by the arm.

"So where have Mistaire Dousman go?" she asked in a low voice. "He should be here—at my side. But business is Mistaire Dousman's firs' love!"

Hercules smiled and patted her hand.

"See, already the guests prepare to go," Jane went on.

The Reverend Alfred Brunson came up to bid them good night as she spoke. The lights gleamed on his high, balding forehead so that Hercules was almost unaware of his piercing, pale blue eyes, shadowed over by bushy brows. He spoke effortlessly in answer to the clergyman's small talk, but he was counting the number of candles reflected from the great chandelier in the hall on his bald head, and he was thinking at the same time of how the Brunsons had brought their house in sections by flatboats all the way from Meadville, Pennsylvania, down the Ohio and up the Mississippi to put it up into a substantial building in Prairie du Chien. How long ago? A dozen years!

The clergyman only led the exodus. Hercules got no farther than the hall. There, with Jane at his side, he saw his guests out. The baby had been taken away at Dr. Foote's insistence; he was long since asleep upstairs, away from the noise of the party, with Eugenie in attendance until Jane could be near him. Now the guests moved slowly past, making small pleasantries, predicting that the new son was but the first of a long line to be sired by Hercules. It was already past eleven o'clock.

As the last of the guests stepped off the veranda, Jane turned toward the stairs. "Do you come now, Mistaire Dousman? Or is there still some mattair require your attention?"

"No, no—I'm coming."

But he did not sleep.

He lay beside Jane in their long bed, his mind crowded with casual thoughts of business, with the journey he must make to Madison to hear Governor Dodge read the formal proclamation of Wisconsin's statehood, with the new man in the office, Jonas Sark, with what Souligne had said to him. After Jane slept, he got up and wandered around the house in his nightgown, descending even to the cellars, which, by lamplight, were shadowed and ghostly—like a man's mind, aging, he thought, and filled with the shadows of all that had been and might have been—to look at receipts and documents stored away for years. But it was the thought of the boy, George Brunet, that kept him awake.

He was up before dawn.

He went out by the west door and across the veranda, which ran almost completely around the house from the west entrance, around across the south and east face of the building. The gray light of morning lay softly on the red brick of the walls he had watched going up five years before, anticipating his marriage to Jane, the red bricks which had come all the way up the Mississippi by steamboat. The house rose proudly out of the grove of young trees Hercules had had planted a few years ago; some day they would tower above the house, but Hercules did not believe that even then they would diminish it. It stood in the middle of ten acres, almost three stories high, what with its deep cellars, its two floors of high-ceilinged rooms, its generous attic. Its chimneys, two at each end, reached for the morning sun.

Grass flowed down to the gate on the east, and under it to the road outside; it greened the earth to the edge of the Mississippi on the other side of the house, broken by Jane's grape arbors and flower beds, brown rounds and rectangles on the near edge of new growth. Hercules walked across to the river's shore, every nerve responding to the exhilaration of the April morning, so fresh, so filled with the smell of growing things—of leaves unfolding, of earth turned somewhere, of water carrying the thaw smell of melted snow from the north. At the Mississippi's shore he turned and looked back. This was his house—it was no mistake to say it was perhaps the grandest in all Wisconsin. He had worked a long time, many years, to achieve it. Its walls sheltered Jane and his son, but he thought only: did Julie Brunet mean to threaten it with the existence of George Brunet? Did she wait to challenge him with his son by Cecile Gardepi?

He had to see the drawings again.

He crossed the lawn toward the north, hastened around the

house, and turned toward the office. Then he saw that someone sat cross-legged before the office door.

It was the Winnebago, Thunder Walker. This seemingly ageless Indian had served as Hercules' ears among the Winnebago during all the councils with the government about the sale of their lands. He had brought their grievances to Hercules and he, in turn, had investigated them and done all he could to satisfy them. But Thunder Walker was more than an agent; he had become an old friend. The two men understood and respected each other, even had a kind of affection for each other.

Looking at Thunder Walker's scant attire—the Indian wore leather trousers, arm and head bands, and moccasins, nothing at all between his bronze waist and neck—Hercules said, "The night was pretty cold for traveling like that, Thunder Walker."

The Winnebago only grunted.

"Come in," invited Hercules, unlocking the office.

Dusk still lay inside. The sun had not yet risen, and everything wore a kind of iridescence, as if illumined by fading moonlight. Hercules crossed to his desk; the Indian simply squatted on the floor, as was his custom.

As soon as Hercules sat down, Thunder Walker began to talk. He had come in from deep in Iowa, he said, from the neutral ground where many Winnebago still were, and at Fort Atkinson, in Iowa. He had also been up along the Wisconsin and the Fox rivers; he had been on the Kickapoo and the Lemonweir and at the settlement of La Crosse, visiting his people. He had talked with many Indians—Sac, Fox, Winnebago, even Sioux. There was much talk of being sent farther west. Was there no end of the Great White Father's wish to push the Indians ever westward?

Hercules smiled. How often—and frequently, how justly—the Indians complained of the white men's duplicity! "Do you remember all those troubles we had when the Indians were still encamped in numbers here in this territory?" he asked, expecting no answer.

Troubles were not over with the Indians, said Thunder Walker ominously. Even now there were dangerous mutterings among the Sioux in Minnesota. And there were Sioux up along the Mississippi; they ought not to be forgotten. There was unrest among the Menominee, too. But he had not come to speak of this, he went on. He wished to ask why the soldiers led by Lieutenant Fonda of Fort Crawford were moving among the Winnebago, disarming them, and making them ready to move. He wished to know why it was that Moses Pauquette, who had been for so many years a ward of his friend, Dousman, was among them —with Simon Lecuyer and John La Ronde and Theodore Lupient, Pauquette's half-brother—also seeking to persuade the Winnebago to move into Minnesota. Was it because of the treaty the Winnebago had signed in the Moon of Falling Leaves almost two years ago?

Hercules explained patiently that he had no jurisdiction in this matter. Pauquette, who was no longer his ward, was now of age; he had worked for Henry Rice, and Rice had a contract to remove the Winnebago from Iowa and Wisconsin to Long Prairie, Minnesota. Rice had obtained some fine land there from the Ojibwa Indians. Lieutenant Fonda had been ordered by Fletcher, the Indian Agent at Turkey River—he was soon to go to St. Paul, and would serve the Winnebago from there, once they were in their new reservation in Minnesota—to help round up the Indians in Wisconsin. The government had not approached him in this removal, so he could do nothing about it.

"When must they go?" asked Thunder Walker.

"I believe they are to be removed early in June, this year."

Could not Hercules persuade Rice that the Winnebago would not like Minnestoa? Could he not make the Great White Father see that the Winnebago loved only Wisconsin?

Hercules shook his head.

Many of the Winnebago would not go, Thunder Walker went on. Kayrahmaunee would go, but he would return; he would not leave his old lands at the head of the Kickapoo. Old Dandy would not go. He would not even appear to go, only to return. He could not speak for old Chachipkaka.

Hercules said nothing. Since there was nothing he could do to halt the removal of the Winnebago, there was nothing he could say. After a while he hardly listened. Thunder Walker's voice went on, now fierce with anger, now lulling, now flat and monotonous, but Hercules had moved the ledger and exposed the pictures of George Brunet. He sat looking at them. In the growing light, the features were all the more unmistakable. He felt that if he should see this boy he might do something rash enough to expose himself. A kind of possessive paternity mushroomed up in him; it took effort to control it. Why should sight of these drawings affect him so? Cecile had not meant so much to him. Just the same, the drawings gave renewed life to that week, which perhaps seemed to him now all the more halcyon in direct proportion to its sharply felt brevity, the hurried, impassioned experience which had been brought so suddenly back to the present from the past in which it had been buried.

Thunder Walker stopped talking. He was aware that Hercules was preoccupied. He sat patiently waiting, with that ancient stolidity so much a part of his race. For him, there was never any need to hasten; time would go on to solve all things.

Hercules turned abruptly and thrust the drawings at the Indian. "Look at these."

Thunder Walker spread the papers in his hands. His dark face remained expressionless. Nevertheless, he divined at once that these drawings troubled his old friend. He grunted.

"Your boy," he said flatly.

"I believe so," answered Hercules.

Thunder Walker regarded him inscrutably; his face had the appearance of heaviness, but there was no fat in it, the skin was tight over his strong jawbone and his high cheekbones, and his eyes were deep. He waited for Hercules to explain. Hercules was already thinking how Thunder Walker might be of use to him in this as he had been in so many things during the years gone by.

"Do you know the house where Souligne lives?" he asked.

Thunder Walker nodded.

"This boy lives next door. I want you to go to Souligne's house and look at the boy. Watch him. See how he acts, how he talks, walks—everything."

Thunder Walker was amazed. His eyes widened. "You want this boy?" he asked with simple directness.

Hercules parted his lips to answer. But how could he say what he wanted? He did not know. He shook his head. "No, no—I only want to make sure. He doesn't bear my name. Just the same—he may be my son."

Thunder Walker gave an explosive grunt. If he wanted the boy, it would be easy to take him.

"Your methods wouldn't do any good in this case," Hercules explained dryly.

Thunder Walker shook his head. The ways of the white men were incomprehensible to the Indian. He made no attempt to understand them. He did not think white men knew what they were doing half the time. Nevertheless, he would do as Hercules asked. He got up as he spoke and started for the door.

"Hold on!" cried Hercules. "Not so fast. I wanted to say I might not be here for a day or two. Stay with Souligne, if you like. Say to him I sent you."

Thunder Walker's eyes gleamed as he ducked his head and walked from the office.

Hercules got up and retrieved the drawings from the floor where the Winnebago had left them. He stood for a moment looking after Thunder Walker where he strode across the lawn. The sun had now risen; the long shadows of the trees stretched across the grass toward the house; already there was the hum of life from the village—dogs barking, voices raised, wagons moving. From the steamboat landing south, beyond the island, at Fort Crawford, came the blasts of a whistle.

I should be going myself, Hercules thought. But he was divided against himself. Part of him wanted urgently to hurry to Souligne's house and sit watching for the boy; part of him feared to go, did not wish to know, was satisfied only to harry the doubt about the identity of George Brunet's father.

But it was ridiculous to waste his time and his thoughts like this. He turned back to the desk, thrust the drawings away, and drew out Kilbourn's letter again. He read it to the end, where he was reminded in Kilbourn's terse words that they would very probably meet at the governor's proclamation the day after tomorrow. That would mean he had to go to Madison before he did anything else; the matter of George Brunet could be allowed to simmer a little longer. Perhaps by that time he would know what to do.

As he sat pondering on the money Kilbourn and his fellow directors would need to construct the railroad, even to Waukesha, he heard shouts from the east channel of the Mississippi. He went outside at once, crossing toward the house so that he could see the river.

Benoit was there in his canoe with a load of furs. Seeing Hercules, he shouted all the louder. He was a big man, clad in the colorful shirts and caps of the *engagés;* in the early sunlight he looked fierce with a month's beard on his ruddy face. Hercules waved.

"Ho! M'sieu' Dousman—do I tak dem on to de warehouse?" Benoit shouted.

Hercules motioned him south along the river, in the direction of the warehouse. "I'll be right down," he promised.

The trader pushed on downstream. Hercules could not recognize his companion, whom he saw suddenly, hardly visible among the furs piled in the canoe. It was probably a *voyageur* Benoit had picked up somewhere to lend a hand for the down journey.

Hercules followed on foot. Sunlight had brought the morning to life. The very air seemed to spring with joy. It was as if a thousand birds sang. Killdeers cried along the river; bluebirds made their chortling, bubbling songs from on wing; robins scattered before him from their feeding on the ground; song sparrows filled the riverside willows with their threnodies—and there were countless songs Hercules could not identify. Ducks flew up before Benoit's canoe, scattering toward the islands in the Mississippi and the sloughs which filled the bottoms in the vicinity of the Wisconsin's mouth, where that river emptied into the Mississippi to the north. The sunlight seemed to draw the blade from the earth, the leaf from the bough. Here and there early dandelions shone yellow in the grass.

The stone warehouse was not far south of the house on the mound. Its old walls were soft in the sun; the yellow stones had faded to a kind of drab cream color, but nothing diminished the sturdiness of the building. Benoit was already at the landing, unloading the furs, as Hercules came up.

"Dis might be las' trip," he said. "Vair' warm to paddle."

His companion scuttled unobtrusively from the canoe to the warehouse and back; Benoit paid him no attention, and Hercules did not ask who he was.

Hercules bent over the furs. Beaver pelts—three packs. Two of otter. Three of marten. And mink. Even some buffalo robes. "These are fine furs, Benoit. Where did you get them?"

"Some from Winnebago. Othairs—you know Frenchman on de Sac Prairie? Pierneau? Frien' of Lapiage and Souligne?"

"I know him well."

"From heem I get othairs. His man Clement, he bring in fine furs from wes' country, where he trap. Dey have dem in de storehouse on de hill behin' house."

"I thought the Indians were gone from that place."

"Mos' are."

So Benoit had been up the Wisconsin. "You came down all the way from Mackinac?"

Benoit shook his head. "I was at La Baye."

"But you never got buffalo robes there, Benoit."

Benoit grinned. "No. I had dem—before de wintair—w'en I was at St. Ant'ony up de Mississip."

Then Benoit had spent the winter at Green Bay. The Winnebago with whom he had traded had probably been in the vicinity of Lake Winnebago, in Menominee country. Hercules did not ask. He was satisfied with the pelts. They did not often come in such quality any more. The fur trade had been in a steady decline for some years; it would last, still, for some time —at least for the entrepôts here and in St. Paul—but, as more and more settlers came into Wisconsin, it was certain to diminish to a point, at last, where it would no longer be a profitable business. In a few years wheat would be the mainstay of the business for him at Prairie du Chien; wheat and the land and the shipping on the Mississippi and the railroad. But he said nothing of this to Benoit, for what would Benoit do if he could not move profitably up and down the rivers and the lakes as he had done since he was a boy? He would probably go west with the trade, up to Pembina or out to the upper reaches of the Missouri, to Astoria.

As was his custom, Hercules set aside the packs of marten furs for his closer inspection later.

Benoit saw him do so as he turned; he grinned again. "Dose are not de bes', M'sieu' Dousman."

He crossed to the canoe, stepped back into it, and from the prow of the craft he took out a small package carefully wrapped in canvas. He brought it proudly to Hercules.

"Compliment of Pierneau," he said.

Hercules untied the package and opened it. The sunlight gleamed upon two fine pelts, dark almost to blackness. Hercules knew at a glance that these were superb, flawless furs. He looked up at Benoit.

"For Madame," said Benoit. "Las' Octobaire, w'en I stop at de house on de hill, I tell Pierneau how—two, t'ree year now—you look for de fines' sable to make de coat for Madame. So, w'en he tak dese, he remembaire you."

"I'm in his debt. These are remarkably fine furs."

"De bes'!"

Benoit was as proud of having brought them to Hercules as if he himself had trapped the animals. He explained again, speaking swiftly, for he sensed that Hercules was eager to be away, that trappers all up and down the valleys of the Fox, the Wisconsin, and the upper Mississippi knew that "M'sieu' Dousman" was looking for flawless sables. He, Benoit, had passed along the word, and so had others among the traders.

Hercules thanked him. This talk of the coat or cape he planned for Jane reminded him that Jane would be up now, breakfast would be waiting for him and Jane. He told Benoit to store the furs—particularly the sables from Pierneau—and to come to the office afterward for his pay. Then he turned back toward the house.

Jane was at the breakfast table. How pretty she still is! thought Hercules—with her lustrous eyes, and her dark hair, and the petiteness of her face! She made a moue of displeasure at his appearance.

"Three time I call Mistaire Dousman," she complained with a smile, "an' each time, no answair." She cocked her head at him, her dark eyes mockingly sad. "Can it be I have los' my charm?"

"I was busy with Benoit at the warehouse." He bent and kissed her. "He came in just before with a load of fine furs." He sat down.

"Ah, yes, *now,*" Jane went on. "But where was Mistaire Dousman mos' of the night?"

"Jane, I have a great many things on my mind."

"When have Mistaire Dousman not many thing on his min'?"

He smiled ruefully. It was true, he might be accused of neglecting his wife now and then. Business affairs pressed him hard. A hundred small matters constantly jockeyed for his decision. This was a time of change in Prairie du Chien as in all Wisconsin. He had to think not only of his own Emily, but also of Jane's son Joe; until recently he had had the two Pauquette children to see to. And the Indians . . . He had said all this to her before, but no matter how often he said it, she was willing to hear it again.

"Jane, I must go to Madison in the night. I'll be gone several days. Governor Dodge is proclaiming statehood, and it'll be an opportunity for me to see several of the men from Milwaukee there. I'll not have to go to Milwaukee then."

"Mistaire Dousman will have an excite' time?"

He shook his head patiently. "Hardly. Business isn't exciting. We'll talk about the railroad they're projecting for Wisconsin.

Such matters. I'd ask you to go along, but the party was quite enough strain so soon after the boy's birth."

"You wish me to go?"

"I want you always to do as you like, Jane."

She pondered for a moment, then shook her head. "No. I cannot. I do not wish to leave Dédé. Besides, tomorrow I am to see a lady. I have made the appointment to see a Miss McCleod who wish to start a school here for young Catholic ladies. Father Gaultier say she desire to see me."

"She'll want some money, no doubt."

"No doubt," she agreed affably. "You do not want her to have it?"

"You do as you like, Jane. Whatever you do"—he shrugged—"it's all right with me."

"Mistaire Dousman give me too much rope!"

They laughed together.

As they ate, she glanced at him from time to time. Something held him away from her this morning, as last night. She sensed it. Some matter of business, perhaps, troubled him. She was too wise to speak of it; if Hercules meant her to know it, he would mention it himself, all in good time. There had never been any important difference between them, never a quarrel of any kind. She could see in Hercules still the brash, somewhat diffident young man who had first come to her home seeking for her husband, his employer—a boy, little more, fresh from Mackinac, who had mistaken her for Rolette's daughter. He had been but twenty-six then, and looked younger—and, by his actions, a stranger to women.

But what a difference his coming had made in her life! He had been so circumspect while Joe lived, so patient! But then there had been his Margaret. And perhaps other women. She did not know for certain. She knew only that being the wife of Hercules Dousman was far different from being the wife of Joe Rolette, for Joe had left her virtually isolated in their house with their children, sometimes for months at a time, and Hercules had imposed upon her a way of life in which she herself was largely responsible for the way in which she spent her time, whether in charitable works or among the birds and flowers in the conservatory on the south wall of the house. And now, of course, there was Dédé.

Hercules glanced up suddenly and caught her regarding him thoughtfully. He looked almost guilty, she decided.

"One of these days I'll have to go down to St. Louis," he said. "I'll go by one of the packets, most likely. If you'd like me to, I'll see Stambaugh about some new clothes for you."

"It seem all my life Mistaire Dousman has buy my clothes—even when M'sieu' Rolette think he pay for them."

"Joe didn't have any money those last years; you know that, Jane. It was a kindness to him."

"An' to me." She shook her head. "Me, I have too many clothing now. There are othair thing. I will think of them."

Hercules made no reply. He smiled to himself, seeing the expression of intent concentration grow on Jane's face. He knew she was already putting together a list of things she wanted.

When he returned to the office, half the morning had slipped by. Benoit was there, waiting for his pay, and eager to go up into the village, where he would likely spend most of the day at a tavern, and all night in pursuit of some woman. Hercules paid him, and he departed, singing in a shouting voice: "*En roulant ma boule roulant, En roulant ma boule. En roulant ma boule roulant . . .*"

Jonas Sark was also at the office. Sark was in his middle twenties, a dark young man with fair skin. His hair was in black ringlets close to his head, save where it was long; his eyes were a blue-black and seemed to dance perpetually to the accompaniment of a ready smile which hovered forever at his slightly pouting lips. He was just short of six feet tall, and dressed with a certain elegance. His long fingers at the moment held a pen, for he sat bookkeeping. He had come down the Fox-Wisconsin waterway with the first boat that year—a roundabout way from Sibley in St. Paul, carrying recommendations from Sibley, who had as much voice in the fur trade as Hercules —and had applied without delay for some kind of work at the Company office, although, as he had explained to Hercules, "I'd rather not go out trading." Hercules had tried him at the books and found him apt at learning, diligent at work, and good company besides. But Sark had disclosed little of himself, except that he had come from New York some years ago and had been in the wilderness since then. This morning one side of his face wore a long scratch, which showed up redly against his fairness. He had made some attempt to cover it with powder or flour.

"Who was it last night, Jonas?" asked Hercules, grinning. "Mademoiselle Famechon or Miss Lockwood?"

"Neither," said Sark, without looking up. "This one is a spitfire, Mr. Dousman."

"You're too impetuous. You ought to take your time with the ladies."

Sark said nothing. For a few moments the scratching of his pen was the only sound in the office. Hercules sat still. He wanted to look at the drawings of the boy again, but he would not do so while Sark was there. He was by nature cautious; he did not know enough about Sark, and he was unwilling to reveal to him anything at all which might be turned against him.

Sark looked up. "You paid Benoit a good price, Mr. Dousman."

"They were good furs. Besides, Benoit is an old-timer with the Company. There aren't many left. Lapiage, Benoit—that's about all, now that Souligne doesn't go out any more."

"You can't do business on sentiment, Mr. Dousman."

Hercules laughed. His laughter came rumbling up from deep inside him. It tickled him to hear this youngster, so new to the business, telling him how it should be run. Sark looked at him aggrievedly, offended at his levity.

"You may live long enough to find out that a little sentiment with the right people and at the right times will buy you far more good will than any amount of money, Jonas," said Hercules, as his laughter subsided.

"After all, Mr. Dousman, the business is in a decline—you said as much yourself more than once."

"So I did. But the fur trade has been declining for twenty years or more. It will take perhaps another twenty—ten, at least—for it to become worthless for us. Of the three of us in the Company, Jonas, Chouteau and Sibley have it better than we do. Chouteau has Manuel Lisa's old lines—he has the valley of the Missouri to draw upon. Sibley draws from the Red River settlement. You'll see by your records that one day in July last year no less than a hundred twenty carts traveling together in single file brought buffalo robes to St. Paul from Pembina. As long as that kind of trade continues, we're in business.

"Prairie du Chien, on the other hand, is already over a century old, and everyone in the trade knows that when the Indians pull back and the settlers come, the animals diminish in number, too. The Indians never killed more than they needed—that isn't so of white men. Today Prairie du Chien and St. Paul are the only entrepôts on the entire upper Mississippi; twenty years ago there were a dozen stations."

"I should have gone to Astoria. Perhaps some day I'll go," said Sark.

Hercules looked at him quizzically. How curious it was that he should talk so often of Astoria—of Astor, of the old American Fur Company that was Astor's before Dousman, Sibley, and Chouteau had bought him out.

"You like the trade that well, Jonas?"

"It draws me," said Sark shortly.

What Sark said did not ring true to Hercules, but he said only, "Business is business. You sit at a desk in any other just as well. With less to do, perhaps, too. It's one thing to be a *coureur de bois*—I can understand how that part of the trade could get into a man's blood—I've known enough of the traders. But for what you do—why, you might as well be in a counting-house in New York."

Sark did not reply.

Hercules shrugged. "We have a great many things to do today

if I'm to get off to Madison in the night. First thing, Jonas—take Benoit's list and check it against the furs in the warehouse. They're set apart, near the door."

Sark took the list and went out.

Hercules left his desk, walked past the filing cabinet and the letter press to Sark's desk, which stood next to another cabinet in the southwest corner of the long, narrow room. Beside it, along the north wall, between it and the door, were an easy chair and a stove. Hercules, made curious by Sark's talk of the decline in the fur trade, wanted to check the number of furs brought by Benoit on this first trip of the season against those he had brought on the same trip last year.

The ledger open on Sark's desk had been begun only a week before, Hercules saw. He crossed to the cabinet nearby, where the journals and ledgers were kept. He found the one he sought, brought it to Sark's desk, and let it fall open. The ledger opened at a page where an envelope had been laid in; it was an envelope upon which Sark had evidently started to write an address, but had made a bad blot of ink on the second line. He had sprinkled sand on it to dry it; a few grains still stuck to the envelope; they fell off with a rustling sound as Hercules picked it up.

He read the name on the envelope with amazement. "Aubrey Ferrier, Esq." The address was too blotted to read. Nevertheless, it did not matter; if this were indeed the same man of this name Hercules knew, he himself could supply the address. Ferrier was the man in charge of Astor's western division, a kind of manager who kept his fingers on the pulse of the trade. But what would Sark be doing, writing to Ferrier?

Hercules forgot about Benoit. He replaced the envelope—Sark had undoubtedly forgotten it there—and restored the ledger to the shelf. He felt sure there might be a perfectly natural explanation for such a coincidence as this, but he could not overlook the possibility that Sark might have been sent to spy on the Company, now that Astor had sold his interest. Absurd as it was, it would be typical of Astor to want to know how his old Company fared, without troubling to ask directly.

But Sark seemed so intent upon learning everything he could about the trade that his very sincerity made it difficult for Hercules to believe that he was here in any other capacity but that of clerk. There was nothing, after all, he could find out that Hercules would mind Astor's knowing.

When the time comes, I'll ask him about it, he decided.

He went back to his desk and hurriedly drew out the drawings of George Brunet. In the high light of late morning he thought it could have been his own youthful face looking up at him from the white paper.

Sark, meanwhile, had set out briskly from the office. His briskness, however, soon evaporated; he slowed to a leisurely walk, unmindful of the fact that he was not yet out of sight of the office if Hercules chose to look after him. Hercules was no martinet; time mattered little to him, so long as a man's appointed tasks were done when they needed to be.

He was not thinking of the furs. To tell the truth, Sark hated everything that had to do with the trade. He could not tell as much to Hercules for reasons he would not reveal. As he walked along, exhilarated by the freshness of the morning—the cries of men on the river, the shouts of the men manning Alex McGregor's ferry and the rival ferry run by Jean Brunet when he was not too busy in his tavern, the voices of water birds moving up and down the Mississippi, the soft, lingering touch of the rising south wind—he kept looking east, toward the village on the island, among the houses of the French families who lived between the shore of the river and the bank of that long arm of brackish water called the Marais de St. Feriole—a slough, little more, thought Sark, now bridged over—to where stood the house of Emile Gaucher—and his daughter, Annette.

He was tempted to turn and go to it, but no, he would not. His job first. Afterward, he would see.

He reached the warehouse, unlocked it, and went in. The furs were there, just beyond the door. Benoit and his fellow trader had piled them in such a way as to make the counting easy—

all the beaver pelts together, then the otter, and so on. Sark left the door stand open; the interior of the warehouse was cold; it sent a chill into him, coming in from the rising warmth outside. Besides, this way he could look out upon the east channel of the Mississippi.

He counted rapidly, sharply conscious of the looming piles of furs towering up along the walls. The warehouse was dark with them, waiting upon the steamboats; their strong musk filled the enclosed space against the time when the boats could carry them away, now that the lake route was all but abandoned. There were thousands of furs here, but already Sark had learned that not only had their quality diminished, but the numbers of the best had thinned; furs scorned twenty years ago were now eagerly sought after, while those of the best of that time were seldom found today. But to some extent the markets in the east were changing, too. In but a few days now, Sark knew, he would be kept busy here, loading these furs on to the steamboats for the Ohio waterway and the east.

The list was correct; everything jibed. Sark moved the furs back with the others, piling them compactly in their proper places, keeping the different kinds separate, in accordance with Hercules' wish. Then, satisfied that he had accomplished his task, he left the building, locked it once more, and hurried up toward the Marais de St. Feriole.

A fence separated the Gaucher land from the lane behind it. Sark raised himself cautiously so that he could look over the staves into the garden.

Annette was there, as he had expected her to be. She had said she planned to spend the morning working over the garden, getting the ground ready for seeds. Her slight figure was bent over a hoe, but even in this pose it could be seen that she was lithe, with swelling breasts which the carelessness of her attire did not conceal. Her well-turned legs were bare to the knees because her naturally long skirts had been tucked up. Her face was small but fair; her hair and eyes were so black that her face by comparison seemed almost colorless. Her provocative, pouting mouth was pale. In her concentration on her task she was not immediately aware of being observed.

Sark clung to the fence, folding his arms around two staves, and watched her. Her lack of artifice only enhanced her desirability. His shoe scraping on the fence brought her head up suddenly.

She saw him.

"Good morning, Annette," he said urbanely.

"So!" she cried out. "You spy on me."

"I? I was merely passing by—I recalled your saying you'd be at work in the garden—let me see, was that before or after you gave me this proof of your affection?" He caressed the scratch on his face, even rubbing a little of the powder off so that she could see it more clearly from where she stood.

"Monsieur Jonas Sark!" she cried. She pronounced it "Shark."

He immediately bared his teeth in a wide grin. "You see, I am incapable of being a shark. I don't have the teeth."

She refused to smile. "I am sure Mr. Dousman doesn't pay you to hang on my father's fence."

"When you tell me when I may see you again, I'll drop with happiness—and were it ten feet instead of two."

"You're making sport of me," she cried angrily. "I tell you, Monsieur Sark—this hoe"—she gripped it tightly and half raised it—"will make more of a mark than my nail."

"Could you be that fond of me?" he asked mockingly.

With the hoe held menacingly, she walked three steps toward the fence where he clung. He cocked his head judiciously to one side and nodded.

"With your arms upraised—just so—yes, that's right—even in that dress, Annette, you're a dream for the gods."

She flung the hoe at him.

He dropped. The hoe came sailing over the fence.

He picked it up and came to the top of the fence again. He held the hoe out to her. "I believe Mademoiselle has lost a hoe?"

She had to smile in spite of herself.

"Tonight, Annette?" he asked.

She shook her head.

"Tomorrow then?"

"No."

"This day week?" he begged.

"If you do not go, my father . . ."

"Ten days?"

She burst into a spate of French, most of which he did not understand, although he cocked his head inquiringly, widened his eyes, and grinned again.

When she lost her breath, he put in quickly, "I thought ten days was too long myself. I'm glad you agree. Let's say this day week, then, eh, Annette?"

She shot an apprehensive glance toward the house behind her. Then she shrugged her shoulders, sighed, and nodded. "Next week—all right, Monsieur Sark. I shall have my nails—like the razor, so sharp."

"It will seem like a month."

"You have said all these things to so many ladies you think they will all believe you."

"Well, almost all, Annette. Not you, of course."

"Of course not me." She flashed another glance behind her and urged him, "Go now. In one week."

He dropped from the fence and went whistling his self-confidence down the lane, hurrying back to the office of the American Fur Company.

Hercules got up in the night and made ready for the journey to Madison. Jane sat up in bed, a shawl over her shoulders, watching him.

"It seem to me that Mistaire Dousman have always to go some place," she said. "Firs' it is St. Paul—then Milwaukee—then St. Louis. Nex' it is New York. Now it is Madison."

"Business carries its obligations," answered Hercules. "I'm compelled to go."

"Sometime I think I have marry not jus' Hercules Dousman but also the American Fur Company—the steamboats and the

Packet Company—and the wheat-shipping business—and now the railroad," she went on, a smile on her lips.

He crossed over and kissed her. "You have, Jane. You're just as much Madame the American Fur Company as Madame Dousman. That ought to please you, though it would be an awkward form of address."

"Oh, you are all time make the joke of me, Mistaire Dousman!"

"I always thought it ought to be enough that you're so pretty, Jane—and so efficient at everything you undertake—and such a good housekeeper and mother—could a man ask for more? Do I ask you to skin beavers?"

She laughed heartily. Her eyes danced. "I say to myself a long time ago—before M'sieu' Rolette die—I would have marry you for those pretty speeches you make, Mistaire Dousman."

He thanked her gravely, kissed her again, and said, "I'm ready now, Jane. I'll be home as soon as I can—in three or four days, perhaps. If there's anything you need—and Eugenie can't serve you—send Jonas. I'll be at the Madison Hotel."

She would have got out of bed to follow him to the door, but he would not permit it.

He took the fastest horse in the stables. Madison lay almost a hundred miles east, and a very little northward from Prairie du Chien, halfway across the Territory. The journey usually took two days on horse, by easy stages, but Hercules did not intend to stop between Prairie du Chien and the capital. He took the high road, which was the military road; it led north of Fort Crawford in Prairie du Chien to the Wisconsin River, where Hercules roused the ferryman from his sleep and crossed the river. The road from there went up a long, meandering hill slope to the top of a ridge. Once there, it wound eastward almost all the way along the ridge to Madison.

The night was balmy. The moon had set, the stars of the winter heavens had long vanished below the western rim, but in the east Venus, the morning star, shone with supernal beauty. Once on the ridge, Hercules rode directly toward it; the planet hung like a guiding light before him, as bright to the eye as any light made by man. All was yet in darkness; the starlight alone lit the night; only the very first blush of day trembled along the eastern horizon. No bird had yet begun to salute the coming day, and there was no sound falling to ear but the clop-clop of the horse's hoofs as he rode along. A faint stirring in the air gave evidence of the rising of a south wind which bore to his nostrils the fragrant exhalation of the deep woods darkening the valleys of the ridge—a stimulating perfume compounded of last year's fallen leaves, new blades and leaves, the musk of turned soil, and the distillation of watery places.

The thought of Jane snug abed in the house on the mound warmed him. But slowly, insidiously, an image made a faint shadow across the picture before his mind's eye—it was the pale likeness of Cecile Gardepi—and beyond her, of the boy, George Brunet. He thrust the thought of them from him; he shook himself free even of his affectionate regard for Jane, and turned his mind instead to what lay immediately before him—the meeting with Kilbourn and Governor Dodge's proclamation.

He pushed his horse hard. Ahead of him the darkness began to thin; he was already then two hours out of Prairie du Chien. The gray rim of sky fanned upward, turned slowly to magenta, to shell pink, to lemon. And all around him the matins of the birds began to rise like a great symphony; the passenger pigeons rose from their roosts and flew in great clouds northward; the prairie chickens ran crying among the grasses; the day was born.

It was evening when he reached the capital.

Madison was a young, sprawling town. It was scarcely ten years since the first log cabin had been built upon its site; it was less than that since the wily James Doty had so skillfully maneuvered that the Territorial capital had been removed from Belmont in the south to the place of the four lakes which was named Madison after the vivacious Dolly, whom Doty had known in Washington. The capitol building—as yet unfinished—stood on a knoll only a little way up the shore of one of the four lakes surrounding the settlement. Streets radiated away from the square occupied by the capitol, but apart from those of the square itself, opposite the park of slender young trees around the capitol building, few of the streets were built upon. Most of them were muddy lanes, far more accustomed to the traffic of pigs and geese than of horses and stages, and forbidding, in inclement weather, to foot travelers who were at all sensitive to difficulty in moving about.

But for all that it was young and rough, the settlement was vigorous, as if it were confident of its destiny as Wisconsin's capital. Horses, wagons, and foot travelers crowded the streets around the capitol park; groups of men passed from one tavern to another, from one inn to another, for there was no dearth of them in the immediate vicinity of the capitol.

Hercules went directly to the Madison Hotel. He rode around to the stables and left his horse there. Then he went back to the front of the hotel and went in.

He found himself immediately in a crowd of people, and stood for a moment to get his bearings. Before he could press forward, the proprietor himself was at his side.

"Mr. Dousman. You honor my house," said Colonel Augustus Bird, his heavy face lit up by his broad smile.

"Do you have a room for me, Bird?"

"We certainly do, Mr. Dousman."

"Is Byron Kilbourn here, Colonel?"

"No, sir. I believe he's at the American."

Hercules was impelled to go to Kilbourn at once, but he was now very tired and also hungry; he thought better of it. Colonel Bird's big, broad-shouldered frame leaned almost obsequiously toward him, waiting upon his decision.

"I'll take supper and go to bed. I can see him in the morning. When is Governor Dodge making his proclamation?"

"At or just after noon, I believe."

He went to his room, washed up, and came back down to the dining room. Several tables were occupied with but one diner each, while most of the others were filled or all but filled, despite the lateness of the hour. Hercules stood at the threshold glancing from one to another of the diners until he saw someone he knew; then he crossed to his table. He had recognized an aide of Governor Dodge—an enigmatic young fellow, darkly handsome, who went about constantly attended by an Indian companion of his own age, although Soaring Hawk did not seem to be present on this occasion.

"Do you mind, Lieutenant?" he asked, drawing out a chair.

Lieutenant Nathaniel Parr looked up, startled, then smiled. Something on his mind, thought Hercules fleetingly. "By all means, Mr. Dousman. Be my guest."

"Thanks. I won't impose on you. I'm staying for the night. Is Sunday night always so crowded at the Madison?"

"No, sir. It's the governor's proclamation tomorrow, and everyone who has an ax to grind is here to grind it before the elections next month." He smiled engagingly. "What ax are you grinding, Mr. Dousman?"

Hercules laughed. "Mine isn't with the governor, Parr." He did not think it necessary to say more of his reason for visiting Madison; what with all the rivalry between opposing groups jockeying for position in the rush toward the establishment of railroad companies, no one could be sure where anyone stood. And Parr might be in a position to influence Dodge or those close to him.

As they ate, Hercules thought about Parr. There was some mystery about him, he seemed to recall, something about his birth. And from this he went naturally back to thinking of the boy George Brunet, and grew irritated with himself that he could not push this matter from his thoughts for even so little a time as the hour of this evening meal. He grew monosyllabic in his replies to Parr's conversation, and presently Parr made his excuses and stood up.

"We both seem to be occupied with problems of our own, Mr. Dousman," he said pleasantly.

"You must overlook my silence, Lieutenant. I'm tired after the long ride from Prairie du Chien. I made it in just under eighteen hours—virtually without stopping to rest." Then, moved by a sudden impulse, he went on, "You get around the Territory quite a bit, don't you, Parr?"

"I guess you could say so," said Parr cautiously. "I move down as far as Kentucky and over into Iowa."

"Tell me—have you ever run into a young fellow named Jonas Sark?"

"No, sir, I never have," answered Parr without hesitation.

They bade each other good night.

Soon after Hercules finished his meal and rose. He went directly to his room. Within a few minutes he was sound asleep.

He got out of bed early, as was his habit, dressed, and took breakfast downstairs. After breakfast, he walked down the street to the American House in search of Byron Kilbourn.

Kilbourn, however, had already gone, leaving no word as to his destination. There was nothing to be done but find him; fortunately, Madison was not large, and he could not be far away. Hercules went out into the square of streets once more, trying to think of where Kilbourn might have gone. Certainly not yet to the capitol—Dodge would be busy working on his statehood proclamation, as Dodge was accustomed to doing most things at the last minute. Yet Kilbourn would ultimately go there, because he had not come primarily for the formality of the proclamation, but because he wanted to press the interests of the railroad, Hercules knew.

He started back toward the Madison Hotel, thinking that Kilbourn might have sought him there. Almost at once he heard himself hailed from the road. He looked toward a rider on a horse; even as he looked, the rider dismounted and came toward him—a slender man of middle age, fine-featured, wearing a slight pointed beard.

"Pierneau!" exclaimed Dosuman, delighted.

He clasped the extended hand with pleasure and shook it vigorously.

"Are you, too, here in protection of your interests, Hercules?" asked Pierneau.

Hercules laughed. "No, sir. But you?"

Pierneau shrugged. "I came down with my cousin, Brogmar. He has some matters to attend to—perhaps you haven't heard—there are rumors they've discovered gold in California, and Augustin is bound to go out there before the year's done."

"I heard those rumors, yes. More important to me—while I see you—I'm reminded I owe you many thanks for those fine sables you sent me by Benoit."

"I wish there could have been more. Will you soon have enough?"

Hercules hunched his shoulders. "At the rate I've been collecting them, it'll take again as long. Three years or so."

"I wish I could promise you more. But there aren't as many furs as there were but ten years ago. You know how it is. Everywhere at Sac Prairie the land's being broken, the grain's going in—the very face of the place changes from year to year."

"It's the same at Prairie du Chien. The fur trade is in the west now, Chalfonte. But there are other things. Do you get down toward our town? If so, come see us some time. You know I've had a son?"

"No! Congratulations!" exclaimed Pierneau heartily, his serious eyes for the moment lively with pleasure. "Someone to follow in your footsteps, eh?"

"I hope for it," answered Hercules soberly.

While they talked, people moved all around them, but a general movement toward the capitol was beginning. Hercules sought constantly for Kilbourn, but in vain. Observing that Hercules looked for someone, Pierneau presently made his excuses and they parted.

Hercules returned to the Madison Hotel. But Kilbourn had not been there, so he could do nothing other than make the rounds of all the likely places in search of him. He set out once more, and was stopped almost at once by an acquaintaince from Green Bay.

It was noon before he caught up with Kilbourn in the capitol. He caught sight of Kilbourn's high, gleaming brow and soft, clean-shaven face in the crowd gathered in the legislative chambers to hear the governor's proclamation. Hercules pushed his way through the crowd, his eyes fixed on the Milwaukeean. Kilbourn was a large man; his soft face was decorated with sideburns which were so full and so long that they could readily have joined to become a Quaker beard and would in all likelihood ultimately do so. Out of his pink face looked eyes of a guileless blue, widely separated by a prominent but not overlarge nose above a tender, full-lipped mouth.

Just as Hercules reached Kilbourn's side, Governor Dodge entered the chamber to address the Territorial Legislature. Immediately silence spread among the throng.

"Gentlemen," began the governor in a ringing voice, "I have today caused to be published the following proclamation—'To All to Whom These Presents Shall Come, Greeting: Whereas, the people of the Territory of Wisconsin did on the first day of February, 1848, by a convention of their delegates, assembled at Madison, the seat of government, form a constitution for a state government . . .' "

At this moment Kilbourn turned and saw Hercules.

"Ah, Dousman, I thought you'd be here before this," he whispered.

"I looked for you all morning," answered Hercules dryly.

Kilbourn chuckled. "Come, let's move to the back where we can talk."

They began to move back through the crowd as the last of the governor's proclamation rang out: " 'I have hereunto set my hand and caused the Seal of the Territory to be affixed, at Madison this tenth day of April, in the year of our Lord, 1848. Henry Dodge.' There, Gentlemen—that battle has been won. Now for others."

A prolonged bedlam of cheers and applause broke out. Many legislators stamped their feet in loud approval, although the bailiffs signaled angrily for order. Gradually the furore subsided.

Hercules and Kilbourn reached a place near the doors where

they could still hear Governor Dodge and yet converse without disturbing others.

"I know you too well, Kilbourn, to think you came just to hear what you could have read in tomorrow's papers," said Hercules. "What progress have you made here with the railroad?"

"With Dodge—none. Dodge will be of little further use to us. He's standing for the United States Senate, and his election is certain. Our man now will be young Nelson Dewey—he'll be our first state governor, unless I mistake the temper of the people. Just the same, I haven't been idle."

Hercules smiled. He knew very well that Byron Kilbourn could not be idle if he tried. Yet, likeable as Kilbourn was, there was a vein of recklessness in him, something occasionally akin to bad judgment—perhaps the two things were indistinguishable—and he felt always a kind of cautious pause in Kilbourn's company. Had Kilbourn lived in European courts, he would certainly have been an ambitious intriguer—a willing servant of a Richelieu or Mazarin or Cromwell.

"You know we're soliciting subscriptions—not only money, but land, even labor and goods," Kilbourn went on. "The canal is done for—I think I wrote you as much—I gave it up with reluctance." He shrugged. "But one must move with the times, and the railroads will supplant all the canals in the nation soon enough without building more waterways. But there are people —I'm frank to admit I'm one of them—who are troubled by this madness in Washington."

"What is it now?"

"The Democrats are screaming for the annexation of all of Mexico. They aren't satisfied with the northern provinces—they insist we should go back and take all the rest of the country. And most of the newspapers in the East—to say nothing of the Southwest and West—agree, loudly. If this keeps up, we'll be in another war, and you know as well as I our Wisconsin development will have to wait on it, just as our statehood had to wait on the Mexican War."

"I never permit myself to be troubled by political oratory in an election year," said Hercules. "You know you may count on me for a subscription—but only on condition that the line from Milwaukee ends at Prairie du Chien on its route to the Mississippi."

"Is there any other terminus that's feasible?" asked Kilbourn. "Prairie du Chien is the gate to Iowa and Minnesota—and by extension, to the entire west north of St. Louis."

Another burst of applause interrupted them.

"Now what is he saying?" demanded Kilbourn petulantly.

"We'll listen and find out."

As the applause died away, Governor Dodge's voice sounded again, with a clarity that belied his advancing years. "I commend to your attention, Gentlemen, that the election is now less than a month away—by two days. I expect to be leaving for Washington just as soon as the votes have been counted."

Shouts and cheers rose again, together with the stamping of feet. Voices called, "Hear! Hear!" Still others proposed an organized cheer for "Senator Henry Dodge."

Kilbourn took Hercules' arm and steered him toward the door. "Come on. We can't talk here."

Outside, in the wide corridor, Kilbourn walked up and down with Hercules at his side. Kilbourn talked energetically and with great enthusiasm. The railroad company they proposed to organize in Milwaukee in the spring would be capitalized at a hundred thousand dollars; subscribers to shares would pay for them at a hundred dollars a share. He was confident that the emendation of the charter to extend the proposed line to Madison and thence to the Mississippi . . .

"At Prairie du Chien," said Hercules firmly.

"Well, in point of fact," answered Kilbourn, "we'll have to let our surveyors and chief engineer determine that. The Mineral Pointers are urging us to go in that way; their Moses Strong has a loud voice in Council."

"The hills in that direction will triple your costs," Hercules pointed out. "And southwest from Madison, the Wisconsin affords a natural valley for the rails."

Kilbourn nodded and went on to talk about his plans, confiding that he had a great vision of ultimately reaching the Pacific at San Francisco.

Hercules listened without further interruption. He was filled with doubts of which he did not now intend to speak. He did not believe that a hundred thousand dollars would pay for the railroad even as far as Waukesha, and as for San Francisco, as an ultimate terminus for the line, it was too remote even to dream about. Kilbourn's enthusiasms blinded him to reality, just as his insistence on the Rock River Canal had done. All his work for the canal was now worthless, but it troubled Kilbourn not at all; he was as confident of the success of the railroad now as he had been of the canal less than a decade ago. Kilbourn's youthful eagerness—he was now in his early forties, but his spirit was that of a younger man—his flamboyance, his arrogant certainty that every decision he made was right, his pride and obstinacy—all shone through his glowing words, convincing Hercules anew that Kilbourn was not a man to bind himself to too strongly, too irrevocably.

"The main purpose of our haste ought to be obvious," concluded Kilbourn at last. "Our only rival is Chicago—whichever of us first puts rails into the west and northwest is likely to grow into the greater city. And I mean Milwaukee to be a great city, Dousman."

"I suppose other Milwaukeeans are at one with you in that. Will the same men serve as directors of this company as served for your canal company?"

Kilbourn shook his head. "No, no—time has passed most of them by. We'll have Tweedy and Holton, Kneeland for sure—I'm hoping to persuade Alex Mitchell to come in—but he's canny; he doesn't say much; he never tells a man what he thinks if he can help it."

Behind them, the doors of the legislative chambers opened.

Visitors and legislators began to pour out into the corridor. Kilbourn took Hercules' arm again.

"Enough of this talk for now, Dousman. There are some men here you must meet. Do you know Nelson Dewey?"

He did not wait for Hercules to answer, but pushed him eagerly into the throng.

Hercules reached home in the early hours of Thursday morning. He had started out on Wednesday from Madison, riding more leisurely than he had come. Just three miles out of Prairie du Chien he had ridden into a downpour of rain which had held until he reached the outskirts of the village, after which the clouds had drawn away once more. By the time Hercules rode across the bridge over the Marais de St. Feriole, the moon had come out, and all was once more serene and gleaming with raindrops. But Hercules was soaked to the skin and chilled when he reached the house.

Despite his caution, the squelching sounds of his rain-soaked boots woke Jane. She met him at the head of the stairs, holding high a candelabrum of flickering candles.

"Mistaire Dousman is wet!" she cried at sight of him.

"I'm all right. Just an April shower. Let me get to bed."

Jane went immediately to cry up Eugenie.

While Hercules was undressing, she came back to their room and began to help him.

"Eugenie have go to make some hot watair. Mistaire Dousman mus' have a bath at once."

He suffered her to lead him to the bathroom and to the tin tub. He got in. It was cold to his feet.

"All I need is some sleep," he protested. "I've been riding a long way."

"A hot bath," she insisted. She would not be moved. "Besides, you are late—a day more so than you say to me. You have much business, eh? And that Indian . . ."

"Thunder Walker."

She nodded vigorously. "Three time he have been here today

—no, yesterday it is now. I say to him to come tomorrow—today, I mean."

"He'll be back."

Presently Eugenie came, carrying two pails of hot water. Unmindful of his protests, Jane pulled his robe from him and began to pour the water over him.

"I have not wait so long to marry Mistaire Dousman to have him now be take from me by the lung fevair," she said vehemently. "Men—they are all alike—they think the worl' cannot get along without them—but the women and the children—of them they do not think at all!"

Hercules submitted to her ministrations. The hot water cascaded down his body and into the tub, warming it. He sat down at last, gingerly. Eugenie came with two more pails of water, hotter this time. These, too, Jane poured over him.

"When you are well again . . ." she began.

"Good God! Jane, I'm not sick."

". . . I want you to meet Miss McCleod."

"Miss McCleod?"

"I tol' you," she said impatiently. "Father Gaultier ask me to see her about her school for young ladies. Mistaire Dousman—she is a traisir! I mus' have her."

"Have her? What the devil do you mean, Jane?"

"When Dédé need someone to look aftair him, Miss McCleod will be that one. An' for the house—Mistaire Dousman, I am convince' she is the pairfec' housekeepair."

"A schoolteacher!"

"Wait till you see her. Someday I will ask her to dinnair, and you shall see for yourself. She is made for this house an' this house is made for her!"

"That will be interesting," said Hercules dryly. "I made this house for you. I didn't think there was another woman like you. Now you've interested me."

"Miss McCleod is not at all like me, Mistaire Dousman," said Jane stiffly.

Hercules began to laugh. He laughed until Jane seized a pail of cold water newly brought by Eugenie and emptied it over his head.

Sputtering, Hercules came to his feet. "Enough!" he cried.

As she dried him, Jane complained. "Mistaire Dousman has not say one word of the news in Madison."

"You haven't given me a chance," grumbled Hercules. "Besides, you aren't interested in what men talk about, and I don't take much notice of the fashions. There weren't many women there, anyway. But I did hear something about Taylor—you remember General Taylor who was at Fort Crawford?"

"Mistaire Zachary!" she cried. "An' his Knoxie, who run off with Lieutenant Jefferson Davis. She marry him, too, no mattair what Mistaire Taylor say."

Hercules smiled. "Yes, that's the man."

"Where are they now? Somewhere in the South, is it so?"

"Oh, the devil with them! I don't know anything about them. It's about Taylor. The Whigs are planning to draft him to run for President—as soon as he'll say which party he belongs to. He hasn't said yet. They're getting out daguerreotypes of him standing beside the white horse he rode in the Mexican War."

"Thirteen years!" cried Jane. "It was thirteen years that they elope! So long ago! They mus' have a family by now."

Hercules laughed. "You haven't heard a word I said. No matter—I want to sleep a little."

"I'll come, too."

He crept into bed and she crawled into his arms, snuggling against him, making him think of her again as he had thought when first he saw her, a girl almost too young to be a mother.

Thunder Walker sat cross-legged on the grass before the office when Hercules came out of the house late in the morning. He sat so passively that he did not trouble to brush away a fly crawling over his face. As Hercules approached, he looked at him with mild disapproval for having slept so long.

"Come in, Thunder Walker," said Hercules, striding past him.

The Winnebago came to his feet without effort and walked directly after Hercules.

Jonas Sark was at his desk.

"Good morning, Jonas," said Hercules, crossing to his own desk.

"Good morning, sir."

"Jonas, go over to the cellars and find me the papers concerning our agreement with Astor at the time of the sale."

Sark got off his stool with alacrity, turned, and almost fell over Thunder Walker, who had squatted on the floor behind him so noiselessly that Sark had not even been aware of his entrance.

The Winnebago grunted explosively.

Hercules chuckled as Sark backed away, apologizing.

As soon as they were alone, Thunder Walker began to talk, keeping his guttural voice low, as was his custom. He had seen the child, he said. He had done as Hercules had asked him to do. He had done this out of respect for their brotherhood. He had seen the boy, George Brunet, not only once, but many times, for three days.

"Yes, and what do you think?" broke in Hercules.

"He your son," said Thunder Walker, nodding weightily. "He look like you. He act like you. He stand so"—he rose and demonstrated—"like you do. He do not say much. He watch much. He has hair like you. His eyes—his mouth—they are yours."

Hercules had really expected nothing else. Souligne would never have come to him in the first place if it had not been certain, he was sure of so much. He got up and paced the length of the office and back, his hands clasped behind him.

Thunder Walker watched him out of narrow, inscrutable eyes. He grunted impatiently. It would be an easy matter to take the boy, he said. If Hercules would but say the word, he, Thunder Walker, would bring the boy to him.

Hercules shook his head impatiently. "We can't do it, Thunder Walker. That's not the way white men do things."

That he understood the white man's inferiority in these matters Thunder Walker clearly indicated by a wintry smile.

Hercules sighed. "Well, there's nothing for it—I'll have to see him for myself—I must be sure."

Thunder Walker said solemnly that he would see even as he, Thunder Walker, had seen, and Souligne before him. This boy was the fruit of Hercules' loins. How could he have lost him? How was it that white women could bear a child for a man and lose him?

Hercules only shook his head, motioning Thunder Walker to silence. Out the window he saw Sark at the door of the house, talking to someone. He had already found the papers.

Hercules crossed to Sark's desk, sought among his ledgers, and, finding the one he wanted, pulled it quickly out to riffle through its pages. The envelope addressed to Ferrier was gone. He pushed the ledger back into place.

Thunder Walker watched him closely. "He trouble you?" he asked, his face darkening. He made a significant gesture toward his throat.

"You bloodthirsty devil, Thunder Walker! No, Sark's a good man—there are things about him I don't know; that's all."

Sark came in and put the Astor agreement down on Hercules' desk.

Hercules turned to Thunder Walker. "Go to the house and get yourself something to eat. Go straight to the kitchen. Say to them that I sent you. I'll talk with you again."

Then he turned to look over the papers Sark had brought him, though he knew what was in them; he had sent Sark only to get him out of the office while he talked with the Winnebago. He sat looking down with unseeing eyes, asking himself what of the boy, asking himself what Sark had done with the envelope? Destroyed it? Mailed it? What could he have to do with Ferrier?

All in good time, he thought.

By the scratching of Sark's pen, Hercules could tell that he was setting down a column of figures. Whatever he was about,

Hercules decided that he was easy in mind. He could not say as much for himself.

Early one morning in May, Hercules went over to Souligne's house. The house was low, of one story, set right next to a path going by, separating it from the road beyond. It was partly of stone, partly of wood, and in the dawn light it blended its gray, unpainted walls into the landscape like something that had always been there, together with the trees and the earth itself.

Hercules knocked on the back door.

He could hear Souligne moving about and coughing inside. The old *voyageur*'s cough had grown worse, he thought. Perhaps Souligne was right in thinking he was not long for this world. He was slow coming to the door. Hercules knocked again, conscious of the smell on the wind of wild plum and cherry blossoms.

The door opened, and Souligne, still but half-dressed, stood aside wordlessly for him to enter.

"You were a long time coming," he said, when he had shut the door. "I thought—after the Indian . . ."

"I know," answered Hercules shortly. He did not want to talk about it—how he had been pulled this way and that, wanting to come, afraid to come, putting off until he could not put it off any longer knowing for sure what he knew had to be. Now he had come without any plan; his curiosity had gnawed its way through every obstacle, forcing him to slip silently out of bed, to dress in the half-dark, to slip out of the house and come here at this hour, without a word to anyone, not caring what Jane would think—but she would know his ways—or what wonder might fill Jonas Sark when he did not come to the office.

"Six weeks," murmured Souligne.

It had been six weeks—even a few days more. May was almost done. Every day Hercules had been putting it off—one more day—but yesterday had been the last, and here he was.

"Now I'm here," he said. "I picked a Saturday because I didn't know whether he went to any school, or what he did. I said I'd come when I could."

Souligne led the way into the front of the house, which was without light other than that which came wanly in through the two small windows. He picked up a chair and carried it to one of the windows.

"You can watch from here, Mr. Dousman," he said. "This way, she can't see you. You can see the yard."

Hercules thanked him and sat down.

Souligne went on talking in a quiet voice. He had seen, he said, that Julia Brunet was very close to the boy—he obeyed her instantly whenever she called—he ran to her with his problems—those of any small boy . . .

But, since Hercules did not speak, Souligne, too, lapsed into silence. He moved over to one side and leaned up against the wall, pulling together his trousers which he had been holding up, and buttoning them over his shirt, buttoning his shirt, too. He fished a splinter of wood out of his trousers pocket and began to pick at his teeth, his eyes fixed on Hercules.

Hercules, having settled himself, sat motionless. He was as tired as if he had not slept all night. To tell the truth, he had tossed about in his sleep; he had made up his mind the night before that he would go to Souligne's house this morning, yet he fought against his decision, as if by turning his back on it he might turn his back on the boy and the problem of what to do about him.

"George is a name I'd have given him myself," he said softly into the growing light.

"Eh?"

Hercules did not answer. "What time does he usually come out?"

"Sometimes as early as the sun comes up. It's a fine morning. Going to be warm. He'll be early."

Hercules stirred restlessly. Having at last come to this place where he might see the boy, he was impatient for him to appear. He had had six weeks in which to see him; he had made no move to come here. Perhaps what he should have done was to go directly to the Brunet house and demand to see the child. But, no, that would have been wrong. It would be better for Mrs. Brunet to make the first move. He did not doubt that she would when she was ready for it. If the child were his—if she could prove it. It might not be so at all; it might be only a monstrous coincidence. But he was sure in his heart that it was not. In the six weeks just past he had had plenty of time to think about it—to recall Cecile Gardepi, to know her again in memory as he had known her that impassioned week—and he knew this was just the thing she would have done, gone away to have her child, saying nothing, telling no one, because she would not want his help, his feeling an obligation. Perhaps she might have intended someday to reveal his child to him, but he could not be sure, and circumstances had made that forever impossible.

He took two cigars from his pocket, handing one to Souligne. He lit the other.

"Why do you just stand there, Souligne?" he asked. "Why don't you sit down? Better still—go on about your work—whatever you do—so they don't think, over there, something is different here with you today."

"Me? I do nothing, Mr. Dousman. I just—wait."

Hercules flashed a glance at him. How pale he looked! He turned away. "I want you to see Dr. Foote. Tell him I sent you. Tell him I send you at the Company's expense. Today, without fail."

The sun came up. Its light lay in a soft peach against the Brunet house. Even as Hercules watched, the light grew stronger; the last of the night was gone. Across the way a window went up and back down again, and voices were raised. A door slammed, as Jean Brunet hurried out of his house and went off to his tavern.

Now, on the threshold of seeing the boy, Hercules felt an impulse to get up and go the way he had come without waiting longer. Once he had seen him, all possibility for self-deception was done with. Until then he could assuage his curiosity by telling himself someone might have made a mistake. But he would not. He began to fill with excitement, a sense of discovery, which was none the less strong because he was convinced of what he would see.

He waited. Nothing happened.

The sun pulled up the east. It lay strong in the yard of the Brunet house. The day was clear; not a cloud was in the blue. The morning air was filled with the sensuous murmur of mourning doves, with the carols of robins, with the high, defiant cries of flickers. Dogs barked. There seemed to be as many dogs in Prairie du Chien as there always were in the Indian villages, and all seemed to be barking at once.

"There, Mr. Dousman," whispered Souligne.

The back door of the Brunet house had been flung open. The boy came running into the yard, so fast that Hercules at first saw nothing but moving arms and legs.

Mrs. Brunet appeared in the doorway.

"George, you come back here!"

The boy stopped, half-turned. The light fell full into his face. Hercules looked at him. There could not be more than a hundred feet between them. The bright sunlight in the boy's face left nothing to Hercules' imagination, nevertheless he fought to escape what was so evident. Try as he might, he could not look away.

The boy began to walk slowly toward the house, dragging his feet, scuffing at the grass. He was tall for eight years. His shock of dark hair was as unruly as Hercules' own had been as a boy—the same hue, the same direction—down over his high forehead. His nose was long, his mouth wide, his eyes brooding.

"He comes over here to play sometimes," Souligne said in a soft voice. "We're good friends—he and I."

Hercules felt suddenly stifled. He thought he was looking across forty years where in a glass darkly stood the boy he had been, and the distance between them forty years, too. I could almost touch him, he thought, but I couldn't reach him. Not now. What has that woman done to him? He was certain, without knowledge of it, that a dark abyss yawned between them, one not of his own making, one not given substance by anything Jane might say, what anyone at all might think.

The boy went into the house.

Hercules pushed back the chair. He stood up. He wiped little beads of perspiration from his forehead.

Souligne waited respectfully, saying nothing.

"The boy is mine," said Hercules hoarsely. After a moment he added, "But I'll wait. I want to see him again—I have all morning—all day, if I want it."

But he knew even as he said it that no matter how many times he saw George Brunet nothing would be altered now, the boy was his, he knew it with the force of a wounding blow. And he knew, as surely as if she herself had told him, that he must wait upon Julia Brunet to make the first move in the hope that she might betray herself. He hoped she might do so now, at once, but he had a strong feeling that, having waited so long already, she would wait longer yet.

But why? Why?

Upon that knowledge, too, he must wait.

2. *Cry Grace*

Spring, 1849

HERCULES WAITED IN VAIN.

Now that there was no longer any doubt in him, no longer any refuge for his willingness to disbelieve, it was as if he had declared himself to Julia Brunet as well as to the boy; he expected her to approach him, perhaps even to strike at him through Jane, if her motive were to avenge what she fancied a wrong done her late brother. But Julia Brunet made no move, and her very silence at first disturbed Hercules profoundly, then lulled him.

He went twice that summer to watch the boy, but resolutely held himself from going again, partly because his pride stood in his way, partly because he feared to arouse suspicion, lest some harm come to Jane and Dédé, partly because to go was a kind of self-torture, and partly also because Souligne grew increasingly unwell, and he did not want to impose on him. Dr. Foote had diagnosed Souligne's illness as consumption, and the old *voyageur* seemed to fail slowly but steadily.

Summer turned to autumn, and soon once more the snow blew. Now it was spring again, the rivers opened up, and the traffic began anew. Young Joe Rolette came down from Pembina to stay a few days, the steamboat traffic resumed, and one afternoon in May Eugenie came hurrying from the house to the office.

"Mistaire Dousman, a man to see you is at the house," she said breathlessly.

"Tell him to come here. He knows where I am."

Sark looked across toward Hercules and grinned.

"Sair, he is a strangair. He do not come on business. He come new from the steamboat—all the way down the Ohio, he tell Madame, and up the river from there."

"All right, Eugenie. I'll come."

Eugenie ran back to the house, lifting her skirts from her ankles so that she could run faster.

Hercules followed more leisurely.

In the drawing room he saw a tall, handsome man, with a dominant nose over a firm, sensuous mouth, and strong blue eyes under a broad brow surmounted by rather long hair parted on the right side. He was clad in a black frock coat and wore a black tie in a bow at his neck. A Scottish face, guessed Hercules.

Jane, who was talking with him, turned as Hercules came in. "Here is my husban' now, sair," she said. "If you gentlemen will excuse me, I will go."

The visitor bowed, and turned to Hercules. "I have the honor to address Colonel Hercules Dousman?"

"You do, sir."

"Permit me." With an almost formal politeness he drew a letter from his pocket and handed it to Hercules.

Hercules broke the seal and opened it. He glanced down at the signature. Senator Cameron. Then he looked back at the beginning of the letter, dated April 26, and read:

My dear Sir:

I have pleasure in bringing to your acquaintance my friend, Alexander Ramsey, who will pass through your place on the way to his new home in Minnesota, to which Territory he has just been appointed Governor. He is a native of Harrisburg, of Scotch, Irish, and German descent. His father was an officer in the War of 1812. He served as clerk of the House of Representatives in Pennsylvania, and from 1843 to 1846 Alex was in the House here in Washington. President Taylor has just appointed him Governor of Minnesota Territory. No man has ever left our neighborhood more respected. I want you to be acquainted with him intimately, for I am satisfied that you can be to each other of much service. He is a man of sense and of integrity with unfailing attachments to his friends, and from what he has heard me say of you, he is prepared to have a high opinion of you. With many wishes for your continued health and prosperity, I am, sir, yours very truly,

Simon Cameron

Hercules held out his hand. "Governor Ramsey—a pleasure."

They shook hands.

"I hope we'll have the honor of your company for as long as you'd like to stay," Hercules went on.

"Thank you, sir. But I'm afraid I must set out again in the morning. There are many things Senator Cameron thought you could help me with before I set foot in Minnesota Territory."

"I'll have Eugenie make up a room for you, Governor. And of course I'll be happy to prepare you for Minnesota in any way I can, although I'm afraid the senator overrates me. Just the same, my stepson—Joe Rolette—happens to be here from Pembina, which is in your territory—as a matter of fact. I believe he may be shipping out on the same boat with you tomorrow—and I'll wager he can tell you a good deal about the country in your charge. Now, sir, I'm at your disposal."

Ramsey held up a protesting hand. "I wouldn't think of troubling you now, Colonel. Perhaps I might rest a little. Then, later . . ."

"I'll see to it at once, if you'll excuse me."

Hercules went across the hall, through the library, and out into the kitchen. Neither Jane nor Eugenie was there, so he returned to Jane's morning room in the southwest corner of the house. Jane was there, waiting expectantly.

"Such a handsome man, Mistaire Ramsey!" she cried out in a soft voice, lest he hear her. "Do he stay with us?"

"Overnight. Send Eugenie to make up his room. He wants to rest awhile."

Jane clapped her hands in glee. "It give me much plaisir to have company!" she cried.

Hercules laughed. He caught her to him, as she hurried past, and kissed her. Then he went out of the room to the west door of the house.

As he descended the steps of the veranda to the walk below, he saw his stepson coming toward the house from the bank of the Mississippi.

Young Joe Rolette saw him at the same time, raised an arm to hail him, and shouted, "Wait a minute, Mr. Dousman. I want a word with you."

Hercules waited, resigned. He'll want more money, he told himself. Always money, no matter how much Jane sends him.

Young Joe—he was always called so, although he was in his twenties—was of medium height, as his father had been. His face was less broad; he had been given something of the finer features of his mother; but his hair was thick, dark, and somewhat curly, as Rolette's had been. He was thick-shouldered, and powerful of frame. In his dress he revealed little of his eastern schooling; he looked far more like a *voyageur* than the stepson of Hercules Dousman.

"I wanted a chance to speak to you alone," said Young Joe, coming up. He took Hercules familiarly by the arm and fell into step at his side, walking north toward the office.

"One thing," said Hercules. "I want you to dress for dinner tonight. Governor Ramsey of Minnesota Territory is our guest."

"Good. I'll dress. I'll be happy to meet him. You know I'm interested in the political life."

Hercules laughed. "Oh, you're interested in anything which promises an easy living, Joe. I suppose you need money again."

"I always need money, Mr. Dousman. I know I'm a thorn in your flesh—but better yours than Mother's, eh?" He laughed heartily. "Just the same, I didn't intend to ask you for money—although I'll take it, you can be sure of that—no, it's something else. I've been wondering about it ever since I first laid eyes on him ten days ago. Where did you get that fellow Sark?"

Hercules told him.

"You're sure his name is Sark?"

Hercules stopped and faced his stepson. "No, Joe, I'm not. What's on your mind?"

"He reminds me of someone—although I suppose time and memory could be playing a trick on me. Long ago, when Father was still alive—I went with him once in a while—not often—Mother saw to that, as you know. On one of those rare trips we had a run-in with an independent—I can see him yet—a fierce-eyed man, quite good-looking; he and Father had words. I was too young to understand it, but I know they were almost at each other's throats. The other fellow started it by saying something about Astor and the Company."

"Yes, yes," Hercules interrupted impatiently, "but what has this to do with Sark?"

"They look so much alike—that fellow and Sark. His name wasn't Sark, though—it was Saquin—Germain Saquin."

"Where was this, Joe?"

Rolette shrugged. "Somewhere upriver—I don't remember. Father explained what an independent trader was; I didn't know before."

"Well, Sark's been a good worker. He's a ladies' man, I understand, but he doesn't drink, doesn't even smoke, keeps reasonably sensible hours, and doesn't come late to work. I couldn't ask more of him. Just the same, I'll keep that in mind. I'll make a few inquiries. Now go and make yourself presentable, Joe. And don't disturb Governor Ramsey; he's resting. I'll see that you'll have some money before you leave tomorrow."

Rolette thanked him and turned to run back toward the steps.

Saquin, thought Hercules. It was a name that stirred a distant echo deep in memory. He stood trying to order his thoughts, trying to bridge memory, but he could not; the name remained isolated in space and time. Nevertheless, he resolved to probe a little—perhaps someone at the Astor office would recall him from the time of the struggle with the independents.

He went on to the office.

At dinner that evening Governor Ramsey was refreshed. He was now elegantly dressed, and Jane's eyes shone to look at him. Young Joe, too, was in his best clothes and on his best behavior; Hercules had some misgivings, watching how Joe waited on Ramsey's words, convinced that Joe already had plans for the governor of which Ramsey knew nothing—and which he would probably not have liked if he knew.

For his part, the governor was impressed with Jane's table. "Madame, I'm forced to say in truth that this table would do justice to any in Washington—not even excepting the White House," he said. "I'm astonished to discover such a variety of viands in"— He hesitated, then added "—in Wisconsin."

Jane's laughter rang out with a bell-like quality. "Oh, Governor, I know what you would say—in wilderness, not so?"

Ramsey's laughter joined hers. "I admit it. In the east we tend to think ill of the west, I fear. We have an offensive self-satisfaction—we think civilization ends with the Appalachians, and of course it isn't so. Just the same, we're surprised, you see, whenever we come to proof of our errors." He turned to Hercules. "But what must it be like, then, in Minnesota, Mr. Dousman?"

"You'll find it livable enough, Mr. Ramsey. We did."

"Oh? You lived there once?"

"No, sir. But Wisconsin was the frontier within my time, and Minnesota isn't different now."

"Are there Indians?"

"Yes—a great many. We've only just moved a large body of Winnebago from Iowa and Wisconsin to Long Prairie in Minnesota; that's Chippewa or Ojibwa country, and I understand from the Indian Agent there—Fletcher—that the Winnebago aren't getting along well with the Chippewa and want to move south. The Sioux are in the south and west from there, and in the Northwest, the Assiniboin. I don't think you'll have trouble with any of them except possibly the Sioux."

"Oh, they always talk uprisings," put in Joe.

"In dealing with Indians, Mr. Ramsey," Hercules went on, "only remember that they, too, are human beings, with as much dignity as white men, and, I must concede, oftener a stronger sense of honor and justice."

"Surely you exaggerate, sir!"

"No, sir, I don't. The Indians are honorable men. Our government hasn't treated them honorably. I saw how they stole the Winnebago lead country. I saw how they mistreated the Sauk under Black Hawk. Nor are the fur traders without blame. But these are past things, although I'm afraid the government doesn't learn very readily. If you have any trouble with Indians, don't hesitate to send for me, if you feel I can help."

"Thank you, sir."

Jane leaned forward. "Mistaire Dousman, he have all time many Indians work for him. He know Red Bird. He know Black Hawk. He know Caramaunee. He know Wabashaw. He still have Thundair Walker work for him. He is all time great friend of Indians."

"Sometimes they're difficult to handle," added Hercules. "Even now there are a hundred or so of the Winnebago still in Prairie du Chien; at the last moment they refused to ship out for Long Prairie last June—so here they still are. Fletcher will have to come down himself or send someone to talk to them. As far as the Indians are concerned, if you'd come a year ago, I know just the man to advise you—our partner, Henry Sibley. He built in Mendota the first stone house in Minnesota a dozen years ago; he was our agent till last year, when he was called to act as delegate to Congress from the Territory west of the St. Croix. So he's now in Washington. Of course, my stepson can undoubtedly be of some service to you." He turned to Joe. "If he will."

"It will be a pleasure," assured Young Joe.

"Only, Mr. Ramsey, you must take into account that Joe's interested in politics himself, and may need some restraint laid upon him now and then. I hope you'll not hesitate to exercise your authority."

Governor Ramsey smiled almost paternally.

"Joe is a good boy," said Jane defensively. "He is so impulsive —like his fathair was."

Minnesota, Hercules went on, was a beautiful land. It abounded with game—the governor would find buffalo still in the western part of the Territory, and elk in the north. Many bear, deer, raccoon, lynx, marten, and game of every description filled the woods and prairies. Wild ducks and geese thronged the waterways and the thousands of lakes, and the fish were plentiful. The northwest corner of the Territory, part of the old Selkirk Settlement, with the post at Pembina, sent great loads of furs by oxcart to St. Paul; the entire Red River Valley was a source of great wealth. The country, though wild, was pleasing to the eye, all the way from the land around St. Peters north to the British line and west to the headwaters of the Missouri River's tributaries.

"I fear it won't remain wild for many more years," said Ramsey.

Hercules agreed. The westward movement into Wisconsin through Milwaukee alone had more than quadrupled in the past year, and the steamboats were bringing thousands more up the Mississippi. Now the rise of another Buonaparte in France and the trouble in the German states would bring even more immigrants to America. Many would come west.

"Even while our own people go west themselves—to California after gold," mused Ramsey. "It seems all mankind is moving west."

"Do Madame Ramsey come to Minnesota, too?" asked Jane.

"Mrs. Ramsey and our daughter Marian will join me later, Mrs. Dousman. I hope in the not-too-distant future, for I don't like to be separated from them. However, if the country's too dangerous . . ."

"I have survive' it," said Jane simply.

"Madame could hardly offer better evidence of its healthfulness," replied Ramsey with a little bow.

"Oh, you make the pretty speech like my husban'," cried Jane.

"Tell me, Mistaire Ramsey, what do the ladies wear in Washington?"

A touch of color came to the governor's cheeks. "I suppose, Madame, they wear all the latest fashions to be found in *Godey's Lady's Book,* which I see you subscribe to."

"Oh, he flattair me!" said Jane. "But it is true—Mistaire Dousman subscribe for me."

The conversation diminished to pleasantries, while on the table the amounts of food grew less. The roast duck was almost gone, the wine, not too frequently replenished, lowered in their glasses, the dandelion salad was eaten. Soon, with the surfeit of appetite, conversation came to a lull.

Young Joe turned to his mother and said casually, "By the way, Mother, I finally managed to call on Aunt Julia this afternoon."

"Good! I do not wish her to think I keep you from her. She do not love me."

"Where did she get that strange boy?"

"I do not see him, because I do not see her—evair since your fathair die," said Jane. "I do not know."

"He was so quiet, I thought he was unable to talk," Joe went on. "I tried to make friends with him, but it was no use. He just sat and looked at me when Aunt Julia told him I was his cousin."

"They say she adop' him in Green Bay," said Jane.

"She calls him George. Says he's nine."

"But surely you've seen him before."

"I haven't seen Aunt Julia or Uncle Jean—oh, it must be six years—before you were married. And then he'd have been three or so, and I wouldn't have noticed him."

Hercules said nothing. A little knot of apprehension flowered in him. If Young Joe had noticed a fancied resemblance between Sark and a fur trader named Saquin seen but once years ago—as much as a decade—how much must he have noticed the resemblance between his stepfather and the boy at Brunet's! He did not want to speak, as if by keeping silent and not drawing attention to himself he might prevent the thought from occurring to Joe. Yet he listened fascinated as Joe described the boy —his dark head, his brooding eyes, his wide mouth, and high forehead. Doesn't he realize he's describing me? Hercules asked himself. Momentarily he expected Jane and Ramsey alike to cry out that, of course, it was Hercules Joe described, but no one said anything. Ramsey listened politely, and Jane seemed disinterested.

"Haven't you ever seen him, Mr. Dousman?" Joe asked suddenly.

Hercules felt himself the focus of all eyes. "I've seen the boy. I believe Julia found him in Green Bay. They say his mother died not long after his birth."

"Funny thing," Joe went on. "He looks like someone—I feel as if I ought to know him." He shrugged. "But I suppose that's a common feeling. I had it earlier about that fellow who works in the office. Now this boy . . ."

"I'm sure Mistaire Ramsey is not interest' in family mattair," said Jane.

Ramsey turned to Hercules as Young Joe fell silent, and asked whether it was true that Hercules was responsible for having given Minnesota Territory its name. "I heard that from Henry Rice, whom I met when he visited in Washington. Senator Cameron confirmed it."

Yes, Hercules admitted, he had named the Territory, given it an Indian name. But it was clear that he did not wish to talk about it, or, indeed, about much else; he was anxious to leave the table, and Jane, sensing this, excused herself, so that the men might follow.

That night, in bed, where Hercules had lain sleepless for more than an hour, Jane spoke suddenly.

"What is it bothair Mistaire Dousman? He have lie here res'less, he do not sleep."

"Nothing, Jane. Go to sleep."

"It do no good to speak so. Mistaire Dousman has something on his min'. I have not live with him so long not to know this."

"Jane, dozens of things trouble me always, you know that," said Hercules patiently.

"I notice at table tonight, as soon as Joe talk, Mistaire Dousman say no word. Has Joe again ask' you for money?"

"Yes. I told him I'd give him some in the morning."

"He ask' me, too."

"Young Joe promises to be as improvident as his father was. He comes to us both for money. He worries you by letter once he's gone. When is it going to stop?"

"Do Mistaire Dousman worry about the money?"

"No, Jane. I worry about him. The money's nothing. But it's time for Joe to settle down and assume some responsibilities. What will become of him?"

"If that is all that trouble Mistaire Dousman, he may res' peaceful. Who can do anything for anybody else? You try it with M'sieu' Rolette—now it is Young Joe—an' you still try. For why you do this? You know it do no good. Now you worry about it, you do not sleep, you let it spoil your dinnair . . ."

Hercules did not disabuse her. If she chose to think he was troubled about Young Joe, he would say nothing to let her think otherwise. It was true that Young Joe's lavish spending and irresponsibility disturbed him from time to time, but he had never lost a moment's sleep about him, and he never would. Joe, like his father before him, would somehow manage to take care of himself.

It was the boy, George Brunet, who occupied his thoughts. It seemed to Hercules that there must be talk in the village, or was it that it was only to him, who knew the boy's parentage, that the facial resemblance to him was so marked? Whether or not anyone else had noticed the resemblance between them, the time was approaching when Hercules must do something about the boy. It was an obligation he could not avoid, despite the nebulous reasons he could adduce for making no move.

If only he knew what lay hidden in Julia Brunet's mind! He could not deceive himself about her dislike of him, which made him wonder all the more why she should make a home for his son. If she had mistreated the boy, in an effort to hurt Hercules, he could have understood it, however warped and vengeful it might have been. But she had not; Hercules had been careful to ascertain as much; Souligne had watched and listened. The boy was as close to her as her own son might have been, had she had one. And if she meant to strike at Hercules through the boy, why had she made no move to reach him?

It was incomprehensible to Hercules. Nine years! How could a woman raise the child of a man she hated, without so much as letting that man know she had the boy?

He turned uneasily and lay peering into the darkness of the room, where the wardrobe loomed in one corner, its mirrored doors giving off a kind of dim light. His eyes fixed on his desk in the middle of the room off the foot of the bed, but this reminded him of the unanswered letters in the office, and he turned again to the other side, where he could see only the window in the dark wall, a few stars, and, spectral in the near corner, Jane's *prie-dieu.*

Jane sighed. "Go to sleep, Mistaire Dousman. If your conscience trouble you, confess it. Ever'thing else will be take care of by time—you need but to wait."

A thin wail started out of the darkness of the adjoining room, and Jane instantly threw back the covers. She slipped out of bed.

"I go now to look at Dédé. He is the only one who may disturb *my* sleep, Mistaire Dousman."

Hercules smiled in the darkness. And how would any acknowledgement of George Brunet as his son affect her? How simple it would be if he were not married! Then he could go straight to the Brunets, claim his son, and not care what anyone said. But it was not to be. Cecile Gardepi was dead; she had never had his heart—only Jane had had it always, despite his body's needs, and he could not hurt her so by taking the boy as he was of a mind to do, despite the clack of tongues which could not touch him but might hurt her.

He feigned sleep when Jane returned, and presently slipped into a light slumber.

May turned to June, and the first signs of summer came to the river and the prairie. Already the hills along the western shore of the Mississippi were turning a dark green, the color of summer leaves. At the house on the mound Jane waited day after day for the arrival of her uncle from Canada; she had had word of his coming weeks before, but now she had begun to think something had happened to him. As for Hercules, the resolution so readily arrived at during Ramsey's visit dimmed before the pressure of events; he found it too easy to put thought of George aside. Governor Ramsey had scarcely gone when Hercules had a letter from Fletcher, the Indian Agent at St. Paul, requesting him to speak to the balking Winnebago near Prairie du Chien and either persuade them to join the other Winnebago at Long Prairie or tell them flatly that the commandant at Fort Crawford would be instructed to remove them by force. Hercules went out and talked for an hour with the leader of the Winnebago band, Maukeektshunxka, who styled himself a grandson of old Caramaunee, but failed to move them; so he reported the matter to the garrison at Fort Crawford. He spent several days inspecting the land he owned—the Mill Coulee Farm, the Bluff Street Farm, and the Campbell Coulee, to which Jane had gone in March, as always every year, to tap the sugar maples there and make maple syrup, now that Indians with their mocucks of maple sugar no longer came to Prairie du Chien. And every week he received supplies by steamboat, and shipped out a part of the furs brought in during the winter when the Mississippi was locked in ice. So the spring of that year moved toward summer.

One night that month Jane started from sleep with a cry of alarm.

"What is it?" asked Hercules, sitting up beside her.

"I hear Uncle Alex Fisher's voice!" she whispered.

"You're dreaming."

A shout from outside interrupted him. "Hallo, the house!" The great voice came booming in from the river side of the house. Hercules slipped from bed, groped for his trousers, and got into them, while Jane put on a robe and made a light.

"It *is* Uncle Alex!" she cried. "He have come at las'."

"He's not alone," said Hercules, who had heard other voices below.

They hurried down the stairs. As he went past his father's tall old wooden clock on the landing, Hercules saw by the light of the lamp he carried that the hour was just past midnight.

"At this hour!" he cried out.

"That is jus' like Uncle Alex," Jane called back.

Downstairs, Eugenie was already up and about with a lamp. She was opening the west doors, beyond which, below the steps, stood four figures, lit by a fitful orange glow from torches two of them held aloft.

There was no mistaking the towering figure in the middle—a great, thick-bearded man, dark and gray mingled with his hair. His eyes gleamed out of folds of flesh. He stood with arms akimbo, and beside him, almost lost in the shadow of his massive body, was a lithe boy, thin, almost frail. On either side of them stood *voyageurs*—Benoit and Lapiage—the sturdy Benoit, his face broken by a wide, toothy grin; Lapiage short, still fat, though not as fat as he had once been, swarthy and oily; his face fairly shone in the torchlight.

Jane flew into her uncle's arms.

"Uncle Alex! We were afraid you were los'—you write so long time ago—you do not come! Welcome to Château Briliante!"

He smothered her voice in his arms.

"Dis man after my own heart," cried Benoit. "M'sieu' Dousman, de dark do not stop heem. I lak dees."

Lapiage found it possible to contain his enthusiasm; plainly he had not relished driving so hard after sundown, especially through the lower reaches of the Wisconsin. At least he had managed to avoid the confusing sloughs that led to the Marais de St. Feriole and had come up the Mississippi instead.

"We came so far, I saw no need to stay away only six hours from the house," said Fisher.

"Come in, come in," urged Jane, hurrying back up the steps. "You mus' all be famish'. Eugenie, Eugenie! Wake Giselle—tell her to prepare dinnair."

The *voyageurs* turned back to bring Fisher's baggage from the canoe. Fisher himself followed Jane and Hercules into the house; the boy came silently after.

Fisher talked volubly, describing his journey in short, jerky sentences. He brought Mackinac to life again for Hercules. How long had it been since he had been back to Mackinac? Hercules asked himself. Fisher brought to vivid immediacy again the route down Lake Michigan, the long Green Bay, the Fox-Wisconsin waterway.

Not until he had lowered his bulk gingerly to one of the chairs at the table in the dining room did he think of the boy. He sprang to his feet, reached out to where the boy stood silently at his side, and turned him about to face Hercules.

"My poor Louis!" he boomed. "I forgot him. He's been with me so long I think he's my shadow. Louis, here is Mr. Hercules Dousman, and his wife, my niece, Jane. They'll treat you well. I'm going to leave Louis LeBrun here with you as long as he'll stay or you'll keep him—whichever's the longer. His mother is dead, and his father was killed by Indians. He needs a better home than mine."

The boy stood wordlessly. His light brown hair was touseled, as if it had not seen a comb for weeks. His eyes were bright and alert, but his cheeks seemed a little hollow, and his face was a uniform tan in color—it had been punished by the sun on the long journey. His mouth was sensitive. He was shy but unafraid.

The silence was broken by Lapiage and Benoit coming in laden with baggage.

"W'ere do dees go?" asked Benoit.

Eugenie hurried forward to take charge of them. "Follow me. And watch where you go."

"He hasn't said anything because he speaks mostly French. His English isn't very good yet," said Fisher. "You'll have to teach him, Jane."

Jane came over to Louis and took his hand. "You mus' be scarcely fifteen, Louis," she said gently. "We're happy you are come to be with us. You will like it here?"

His eyes darted from Jane to Fisher and back.

Jane spoke again, repeating what she had said in French.

"*Très bien!*" he answered, and smiled radiantly. He added, "I work hard."

"He'll make a good houseboy," said Fisher. "You could even use him in the office, Hercules, if you've a mind to."

"Without training?"

"Aye. Train him yerself, Hercules. Once he learns English, he'll be as honest and good as anybody you could hire, I'll warrant you. I've had him two, three years."

Eugenie came back. "Where do this boy's things go, Madame?"

"Oh—yes, he stay here now, pairhaps for good. Let me see." She thought for a moment. "He may have the little room jus' down the hall near to the kitchen on the eas' side. Jus' put his things there." She took hold of Louis' hand once more and pulled gently. "Come, Louis—I show you—come this way."

He followed her obediently. His room was less than a dozen paces from the dining room, and Jane's voice drifted back.

Lapiage and Benoit came in. Lapiage's hard eyes fell to the table, to which Giselle had begun to bring food.

"I suppose we should be on our way now, Mr. Fisher," he said.

"No, no," cried Hercules, "you'll stay and eat with us."

"In de kitchen, den," said Benoit.

"Nonsense! Do you men think because I've changed houses I've changed my feathers?" asked Hercules. "You'll eat with us here at this table."

"But, M'sieu' Dousman, we are not dress'," protested Benoit.

"Neither are we," said Hercules.

Jane and the boy came back into the room.

"Of course you mus' stay—jus' as you are," she said. "You have paddle' vair' hard to bring me my uncle—you are pairhaps more hungry than he." She turned to the boy. "Come, Louis—you sit here, beside me. Tomorrow I begin to teach you the English, so we may all talk togethair." She called to the kitchen: "Giselle! Eugenie! We are ready to eat."

Giselle followed hard upon her words with a great platter of fried ham. Eugenie came after her with another of fried eggs.

Without further argument Lapiage and Benoit sat down to the table.

Outside, in the windy night, Jonas Sark and Annette Gaucher passed by on the east, on their way to the Gaucher home. From where they walked, Sark saw the lights in the house on the mound. He stopped in wonderment.

"Look at that!" he cried.

"Perhaps they have a party," said Annette.

Sark shook his head. "He'd have said something. One never knows what goes on next."

"Do you like to work for him, Jonas?"

He nodded vigorously. "But I won't stay. Some day I'll go—that way." He gestured to the west. "And when I go, will you go along?"

Annette shook her head.

"Is that no or yes?"

"Neither. I haven't made up my mind."

"Perhaps I'd better take you back where we were."

"Among all those gravestones!" she cried. "I think you did deliberately take me to the French cemetery to frighten me—and you learned I don't scare easily. Besides, one has nothing to fear from the dead—only the living, like you, Jonas."

He stood looking west to the house on the mound. The night was mellow. The soft southwest wind bore on it the musk of the sloughs along the Mississippi, the perfume of locusts in blossom.

In the east, the waning moon shone orange. All the night was still, save for whippoorwills and herons calling from along the river, and the occasional *cree-ee* of a wood duck.

"What can have happened?" he wondered aloud. "I know the house was dark when we went by before."

"If I'm not home soon—if my father hears me—you'll have more than Mr. Dousman's lights to think about," said Annette impatiently. "Come on."

Sark made no protest. He allowed himself to be drawn along, but his thoughts were elsewhere. He had several times of late seen Mr. Dousman looking at him with such speculation that he wondered if there were any reason to think he had been found out. Hercules could have no dissatisfaction with his work; he had learned enough now so that he could go at any time into the West and find no trouble obtaining a position with the Astor outfit in Astoria. But something held him back; he was not yet ready; in part it was Annette, in part the too easy acceptance of his comfort here.

They moved silently through the moonlit darkness, pausing now and then to kiss. In the past year Sark had grown so fond of Annette that he had ceased to pay much attention to other women, although he would not say as much to Annette. They were late tonight—they were not often so late; but time had passed so fleetly in the cemetery where the wind had held off the mosquitoes that, as for the dead all around them, time had lost its meaning for them.

And time had blunted the edge of his compulsive drive, the purpose of his coming to Prairie du Chien, and of his yearning for Astoria.

One morning, a week later, as Hercules walked in the village, he approached the steepled structure of St. Gabriel's. He paused to admire again the little church's classic lines, the work of its former rector, Father Samuel Mazzuchelli, the hot-eyed Italian whose second love had been architecture. It was more than a decade now, thought Hercules, since he had witnessed the deed in the priest's company, after giving him the land for the church. Mazzuchelli had gone on to begin a college at Sinsinawa Mound, and then he had gone from there. Where was he now? Someone had spoken of him as in Kentucky—far from Prairie du Chien and Iowa, the country which had known the priest best. Hercules felt again that the past years were slipping too swiftly from his grasp.

At this moment the church doors opened, and the people who had been attending early Mass came out. There were not many. Hercules would have hurried past had he not suddenly seen Julia Brunet—and the boy at her side. He stood where he was until he saw that they had turned in his direction. Then he walked slowly forward, watching the woman rather than the boy.

She saw him when they were less than twenty paces apart.

Hercules touched his hat. "Good morning, Julia."

She stopped before him, holding the boy by the hand. "Mistaire Dousman, I thank you to let my nephew pay his respects to me."

"Don't thank me, Julia. The boy's his own master. I pity anyone who tries to order him about."

"Why, then, has he not come to see me before this if not because you keep him away?"

Hercules shrugged. "You ought to know young people, Julia. Even his mother sees less of him than she would like. Now he's gone again—back to Pembina, perhaps. Who knows? He went with Governor Ramsey of Minnesota Territory—and with his eye on the first chance to get into politics himself."

"Joe should not have died," said Mrs. Brunet with an edge of scorn in her voice, her black eyes snapping. "He would know how to handle Young Joe."

Hercules wanted to say that her brother had not been able to manage his business nor his family for years before his death, but he held the words back. There was nothing to be gained by antagonizing her any further, for clearly she held an opposite view. She had never made any move to help her brother when troubles beset him, perhaps because she had never had the means;

but at least she could have shared Joe's problems by giving comfort to her sister-in-law. But no, she had permitted Jane to lean on Hercules.

"We told Joe each time he came home to call on you and Jean. We said to him he must not neglect his relatives."

Julia Brunet tossed her dark head. "It is easy to say, but he do not come."

"I think sometimes he comes home only to ask for money," said Hercules frankly.

"You do not give it him?"

"Of course if he needs it, we give it to him."

"So! Jus' so it was with Joe, his papa. You spoil the boy, jus' as you spoil' the fathair!"

Hercules smiled mirthlessly. "No matter which course I took, it would be wrong with you, wouldn't it, Julia?"

Now for the first time he allowed his eyes to drop to the boy. George looked at him out of grave eyes. There was not a hint of expression on his face; it might have been a mask. He stood still, clinging to Mrs. Brunet's hand, looking fixedly at Hercules. Hercules could see Cecile looking out of his eyes, but the rest of him wore his own youthful face.

He looked up. Julia Brunet had observed his glance. A little smile touched her lips, and in her dark eyes there was an unmistakable glint of triumph. He met her gaze tranquilly. Now is the time for her to declare herself, he thought.

Her mouth pursed into a straight line, emphasizing the growing wrinkles radiating from her lips. Her hand tightened on the boy's, and she moved to step around Hercules.

"Come, George," she said.

Hercules did not risk a glance after them, lest other eyes be watching. He went on, keeping his gaze in front of him. But he was shaken. Perhaps she knew that he wondered—possibly even suspected—but she gave no clue to her plans for the boy. Or for Hercules, for he was sure she had considered him when she took the boy.

As he went on, a slow anger grew in him, born of the frustration which tied his hands. He was not accustomed to this; he was a man of action, not one to sit waiting upon such events as this. Soon, he promised himself, something must happen.

On the last day of that spring, late in the afternoon, a boy came running to the office of the American Fur Company, darted inside, past Sark, to Hercules' side.

"Mr. Dousman—Dr. Foote says to come quick," he said breathlessly.

"Come where?"

"Mr. Souligne's place." He waited only to see Hercules rise from his chair then he turned to go out again, resuming his explanation. "He's real sick. He asked for you."

In passing, Hercules told Sark to tell Jane where he had gone, then he hastened after the boy.

Dr. Foote met him at the door. He shook his head, and motioned toward Souligne's narrow little bedroom, which opened out into the sitting room from which Hercules had watched George Brunet several times. Hercules went through to the bedside.

Already the house was shadowed. Clouds had come up over the westering sun, darkening the sky, threatening rain; they were built up into great thunderheads over the hills west of the Mississippi, and now their shadows lay upon the house of Souligne and all that part of Prairie du Chien, though to the east the bluffs still shone with sunlight. Souligne lay in his bed in this cloud darkness as if he had already been given over to the last dark.

He was thin and wasted. Hercules silently rebuked himself for not having come to see him before this. He had known of his illness for a long time.

"Mr. Dousman." Souligne's voice was barely more than a whisper.

Hercules pulled a chair over to the side of the bed and sat down. "I'm sorry to find you like this, Souligne."

"I knew it was coming," said Souligne. "It's no matter."

"Is there anything I can do for you, Souligne?"

"Yes. I think of you—Lapiage is gone out again. Benoit, too. Say to them I thought of them. Those were the good years." He rested for a little while. Hercules was aware of Dr. Foote standing at the threshold of the room. "Doctor," said Souligne in a peevish voice, "I want to talk to Mr. Dousman alone."

Dr. Foote withdrew.

The effort of speaking seemed to have exhausted Souligne. He coughed a little, then lay quiet, breathing loudly in the silent room. Outside the clouds thickened, grew blacker as the storm approached, and the room grew more dark. Souligne seemed to recede visibly into the past. His thin body made scarce a mound in the bed, his eyes were dark pools, his face, always narrow and thin, seemed but skin drawn over fine bones. Watching him, Hercules was reminded of his familiar gesture of placing one finger alongside his nose; Souligne was too weak to make it now. In a few moments he spoke again.

"Mr. Dousman—this house. I have no one. Perhaps in Canada, I don't know. It's many years since I've gone there. I want you to have it."

"But I already own thousands of acres, Souligne," protested Hercules, astonished and touched.

"Don't interrupt me—I don't have much time. There's some money, too. That's for Lapiage, for our old friendship. Now reach under the mattress—there, at my feet—the paper's there."

Hercules groped for the paper Souligne had written.

"So you can keep on watching the boy—your son."

Hercules shook his head. "It's no good to watch him, Souligne. It adds up to nothing. I'm satisfied."

"You'll want him. You'll see," said Souligne.

Hercules made no answer.

"I was afraid when the cough began what it was," said Souligne then. "Two years. A long time to die." He sighed. Then, after a moment, he added, "Tell the doctor to go, Mr. Dousman. He needn't stay."

Hercules got up and went out to where Dr. Foote stood on

the back stoop watching the storm drawing in over the valley of the Mississippi.

"Has he had the priest?" asked Hercules.

Dr. Foote nodded.

"I'll stay with him, then. Unless it'll take quite a while."

Dr. Foote shrugged. "Not more than an hour, I'd guess, Mr. Dousman. Sure you want to stay?"

"It's the least I can do."

He went back to the bedroom.

Souligne still lay, breathing shallowly, otherwise motionless. Aware of Hercules, he roused himself and asked, "The paper?"

"I have it."

"Put it in your pocket. When the time comes, read it." He strove to push himself up on his elbow, but he was too weak. "Why is it so dark in here?"

"There's a storm coming up. It's likely to break any minute."

Souligne rolled this knowledge about in his thoughts. "I remember once," he began, speaking jerkily and coughing, "a long time ago—we had just left Pierneau's place on Sac Prairie—we were down the Wisconsin, past those bluffs where Black Hawk fought that time—sixteen years ago, that was how long—a storm came on us, Lapiage and I—we couldn't get to shore in time, to get under the canoe—we were soaked—had to stop, build fire, dry out . . ."

Thunder rolled outside. It came off the hills along the Mississippi, bounded over the broad river, shattered the waiting hush of the village. Lightning flashed. Presently came the first tentative drops splashing against the house, then the downpour.

From time to time, Souligne roused himself to ask whether Hercules was still there. Each time, on being reassured, he would recall some memory remote in the past—of his childhood in Canada, of the bustle of Mackinac in the season, of Indians, and the fur trade—bringing back his life a little at a time.

Hercules listened, thinking how strange it was to hear a dying man speak of the things that were meaningful to him. Nothing of recent years was in Souligne's talk—only the far years, those gone long ago, the years of his childhood and youth, his young manhood.

"This boy," said Hercules suddenly. "This son of mine . . ."

"George Brunet, she calls him," said Souligne.

"Did you ever talk much with him?"

"He came sometimes—he played here—we were good friends. She didn't care. But he never spoke much. A strange boy—much to himself. But in every other way your son, Mr. Dousman."

The storm spread low over the village. The room was almost dark. Only the white sheet on the bed, turned back over the brown quilt, and Souligne's face dark on the pillow, stood out in the room. Hercules sat listening to the storm as it spent itself, and Souligne listened, too, speaking less often.

But his intervals of speech were shorter now—only a few words—always with much effort. And his breathing, which Hercules could not help hearing, changed slowly to deep draughts, and the breath issued from Souligne's lips in long-drawn-out sighs. Souligne seemed to sleep; he was no longer aware of Hercules' presence, and from time to time Hercules went out to the back door to look at the storm. Most of it had moved east now, the wild waving of the wind-bent trees had stopped, and a light was beginning to shine behind the thinning clouds in the west, in contrast to the retreating clouds black along the eastern rim. Everything lay wet and gleaming, and pools of water stood in the road.

Just as the sunlight broke through to shine redly upon the village at setting, Souligne died. Hercules had come back from the doorway and had taken his place once more at the bedside when he was aware that Souligne no longer breathed.

He got up again at once, leaned over, and closed Souligne's eyes, then drew the sheet up over his face. He looked at Souligne's clock. He had been there a little more than two hours. He set out immediately for Dr. Foote's, stopping on the way to notify Father Gaultier that Souligne had died. Since Souligne had no known relatives, the funeral could be held next day.

That evening he went to the office to read the paper Souligne had bidden him to take. It had not been sealed, and was badly wrinkled, from having been under the mattress so long. Yet it must have been written within the last year. Yes, there was a date—"Feb'y. 7, 1849"—barely legible. The will was written in pencil.

I, Amable Souligne, being made aware that I am about to die, wish it to be known that I desire these things to be done. Some money, kept in a leather pouch in my cupboard, is to be given to my old friend, Lapiage, after expense of my funeral has been taken from it. He may have also any of my other effects he likes, other than my house. What is left shall be given to the poor.

My house and land shall be given to Hercules L. Dousman, to do with as he may like. In return for the same, he shall have some Masses read for me. Mr. Dousman shall see that these wishes are carried out.

Amable Souligne.

A simple document, admirably clear.

Would not people wonder that Souligne should bestow his home upon a man who already owned so much property? Hercules asked himself.

He looked at the will again. It would be easy to make alterations in it. He could imitate Souligne's handwriting, especially since the will had been written with such manifest effort.

Carefully he erased his name from the bequest of house and land, and with infinite pains wrote in "George Brunet."

All in good time he would make it public, but only after he had satisfied all the other directions of the will.

3. Leave to Ponder

Autumn, 1849-Spring, 1850

STAMBAUGH WENT DOWN TO THE BOAT WITH HERCULES. IT was too early to open the store, he maintained, and the October morning was so pleasant that it was good to be out in it before the day's confinement. Besides, Hercules was a customer of many years' standing. Stambaugh was a tall, saturnine man, with a sharp look about him, gaunt-faced, with a kind of tic below one eye, which caused his skin to twitch from time to time. His hair was graying, and he walked with hands clasped behind him, in the manner of a man given to age.

"I said to myself the other day," he said in his reedy voice, "it's more than twenty years that Hercules Dousman has been buying from me. I remember you sort of took over Joe Rolette's account." He chuckled. "Then his wife, eh? Oh, all right and proper—don't mistake me, I don't mean any disrespect."

"Don't apologize," said Hercules shortly. "Just don't forget to send those new dresses for Madame before we freeze in for the winter."

"If they get here in time, Mr. Dousman, certainly," said Stambaugh. "How have you found St. Louis, sir?"

"Growing—as is all the Middle West."

" 'Middle West,' " repeated Stambaugh, tasting the words. "Now, that's good. St. Louis has always been the gateway to the

West—I suppose, when you think it over, we're not the West at all."

"Far from it."

They reached the docks. Here, for all the bustle of activity, the hour might have been midday. The river outward from the landing was a sea of stacks, most of them belching black smoke into the morning sun. Some barges were to be seen, but not a keelboat, not a flatboat, not a bateau was in sight. The Mississippi, which had once been the province of canoes and bateaux, then of pirogues and keelboats and flatboats, was now the domain of steamboats. Even as keelboats had once increased travel and commerce on the river, so now the steamboats were bringing vastly greater traffic to all the rivers in the Middle West. The sea of smokestacks was testimony of the steamboat's popularity.

Observing Hercules' calculating glance, Stambaugh hastened to say, "Most of these are for the upper Mississippi trade, Mr. Dousman. Fully seven hundred boats docked here last year—all from the upper Mississippi—and that was just about a quarter of the total we had from the lower Mississippi, the Ohio, the Illinois, and the Missouri, together with the upper Mississippi. And this"—he gestured—"this has been a common scene throughout the entire season."

Stambaugh referred to the patient crowds of immigrants. Men, women, and children, standing or sitting among all their worldly possessions, were to be seen the length of the docks, waiting to board the steamboats, anxious lest they be left before the season closed.

"Some are going West, but most of them are heading for points north," said Stambaugh. "Minnesota Territory, particularly. A great many Germans, but a lot of Irish, too. The Irish are replacing the roustabouts up North—you've probably noticed. After all, a nigger has some cash value, but an Irishman hasn't any." He grinned. "I don't mean to run down the race, Colonel, but the fact is the nigger costs money—he represents a cash investment—and the Irishman works for a wage, and not much of that. If the nigger gets sick of the cold—and they're sensitive, mighty sensitive—it's too big a risk to take; a man could lose up to a thousand dollars on one nigger."

"Where's the *Galena Belle?*" asked Hercules.

"Over this way. I see her, Mr. Dousman."

The boat on which Hercules had taken passage stood on the ready. Smoke poured from her twin stacks. She was a sternwheeler, destined to travel no farther north than Prairie du Chien, under the command of Captain Albert Dreiburgh. Roustabouts were loading her, and the ship's clerk was measuring wood to be taken aboard. Immigrants already crowded her lower deck.

"I hope Phillips hasn't forgotten to get my piano on board," said Hercules.

"Ah, you bought Madame a piano, Mr. Dousman?"

"A Lemuel Gilbert—one of the best, I'm told, although, being no hand at playing myself, I wouldn't know."

"Trust Phillips, Colonel."

"I have to. I paid three hundred fifty for it. That's a good price, and I expect a good instrument."

"What is the wood?"

"Rosewood."

"Oh, fine, fine! Couldn't do better. Phillips has done himself proud. You'll never regret it, sir! That piano will hold its tune. It will serve you a hundred years, mark my words."

"Not me, it won't," said Hercules with a grin.

"That boy of yours, then."

"Well, I'd better get on board, Stambaugh. I'll look to you for your customary service, sir."

"I've never disappointed you yet, Mr. Dousman. I won't start now. Some of your goods have been loaded, and the rest will follow just as soon as I can find the space."

Hercules moved down among the roustabouts, past passengers bidding final good-bys to friends and relatives, through a medley of shouting and bawling of orders from boats to shore and back. It was the landing at Prairie du Chien, multiplied many times over. Watching the bustle, listening to the excitement of arrivals and departures never failed to please Hercules; in this lay ample proof of the westward expansion, of the growth of the valley of the upper Mississippi, of the triumph of man over the wilderness, which had once seemed so awesomely forbidding. Yet Hercules never recognized this without a concomitant feeling of regret at the inexorable passing of that wilderness. He remembered how his friend, Baron Pierneau, had railed against the westward expansion, and mourned the loss of his Indian friends, Chief Black Hawk and his Sauk band. He understood now how Pierneau had felt at that time, fifteen years ago. How much had happened to the frontier in those years!

He went on board the *Galena Belle*. He pushed through the immigrants on the lower deck, past bales of goods, and mounted to the upper deck. He found a place at the railing where he was out of the way and stood to look back at the city, glowing in the morning sunlight. St. Louis was now a city of 75,000. The innumerable stacks of the boats tied up along the river were matched by the steeples and spires gleaming in the morning sun. Hercules counted more than a dozen church steeples before he stopped. The skyline was dominated by the white dome of the new courthouse and beyond it by an almost Byzantine structure rising up among rows of red-brick houses. The city, below its towers looked, like an army of chimneys flowing back from the river's edge. Adding to its color, the city's trees were resplendant in yellow and claret, at their height of brilliance before the season turned. How well Pierre Liguest had chosen, when he picked the site of St. Louis almost a century ago!

Hercules left the rail and sought out the captain. He found him down off the texas, watching the last load being put on board, tense and impatient. Captain Dreiburgh was a short, pudgy German, with a florid face and a fierce mustache which jutted forth on both sides of his mouth. His sharp eyes saw Hercules coming.

"Yes, Mr. Dousman," he said before Hercules could speak, "your piano's on board—and precious room it took, too!"

"Thank you, Captain. That was what I wanted to know."

"It's the first piano I've taken North, Mr. Dousman."

"It won't be the last."

Hercules looked across to the neighboring steamboat, which had come in to unload. It was the *Dr. Franklin II,* under the command of Captain Daniel Smith Harris, one of the most daring and skillful captains on the upper Mississippi. The boat had come in from Galena, for the roustabouts were carrying lead down her planks. Beyond her another side-wheeler was pulling out. As far as he could see in either direction steamboats were loading or unloading; Hercules estimated that at least forty boats were in dock; others stood offshore waiting to come in. The complexion of the dock had not changed since his arrival; some of the immigrants had got on board; others had moved in to take their places, waiting; draymen, boatmen, roustabouts swarmed over the docks, voices raised in songs or curses. Barrels of flour, bags of corn, piles of lead, hogsheads of tobacco, barrels of whisky and cider, lumber, farming implements, brick, crackers—all were stacked waiting to be loaded for the journey upriver or the Ohio River run, and the activity from one end of the docks to another, between boats and landing, was indescribable.

A shout from below interrupted his reverie. The last load had been brought aboard; the roustabouts were signaling to the captain. Captain Dreiburgh immediately cupped his mouth in his hands and shouted, "All aboard! Up Planks! Loose the ropes!" The roustabouts fell back; some ran to the ropes to loosen them; the two planks at the head of the *Galena Belle* were raised to stand out at an angle. The departing bell began to ring. Captain Dreiburgh turned toward the pilothouse. "Are you ready, Mr. Brown?" The pilot waved his hand.

The *Galena Belle* backed out into the current, widening the water between her head and the dock. A roustabout stood at the bow with a measuring line in his hand, although there was no need for him in these familiar waters; yet he stood ready to call back the water's depth to another black beneath the pilothouse. The paddle-wheel churned water, brown with silt, into yellow and white foam. The boat moved out among others standing off, carefully edging past another boat bound upriver with a barge filled with cattle lashed to its side, and swung out into the current, pointing upriver.

Hercules looked back. Already St. Louis was diminished in perspective. Across the river, on the east shore, Illinoistown looked like the merest hamlet by comparison; beyond it the low, rolling country of Illinois stretched limitlessly away toward the horizon, lost in the blaze of the morning sun. Blue herons and white sandhill cranes flew along the river's shore, sunlight gleaming on their wings.

The boat leaped forward, filled with life; the throbbing of the engines made a steady pulse; the smokestacks began to sigh; the movement of the water seemed to communicate itself to the boat.

Captain Dreiburgh leaned past the upright to which he clung, swinging out over the water. "Tell me, Mr. Dousman, is it true you're thinking of starting a line?"

Hercules smiled. "I take it you've been hearing talk. Captain, I've had a hand in the game for a long time. Captain Throckmorton and I bought the *Chippewa* nine years ago; she weighed in at a hundred seven tons. Four years later I owned half the *Lynx*. But it's true, I am thinking about expanding my steamboating interests."

"The way the river towns are growing—I don't know of another investment that pays off so well."

"Is that so?"

"Take it from me, Mr. Dousman—the average steamboat plying the upper Mississippi—that is, if she's kept up and keeps her engagements—clears about eight thousand a season."

"That's an impressive figure, Captain," said Hercules, who had reason to know that the average earnings of boats were closer to twelve thousand.

"I say we're just beginning on the upper Mississippi, Mr. Dousman."

"You may be right, but, remember, the keelboats had hardly begun when the steamboats came along. And now the railroad's pushing toward the river."

"That won't matter." He swung around again. "Stop in at my cabin any time, Mr. Dousman."

"Thank you, Captain."

Hercules made his way to the main cabin, and into his stateroom, which opened off it. The day glowed with sunlight; the trip North promised to be swift and easy.

In the early hours of the fourth morning out of St. Louis Hercules woke. He lay for a while in his bunk, listening to the sounds of passage he had come to know so well—the lulling churning of the water, the soft chanting of roustabouts singing a spiritual as a kind of obbligato to the ruminative sighing of the smokestacks, the voices of the roustabouts at the bow and below the pilothouse, calling out one after the other to the pilot, "Oh, mark four! Mark four!" and, in a little while, "Quarter less three!"

Hercules lay for some time drowsily listening. But he had had enough sleep. The *Galena Belle* was moving less swiftly now, and he guessed that they were coming either to a difficult channel or toward shore to wood up. Without interrupting incident they would be in Prairie du Chien by noon, for they were already north of Savanna. The roustabout at the bow was calling oftener. "Half twain!" and again, "Mark twain!" The boat was moving uncertainly into shoal water.

He guessed that they were pausing to take on wood, and lay waiting for confirmation of his guess. They would be somewhere along the Illinois shore, where great stacks of cottonwood and poplar lay cut in cords for the steamboats. The *Galena Belle* headed in to shore. He heard the sounds drifting in from outside He followed the clerk off the boat to measure the wood to be taken on; the conversation between the seller and the clerk was indistinguishable, but presently came the sound of the wood being loaded. Hercules listened. More than ten cords, he guessed, and less than twenty. Probably fifteen cords were taken on before the boat backed out into the river once more.

He got up and dressed in the darkness. He went out on deck, and stood there in the darkness. The waxing moon, not yet at first quarter, had gone down hours ago; already Venus and Jupiter rode the eastern heavens to signal the dawn. The morning air was fresh, almost cold; the steamboats would not long be moving this far north before ice would make passage too dangerous. The roustabouts were still, except for the two marking the depth of the water; they began again as the boat swung into the current. But the shoal had been passed now, and the *Galena Belle* was once more in safe water.

Hercules mounted to the pilothouse. Jedediah Brown, a ruddy-faced, pale-eyed man of forty, wearing a Quaker beard, nodded curtly at him, without more than a momentary glance away from the dark water below. No light burned in the pilothouse, lest the skilled vision of the pilot be impaired in his constant search for familiar landmarks along the line of earth and sky.

Hercules spoke to the pilot's back. "Where are we, Mr. Brown?"

"Comin' to Galena, Mr. Dousman."

"How long do we tie up there?"

Brown shrugged. "Don't reckon too long. Galena ain't the town it was—they ain't shippin' the way they used to before they found gold in California and they were sendin' all the lead we could carry down the river. I figure the town's only about half as big as it was five years ago, that's a fact."

The cries of the roustabouts rose from below. "Quarter less three! Quarter less three!"

"We've got better'n sixteen feet," said the pilot. "The river's a little low, but not as low as she was in August and September." He grinned at Hercules, relaxed now.

"What do you think will happen to the river traffic once the railroads push to the Mississippi up here, Mr. Brown?"

"Oh, I don't know. I reckon, though, it'll take quite a while before the railroads make much difference, and at first, why, it'll boom it. The old Miss' is just openin' up for St. Paul—every trip we make that way, we're filled up with people from the old country, and we come back crammed full of furs, buffalo robes, and, if we've got any room left, we stop for lead at Galena."

Hercules said nothing more. The pilot was now peering intently into the lessening dark, searching for some landmark. Hercules agreed that the pilot was undoubtedly right—river traffic on the upper Mississippi would not appreciably diminish until rails reached all the way to St. Paul. That would take a while.

Outside now the dawn was beginning to break; Venus and Jupiter still glowed high up in the east, but the rising light along that rim had dimmed and paled the other stars. Hercules turned and slipped quietly out of the pilothouse.

Just after sunrise the boat turned into the mouth of the Fever River, up which it made its way slowly, for the stream was narrow in comparison to the Mississippi. Galena loomed not far up the river. The town lay beautifully compact, sweeping up the rocky hill slopes from the river's edge so steeply that at times the *Galena Belle* rode beneath the windows of houses where children leaned out waving and shouting at the boat. Unlike so many new towns, Galena was not barren of trees; they rose up along the streets, scarlet and chrome, more brilliant than the trees of St. Louis, and all around the town, across the river as well as in an arc behind it, the groves of trees made large patches of riotous color among the barren crowns and slopes of the encircling hills. Here, too, Hercules thought, the church spires, the warehouses, and the smokestacks boasted of human enterprise.

They were two hours in Galena. Many of the passengers got off to stretch their legs in the village, though most of them, Hercules had learned, were bound for Iowa and would leave the *Galena Belle* at its next stop on the western side of the river. A great deal of freight was taken off the boat, but none was loaded, since the *Galena Belle* meant to go no farther north than Prairie du Chien on this trip, and would return to pick up freight bound for St. Louis and the East. But at last they were off again, bound for Dubuque.

It was late in the day when the boat reached the dock at Prairie du Chien. Captain Dreiburgh assured Hercules that as soon as the boat had unloaded here, he would bring the *Galena Belle* up the east channel of the Mississippi to Hercules' private wharf just west of the house on the mound and unload his supplies and the piano he had bought for Jane. The roustabouts would bring the piano to the house. Satisfied, Hercules hurried home.

Jane saw him coming and flew to the door to greet him, throwing her arms around him and kissing him.

"Mistaire Dousman do not come with his arms full of dresses!" she cried. "He have reform'."

"Don't speak too soon. I just couldn't carry them, that's all. You'll find a few things for Dédé, too, when the boat comes around to our dock."

"Ah, no doubt." Her slender fingers searched his pockets rapidly, while he stood patiently waiting. Her eyebrows raised. "No jewel? No necklace? No ring?" she laughed. "Madame Dousman has los' her charm." Then she shrugged. "But come—suppair is wait'. I have wait' dinnair and suppair for two days now. Pairhaps you will feel bettair after food."

Hercules only smiled. He suffered himself to be led to the table. At such moments as this Jane was still a girl, wearing a kind of enchantment which, he was positive, would never permit her to grow old; at such times he found it difficult to believe that she was almost his own age. He sat down at the head of the table; she went around to the foot, where, in a small chair of his own, sat Dédé, watching Hercules' every move with great, round eyes and an adoring smile. Hercules waved at him and aroused his excited laughter; he bent and kissed him, at which Dédé cried out happily, "Papa! Papa home!"

Jane hushed him as she sat down and said to Hercules, "Mistaire Sark is vair' anxious to see you."

"Oh, bother business. I can always see Jonas."

"He want to see you as soon as he can aftair you come back from St. Louis."

"After I look over the mail, then."

"If that is all . . ." Jane turned and called. "Eugenie!"

Eugenie appeared and looked questioningly into the room.

"Eugenie, go at once and get Mistaire Dousman's mail from the office."

Hercules' protest was in vain; Eugenie had vanished instantly.

Giselle came in with a roast, setting it down for Hercules to carve. He was still at it when Eugenie returned and put two dozen or more letters down beside his plate.

"Now read your mail, Mistaire Dousman," said Jane with comic asperity.

Hercules handed Jane's plate to Eugenie, who took it to her. Then he turned to the letters, letting Eugenie serve Dédé. He went rapidly through them, disdaining to open them, until he came to a sealed letter from New York. This he turned over; it came, as he suspected, from the Astor office. Hercules had written early in the summer to young William Astor, who, he supposed, was in charge of the trade since his father's death a year ago in March, to ask about Saquin; he had turned over what Young Joe had told him until that time; then he had written impulsively, not only to ask about Saquin, but about the possibility of a son of that trader working for the Astor Company. This, doubtless, was their answer, long put off—as long as he himself had put off writing. This letter he opened.

It was brief.

"I suppose my father might have known the man Saquin, but the name means nothing to me. We do not have any record of having employed any man of that name. You describe him as an independent, and I suppose that was what he was, in which case he would not have been likely to become part of our organization. Nor a son, if there were one.

"Our best wishes to you, as always . . ."

Hercules thought it evasive. It was a feeling he had, because certainly William might not have known anything about Saquin. Yet William was now—he made a rapid calculation—fifty-seven—he could have had some knowledge of Saquin.

He restored the letter to its envelope. The rest of the letters could always be looked at; they were from his bankers in Milwaukee, from Byron Kilbourn—letters about investments, letters of information, a few bills. One other caught his eye, this one from Milwaukee. He opened this hastily, recognizing the handwriting of his daughter Emily.

"Dear Papa, I am giving up my place here and coming home. I have a surprise for you. I hope it will please you. If I may, I will come to the house. Perhaps my stepmama will not care if I am there for a little while. Love to you both, Emily."

Hercules handed the little note to Jane without comment.

"I am glad she is come'," said Jane. "We mus' make her welcome, Mistaire Dousman. She have stay' away too long with your brothair in Milwaukee, an' your fathair in Mackinac—everywhere but this house which should be her home."

"Emily has a mind of her own."

"She would not be Mistaire Dousman's daughtair if she do not have."

He restored Emily's letter to the pile at his elbow, musing, "She's eighteen now! I'm ashamed to say I hardly remember what she looks like—it's been so long since I've seen her."

"Mistaire Dousman ought to be ashame'," said Jane with spirit.

"She was happy where she was. Now she's made up her mind about something else—and we'll hear about it."

"Why do not Mistaire Dousman open all his lettairs?"

"I know pretty well what's in them."

He cut himself some beef and began to eat.

They were still at the table when the men came with the piano. Hercules had heard the *Galena Belle* moving in to the wharf, followed by the voices of the roustabouts unloading the supplies for the trade—the blankets, cloth, strouding, coats, pantaloons, wampum, armbands, broaches, earbobs, soap, nail rods, flatirons, linseed oil, nails, and footstuffs. Jane must have heard them, too, but thought nothing of them, recognizing the sounds so familiar to her when a boat came to the landing. It was she who heard the men at the west door.

"Pairhaps that is Mistaire Sark. Shall I say to him you will see him now?"

Hercules knew Sark would not interrupt his meal, unless the matter was of singular urgence. He could not conceive of such urgence. "Tell him I will not," he said, suspecting what awaited Jane when she went to the door.

She rose determinedly, saying, "You mus' not keep him wait', Mistaire Dousman. He, too, may need your help."

She reached the door and pulled it open.

Her squeal of delighted surprise pleased Hercules. He got up and followed her.

"Where will you have it put, Jane?" he asked.

She spun around and embraced him, burying her head in his chest.

"I knew I nevair make a mistake to marry Mistaire Dousman!" she cried. "I mus' have it in my morning room—here!" she gestured to the men, pointing to the door at the right of the outer doors.

Hercules opened both of the western doors, so that the piano could be brought in. In the lamplight it shone with a deep roseate glow. Jane stood with hands ecstatically clasped, her eyes shining with happiness, watching every move and maneuver of the men bringing in the piano. She was so enthralled by the sight of it that Hercules had to precede it into her parlor to make room for it.

"Where, Jane?" he asked.

"Ovair on the eas' wall. Put the table in the middle of the room." As she spoke, she edged into the room herself, casting an anxious glance backward at the piano; she took hold of the table and moved it. "So—and the chair nex' to it. Now, see, it stand undair the picture of my Vairginie!"

Hercules watched the piano put into position. The oil portrait of Jane's dead daughter—that dear child who had died so tragically on her way home from school in the East; he remembered as if it were yesterday Jane's grief at learning from the captain of the boat of the death of that child she had been waiting at the landing to greet—looked down above the piano. Indeed, it was well placed.

Jane sat down to it, trying the keys with a French lullaby.

"Oh, it is pairfec'!" she cried. "It is so much bettair than rings or dresses. I thank you from the bottom of my heart, Mistaire Dousman."

"If it pleases you, Jane, I ask no more."

He stepped into the hall where the men waited, paid them, and saw them out. He closed the double doors once more. Eugenie came out of the dining room with the baby held against her shoulder. She crossed to Jane's parlor and went in, talking to Dédé.

"See, boy—your maman play piano."

The piano sounded pleasantly; it echoed in the hall, up the stairs; Jane filled the house with music. Hercules stood for a moment to listen, picking out the tune, trying to name it; then he went back into the dining room, gathered up his letters, took another draught of tea, and went through the kitchen outside.

The door of the office was unlocked. Sark would not have left it so. He must then be inside, in the gathering dark. Hercules opened the door and stepped in, his eyes probing the dusk.

"Jonas?"

"Yes, Mr. Dousman."

Sark got out of his chair, crossed to Hercules' desk, and lit the lamp there, dispelling the faint glow of moonlight from the waxing moon in the southwestern sky, which lay in a parallelogram along the floor near the door.

Hercules flashed a glance at Sark's face; it told him nothing. He dropped his letters to his desk and sat down, turning to face Sark.

"I had to see you, Mr. Dousman."

"I'm here."

"Mr. Dousman, did you write the Astor office to ask about a trader named Saquin?"

Hercules was astounded. But his astonishment quickly gave way to caution. Sark could not have known from anyone here in Prairie du Chien that inquiry had been made about Saquin. Young Joe could not have told him before he went North, because even Hercules had not known then that he would write to Astor. Sark could have learned only from someone in New York. Hercules recognized abruptly that there was more to the riddle of Sark than he had supposed.

"Why do you ask, Jonas?"

"I've a good reason for asking, Mr. Dousman. I'm told you wrote—I learned it on good authority."

"By whom? Ferrier?"

It was Sark's turn to be surprised. "Ferrier," he repeated.

Hercules took advantage of Sark's silence. "I know you've been writing to Ferrier—so it must have been he." He was impelled by Sark's patent perplexity to add gently, "I happened to see an envelope addressed to Ferrier in your hand one day over a year ago."

Without a word Sark pulled a letter from his pocket and handed it to Hercules, who unfolded it and glanced at the signature: Ferrier. He read it; it amounted to a terse order.

"Sark: Mr. Dousman has been making inquiries about a trader named Saquin thought to have been involved with the Astor Company at one time. Ascertain why he is making these inquiries, but do not betray yourself."

Hercules looked up, his eyes narrowed. "But you *have* betrayed yourself, Jonas."

Sark shrugged. "I don't care about that, Mr. Dousman."

"But I do, Jonas. I think now I have a right to know what you've been writing to Ferrier since you came into my employment."

Sark sat for a few moments in silence. Then he spoke thoughtfully, as if choosing his words. "Mr. Dousman—I should have told you right away—only I didn't know you well enough then, and later on, somehow, I didn't feel right about it. The fact is, I hired out to some agents of the Astor Company. It was my business to pass along to them anything I could learn about your affairs—I don't suppose they were as much interested in the furs any more, because they knew as much as I that most of the business went through St. Paul and St. Louis, from the West—but just your general affairs. You know how they like to keep informed. I know they could have asked you, and you'd have told them, but that isn't the way they work."

Hercules withheld a chuckle. It was like many eastern business interests to follow just such a course, as if they were fearful that some source of making money might have escaped them. "What it amounts to," he said, "is spying."

"I guess you'd call it that."

"But that isn't all," continued Hercules shrewdly. "You're upset now—it looks like more than conscience to me. Why come to me? You sought me out. Did they send you?"

"Well, yes—and no. I suggested you."

"Why?"

"I knew your reputation. I wanted to learn something about the trade before I went West. *My* purpose in coming here wasn't to spy on you, Mr. Dousman, it was to inform myself as much as I could, so that I could move about freely and feel at home in the trade. I did that for two reasons—secondarily—if I fail in my first—to do what damage I can to the Astor Company, but primarily—to find the two men in Astor's employment who murdered my father and his Indian guide one night seventeen years ago."

"So then you're Saquin's son?"

"My right name is Jean Saquin, yes. What did you know of my father, Mr. Dousman?"

Hercules took a few moments to orient himself before he answered. Sark was neither a friend of the Astor Company nor a foe of Dousman's interests. "I never knew your father, Jonas. The first time I heard his name mentioned was last spring, when Young Joe mentioned him, said you resembled him. He had seen your father when he was along on a trading trip with old Joe—we were still with the Astor Company at that time; we didn't buy out until 1834, as you know."

"I know that, yes."

"Then you also know how little of the trade is left—that most of my business lies in investments of one kind or another in the future of this Middle Western country. And you ought to know, too, that striking blindly against the Astor Company is a poor kind of vengeance to achieve. Astoria's been nothing for Astor but a sequence of accidents and disasters. You couldn't have done Astor as much harm as has happened to him in Astoria, if you'd been on the spot from the beginning—and that was back in 1812, before you were born. Besides, the old man's dead now." He leaned forward earnestly. "I don't approve of vengeance, but I don't presume to judge. The fact is, you went about this the long way round. You should have directed your energies to finding the men who killed your father and forgetting the Company."

"Mr. Dousman, I did everything I could to find out who they were. Besides, if the Company didn't order my father killed—and I have reason to believe they did—they at least condoned it." He tapped Ferrier's letter. "Now what am I to do about this?"

"Nothing, I think."

"But I'll have to answer him."

Hercules shook his head. "My boy, I knew for a long time how men in the Astor Company acknowledged murder as a weapon to bring the independents into line or get rid of them. I never approved such methods. I never approved the way in which they debauched the Indians, either, only to cheat them. I think you'll find that this post under Rolette and myself was always fair with the Indians. Some of the Astor people had hired assassins—it needn't have been Company policy—and if I know them, they'll still have these people on their pay roll; they don't dare fire them for fear they'll talk. If your father was killed by Astor Company assassins—the murderers, if they're still alive, will be here somewhere in the Middle West—not in Astoria."

"Sir, I've looked."

"Blindly. You should have made them come to you. I propose to write Astor a letter and tell him I have a young fellow named Sark in my employment whose true name I believe to be Saquin. Let us just see if they'll take that bait."

Sark looked dubious. "Seventeen years is a long time, Mr. Dousman. I've thought about this almost all my life . . ."

"Nursed it along, you mean. You're young—life is more than a coddling of old hatreds, Jonas."

"My father was all I had, Mr. Dousman."

"You couldn't have been more than seven years old when he was killed. Hatred warps a man, Jonas."

Sark did not answer.

Hercules saw that he was reluctant to abandon his goal. He determined to speak to Sark later. Let him think over what he had said. He turned his back on Sark.

"Let me alone now, Jonas. I want to think about this."

"All right, Mr. Dousman." Sark got up. "It looks, though, as if I'd better be thinking of moving on."

"Not yet," said Hercules crisply. "Let's just wait and see what comes of this. I'll write."

"But not to Astor. It won't mean anything to him, now the old man's dead. It might have to old John, but not to William. If you have to write, write to Ferrier—Ferrier's been with them for fifty years—he'll know about Saquin, if anybody will."

Of course Jonas was right, thought Hercules. He nodded curtly. After Sark had gone, he pulled paper over to himself and began to write rapidly.

My dear Mr. Ferrier:

I dislike to trouble you, but with your access to the Company records and papers, you may know the answer to a riddle which has been bothering us here. I have in my employment a young fellow named Sark whom I believe to be the son of Germain Saquin, an independent who vanished some years ago. Do you know anything about him? . . .

That should bring in something, he thought. But he was already resigned to the ultimate loss of Sark, for of course he could not stay.

Sark went out into the moonlit night and walked in the direction of the Marais de St. Feriole. What was Dousman about, he asked himself, if not to set the dogs on him? Was that what his employer wanted? He could not believe it. What he had come to know about Hercules had revealed not only a shrewd and able businessman but also a man of great vision and great generosity, of soul as well as of purse. His access to Hercules' books showed him that Hercules was as rich as he was influential; indeed, he knew of no one, in fact or in reputation, richer than Dousman in the state of Wisconsin. He was nevertheless a little apprehensive about Dousman's plan to betray him to Ferrier.

Just the same, he was relieved that Hercules knew who he was and what he was doing in Prairie du Chien. However self-satisfied he had been at coming, his opinion of himself had undergone some alteration in the face of Hercules' unfailing consideration for him. The town itself had mellowed him with its easy acceptance of him, and Annette Gaucher had played no small role in this. He turned his steps in the direction of her home.

But half way there he paused on the bank of the slough and sat down on a stump, looking across the water into the mainland town and to the hills and the sky beyond. The moon touched the hills behind him; ahead, the Pleiades and the red orb of Aldebaran were pulling up the buttes of heaven, but Stark did not see them. He was immersed in his own thoughts, trying to temper a fierce reluctance to alter his plans, as Hercules had suggested.

Although he sat there for an hour, he came to no decision save to wait upon events. He knew Hercules had told the truth when he inferred that a stroke against the Astor interests in Astoria would be hollow triumph indeed, for destiny had not been kind to that venture. But he could not yet convince himself that the abandonment of his goal was not an act of disloyalty to his dead father.

He rose abruptly and strode along the bank of the Marais to the Gaucher house. He knocked boldly.

Gaucher came to the door in stocking feet, peering into the darkness. "Oh, it's you," he growled. He turned and called out, "Annette!" Then he went off without a word and left Sark standing there, not inviting him in, which did not matter to Sark, for he did not want to come in.

Annette came and stepped outside into the crisping night, pulling the door shut behind her but clinging with one hand to the knob.

"M'sieu' Sark—Jonas," she whispered. "I do not expect you."

"Say to me only one thing, Annette," he asked urgently. "If I must leave Prairie du Chien—tomorrow, next week—perhaps even tonight—would you go with me?"

She stood gazing at him, trying to determine what urgence impelled him to ask.

"Only answer me," he begged.

"All right, I tell you. I ask you why afterward—but yes, I would go."

He caught her to him, kissed her fiercely, and ran off into the darkness, leaving her agape on the stoop.

Emily came the following week. Hercules did not observe her arrival, for he was busy answering letters, but presently Louis LeBrun came to the office for him.

"Mr. Dousman, Miss Emily's here," he said politely.

"Thanks, Louis." He got up to follow the boy out of the office. As they walked across the lawn in the mellow October sunlight, he asked curiously, "Tell me, Louis, now you've been here a while—do you like it?"

"I am happy here, Mr. Dousman."

"Good! We shall keep you so."

Looking at Louis as he walked sturdily ahead of him, Hercules saw that he had filled out a little since his coming. He looked healthier, he had more color, and he had lost much of his shyness, which had been replaced by a quiet self-assurance that rose from knowledge of security—he had a home, and he had been made to feel that he belonged here.

They went into the house.

Emily Dousman was not alone. A dark-haired, dark-skinned young man stood next to where she sat with Jane in the morning room. Hercules scarcely looked at him; he had eyes only for his daughter, whom he had last seen five years ago, at his own wedding to Jane. She stood up as he approached. She had grown into a girl of medium height, with long black hair —like her mother's—and intense eyes which were also like her mother's had been. Her skin was less fair than dark, as if tanned by the sun. Her manner was grave, almost staid. She received her father's kiss coolly, but her embrace was tight.

"You've grown into a young lady, Emily," said Hercules.

"Yes, Papa."

"And given up your place, too!"

"Papa, I want you to meet Charlie Barrette," said Emily with simple straightforwardness.

Hercules turned. The dark young man held out his hand.

"How do you do, sir. You must remember me."

"Why, you're Peter Barrette's boy, aren't you?" said Hercules as they shook hands.

"Charlie and I are going to be married," said Emily.

Hercules did not know, for a moment, what to say.

"That is, if you have no objection, sir," said Barrette.

"None, none at all. My congratulations! I can hardly believe it! How the world does grow away from us! And what do you expect to do, my boy?"

"My father has given us a good tract of land north of Prairie du Chien. I expect to farm it."

"Is there a house on it?"

"Not yet."

"Perhaps you'll let me build one for you? One of good size, with a veranda on three sides—I'd like to give you that for a wedding present."

Jane spoke suddenly. "And the furnishin', Mistaire Dousman."

"Thank you, Papa," said Emily. "But we expect to be married as soon as we can. Perhaps in two weeks, if Father Gaultier will permit it."

"Mistaire Dousman and I would, of course, give you this wedding," said Jane. "I especial' would love to have your dress made, Emily, and to see to it all the arrangement' are made for your dinnair and your reception."

Emily bit her lip. "But I'd much rather have a simple little wedding—nothing so grand. The dress, yes—I know it would be beautiful. Perhaps even dinner."

"You mus' eat, my child."

"But no big party, please. We would like just a quiet wedding —just Charlie's people, and you, and perhaps Uncle John, if he would care to come from Milwaukee, and Uncle George. But I do not think they would come all the way here."

How self-assured she was, how poised! thought Hercules. Their blood was the same, but they had grown apart. Just as he himself had done early in life, she had made a place for herself, charted her own course, and meant to follow it.

"Your wedding will be just as you want it, Emily," he said. "Jane will have your dress made, the dinner will be here, and we'll dispense with any party."

"Thank you, Papa."

"And as soon as we can, we'll make plans for your house, and I'll build it just to suit you both. Now for the time being you'll stay here, of course—it wouldn't look well for you to be somewhere else—and Charlie will be welcome to be here as much as he likes. Perhaps some evening he and his parents would like to come to dinner."

"Yes, we mus' all plan so your wedding will be a success," Jane put in.

"It will be," said Emily with a confident smile.

Two weeks later, as Hercules walked down the aisle of St. Gabriel's and gave his daughter away, then knelt to watch the ceremony, he knew as well as any man might know anything, that Emily's marriage would be successful. She had put her girlhood behind her; she was a young lady at eighteen, fully capable of being Charles Barrette's wife, ready to assume the duties of running her own home, of motherhood and the added maturity it would bring. She had prepared herself with little help from him, she had planned her life with the same care he had planned his own, and in this she was fully his daughter.

No answer came to Hercules' letter to Ferrier. Hercules was not surprised. Ferrier would answer only when he had decided upon what action to take. The son of Germain Saquin, probing into what had happened to the trader, was not someone Ferrier would like about, certainly not on the payroll of the Company.

As the days passed, Hercules pushed the problem of Sark into a recess of his mind, once having quieted Sark's anxiety. There were other affairs demanding his attention. He had to see to the building of Emily's house along the road north to the Wisconsin River. He had to go to Milwaukee to look at the first rails of the new railroad being pushed out of Milwaukee toward Waukesha; Kilbourn's insistence knew no alternative. So he went, spent a day studying the maps of the proposed route, noticing that no western terminus of the projected road had as yet been established, although all signs pointed to Prairie du Chien. He had to act for the government and make a short journey up the Mississippi to talk to a band of Sioux and Winnebago chieftains and listen to their grievances.

Jane, too, had plans for him.

"Tonight Mistaire Dousman mus' be home for dinnair," she said one November morning. "We are hav' important guest."

"Who is it?" he asked.

"Mistaire Dousman will see. But until then, he will not know. Yet he mus' come; it is vair' important to me pairsonal', an' I know he will not disappoint me."

Hercules could deny Jane nothing. He altered his plans so that he could be home for dinner.

Jane's guest was a reserved young woman of medium height,

with light brown hair and alert, bright blue eyes glinting with good humor. She had a mouth that wore authority well, but not unpleasantly, and self-assurance was so much a part of her that it seemed to envelop her, like some sort of invisible but tangible garment. Good nature radiated from her face. When Hercules walked into the drawing room, she gave him a quick, measured glance of appraisal.

"Miss McCleod, my husban', Mistaire Dousman," said Jane proudly. "You remembair, Mistaire Dousman, long time ago I say to you Miss Penelope McCleod is a traisir, and here now is this traisir."

Miss McCleod held out her hand with easy naturalness. "I hear so much about Hercules Dousman," she said simply. "One could not live in Prairie du Chien without doing so." Her voice carried a strong Scottish burr.

"I assure you, Miss McCleod, I've had *your* virtues dinned into my ears ever since you first set foot in this village," replied Hercules.

So this was the woman Jane wanted as governess and housekeeper! Hercules examined her as unobtrusively as possible. She had a trim figure, and her manner was quietly confident. She was not unattractive, with her brown hair worn in ringlets at her temples and mounded on the back of her head, allowing three curls to escape the coil of hair. Her dress was conservative, perhaps as befitted her profession.

Jane chattered happily on as they walked in to dinner. Miss McCleod was still teaching in Father Gaultier's school, she said. She had made a great success of it, and she would be asked to teach there as long as she liked. But there were now enough other teachers, and Miss McCleod no longer felt the responsibility toward the school that she had felt two years before and for some time thereafter.

Hercules noticed with amusement he did not betray that Jane had placed Miss McCleod at table between Louis LeBrun and Dédé, with Eugenie across from her, as if to test her at once. Miss McCleod evidently did not share Eugenie's faith, for she did not cross herself at the prayer, but she bowed her head as meekly as Eugenie and Louis and Jane.

"Is she not a traisir!" cried Jane as they prepared for bed that night.

"She seems a very competent young lady," agreed Hercules. "I don't know that 'treasure' describes her. She knows her mind and means to exercise it. She has a very pleasing personality. From what she says of books, she has evidently kept up with new writing as much as possible."

"Mistaire Dousman," Jane challenged him, "do you like her?"

"I don't know her well enough," he protested. "After all, you've seen her a dozen times to my once."

"Mistaire Dousman know vair' well he have reputation for make the quick and accurate judgment. So, say!"

"She ought to be good for Dédé. I saw how you put her next to him."

"And with Louis, too."

Hercules shrugged. "Louis can do very well without her."

"Then I may ask her to come stay with us?"

"As what?"

"She is to keep the house," answered Jane immediately, showing that she had pondered Miss McCleod's role a long time, "an' keep care of our Dédé, and Louis, and Eugenie."

Hercules laughed. "And Mistaire Dousman, too," he mimicked her. "In short, to be in general charge. I hope you do plan to allow us a little freedom."

"You laugh at me, Mistaire Dousman."

"Shouldn't I? Very well, ask her to come."

"I have already ask' her, and she is to come when she can be release' from the school. I was so sure Mistaire Dousman would like her, too, as soon as he see her."

The season rolled over, the long hard winter closed in, and in time, too, passed. The rivers opened again, the steamboats came in to begin the new season, the leaves began to unfurl and give their delicate perfume to the spring air, and one April day

Thunder Walker made his appearance at the house just as Hercules came downstairs to breakfast.

He invited the Winnebago into the kitchen, where he proposed to take his breakfast. "Join me, Thunder Walker," he said.

The Winnebago shook his head and sat down in his familiar cross-legged position on the floor to watch Hercules eat. He had never been in the kitchen before, and he was wide-eyed with amazement at sight of the great stove, the ovens, the cupboards, and all the devices which white men used to make themselves more comfortable in body.

"Are you just in?" asked Hercules.

Thunder Walker shook his head and held up two fingers.

"You've been here two days!" cried Hercules. "And you're just now coming to see me?"

The Indian answered in his own tongue, pointing to Giselle who stood at the stove preparing Jane's breakfast, to explain why he chose the Winnebago language in preference to his broken English. "I have followed two men," he said. "I saw them first up the river. I believe I know them. Many years ago, when my cousin, Walks Sideways, went with a trader to help him with his traps, both were killed. I believe these are the men who killed them. I saw them at the traps after Walks Sideways was slain."

"White men?" Hercules, too, spoke Winnebago.

Thunder Walker nodded. "I followed them eight days. They came here. Here, for two days, I watch. I see a strange thing."

"What is that?"

"They came to this place for a reason, I believe. For two days they watch him who works for you."

Hercules' interest quickened. "Sark?"

"The black-haired one who sits to write."

"They've not harmed him?"

"No."

Hercules abandoned his breakfast. He stood up suddenly and walked toward the outer door, beckoning the Indian to follow him. He strode out of the house, clattered down the steps, went around the icehouse, and crossed to the office. At the threshold he was relieved to see Sark industriously at work at his desk.

"Jonas," he cried, "they've taken the bait!"

"What bait?" asked Sark wonderingly. Then he understood. "You mean—the Astor people?"

Hercules told him what Thunder Walker had revealed.

Sark's face grew grim, but there was no fear in it, only a kind of anticipation that was not of danger so much as of satisfaction.

"Watch your step now, Jonas."

"Mr. Dousman, these men—if they're the Company's old assassins—they're here for just one purpose. You know as well as I they're not here to take me out to lunch and ask me please to go away."

Hercules walked over to the window nearest his desk and stood there looking out, his hands clasped behind his back. "In a way, this is my fault. If I hadn't gone prying into your background . . ."

"Or if I'd made a clean breast of things. I brought it on myself, and that's all there is to it."

Thunder Walker watched and listened. For all the years he had known them, white men were incomprehensible to him. He burst into a flow of broken English, interjecting an occasional phrase in Winnebago. White men were so devious, he did not understand them, he said. If these men were dangerous to him, Sark, why not lure them into a trap and kill them? It was the easiest thing to do, so long as one did not get himself killed. Indians had done this many times. It was folly to walk under fear of death when it was so easy to rid one's self of its cause. After all, he, Thunder Walker, had a grievance against them, too. Had they not slain Walks Sideways?

Hercules shook his head.

Thunder Walker spread his hands and wrinkled his face in disgust. "White man like duck on water. He wait for hunter to shoot."

Sark grinned. "That's about it," he said to Hercules.

"I'd advise you to call on that Gaucher girl in the daytime," said Hercules. "About the time you usually leave her house at night there's nothing much moving in the island town."

"Seems to me if I have to wait for them to make the first move, I'd better carry on the way I always do. If I change my habits now—they've watched me two days, according to the Indian—they might figure I'm wise to them."

Hercules sat down at his desk. If the men had indeed been sent by the Astor Company, and he was certain they had been, they were here for but one purpose—to get rid of Sark. But why should Sark trouble them? The Astor Company had been charged with worse than murder, even to bribing the federal government many times; Sark should pose no threat to them, unless there existed somewhere corroborative evidence which might stand up in court if Sark proffered formal charges. Hercules could not imagine what such evidence would be. Far more likely that the old hands in the Company, such as Ferrier, reacted in their customary pattern: remove any menace or obstruction to the Company as expeditiously as possible. That was the way it had always been with the unfortunate independents who had refused to do business on Astor's disadvantageous terms.

"No," said Sark, "I'll go on just the way I always have. We'll see what happens."

"Well, now you're warned I guess you can take care of yourself." Hercules shrugged. He wanted to add, "Only don't involve me," but he could not; he was already involved; he would not disengage himself now. "If you get into trouble, Jonas, count on me to help."

"Thanks, Mr. Dousman." He added confidently, "I figure, though, if it comes, I can handle it."

"Just the same, don't invite trouble."

"Invite it!" Sark snorted. "It's coming to me."

"That goes for you, too, Thunder Walker," added Hercules, turning to the Winnebago. "I know your inclinations."

Thunder Walker struck his breast. "Manitou tell me here what I do. White friend do not."

Hercules turned to his mail, filled with misgivings. For half an hour he could not concentrate on what Kilbourn wrote of the progress of the railroad and the need of eastern money, nor on what his brokers wrote of the New York market. But Sark worked undisturbed.

At midnight Sark kissed Annette one last time and slipped out of the house. He stood for a moment, looking about him, accustoming his eyes to the strange iridescence of the night. There was a thin overcast of clouds, yet the night was not quite dark because the moon was only a day past the full, and it shone behind the clouds, which were not thick enough to shut away its light, but only to diffuse it, blending light and shadow into an eerie half-dark. All was still; out of the late April night came only the throbbing notes of a whippoorwill from the islands in the Mississippi.

The village slept. He sniffed the air. The smell of thaw water moving down the Mississippi and the Wisconsin was almost overpowering; added to its musk was a sweetness that rose from new-turned soil. The scent Annette wore still clung to him; he was tantalizingly aware of it. The freshness and sweetness of the air exhilarated him. How good it was to be alive! He wondered, as he often did, whether his father had felt this way about the aspects of earth and sky, whether he had had the same interest in people and events . . .

A flicker of movement beside a tree down at the edge of the Marais de St. Feriole caught his eye. He looked in that direction; it was not repeated. He might have deceived himself, since he had been watching for just such movement; he thought not. His pulse quickened. If the one was there, he was sure, the other was, too.

He stepped off the low stoop and began to walk north along the slough, keeping as much as possible to the protection of what trees grew there, making sure that he was not a target for a deftly flung knife. He gazed behind him from time to time, always when in shadow, so that they might not see his face. He was abruptly, disagreeably surprised.

There was not but one follower. There were three.

He had not counted on three. He grew tense. He hesitated. Which way should he go? If he went to his quarters, he would invite attack perhaps along an open lane. Where else could he go? He thought of the office.

Behind him, his followers closed in.

He heard a low command in French, and immediately one of the men began to run up the slope away from the slough. They were trying to cut him off.

He left the bank of the slough and struck out in great strides for the office. Behind him he heard a splash of water, as if one of the men had stumbled and fallen into the slough, but he did not turn. He kept his eye on that one of his pursuers now striving to cut around in front of him.

Sark had the advantage. He was younger—if Thunder Walker's description of the men was to be accepted—almost by half. He was lithe. Even in the semi-darkness it was possible to see that the near pursuer was stocky and ran awkwardly.

Sark bounded from shadow to shadow, keeping behind trees as much as he could. In a short time he reached Dousman's land, which was extensive along the river, but not as wide as it was long. He broke into it just northeast of the house where trees were young and afforded little cover.

Fortunately his pursuer was not close enough to take advantage of Sark's lack of protection, and Sark gave him no chance to catch up. A fleeting glance behind revealed that the other two men had vanished. Had they cut around in front of him? Was he running into their arms?

Sark ran for the east wall of the office. Reaching it, he moved around the building to the north. His eye fell upon the doors to the wine cellar beneath the office. He started to lift the doors, but thought better of it; the space beneath the wine cellar was too cramped; he would be trapped there, and it was not his intention to be trapped. He thought coolly about where he might go. He listened. He thought he could hear someone breathing hard.

He slipped around to the west wall of the office and darted up between the office and the icehouse to the north wall of the house itself. In the northeast corner he lifted the great cellar doors and dropped to the steps, crouching there to look around. Even as he moved, a knife thudded into the wood of the unopened door beside him. He slipped into the darkness, catlike, leaving the door open behind him. The absolute blackness of the cellar beckoned him.

The cellar beneath the house on the mound was divided into three great rooms on three levels. The highest level was at the north end of the house; this was walled off from a lower level under the dining room and library, reached by three stone steps through a wide door in the center of the wall; in similar fashion, the lowest level under the drawing room and Jane's morning room was reached; this, in turn, gave access to the house above. Sark found himself in the cellar at the first level, in such darkness that he was forced to pause until the faint light from the open cellar door defined the room.

Then he pushed cautiously forward, through the first cellar, down the steps, through the second. He took up a station just behind the entrance to the third cellar room, pressing up against the damp limestone beside the yawning black mouth through which his pursuer must come. If he came.

He waited.

The cellar where he stood was so dark that even the open outer door, three rooms away and out of Sark's direct line of vision, seemed bright, lending a kind of spectral being to the great rooms. The earth of the floor was cold to Sark's feet; the stone wall was clammy to his body; the very air seemed oppressive with the smell of potatoes, of old papers, of vegetable roots buried against need in the kitchen above. The cellar rooms were vaultlike, high-ceilinged, and Sark's entrance had disturbed a little group of bats that lived there; they were flying about, chittering in the darkness, making for the open outer door.

A pebble rustled down the outer steps and rolled into the first cellar room. Sark waited in vain for the sound of voices. He could hardly believe that one of his pursuers would come alone, unless his self-confidence overcame his judgment. Yet they could not abandon the chase now, for they knew that Sark was aware of their presence in Prairie du Chien and would have guessed their mission.

Sark groped for and found a fragment of stone. It was not large, but it would have to do, since he had no other weapon. He strove to flatten himself still more against the wall, but then it occurred to him that his pursuer would expect him to do just that; there was no need for such caution; the room, away from the arched openings, was so unrelievedly black that it would be next to impossible to distinguish anyone in the middle of any part of the cellar. He slipped away from the entrance wall, just far enough so as to be out of reach of anything that might be swung around the wall from the adjacent room.

He listened.

There was no sound, nothing at all to give him warning. Perhaps he had failed in his attempt to lure them into the cellar, where the darkness might offset their advantage of being three to his one. He wanted to slip back to the open door, but he dared not do what perhaps they hoped he might do. In the darkness he heard only the beating of his own heart; it sounded so loud that he was sure whoever was on his trail must hear it and be guided unerringly to him.

Then, suddenly, without a sound, his pursuer was in the room. Sark saw him as a shadowy blackness whipping his powerful arms around first one side of the entrance, then another. He caught the gleam, faint in the pale light of the open door three rooms away, of a long-bladed knife in one hand—the left hand. The fellow was left-handed. His gasp of surprise gave him away. He had presence of mind enough to strike the hand that held the knife before his pursuer found him. He heard the knife fall to the floor.

Then he was fighting for his life.

For all his muscular litheness Sark was almost smothered by the rushing bigness of his adversary. He slipped out of a crushing hug which would have forced the breath out of him and cracked his ribs. He came up hard and hit him in the groin, at the same time kicking violently. A grunt was his only answer. The powerful arms reached for his throat; Sark thrust his fingers for the other's eyes, tore his nails down his cheek, wound his fingers into his beard, and pulled. A grunt again—his adversary worked with deadly urgence.

A blow struck Sark on the side of the head; he reeled, thrust out a hand, sent a glass jar to the wall and tinkling into a dozen fragments. Papers and account books rustled to the floor. Another blow hit him, glancing this time. He lashed out viciously, brought his knee up, and caught the other's chin. Then a leg was thrust between his, and he went down. At once his opponent threw himself on top of him, almost knocking Sark breathless. The fellow's face came down; Sark bit him savagely.

Both were breathing hard. Despite his youth and litheness, Sark was at a disadvantage with his back to the floor. Sark groped with one hand for the stone with which he had knocked the other's blade from his hand. He touched something, clasped it tightly and raised it just as big, powerful hands found his throat.

It was not the stone—it was the knife.

Upstairs, Hercules started awake at the sound of breaking glass. He raised himself on one elbow. The iridescence of the night flowed into the room, made a pale glowing on his desk, on Jane's *prie-dieu,* on the bed. Listening intently, he heard sounds from below, muffled, indistinct. He glanced at Jane; she slept on, undisturbed.

He crept quietly out of bed, put his trousers on over his nightgown, and got into his shoes. He went noiselessly out of the room. In the hall he paused to light one of the oil lamps. With this in one hand he went down the back stairs silently, to the door to the cellar. There he stood listening. He thought he heard heavy breathing as from a far place.

He opened the door. Someone was down in the cellar, he was certain. He put down the lamp and went into the library, where in a recess of the mantel he had concealed a pistol. Armed, he went back, took up the lamp, and started down the cellar steps.

The glow of the lamp preceded him.

He came to the foot of the steps. There, over near the stone steps ascending to the second cellar room, stood Sark, pale and disheveled, his clothing torn and dirty. In one hand he held a long, pointed blade, dripping blood. Beyond him, grotesque in the light of the lamp, lay the body of Sark's adversary, still on his face, partly on one side, as Sark had left him after crawling out from under him.

"It was—either him—or me," said Sark jerkily. He dropped the knife. "His knife. I was almost done for."

Hercules thrust the lamp at him. "Hold this, Jonas."

Sark took it, his hand trembling. He put his other hand to steady himself against the stone wall.

Hercules stepped over to the body. He pulled the dead man's shoulder back, turning his head. A small sound escaped him.

"I know him. Jacques Doutard. An old hand at this dirty work. Last heard of him at Prairie La Crosse." He stood up. "Where's the other one?"

"I don't know, Mr. Dousman. They were both after me—more—there were three."

"Three," murmured Hercules thoughtfully.

At this moment there was a grunt behind them.

Hercules spun around, his pistol up. Sark held the lamp aloft.

Thunder Walker stood on the threshold of the second cellar, gazing down at Doutard's body. He saw the knife and the blood on Doutard's back. He shook his head, and jabbed a blunt finger at Sark.

"You not have cunning. Knife show."

"Ah, I see," said Hercules. "What did you do with the other one, Thunder Walker?"

Thunder Walker spread his hands. "No blood. Dirt maybe, maybe water—no blood." He shook his head dolefully. "Poor white man. He have accident. He fall into Marais. He drown. I think maybe better not leave him there. I think maybe he drink firewater. I make sure. I pour little firewater down his throat—spill over on his clothes. He dead. No breathe. I take him to river, put him in."

Sark grinned appreciatively. He knew what had taken place. The splash he had heard was certainly Thunder Walker's attack on his other follower. Thunder Walker had been the third shadow. The Winnebago had simply held him under water until he had drowned, then poured whisky over his clothes and down his throat, after which he had carried the body to the Mississippi. In time the body might be found, but, if soon, it would be assumed that the fellow had got drunk and fallen into the river. And if not soon, it would not matter; the mudcats and turtles would finish him off, and the sand would bury his bones.

All this went through Hercules' mind as well; thanks to Thunder Walker's natural inclinations, the other of the Astor Company's assassins presented no problem. It was Sark's victim he must think of now. What was to be done with him? He could not simply be thrown into the water, as Thunder Walker's had been; the knife wounds would be discovered, questions would be asked, and, however justified Sark's killing in self-defense had been, an inquiry would inform the Astor people as to what had taken place. Silence was their best answer. Of course Sark would have to go, or it would all start over.

"This is the way they killed my father," said Sark with sudden bitterness. "A knife in the back. I'm glad I did it."

"You had no choice," said Hercules curtly. "But forget that for now. We can't leave him here. We haven't much time to think about it, either. It will be dawn in a couple of hours."

Thunder Walker proposed tying stones to the body and sinking it into the Mississippi.

Hercules shook his head. With the Mississippi high because of the thaw water pouring down out of the North, the stones would soon be worked loose and the body would turn up. "This fellow has no family I know of. He's been a solitary most of his life, and chances are the other one was, too. They're the kind the Company always picked for a job like this. No, we'll have to bury him, and I think I know the place—the big island west of the house."

Thunder Walker nodded in approval.

"If you feel up to it, Jonas, take hold of him and help Thunder Walker carry him out. I'll get shovels. Take him down to the boat at the wharf." As an afterthought he added, "Better take that knife, too, Jonas."

Sark bent, retrieved the knife, wrapped it in a handkerchief after stabbing it several times into the earth of the cellar floor, and stuck it under his belt. Then he picked up Doutard's legs, as Thunder Walker lifted the dead man by the shoulders. They carried him from one level to another, the lamplight flickering eerily on the dead man's face. They went out the way they had come in. At the cellar steps Hercules put out the lamp, then followed them outside.

He hurried to the sheds and found two shovels and a spade. Then he hastened after Sark and the Winnebago.

They already had the body in the boat when Hercules caught up with them. He stepped into the boat. Sark bent to the oars, and they pushed out into the swirling Mississippi. Sark fought and pulled against the rushing water.

No one spoke. A light wind had come up, and the trees, which had just begun to unfurl their leaves, made a hushing sibilance which fell to ear above the boiling sounds of the water. Here on the river the smell of thaw water, of snow and ice rotted by sunlight, was a heavy, cloying musk which drowned out all else—the delicate perfumes of early blossoms in the bottomlands of the Mississippi, the pleasant pungences and fragrances of opening leaves, the smell of turned soil—all were lost in the powerful odor of the river in flood.

They reached the first small island, which loomed dark against the water. Sark worked the boat around it. At a point where the water flowed in over the land he crossed it, thus avoiding the rushing current. Beyond it, the water was even more turbulent, but Sark did not tire; the very weight of the boat kept it on an even keel, and Sark was careful to move a little upstream and never to present the broad side of the boat to the churning water.

At last they reached the larger island. This was densely wooded and rose a little higher than the first island, although both would be covered by water when the Mississippi reached its height.

"There's an old tree with many spreading roots just about in the center, near one of the ponds," said Hercules. "I'll lead the way."

The island stood as in a sea of sound. All around it the water tore and swirled; it sang among the exposed roots of trees along the shore; it sucked at the earth of its banks; it vied with the wind's susurrus in the leafing branches overhead; it invaded the ponds and sloughs and made tumult there. Hercules picked his way carefully. Now and then the moon flashed forth as the clouds parted, but even under the thin clouds there was enough light to reveal the undergrowth and show the way they must go. Whippoorwills flew up at their approach; owls abruptly ceased to call as they went by; animals rustled through the undergrowth, unseen, and once what must have been a deer crashed away from them.

At length they reached the tree Hercules sought.

"We'll dig here and put him under in such a way the roots will hold him if the water gets too high," he explained.

All three set to work at once. The tree had no large taproot, and there was enough of an opening among the roots on the north side to make it possible for them to dig until they struck water oozing up.

"How far do you reckon we're down?" asked Sark.

"At least four feet—it's deep enough."

"Five," estimated Thunder Walker.

He climbed out of the grave, pulling himself up by the tree's roots, for the sides sloped, the ground was too soft to permit of a narrow, deep hole; and, once out, he waited for Sark to follow, since Hercules had got out when the Winnebago had slid in, the hole being too crowded for three. Then Thunder Walker pulled the corpse of Doutard contemptuously by the legs and rolled it into the grave. The moon came out and shone for a brief instant upon the scene, glinting from the dead man's eyes where he lay at the bottom of the grave; then the clouds came over again, and the earth began to fall back into the grave, covering Doutard, like time, thought Hercules, covering all things, all men and events, making history.

When they got back to the shore near the house on the mound, Hercules climbed out of the boat and strode away from the river's edge, saying over his shoulder, "Come to the office, Jonas."

"Yes, Mr. Dousman."

The Winnebago faded into the night. He was satisfied with himself and his night's work. Sark was confused; elation mixed with uncertainty, even dissatisfaction. Only Hercules was unhappy; he had known necessities before this; he had not flinched from facing them then; he would not flinch now—or ever, he hoped.

He did not look back to see whether Sark followed; he was sure he did. He went directly to the office, unlocked it, and crossed to his desk by the reflected light of the moon from outside, for the clouds had swept away, and the moon shone once more. He lit the lamp. Then he bent to the safe.

He opened it, took out a heavy box, and from it a leather pouch. The pouch was empty. He inserted two fingers into its neck, opening it. Then he unlocked the cash box, counted out three hundred dollars, and closed it again. He put the money into the pouch, closed and locked the cash box, put it back into the safe, and swung the door shut. He reflected ironically that Sark had helped install this safe, especially built for him only last year.

He rose and turned.

Sark was standing in the doorway, watching him.

"What are your plans, Jonas?" asked Hercules, going back to his desk. He sat down.

"Mr. Dousman, I have no plans. Suddenly, everything—all my plans—I never made any plans beyond . . ."

"Beyond getting even. A thirst for vengeance. Well, my boy,

you've tasted blood—just as those men had your father's. It ought to satisfy you. Now you've time to find out that there's more to life than a quest for vengeance. You want to live now—to eat and drink and love, to work and play—without always the bitter taste of hatred on your lips. I grew fond of you, Jonas."

He flung the bag of money to the desk.

"Take that. It's yours. It's not much."

"Mr. Dousman, I haven't earned it."

"No matter. Count it a wedding present."

Sark's lips parted; he could say nothing.

"Are you taking Annette with you?"

"I hope to."

"You haven't much time. You're going West?" He did not wait for him to answer. "West—but not to Astoria. That's the frontier now—put your talents at its disposal. You'll do well there, Jonas."

He turned his back on Sark, uncapped his inkwell, drew paper and envelope toward him, and wrote rapidly in that fine script he penned so effortlessly. When he finished, he folded what he had written and addressed the envelope. He handed it to Sark.

"Carry this with you, and try to get to that address. Count Brogmar left Sac Prairie over a year ago. He's located in the Sonoma Valley. I understand from his cousin, Pierneau, that the land's very rich—not only in gold. Just remember, Jonas, it isn't gold that sweetens life—it's work."

"Thank you, Mr. Dousman."

"I know you've not had an opportunity to plan," continued Hercules. "Take two of my horses—one for yourself, one for Annette, if she'll go. Ride them to Galena and leave them there with Mr. Southworth at the Galena House; I'll get them there or have them brought up on the next boat. Take the boat from Galena to St. Louis. If for any reason you need help there, see Pierre Chouteau. Tell him I sent you. At St. Louis the West is open to you."

"Mr. Dousman . . ." He faltered, not knowing what to say.

"Jonas, you haven't time to stand there. Take any horse but Major. It's not long till dawn, and with the moon out, the night's almost as light as day."

He held out his hand. Jonas clasped it. With his free hand, Hercules reached behind him for the money pouch; he pressed it into Jonas' hand.

"Good luck, Jonas!"

Sark turned abruptly, jumped from the steps, and ran to the stables. Hercules put out the lamp, locked the office, and stood watching Sark come from the stables, riding one horse, leading another. He stood there in the moonlight as Sark rode by, saluting him with one upraised arm, and watched him go in the direction of the Marais de St. Feriole. Then he shrugged, sighed, and walked back to the house. He let himself in by the cellar door, where he picked up the lamp, lit it once more, and carried it down into the cellar.

At the scene of the struggle he looked carefully for any sign that might disclose what had happened. He picked up the jar which had been broken against the wall, carefully gathering all the pieces, and concealed them, with the resolution to dispose of them later. He gathered together the papers and account books which had been scattered. He scuffed the ground with his shoes to hide the marks of battle. He covered with earth a few places where blood had fallen and tramped it down; but most of Doutard's blood had soaked into his clothes.

Then, satisfied, he went back up the stairs to bed, where Jane still slept. He slipped in beside her and lay sleepless, thinking of Sark and the events just past, wondering what he would do for someone in the office now. In the east the first light of dawn began to push up against the glow of the moon. Sleep would not come.

At the breakfast table Hercules said matter-of-factly, "Mr. Sark has left us."

Jane stared at him. "When do he go?"

"He left in the night. I lent him two of my horses. As a matter of guesswork, I believe he eloped with Annette Gaucher, or else he wouldn't have needed a second horse."

Jane turned this over in her mind. "Why do he go all of a sudden this way?"

"I believe these things usually happen suddenly, Jane," said Hercules, laughing.

"But what will Mistaire Dousman do now?" she cried.

"All my life I've been accustomed to doing for myself. Someone to help me is a convenience—but only as important as someone to talk to, and not much more so. Just the same, I've been thinking about the time Jonas would go; I knew he'd leave us someday."

Hercules turned and looked at Louis LeBrun, who sat quietly at table eating bacon and eggs. Louis had grown from a diffident boy to almost a young man. His skin had darkened, his hair seemed even blacker than it had seemed that first night he had come into the house in the shadow of Alexander Fisher. As he had learned to speak English, he had become more confident and poised.

Jane followed his gaze. "Not Louis!" she cried.

"Why not?" To Louis he said, "Louis, when you've finished, come to the office."

"I'm done now, sir," said Louis eagerly, his bright eyes alert.

"Then come."

Hercules got up, went around the table, kissed Jane and Dédé at her side, bade Miss McCleod good morning, and went out of the house. Louis excused himself and followed.

At the office he bade Louis sit at Sark's desk until the mail could be examined. Louis sat down expectantly, his eyes following Hercules' every movement. He was aware that Hercules had plans for him that went beyond his status as houseboy, and he waited patiently while Hercules went over the letters on his desk.

Hercules did not intend to do more than ascertain where the

mail had come from, but among the little stack of letters was one without one of the new stamps which had been in use for a few years now, nor did it have the scrawled fee written by a postmaster in such part of the western territories as stamps might not yet have reached. It was a free letter from Washington.

Hercules slit it open. It came from the Commissioner of Indian Affairs. He looked past the superscription and the initial paragraph, which he knew by experience would be a compound of formal introduction and not so subtle flattery.

We believe, in view of your many past services to us, that you are the man best fitted to represent us in two matters. The one is as yet in the future—perhaps next year—and that is the matter of the Sioux lands west of the Mississippi in Minnesota Territory. There is some reluctance on their part to sell. [No wonder, thought Hercules, at the exchange offered!] . . . The other, however, is more imminent, and I propose to outline it herewith. We are trying to persuade the Menominees under Chief Oshkosh to move into the Crow Wing country of Minnesota Territory. This is the same general region to which the Winnebago we put at Long Prairie have now gone. Oshkosh has proved extremely unwilling to leave his ancestral lands about Lake Winnebago, but he has at last consented to go with a party of his Menominees to look at the Crow Wing country. He will come down to Prairie du Chien with his party by wagon early in June, and expects to go up river from Prairie du Chien on the seventh. We do not know the day of his arrival in Prairie du Chien, but we will try to find out and let you know. Once they reach Minnesota, Fletcher will take them in charge.

Will you use your good offices to talk with Oshkosh and do what you can to put him into the proper frame of mind so that he will be amenable to our suggestion that he remove his tribe to the Crow Wing country? He is a stubborn man . . .

And who would not be? thought Hercules wearily, against such a history of unfairness and duplicity practiced upon the Indians. He put down the letter and turned to Louis LeBrun.

"Now, Louis," he said, "we begin."

Louis was an apt pupil. In three weeks he had learned all Sark's office work, and Hercules did not doubt that he would be as quick to learn what he had to know about furs and the trade. Hercules rapidly grew accustomed to him, and as the days passed Sark become inexorably part of past time—only one brief message came from him, sent from Fort Laramie, then no more; and it began to seem as if Louis LeBrun had been part of the office for a long time.

One day late in May LeBrun came for Hercules just as Hercules had got out Major and was preparing to mount.

"Mr. Dousman," he said deferentially, "I know you said not to bother you, but there's a man at the office who says he must see you. I thought, sir, since he's the sheriff . . ."

"That's right, Louis. Go back and tell Mr. Fonda I'm at his disposal."

The boy ran fleetly back. Hercules followed more leisurely, on his horse. He dismounted at the office just as Sheriff Fonda came out of the building.

"Sorry to disturb you, Dousman," said the sheriff. "But as you know most of the *voyageurs,* I wonder if you might be able to identify a body Alex McGregor turned up over at his ferry landing on the other side of the river. Man been dead some time—been in the water at least six weeks, Dr. Foote said."

"Oh, Foote's had a look at him, has he?"

"I called him."

"What's his verdict?"

"Drowned. Misadventure, he called it." He grinned under his discolored mustache. "You've got a suspicious mind, Dousman. This fellow just drowned, that's all. Probably got pickled and fell in—you know what a rough and fast life those men lead."

"I'll take a look at him."

He thought he might recognize the body; he might be known to him, as Doutard was; but he had forgotten that the river was not kind to flesh—the face had been partly eaten away, and the limbs as well. Hercules did not know him, or, had he once known him, he could not identify him. The body was that of a *voyageur*, judged by such of his clothing as still remained with it, a man over fifty, Dr. Foote had said.

"I'm sorry," he said, after looking at the body. "I don't know him."

But he had no doubt that this was Doutard's companion, Thunder Walker's victim. So this was an end to that matter. The body would be taken out and buried with no name on the stone above it—if a stone were put there: a fate which had once come uncommonly often to the independents who fought the Astor Company, and which now came, thought Hercules, with fitting irony to one of the men who had not hesitated to murder the innocent individualists who had stood fast by their idealism in opposing Astor.

On the tenth day of June the Menominee party reached Prairie du Chien to rest but a night before embarking by steamboat for St. Paul. Hercules went over to where they were encamped. There were eighteen men in the party—eleven Menominee chiefs, headed by Oshkosh and Carron Glaude, two braves, and five white men, including the interpreter, and the Indian Agent, William Bruce, a young man who seemed earnestly convinced that the Crow Wing country of Minnesota Territory was the ideal place for the Menominee to go. After five minutes' conversation with him, Hercules was not convinced that Bruce knew much about either the Crow Wing country or the character of the Menominee, although he was sincere enough.

The Indians themselves seemed passive and resigned. But Hercules, accustomed to dealing with Indians for decades, saw at once that they were glum and hostile. They had come all the way from the Lake Winnebago country in wagons—a distance of more than a hundred miles. Wagons! thought Hercules, when canoes, to which they were accustomed, would have carried them up the Fox and down the Wisconsin to the familiar meeting place at the juncture of the rivers. It was a peculiar kind of madness to which officials of government were prone, to subject the Menominee to this ordeal by wagon, particularly at a time when the government was attempting to cajole them to accept an exchange of property which was not at all to the Indians' advantage.

"I met Oshkosh some years ago when he was at a council here," said Hercules. "But I'm not sure I could pick him out."

Bruce pointed. "He's an ugly one. And if he gets any liquor in him, he's as likely to kill you as look at you."

Hercules paid no attention to this. He decided that Bruce was an easterner. He looked at Chief Oshkosh. True, the old fellow did look somewhat dissipated. Moreover, he was shorter than most Indians, chunky of figure, with a badly wrinkled face. Yet his face was not without character, and his almost absurdly pathetic look might have been the result of the ride he had been forced to take and to which his flesh was unaccustomed. He was dressed partly in tribal regalia and partly in white men's clothing, but he wore his headband and three feathers in it. His black, oily hair glistened in the late-afternoon sunlight.

"I'll talk to him," said Hercules.

"I'll call Powell or Pickett."

"Don't trouble yourself, Mr. Bruce. I don't need interpreters. I can get along in their language. I understand them and they understand me."

He walked over to face Oshkosh, raised his arm, palm outward, and sat down before the chieftain, pronouncing his name for him.

Oshkosh held out his hand. They shook hands.

"I meet Dousman many years ago at this place."

"Are we not old friends?" demanded Hercules. "Have we not looked upon each other before that?"

Oshkosh bent forward and peered into Hercules' face with narrowed eyes, as if seeking some clue to where they might have met before the time of the council to which he referred.

Hercules went on. "Was not the great chief, Oshkosh, then

but a young brave, among the Indians who fought with the Redcoats to seize the Island of the Turtle when the Americans and the Redcoats were locked in battle?"

"It is true," said Oshkosh wonderingly.

"I was then a boy on Mackinac—that is to say, the Turtle. Oshkosh was in one of the boats. He was a brave young Indian, good to look upon. He was with Tomah. He stood out among his fellow braves. He did not stain his tomahawk with innocent blood."

The Menominee smiled, pointed to Hercules, and looked proudly around to the other chiefs who accompanied him. "See!" he cried. "This man is our friend. He has known us in other times." He turned again to Hercules. "You know why we are here?"

Hercules nodded.

"Say to us what we must do, friend of the Great White Father."

"I say to you go to this country of the Crow Wing, look upon it, and do as your heart tells you to do."

Hercules' words aroused a murmur of approval.

Chief Oshkosh sprang to his feet, nodding his head in fierce agreement. "We come here," he said. "We shake hands with you. We do so with a good heart. I have seen many years. I was but a young brave when the Americans came to my place at Green Bay. This was in 1816. This was after they had taken back the Island of the Turtle, where we fought with the Redcoats. The Americans shook hands with us. They told us they had come to live among us and make us happy. They promised us if we followed their counsel we would have no trouble.

"At the council we held in 1827 . . ." He stopped suddenly, and peered intently at Hercules. "It was there that first we saw each other, Dousman."

"It was there."

"At this council," continued Oshkosh, "General Cass said the same thing to us—that Americans were our friends, we should always follow their advice. Again, in 1836, at Cedar Point, we met Governor Dodge, who came to treat with us. He told us that what he promised our Great Father, the President, would perform. We submitted to our Father's wish and ceded part of our lands. Governor Dodge promised that our Great White Father would always protect us as his own children and would always hold our hands in his.

"We always thought much of Governor Dodge as an honest man. We believed all he told us. But he said the government would not ask more of our lands from us. How is this, then, that now these white men come to us and say they have a place in the Crow Wing country for the Menominee, and ask us to surrender our land in Wisconsin for this land we have never seen? How is this?" He turned to his fellow chiefs. "Do I not speak for all of us?" he demanded. "You, Souligny? Na-Molte? Carron? Oshkeehenawniew? Ahkenotoway? Casagascegay?"

Each of the chiefs nodded solemnly as his name was called. Oshkosh turned to Hercules and waited for his answer.

Hercules got to his feet. He began to talk slowly, choosing his words with great care. He explained that many moons had passed since first the Great White Father had spoken to the Menominee. In this time many changes had come about. Many of those who had spoken for the White Father had been gathered to their ancestors. Others were no longer in the government. Even the Great White Father had changed, for now he was that man who had commanded Fort Crawford in the old days, who had taken Black Hawk prisoner, and who had fought with Mexico. Now even he lay ill in Washington. All things must change, said Hercules, for such was the law and order of life.

"The Menominee do not change," cried Oshkosh to the accompaniment of an approving mutter.

Nevertheless, Hercules went on, it was not the fault of Governor Dodge that this request was now made. It was not the fault of General Cass, who had tried to become the Great White Father two years ago but had failed because General Taylor had been the choice of the white men. He explained patiently that many many white men were coming into America from far countries across the sea, that the Great White Father was trying to find more land for them.

"He may send them to the Crow Wing country," said Oshkosh with admirable simplicity.

Hercules restrained a smile.

"We wish to stay in our lands," Oshkosh continued. "We have great love for our lands. We have remained there many generations. We do not wish to exchange for other lands. We are content to die there."

How many times had he heard Indian chiefs express similar sentiments! thought Hercules. Red Bird of the Winnebago! Wabashaw! He recalled with every intonation of the words the moving speech of the Black Sparrow Hawk when he had surrendered to Taylor eighteen years ago. "We loved our land!" Was it not a constant refrain, a continuing lament? It had been spoken by Indians of the eastern seaboard, and was perhaps even now being said in many places west of the Mississippi as the ravenous land seekers pushed toward the West Coast. "We loved our land. We fought for it!"

"Is it our fault that the land around Lake Poygan is coveted by the white men?" cried Oshkosh. "It is our land. Is the land of the Crow Wing rich in wild rice? The blackrobe among us says it is not. We are gatherers of rice. We are not tillers of the soil. We are not farmers. We are hunters." Abruptly Oshkosh shook his head. "Now I have spoken. I will say no more." Then he sat down.

Hercules knew that the government expected him to persuade the Menominee to accept the Crow Wing country. Had they not agreed to go to this country in the treaty of 1848? he asked Oshkosh.

"But only if the country is fit for us—and we shall judge that," answered Oshkosh.

Hercules agreed that this was fair. He could not say to them to obey the wish of the White Father if the agents of the government had accepted the Menominee proposal of approval of the country west of the Mississippi.

"Go then to the Crow Wing country and look upon it. The Crow Wing River is fair. Its valley is good to look upon. I do not know it as a country of wild rice. You must decide as your hearts tell you. I can say no more."

Then he bade Oshkosh and his companions a ceremonious farewell and walked back to where the Indian Agent waited for him.

"What's this about the blackrobe who tells the Menominee the Crow Wing country isn't good?" he asked.

"He's a Jesuit priest—a troublemaker. Father Bonduel. Half these Menominees are Christian, half are not. The Jesuit has a great influence among them."

Hercules shook his head. "They use him, not he them. Mr. Bruce, you're making this journey in vain. These Menominee will never accept the Crow Wing country."

In a way, he hoped they would not. He had seen so many Indians betrayed and misled by the government that he could not help wishing the tables might be turned. In the midst of Bruce's voluble attack on Father Bonduel, Hercules excused himself and walked away, lest it become too clear where his sympathies lay.

For long periods at a time Hercules could put the thought of George Brunet out of his mind. But now and then, stirred by some event, some occasion beyond his ability to control, his mind occupied itself almost obsessively with the boy. This time it was the news that Emily was pregnant and would have her first child in autumn that reminded him that Dédé was not his only other child. And when the awareness of that child of Cecile Gardepi's pressed in upon him, it soon became overpowering; it took possession of him, ruling him, plunging him anew into the complexity of the problem he faced no matter what he did about the boy. And even if he did nothing, procrastinating as he had been doing, waiting vainly upon Julie Brunet to make her wishes known.

On this morning in June he could not free himself from his

concern for the boy. He left LeBrun at his desk and walked over to the house of Souligne. He had already taken care of Lapiage; he had done all else Souligne had asked of him, but though he had had the Masses read for Souligne, he had not yet offered the house to Julia Brunet for George. The time was not yet right.

He let himself in by the back door. Though the day was warm, the house was cool; it had been kept shut for a long time. It was also musty. He crossed to the room facing the Brunet house and sat down a little back from the window.

The boy was playing with others—five in all—in the lane before the Brunet house. Hercules had noticed him as he went by, but had not turned his head to draw attention to himself. Now, seated behind the ragged curtain, out of sight of the Brunet house, he kept his eyes on George.

Save that he had grown taller, he had changed very little since first Hercules had seen him. Two years! The boy was now ten. Between Emily, now virtually a woman, on the one side, and Dédé, now two years old, stood this boy. Dédé, too, had dark hair, like George: both with hair like their father, though his own was thinning now, and if he continued to lose it, Hercules reflected, he would need to order a wig.

George was lively, agile, alert. The boys were playing a game of ball with a bat and a glove. They were in placed positions. As he watched, two other boys came running to join them. George batted the ball and ran for a goal. It reminded Hercules of a game he had seen in the East. But the game itself was of no interest to him; it was the boy who held his eye, and it gave him a kind of satisfaction to be able to watch him like this, even as Souligne had predicted it would. And it filled a void which had been in his life ever since Souligne had disclosed his son's existence to him.

There were times when Hercules had been tempted to go to Jane and tell her of George's nearness. But what could he accomplish without knowing where Julia Brunet stood? He was confident that he could count on Jane's understanding. What would she say to him? Would she want the boy, too? Or would she fear that somehow Dédé might take second place in his affections?

If the boy was taciturn, even sullen, among adults, he was surely not so among other boys. He shouted and screamed with the most active of them; indeed, he moved about so much that Hercules seldom got a very good look at him.

Hercules glanced at the other boys. He knew one or two of them, both older than George. Twelve or thirteen, he thought. They were sons of old settlers, grandsons of some of them; all lived in the neighborhood. They were clearly accustomed to gather together to play games, for they were all easily familiar with one another, and called each other by nicknames. Hercules tried hard to distinguish what it was they called George, but he could not; the window was down; he dared not open it lest he call attention to his presence in the house.

An hour crept by. The number of boys diminished. The ball game was abandoned. George and two others alone remained. They came up into the yard at the Brunet house and sat on a stump there in animated conversation. This brought George closer to the window, and Hercules could not take his eyes off him; it was the old feeling he had, of looking at himself when young, of looking into the intimate past, with all its griefs and joys.

He must do something to bring the boy close to him. But what? He was half afraid to move, lest he learn something he did not want to know. He did not trust Julia Brunet, and with every year that the boy was with her, Julia would have more and more opportunity to bind George to her above all other ties.

Watching George like this, Hercules wanted to get up and go out to him. He wanted to take him by the hand, to say to him, "George, I'm your father."

But he tormented himself. He pushed away from the window. There were little beads of perspiration at his temples, at his lips. He wiped them away.

He forced himself to walk out of the house and away without looking back.

4. *Lose the Name of Action*

Autumn, 1851–Spring, 1852

THE MATTER OF THE SIOUX LANDS WEST OF THE MISSISSIPPI, about which the Commissioner of Indian Affairs had written Hercules, languished for more than a year. Then, late in the second summer, word came from Washington that there continued to be difficulties about the disposal of the Sioux lands; would Hercules travel into the Sioux country and talk with some of the chieftains—Torn Ear, Brown Elk, and Angry Cloud, who were recalcitrant?

Hercules was not anxious to go, but he could think of no good reason for declining. He was surprised that he had been asked, since he had served no purpose in talking with Chief Oshkosh, for the Menominee had returned from the Minnesota Territory more than ever bound to their ancestral lands in Wisconsin, just as Hercules had foreseen.

He set out in September, boarding the *Senator* at the dock at Prairie du Chien, where the activity was as great as it had been all season, despite the proximity of the season's end; immigrants, doctors, lawyers, laboring men, Indians, and Minnesotans returning from buying trips crowded the boat, which carried no less than eighty passengers as well as supplies that ranged all the way from barrels of flour to plows, wagons, even horses.

The low stage of the Mississippi made the upriver trip both

slower and more tedious. Hercules kept much to himself, either in his stateroom or on deck, where he watched the familiar bluffs, river mouths, and lowlands slip by, marveling at the changes which had taken place since first he had made his way up the Mississippi to Fort Snelling—the little villages which had begun to grow on headlands and in valleys where, when first he had looked upon these shores, the wigwams and cabins of Indians had stood; the great piles of cordwood at the wooding stations where once solid, unbroken forest had covered the land. A night storm on Lake Pepin delayed them still more, so that it was not until the sixth day that they reached St. Paul.

Here, too, all was changed since Hercules' first visit. Fort Snelling, which had once commanded the heights in solitary impressiveness, was dwarfed by the town which had grown away from it, spreading back from and surmounting the bluffs that rose from the river's edge. The docks were below the heights, and a broad road wound up into the town.

Governor Ramsey was at the landing to meet Hercules, together with an interpreter, a slender young man who was all sinews and bone. Ramsey was a little more portly than he had been; Hercules noticed also that he was considerably less formal; the frontier had washed away something of the East. His hair was shaggier and longer; it grew now well down along his jaws. He seemed genuinely happy to see Hercules and greeted him as an old friend.

"I hope you don't mind, Dousman—I'm going with you. I want to see at first hand what it is you have to offer the Indians that you're so successful with them."

"I haven't any special quality, Ramsey. I suppose it's just that I treat them like human beings."

"Well, come along. You'll put up with me for the night. Mr. Pickett here is the best interpreter of the Sioux tongue in the Territory, and I understood you didn't know that language as well as you know most of those spoken by your Wisconsin Indians." He added, "You didn't bring an interpreter?"

"No. I expected to find one here or among the Sioux."

The journey was resumed in the morning, this time in two canoes, since steamboat travel was not feasible all the way. The Indian Agent at Fort Snelling went with them, together with two *voyageurs* to assist the Agent and the interpreter at the paddles. One of them was Hercules' old friend and employee, Benoit.

"Long tam, M'sieu' Dousman!" cried Benoit at sight of him.

"I want this man in my canoe, Ramsey," said Hercules.

The governor motioned Benoit to his place. He apologized for the smallness of the canoes, but explained that they would soon leave the Mississippi to go up the Crow Wing River, then through a series of small lakes, and finally overland to a place where a council had been arranged with the Sioux, and the lighter they traveled, the better.

Governor Ramsey's canoe took the lead.

Hercules sat so that he could talk to Benoit. "You've been among these Indians, Benoit?"

"Many tam!" Benoit nodded vigorously.

"How are they?"

Benoit explained volubly that they were "differen'—not lak the Indian we know." It was difficult for him to say exactly what it was that made the Sioux different. For one thing, they were horsemen. For another, they were hunters. They seldom stayed in one place. They roamed the country to the west. They belonged to a vast nation. There were Lakotah Sioux, Arapaho, Minneconjou, Oglala, and many other tribes covering much of the country between Minnesota and the land of the upper Missouri.

The two canoes soon left the Mississippi and turned up the Crow Wing River. They passed through sandy country, with poplar groves and some Norway pine. Though the water beneath them was filled with fish of all kinds—pike, buffalo, rock bass, catfish, and others—there was little game to be seen along shore.

The Crow Wing near its mouth was broad and easy to travel. They made good time upriver. When they stopped for the night, the *voyageurs* netted enough fish for supper, and they all sat for a while around the campfire eating and talking before they wrapped themselves in their blankets and lay under the stars to sleep.

The next day the nature of the country changed. Its sandiness gave place to loam and clay. Burr-oak openings began to show, and tamarack swamps appeared in low places. There were many tracks of bears, and several times bears could be seen lumbering away from the river's edge. Deer bounded away into the woods. And whenever they passed through lakes, ducks and geese scattered before them—not so many, Hercules reflected, as could be seen in the migrating seasons in the sloughs along the Mississippi at Prairie du Chien.

But nowhere was there any rice. It did not surprise him that even the virtues of the country, such as there were, could not overcome the lack of rice for the Menominee who had made this journey the previous year. Yet it was good to look upon, and such Indians as they passed—chiefly transplanted Winnebago who had once lived across the Mississippi in Wisconsin—seemed content, for they were often seen at work in large fields of corn or turnips.

On the fifth day, when Hercules reckoned that they were close to the heart of lower Minnesota Territory, they were met by a party of Sioux with horses for them to ride. Benoit and his fellow *voyageur* were left with the canoes; the others set out with the Sioux.

Hercules had known the Sioux who had lived near Prairie du Chien more than a decade ago. They had been river travelers, like the Winnebago and Pottawatomi who were their neighbors. These Minnesota Sioux were subtly different; they were taller, and their faces were more impassive. They spoke little—indeed, they had spoken only to ask whether it was the party they had been sent to meet; they had indicated the horses they were to ride by almost arrogant gestures. They were big-nosed. They wore little clothing, and seldom more than a single feather at the back of their heads. Such clothing as they wore was heavily beaded and decorated. Most of them had long hair, sometimes worn loose, lending them an unwontedly savage and wild appearance.

After five hours' riding they came to the place of the council. It had been set apart from the Sioux camp, for these Sioux, explained the Indian Agent, claimed a considerable land, but had no true villages, preferring to move about the country hunting, camping sometimes in one place for many months, until game was exhausted, then moving on.

Chief Torn Ear, flanked by Chiefs Brown Elk and Angry Cloud, sat astride horses facing the oncoming party. The chiefs looked very much like the men sent to guide them to this place, thought Hercules, although Angry Cloud wore two feathers in his hair; the others wore but one each. All the chiefs, however, were more fully dressed.

The interpreter immediately made introductions.

Chief Angry Cloud had evidently been chosen to speak, for Torn Ear nudged him forward as soon as the interpreter had finished. Angry Cloud was the oldest of the three; his first words said as much.

"I am an old man. I welcome you in the name of our people."

The interpreter translated rapidly, and Angry Cloud went on.

But all he had to say was simply a speech of welcome. Hercules reflected ruefully that he was no different from most of the Indians he had known. However taciturn and uncommunicative the average Indian, he need only be selected to make a speech to discover a latent ability to say in twenty minutes what he could say more effectively in one. Yet these formalities had to be gone through.

Angry Cloud's speech was only the first formality. Thereafter they had to join the chiefs at a feast, which was followed by an entertainment of ritual dances. Only when all this was done would the Sioux be ready to talk. Unhappily, by this time darkness had fallen, and there was no more time to discuss the proposed cession of the Sioux lands.

The talks began in the morning. Hercules, Governor Ramsey, the Indian Agent, and the interpreter sat in a semicircle facing the three Sioux chiefs, who had been joined in the night by a body of braves; these now sat colorfully behind the chiefs, making violent movements to show their agreement whenever one of the chiefs spoke, sitting watchful and still whenever Hercules replied.

Chief Torn Ear spoke at length on the Sioux grievances. They were much the same as most of the Indian grievances Hercules had heard, but there was a difference. This time there was no complaint that the white men had invaded the Indian villages, but only their hunting grounds. These grounds, it appeared, stretched to westward as far as a bird could fly and east to the great Father of Waters. Torn Ear had yet another and juster complaint.

"I am an Indian, but the white men do not wish it to be so. They want to make a white man out of me. They do not come among us to live as brother with brother. No, they want to change us into likenesses of themselves. Manitou has not put us here to rule the earth, but only this portion of it where we live. But the white men talk as if Manitou is one of them." He defied Hercules to explain this.

"Is not Manitou a red man for red men?" asked Hercules.

"Yes, this is true."

"Then Manitou is a white man for white men," replied Hercules. "Far away, across the great water, there are black men. For them, Manitou is black. Even farther, there are yellow men. Their Manitou is yellow. Manitou is for every man what he thinks Manitou is."

This perplexed Torn Ear. His braves muttered behind him. He consulted with Angry Cloud and Brown Elk. He turned again to face Hercules, grinning.

"Even so, it is true," he agreed. He seemed surprised and delighted to have discovered this truth.

Little by little the underlying complaint of the Sioux became apparent. It was admitted that they had signed and agreed to the treaty of Traverse des Sioux of the previous June. They were perfectly willing to cede their lands west of the Mississippi to the shores of a certain lake well west of where this council sat, explained Torn Ear, but they did not want to be sent to a place with boundaries, conceiving that boundaries impeded their natural inclination to roam.

Hercules promised to study the problem and see what could be done for the Sioux.

There was yet one more matter, Torn Ear went on, and motioned Brown Elk forward.

"Many years ago," began Brown Elk, "one of my people married a trader. They had a son. This boy was to me as my son. His mother was my niece. His father was dear to me. Then one day his father went on a journey and took his son with him. The trader died, and the son was taken by his people. His mother grieves. She wishes her son restored to her. He is in the city white men call St. Louis."

Hercules explained patiently that this was a problem for the Commissioner of Indian Affairs; he had no power to decide it; but he would say to the Commissioner that the boy should be returned. He spoke with such earnestness that Brown Elk was immediately placated; but Hercules spoke in this manner because Brown Elk's story had brought sharply to mind his own son, George Brunet, filling him, as he had been filled before, with remorse that he had not yet moved to bring the boy to his side, where he should rightfully be, and confirming him in his intention to delay no longer.

Thereafter he was eager to start the return journey, and the party started out at once when the parley was done, even though they would have to hasten to reach the canoes before dark.

Yet this resolve, so easily made, so firmly believed in, paled and diminished the closer Hercules got to home. Far west in the Sioux country he had been free of all that bound him from action; but here, in Prairie du Chien, everything reminded him that he could not act of his own free will—Jane, Dédé, even the faithful Louis, as well as his business affairs, had to be considered. The little walk he had intended to make, to visit Julia Brunet, loomed like an interminable journey, beset by unknown perils which were all but insurmountable, concealed in the intentions of Julia Brunet.

He was ashamed of his inability to act, and grew morose.

At table one noon Jane chided him.

"Mistaire Dousman have so much on his min'," she said, "sometime I wondair if I exis', if our son exis' for him."

"Women are much given to such concern. It's always been that way. Unless a man waits on them hand and foot, they begin to think they're no longer loved."

"Oh, I know Mistaire Dousman love me," cried Jane. "But do he think of me?"

"How could I not? Could I not think of flowers in bloom, and the softness of the spring wind, and the beauty of the sunset?"

She sighed happily. "As long as Mistaire Dousman can make the pretty speech, I know he think of me."

Hercules turned to Dédé, who was now a handsome child in his fourth year. "And you, Dédé, would you like to come with your papa this afternoon?"

"Yes, Papa."

"Without ask' where he go," cried Jane instantly. "But, Mistaire Dousman, he cannot go. I wish him to be here where I can watch him so he is safe."

"I didn't intend to take him sailing on the Mississippi," said Hercules reproachfully. He pushed his chair back, went around and lifted his son down from the raised chair in which he sat. "If you don't mind, I'll just borrow him for a little while."

The boy walked proudly along, clinging to Hercules' hand. As they walked through the kitchen, Hercules beckoned to LeBrun, who had just come in.

"Come along, Louis. I want you."

LeBrun followed obediently, his dinner forgotten.

Outside, Hercules turned to him and held out his hand with Dédé's hand in it. "Here, Louis. Teach him to ride a horse."

"He is not too small?"

"I think not."

LeBrun hesitated. "Perhaps better I go get the horse and bring him here. I will get Lady—she is the most gentle."

"We'll wait here then," said Hercules agreeably.

LeBrun ran across the lawn to the stables. Presently he reappeared, leading the brown mare.

Dédé jumped up and down and began to clap his small hands. "I can ride the horse!" he cried. "Can't I, Papa?"

"You may. We'll see if you can."

LeBrun came up with Lady. He came around to Hercules and lifted Dédé to the horse's back. He put the reins into the boy's hands, then walked around to the front and took hold of the halter. Dédé's sturdy little legs pressed close to Lady's sides as LeBrun led the horse away. He shouted with pleasure. "Look at me, Papa! Look at me!"

Jane came out of the house to the back porch steps. For a moment she stood there aghast, as if she could not believe what she saw. Then her face paled. She turned to Hercules.

"Mistaire Dousman! He might fall! He might be hurt! He might even be kill'!"

"That mount is gentler than his rocking horse," answered Hercules imperturbably.

"Mistaire Dousman, he mus' come back."

Hercules gazed tranquilly at her. "Don't you think you coddle him too much, Jane? After all, he's a boy—not a girl—and I want him to grow up so that he'll be able to take hold here when I'm gone."

But Jane was not listening. She left his side to run across the lawn to the horse, which was now near the long grape arbor covering the walk from the west side of the house to the shore of the river. She reached up as soon as LeBrun, who had seen her coming, stopped; she caught hold of Dédé and pulled him down. He protested loudly.

"Papa! Papa! I want to ride!"

He tried to pull back from Jane's hand, but she held him too tightly. She half-dragged him back to the porch steps, paying no attention to his angry tears.

At the steps Hercules took his son. He stopped Jane's protest on her lips. "Madame will go into the house," he said firmly.

For a moment Jane was too surprised to speak. Then her dark eyes flashed fire. "Mistaire Dousman!"

"We do not quarrel in front of Dédé, Jane. Do as I say."

She saw that he would not be moved; he was angry. "If anything happen . . . !" She left the sentence unfinished, turned, and went up the steps into the house.

Hercules turned to LeBrun, who had returned with the mare. "Now, then, Louis. Once again."

LeBrun put the boy back on the horse, and they started away once more. Hercules walked slowly after them. He saw Jane at the window, standing with her fists clenched against the pane, her arms upraised. He looked at her, grinned, and pointed to the boy.

Dédé clung firmly to the horse, his legs kneed in. He was laughing with glee.

Watching him, Hercules was impelled to go for his own mount and ride beside him, but he rejected the impulse because the presence of Major beside Lady might make her less tractable; he could not risk that.

LeBrun led boy and horse down to the river's edge and back. Then they paraded up and down before the west doors, where Jane now stood, still peering out apprehensively.

As they passed before Hercules, he called out, "Enough, Louis."

LeBrun brought the boy back to Hercules, who lifted him from the horse and turned to the house with him.

Miss McCleod stood waiting, primly disapproving. She did not venture to express her feelings to Hercules, simply took the boy's hand in hers and marched off to the nursery with him.

Hercules went directly to Jane's parlor, where she waited.

"I hope Mistaire Dousman is now satisfy," she said.

"Yes, I am."

He straddled a chair, facing her, folding his arms over its back.

"Mistaire Dousman speak vair' harsh to me."

"I'm sorry, Jane, but the circumstances called for it. I didn't order the boy to horse for you to pull him off. I've thought for a while now you tended to coddle him—you and Miss McCleod and Eugenie. He's surrounded by women, and I don't want a woman made out of him, I want someone who'll be able to look after your best interests when I'm gone—and that means all the ramifications of the business."

She put a lace handkerchief to her eyes and held it there. "I suppose Mistaire Dousman mus' start sometime, but he is so young—not yet four."

"After this he'll ride whenever he has the inclination to do so. At first with Louis or me—later, by himself. I'll think of other things for him to do."

"We shall see," answered Jane, tearing the handkerchief from her flashing eyes.

He laughed. "I've always said you are exceptionally attractive when you're angry, Jane."

"Mistaire Dousman cannot always win with pretty words," she said as she got up and swept past him, her skirts brushing against him with a satin rustle.

He swung off his chair. He made no attempt to stop her or follow her, but went out of the house the way he had come in—through the kitchen, where LeBrun now sat eating his belated meal—and on to the office. He sat down at his desk and turned to his work.

But the work did not hold him. The little disagreement with Jane troubled him. Her "We shall see!" had had an ominous sound, because he knew very well that by the nature of things Dédé would be far more in Jane's company—and thus also with the other women of the household—than in his. How could it be otherwise, when he had all his affairs to attend to—his investments, the trade, his loans, and the various projects which engaged his attention, to say nothing of the journeys he must make from time to time?

Jane was attached to Dédé with all the overweening affection of a mother to her last-born. And he was her last; there would be none other. All her children by Joe Rolette were gone—Elizabeth married, Virginie dead, Joe at Pembina and seldom home. Dédé was all she had beside her, and upon him she lavished all that maternal affection which for so many years had had no outlet. He was the dead Virginie all over again; he was Elizabeth and Young Joe as children, all rolled into one. If she had her way with Dédé, would he not in the end be too soft—so soft that when the time came for him to take hold his strength would not be in hand or heart?

He pulled out the ledger in which he had concealed the Catlin drawings of George. He unfolded them, smoothed them out, and sat contemplating them. But the very sight of them reproached him. It was more than three years since first Souligne had brought George to his attention. Souligne himself had been dead for more than a year. And still Hercules had done nothing to challenge Julia Brunet's control over his own son! He told himself that whatever Jane might think, whatever Julia's intentions were, whatever malicious talk might follow an attempt on his part to wrest the boy away from the Brunets—all these things did not excuse his not having taken some step toward him.

Even so, he felt powerless to move. He had not yet acted upon the change he had made in Souligne's will. Even this had been held in abeyance. He had had a hard time fencing with Lapiage, when the *voyageur* had wanted to know how Souligne had disposed of the house; he had had an even more difficult time convincing himself that this indirect approach was worthy of him. Yet he wanted to give Julia Brunet every opportunity to declare herself, and her continued indifference to him troubled him more than he cared to admit.

I'll go to her now, he said to himself.

But he did not. He continued to sit there. Hearing LeBrun

approach the office, he put the drawings away again, and with them went his resolution. . . .

On the day before Christmas an Indian presented himself at the office. He was clad in a suit of elkskin and wrapped in a buffalo robe. It was Brown Elk, the Sioux. Hercules hardly recognized him.

"Brown Elk!" he cried. "What brings you here?"

Brown Elk explained, with some difficulty, since he could not readily understand English any more than Hercules could understand the Sioux tongue, that his people had sent him.

LeBrun watched somewhat apprehensively as the Sioux, with many gestures and elaborations of his hands, as if he were sketching pictures in the air, told why he had come. The Sioux treaty had not yet been ratified. It was not the fault of the Sioux. The Great White Father had done nothing about the treaty. It lay in the city of the Great White Father waiting upon his agreement. Why was this so?

Hercules tried to point out that the politicians in Washington were men of many delays.

Brown Elk had other complaints. The half-breeds had persuaded the Sioux to sell their reservation at Lake Pepin, he said. The Indians were to be paid $150,000. But, since the treaty had not been ratified, there was no money. Now the Sioux wanted to move, since they must, and since the Minnesota Territory was becoming poor for hunting.

"White man," said Brown Elk slowly in English, "kill to kill. Sioux kill to eat." He had evidently painstakingly memorized this.

Hercules could not take issue with him. He nodded in agreement, since there was nothing else to do. The rapacity and greed of many white men were too well known to justify argument.

"What do you expect me to do?" he asked, perplexed.

Brown Elk explained graphically that the Sioux had gone to Governor Ramsey. He had not been able to help them. He had told them that it was Dousman who had spoken for the government at the council three months before. So the Sioux had sent him; they wished Dousman now to use his great influence to see to it that the treaty was ratified.

"It may be that I'll have to go East later this winter," said Hercules. "I could go around by way of Washington."

The Sioux nodded vigorously when this had been made clear to him. He interpreted it as an acceptance of the problem that Brown Elk had brought to him, and he said no more about the matter. Instead, he turned to something more personal. He wished to thank Hercules for what he had done about the boy, his niece's son.

"I go now to St. Louis to see him," said Brown Elk. He was certain that the boy would be returned to him; he was grateful.

"I've done no more than write a letter or two," protested Hercules.

Of what had taken place Hercules had no knowledge. He had referred the problem to Washington, the subagent had also written from St. Paul, and no word of the disposal of the matter had come to either of them. Brown Elk spoke volubly. Evidently the boy was to be restored to his mother, and Brown Elk was going to St. Louis to get him. Of course he would be returned only conditionally, thought Hercules; perhaps Brown Elk did not understand this, and Hercules did not mention it, knowing he would learn of it in St. Louis before being permitted to take the boy.

Having said all he had come to say, Brown Elk immediately made ready to leave. He shook his head in answer to Hercules' invitation to stay for the night.

"It's beginning to snow," Hercules pointed out. "It won't be easy traveling, horse or no horse."

Brown Elk only shook his head. He was anxious to go to the place where his niece's boy was. He wrapped himself in his buffalo robe and stalked to the threshold, where he turned to make the gesture of farewell. Then he stepped out into the falling snow.

"What kind of an Indian was that, Mr. Dousman?" asked LeBrun.

"A Sioux."

"I guess he thinks you're going to Washington."

"It might be, Louis, that I am."

Hercules was not thinking about the Sioux treaty or Washington. Brown Elk's visit had brought forward once more what was now increasingly in the back of his mind—George. The Sioux's mention of the lost son of his niece stirred him, filled him anew with a feeling of guilt, made him chastize himself in his thoughts because, while he, an affluent man, settled and comforatble, had done nothing to bring about a reunion with his own son, this Indian was braving the uncertain, often bitter weather of the Mississippi Valley winter to bring back his grandnephew from St. Louis, hundreds of miles south of the Sioux country.

He was unhappily silent at dinner that night, and later, while he was helping Jane decorate the Christmas tree with which to surprise Dédé in the morning, his preoccupation was so great that she could not escape noticing it.

"Mistaire Dousman ac' like he has guilty conscience," she said suddenly.

Hercules started as if she had prodded him.

She laughed heartily. "Oh, I do think Mistaire Dousman keep some guilty secret," she cried. "What have he do? Have he cheat someone—pairhaps he commit murdair?"

He looked at her through the gay branches of the pine tree. Her laughing eyes mocked him; her provocative smile challenged him to speak. The words were in his throat; he held them back. He could not say to her now that another child of his loins would wake in the morning to a different kind of Christmas. True, he had sent George anonymously a box of gifts, but what were mere gifts to a father's presence, to the knowledge of having a father? He did not know whether George looked upon Jean and Julia Brunet as his parents; perhaps he did; perhaps they had never told him they had taken him from his mother.

"Do not speak," Jane went on, grown suddenly grave. "Do

Mistaire Dousman think a woman who love him can live with him evair' day an' not feel in her heart something trouble him?"

"Many things trouble me every day."

"Say what they may be," she dared him.

"Very well, though these aren't concerns about which you should trouble yourself. For example, there's Mr. Brisbois's store which was destroyed by fire last April, my building—I'm having difficulty collecting the insurance. Then, Mr. Papin's note is overdue, and I don't think he means to pay me; so I'll have to go to court about it. In addition, Mr. Wilkins wants to borrow money to build in St. Paul. At the same time, the Sioux want me to go to Washington to implement the ratification of their treaty—in which I confess to a slight interest since I want to buy some of that land myself as an investment. And, as if that weren't enough, I'm afraid I'm going bald!" Her laughter interrupted him, and he added, "Do you need to hear more?"

"No, not of those things, Mistaire Dousman—but of that othair—what it is that trouble you. Sometime' you wake in the night an' you lie there, not asleep, jus' thinking. Mistaire Dousman, it seem to me evair since Dédé come to be with us you have worry about something. Say to me what it is. Do you fear I love him so much he will not grow up to be a man?"

"Sometimes I do fear that," he answered honestly, and with some relief at being able to answer her this way.

"But sure' it is not that, Mistaire Dousman," she pressed, coming around to stand before him, an ornament dangling from between one thumb and forefinger, a long string of tinsel in the other hand. "When a boy is so little, he need his maman more than his papa. His papa's time come latair."

He took the ornament from between her fingers and hung it on the tree. He draped the tinsel. Then he put his arms around her and kissed her.

"You may yet be sorry you married me," he said lightly.

She shook her head. "Mistaire Dousman know if he has commit murdair, I would help him bury the body. I know my Mistaire Dousman—he would not do this. But what do he do that worry him? This worry me, too. Mistaire Dousman is vair' good man, vair' hones', vair' jus'—he do not do evil thing, he do not do dishonorable thing—so what do he worry about?"

There was no putting her off lightly. He buried his lips in her dark hair and was still.

"An' if he go bald," she went on, smiling, "it do not mattair to me. He is not Samson with all his strengt' in his hair, no?"

He excused himself abruptly. He went out of the house and crossed under the frosty stars to the office, walking between high banks of snow fallen but a day before and glistening now with the snow which had come down only a few hours ago. There he got the gift he had hidden for Jane and carried it back to the drawing room.

"I want you to have this now, Jane—tomorrow is Dédé's day."

She took it, leaning forward to kiss him. "Mus' I open it now?"

"You may open it whenever you like. Tomorrow, next week . . ."

"Oh, you know, Mistaire Dousman, no woman live who could hold back her curiosity ovair night."

She opened it at once and gasped at sight of the sable cape so carefully wrapped weeks before. "Oh, Mistaire Dousman! It is beautiful!" She took it out and put it around her shoulders.

"And you complement it perfectly," said Hercules. "It took a long time to assemble those furs—they're flawless, the best I could find. I thought I'd never find enough."

She kissed him again, snuggling close to him. "I did not eithair," she whispered.

So she had known he was assembling them. He smiled. "How hard it is to keep a secret from you, Jane! I suppose Jonas or Louis let it out and it reached your ears. Well, there was long enough time to find it out."

"But this one secret Mistaire Dousman keep," she said quickly. "What it is that worry him?"

"Jane, there are some things I have to work out by myself," he said soberly.

She gave him a measured glance. Then she went quietly back to trimming the tree. He felt a wild impulse to tell her about George now, this moment, spurred by her admirable aplomb, her calm trust in him and his judgment, her amiability—she did not press, having been put off gently but firmly, neither did she resort to anger or tears. But he did not yield. This was neither the time nor the place to tell her, nor could he speak until he knew incontrovertibly that George was his son—there was still the possibility, however remote, that he had been the victim of some grotesque coincidence which had deceived Souligne as well as himself, though he recognized this as an improbability. But he knew that he could not put Jane off much longer, unless he resolved the problem before the need arose to confide in her. Meanwhile, he must show his feelings less plainly.

And all next day, while he sat among friends and watched Dédé romp among his Christmas toys, there was nothing to betray his almost constant thought of George Brunet and the invisible wall that shut the boy away from him.

As soon as the ice went out in the spring, Hercules departed for the East. He set out down the Mississippi, stopped at St. Louis to place an order with Stambaugh, then went on on an Ohio River steamboat. He stopped again at Cincinnati, then completed his journey by river boat, stagecoach, and rail.

He reached Washington two weeks after leaving Prairie du Chien, engaged a room at a hotel, and sent a note by messenger to Senator Henry Dodge. He dispatched another note to Senator Cameron. Within the hour Dodge's carriage was at the door for Hercules, the driver bearing an invitation to dinner.

Hercules went to Dodge's Washington home as soon as he could get ready; the sooner he accomplished his mission in the capital, the sooner he could go on to New York and complete his business in the East.

He found the senator aged somewhat since last he had seen him—on the day of statehood proclamation four years ago; he was whiter now than he had been, but he seemed more at ease in Washington than Dousman would have thought for a man whose roughness was a byword among the lead-region miners who idolized him. Mrs. Dodge, however, had not altered at all; she was the same gracious woman she had always been, one endowed with poise and charm, without pretension or artifice, simply but becomingly dressed, and not impelled to interrupt the conversation of the men.

"What brings you to Washington, Dousman?" asked the senator when they sat down to dinner.

Hercules explained in detail.

"I'll see what I can do about the Sioux treaty," promised Dodge. "I'll give you a letter to the Commissioner, too, if you need it. You might like to see President Fillmore while you're here. Shall I arrange it?"

"I don't feel I ought to trouble him. What do they think of him here?"

Dodge shook his head. "After Taylor? An indecisive man. Taylor's death left us with a mere politician, I'm afraid. It ought to teach the conventions to nominate men of equal stature for both offices." He shrugged. "But who could have foreseen that Old Rough-and-Ready would die before his term was up?"

Dodge was eager for news of Wisconsin. He wanted to know about the increasing population, about the spreading of the railroads, and the development of the agricultural regions.

Hercules answered him as best he could, but at last he held up his hand to stay Dodge's questions. "I have a few of my own, Senator. Particularly one about the land-grant law."

"What can I tell you about it?"

"Is it possible for us in Wisconsin—say, for the Milwaukee & Mississippi—to obtain grants to help us in the construction of the line between Milwaukee and the river?"

"I don't see why not. The Illinois Central got a grant; so did the Mobile & Ohio line. In all fairness to you, Dousman, I have to admit these things take so much time and patience that your line might be built before the grant came through."

"That's what I was afraid of. We'll have to stay with our

policy of farm mortgages. The eastern capital we need will accept them as collateral."

"A risky business, Dousman."

"I know it."

"For my part," continued Dodge, "I'd like to see the rails reach the Mississippi as soon as possible. The lakes will soon be connected to the East Coast; the Erie Railroad will reach Dunkirk in a month or so, according to information I have."

"Kilbourn's doing his best."

"That fellow's a professional promoter," said Dodge, laughing. "I'm not sure his judgment's always sound, though."

After dinner, when Dodge would have sent for his carriage, Hercules announced that he preferred to walk back to his hotel. Dodge offered to walk part of the way with him, and together they went down the streets toward the hotel. They paused briefly in the soft spring night before the White House.

"Who would have thought, when we knew him at Prairie du Chien, that Taylor would live here some day," mused Dodge. "Strange how the wheel turns. It was the Mexican War that put him there."

Hercules' thoughts went back almost two decades to Taylor at Fort Crawford—the brilliant spectacle of the surrender of Black Hawk—of parades at the fort, and Taylor riding against the Indians. Already it seemed an age ago, so swiftly had change come to Wisconsin.

From time to time Dodge pointed out buildings and places, as if Hercules had never been in Washington before; but Hercules said nothing to stop him, enjoying the mellowness which had come upon the man he had known first as a bold young militiaman, ready to take up arms against the Indians at the slightest hint, fierce in the protection of the lead mines stolen from the Winnebago, who were ever attempting to win them back from the Yankees, the Long Knives, the Cousin Jacks—the New Englanders, Kentuckians, and Cornish who had come in to work the mines all the way from the Wisconsin River at Helena down into Illinois and Iowa.

At last Dodge paused short of Hercules' hotel. They shook hands, and each went on alone.

In the morning Hercules went around to see the junior senator from Wisconsin, Isaac Walker, putting the problem of the Sioux treaty to him, as he had done to Dodge. But he spent little time with Walker, who was gruff and suspicious, certain that the Indians and traders alike were rascals. Moreover, the senator was aware that he was in bad odor with Wisconsin politicians, and was not in a mood to make concessions. Then Hercules went on to have lunch with Senator Simon Cameron, who spent an hour talking about Alexander Ramsey and the opening of Minnesota. Late that same day Hercules visited the Commissioner of Indian Affairs. By evening he was tired and happy to return to his hotel.

He stayed but three days in the capital.

Then he went to New York, resisting a sentimental impulse to visit Elizabethtown, New Jersey, where he had gone to school. Since he had lived for two years in New York, working as an apprentice from eighteen to twenty, he knew the city. He took his time, visiting the sons of his old employers—for the older men were gone now—and spending several hours of half a week closeted with his bankers.

Finally, one day he went around to see old Ferrier at the Astor Company offices. Ferrier seemed ageless. His feral face was unchanged save for a few more lines in its leathery surface and a slight curving of his beaklike nose. His white hair still straggled up, startled, from his temples, lending him a halolike aura—one he did not deserve.

"You're a sight for sore eyes, Mr. Dousman," he said, and cackled with laughter.

"You're no less," retorted Dousman. "They'll have to beat you to death some day."

Ferrier laughed with manifest self-satisfaction, as if his longevity were a feat of his own doing.

"You're keeping well yourself, Mr. Dousman. I well remember the day you entered our employment—1820, it was—and you went back to Mackinac and then to Prairie du Chien, after six years on the island."

They talked for a little while of old times. Then Ferrier came to something that had been sticking in his mind for some time.

"By the way, Dousman, what ever became of that fellow Saquin?"

"We never did know about the old trader," answered Hercules blandly.

Ferrier shook his head impatiently. "No, no—the one who worked for you."

Hercules shrugged. "He left me a year ago. Took off one night with one of the local belles. I've no idea where he went."

"Any hard feeling between you?"

Hercules shook his head. "He did his work. I had no complaint."

"If you hear of him, I'd be obliged to you if you'd let us know."

"Why?"

"Ah, business matters," said Ferrier with deliberate vagueness.

"Not to his advantage, I'll warrant," said Hercules, grinning.

Ferrier made no answer.

After a week in New York, Hercules began the return journey, anxious to be home again.

He reached Prairie du Chien in mid-May.

Early in June four horsemen rode into Prairie du Chien from the north and made directly for the house on the mound. LeBrun saw them first from the door of the office.

"Four riders, Mr. Dousman. Well dressed but dusty."

Hercules came to the door. He recognized the rider in the lead and called out, "Kilbourn!"

Kilbourn came riding up. "Well, Dousman, the Milwaukee & Mississippi has come to Prairie du Chien, in a manner of speaking." He waved toward his companions. "Mr. Anson Eldred—Mr. E. D. Holton—Mr. E. H. Brodhead."

"Come in, gentlemen."

They dismounted and climbed the steps to the office. Hercules motioned LeBrun outside, so that there might be more room for the four men in the office.

"We don't intend to sit here," said Kilbourn. "We've come on business. You'll be glad to know, Hercules, that we've decided to bring the road in from Madison to touch on the Wisconsin River at Arena, and from there down the Wisconsin Valley to Prairie du Chien. Thank Brodhead here for his report."

"It seems the most logical route to take," Brodhead explained. "I believe you pointed that out a few years back, Mr. Dousman. This route lies through arable country, over fairly level ground all the way, and touches the Wisconsin at a place of access to a large tract of country, as the American Fur Company and the Indians before that found out. Moreover, with Iowa filling up, we have excellent prospects to the west."

"I'm happy to hear it," said Hercules. "Now, how can I serve you, gentlemen?"

"Ride out with us and inspect possible sites for the terminus," invited Kilbourn.

"Gladly. Won't you gentlemen have something to drink before we go? You must have ridden quite a way since your last stop."

"You won't have to ask me twice," said Brodhead.

Eldred and Holton nodded in pleased anticipation.

Hercules shouted to LeBrun, who was outside, to go down into the wine cellar beneath the office and bring up some brandy and sherry. He took glasses out of one of the cabinets, explaining that he always kept them handy for occasions like this, adding, "Although if any of you insist on drinking in my house instead of my office, we'll proceed to that place."

"A drink's a drink, outside or in," said Eldred shortly.

LeBrun came with dusty bottles which he wiped before handing them to Hercules.

"Now, gentlemen—your choice."

Half an hour later, Hercules having sent LeBrun for Major, the five men rode south from the house on the mound, crossing the bridge over the Marais de St. Feriole. Hercules rode at Kilbourn's side.

"Eldred and Brodhead seem to think the terminus should be here in the lower town," explained Kilbourn. "We're open-minded—we want to look over the ground."

"I never like talk of lower and upper towns," said Hercules. "It's all one town to me, and rivalry between them—some foolish men try to encourage it—is shortsighted. Just the same, I don't favor the lower town for the terminus."

"Why not?" Eldred called, having overheard him.

"Well, for one thing, if the town's to expand, it can't expand to the west—the Mississippi's in the way. It'll have to go east. It can't go south, because the sloughs and bottom lands stretching to the mouth of the Wisconsin make that impracticable. So it'll have to go north before it goes south. For another—when the Mississippi floods, a great part of the lower town goes under water. I don't call that desirable for a railroad station."

"Nor do I," agreed Kilbourn.

"The lower town site has a lot of backers," said Brodhead.

"I'm afraid with the hardest kind of swearing you couldn't make one man in ten believe it's the serious intention of the Company to terminate at the lower town," said Hercules. "If such a site has a lot of backers, I'm afraid they can hardly be responsible people."

"Well, we'll see—we'll see," said Holton, who had been silent up to this time. "Let's look around before we get to arguing about it. The whole board'll have to decide it, anyway—not the four of us."

"But on our recommendations," Eldred pointed out.

Hercules was not favorably impressed. It seemed to him that at least two members of the group had come with preconceived notions as to where the terminal station should be erected. It would take just so much longer, then, to convince them of error; if they had come to Prairie du Chien with open minds, the disadvantages of the lower town as a terminal site would have been perfectly obvious. The same promptings of caution he had felt before in his earlier dealings with Kilbourn were aroused once more; he was satisfied in his own mind that the management ought to be strengthened. Kilbourn was talking of John Catlin; the Company president had gone to New York to sell the Company bonds. Kilbourn spoke with great enthusiasm, but Hercules was not impressed by enthusiasm. He held his tongue.

The morning was sunny and warm. The air was filled with bird song—vesper sparrows lifted their voices along the river; killdeers flew crying low over the water; bluebirds chortled from high over; and thrushes sang out of the wooded islands in the Mississippi. At the river's edge, while the other three men were estimating the possible height of flood water at the available site for a station, Kilbourn turned instead to look dreamily west.

"We'll have to begin to think of crossing here," he said. "Can it be bridged, Dousman?"

"Oh, it can be bridged. But at what cost?"

"I had that in mind. By the time we reach Prairie du Chien, we'll have to stop and take stock—and wait to catch up on our expenses. We'll be in pretty deep by that time."

"We're in pretty deep now, aren't we? We ran out of money even before we reached Waukesha, and we've been running out chronically ever since."

Kilbourn nodded carelessly. "Think of some way in which we could cross here without the most expensive kind of bridge, Dousman."

"You set me a hard task," mused Hercules, and smiled.

"What are you laughing at?"

"I'm thinking—here you've not yet reached the Wisconsin Valley,—you're quite a while from Prairie du Chien, and you're trying to reach across the Mississippi already."

Kilbourn gestured westward. "That's the way we must go," he cried, his face flushed with excitement. "The one who reaches the west first will achieve the greatest return on the investment."

"Should wealth or service be the goal?"

"Can't we have both? They go together."

"Come on, you two," shouted Eldred, turning. "We're going into the upper town."

They rode for three hours from one place to another in the village, examining several sites for the proposed railroad terminus. None suited all of them, although Hercules fixed on a site across the Marais de St. Feriole, in the upper town. He forbore to speak, however, preferring to listen and observe. Eldred and Brodhead seemed determined to place the terminus on the west end of Farm Lot 36 in the lower town; Kilbourn and Holton were not committed to any one place, but were inclined to heed Hercule's earlier warning about the shifting water levels of the Mississippi, and thus preferred to locate the station east of the Marais. It seemed plain to Hercules that Eldred and Brodhead had been importuned by lower-town businessmen, who put their personal interests above those of the Company.

When they finished, he took them to the house on the mound for dinner and the night.

In the morning they returned the way they had come—back up along the proposed route of the Milwaukee & Mississippi to where the rails terminated, still east of Madison; from this point they would take the cars back to Milwaukee.

One day in July, as Hercules was leaving the office to walk into the village, he saw a little knot of boys gathered in the road, looking toward the house. They stood in animated discussion, and Hercules would not have given them a second glance had he not recognized George Brunet among them. He paused. Should he ask them in? But to what end? They were always at liberty to cross the grounds to the river; asking them in would make them ill at ease. The boys were all in their early teens; some of them had been or were going fishing. George carried a pole, too.

The sight of George stung Hercules. Four years since Souligne had come to him! The boy was now in his thirteenth year. Moreover, at the house on the mound Jane had become increasingly possessive of Dédé. And in all this time, if he had not made a move toward George, Julia Brunet had not made a move in his direction, either.

He turned, went back to the office, unlocked a drawer in his desk, and took out Souligne's will. He put it into his pocket and went out once more.

The boys were moving on now, south toward the sloughs which abounded there in the vicinity of the Wisconsin's mouth; they had evidently been fishing off the island north of the house, and now bent their steps toward the bridge to cross the Marais de St. Feriole for the sloughs. George was still with them. It would be a good time to call on Julia. But now that he had made up his mind, Hercules would have gone in any case, even if George had been on his way home.

Julia Brunet opened to his knock, almost as if she had been expecting him. She looked at him with that same direct and slightly mocking glance, as if behind her dark eyes she laughed at him.

"Mistaire Dousman!" she cried. "You surprise me."

"Good afternoon, Julia. I came on a little matter of business."

"Come in, Mistaire Dousman." She stood aside to let him pass, closing the door after him. "What business can Mistaire Dousman have wit' me?" She walked past him into a spare little sitting room, where she sat down and waved him to a chair. "Sit down, Mistaire Dousman."

"Thank you, Julia." He sat down. "As a matter of fact, strictly speaking, my business is with your boy."

For a moment she made no reply. He sensed her tenseness. Then she relaxed, clasped hands in her lap, and, gazing at him with watchful suspicion, said, "George is not home."

"Well, as he's a minor, I don't really need to talk to him. It's a matter I should have attended to before, but he was so young at the time, not that he's much older now—twelve . . ."

"Mistaire Dousman know?"

"I know only what I'm told," he said flatly.

"What is this business, Mistaire Dousman?" Her suspicion of his motive in coming was heavy in her voice.

"Julia, you'll remember old Souligne."

"He was good man," said Julia Brunet firmly, implying that he was what Hercules was not.

"Souligne used to work for me. When he died, he left a will." But why go on to say this to her, when she could read it for herself? "Here—read it." He took the will from his pocket and handed it to her.

She unfolded it and held it up to the light that streamed in by the single window opening out of the room. She read it with undivided attention, her lips moving, repeating the words to herself. Having read it through once, she read it again before she lowered it and looked at Hercules, baffled.

"But why should Souligne do this?" she asked.

"I suppose because he got along with the boy. He used to tell me he saw something of him now and then. He was all alone. He had no one, only Lapiage, and Lapiage didn't need his house. Perhaps Souligne felt George could use it some day."

"Then say to me, Mistaire Dousman, why you wait so long to come here wit' this." She looked again at the date. "It say February three year ago. Why do you come firs' now? Souligne die that spring—all this time the house stan' empty."

"There were other matters to take care of, Julia," he answered, a little resentful of her attitude. "Lapiage had to be satisfied. I had to make sure the property was free of any indebtedness. These things take time—especially for one who has many other things to see to."

"I do not doubt it," she said coldly. "I am surprise' Mistaire Dousman do finally come wit' it. Who would have know' if he keep it for himself?"

"I would have known. It wouldn't have needed anyone else," replied Hercules shortly. "Besides—what use would it be to me? I already own thousands of acres . . ."

"And some of Joe's, too—you need not say it," Julia was quick to answer.

Hercules was stung. He held back his anger. For a moment he did not venture to speak. Then he began slowly, "I know this has rankled in you a long time, Julia. You've never made any attempt to get at the facts about Joe's property and his debts —you haven't wanted to—you've only wanted to hold against me everything I did for Joe. The plain fact was that in his last years Joe was a very sick man—you never wanted to see it—you wanted to close your eyes to Joe's drinking, to pretend it never happened—but it did, just the same; it wasn't anything to be ashamed of, just because he was your brother. Joe was sick; he was sick and worried; he drank because of that, because sometimes he could drown out the pain and forget his worries . . ."

Julia interrupted him, holding up a clenched fist. "Stop! You have always say this, Mistaire Dousman—not to me, but to othairs—I know, I have ways of knowing—but I, too, knew Joe, and you were his partnair in the business—you started as his partnair, and you ended by owning it all, everything that was his—even in the end, his wife."

"So it's really that that rankles, eh, Julia?" He spoke quietly, but anger lay behind his words; the softness of his tone did not conceal it. "I didn't come here to quarrel; I came to make sure you understood that the house is to go to George. I'll have it entered as soon as I can."

"But why should he do this?" Julia asked again, her eyes clouded with perplexity. "I do not think George was there so often—unless I did not see him."

"Do you watch him, then? Like some of the women, always behind the curtains?"

"You know I do not," she replied indignantly.

"I know nothing of the sort," he retorted. "I didn't even know you had a child"—he paused—"not until some years after."

He said it deliberately, hoping to provoke her into saying something that would force her hand; but she sat quiet, saying nothing, only looking at him with that baffling, mocking air of triumph, as if by the knowledge she held secretly within her she were superior to him.

"If you'll give me the will, I'll take care of it without any more delay," he said then, getting to his feet.

She rose and handed it to him. "I thank you for George," she said stiffly. It was hard for her to mask her dislike of him. He was positive that she bore him a deadly hatred, of such a nature that no truth would prevail against it. Perhaps it was necessary for her to hate him, and to need everything to sustain that hatred, and reject all that would diminish it.

At this moment the back door opened and closed. Quick footsteps moved from room to room, approaching. Then George came into the room and paused just past the threshold, looking from one to the other of them.

"Mama, I was fishing . . ." he began.

Then he made out, in the room's half-light, who stood there with his mother; he stopped talking abruptly, took a step backward, and put one hand out to the door frame, as if to hasten his departure.

"Don't go, George," said Julia. She turned to Hercules. "This is George, Mistaire Dousman."

"I know the boy by sight," said Hercules easily.

He could not believe that his voice was so effortless. He felt in that instant as if he must betray his knowledge, for the boy gazed at him with an expression that seemed to say he held Hercules not only in suspicion but in violent dislike, and Hercules saw at once that the boy was not without some knowledge of him—what knowledge, Hercules was sure he could trust Julia to color to suit her own purpose.

"Say 'Good afternoon' to Mistaire Dousman, George," she commanded.

"Good afternoon, Mr. Dousman," said George tonelessly.

Hercules returned the boy's greeting. Then he looked from him to Julia, gazing at her fixedly. Now, if ever, was her chance to say to him what he knew she cradled in secret, and he waited almost as if she must speak.

But she said nothing except, "I'll be obliged to Mistaire Dousman to take care of the mattair when he wish to do so. The boy is young, as you say—it need not be tomorrow."

Hercules bade her good day, turned, and walked out of the house. He was filled with anger mingled with a confusion of desires—to take the boy; to reject him even as the boy had already rejected him in his heart; to go back and tell Julia he knew who George Brunet was. His anger was directed toward Julia, toward that blind hatred which must be fed at no matter what cost to truth; for the child he felt longing mingled with pity. He wanted him, but he was afraid to say as much. Not only because of Jane, but also for himself. Something was in George that was strange, perhaps inimical. Perhaps Julia had had him too long. Perhaps she did not intend ever to speak, to tell him the truth about George, preferring to take refuge in the satisfaction of having in her trust the child of a man she hated.

He could not believe she would hurt the boy. Would it satisfy her hatred only to have him, to keep him from Hercules—if Hercules did not know? Why had she not spoken? Why did she keep silent even under the provocation which must have been great more than once to taunt Hercules with her possession of him? What lay in her mind?—to poison the boy against him?—to destroy any basis for rapprochement between father and son?

Hercules paused and looked back at the Brunet house. It stood silent. Neither the boy nor Julia was in sight. What went on now within those walls? Was she telling him about Souligne's house? And how, he wondered, did Jean Brunet feel about all this? Perhaps he was too busy with the affairs of his tavern and his ferry to concern himself about the boy. He was positive that Jean did not know about George's paternity; whatever game Julia played, she played it alone, not with her husband's connivance.

He resumed his walk toward the house on the mound. Sometime soon, he told himself, something must be decided. It must not be left to Julia Brunet to decide out of the well of hatred which sustained her.

5. Wheel of Fire

Spring-Autumn, 1853

HIS ANGER COOLED, AND WITH IT HIS RESOLUTION. ONCE BACK with Jane and Dédé, back in the warm affection of life in the house on the mound, Hercules found it too easy to put off a little longer what he had already put off so long. Besides, he seldom had time to think about anything but the affairs in which he was involved; he was content that it should be so; it kept his thoughts from George and the necessity to take a decisive step toward his son.

Autumn gave way to winter.

Soon after Christmas Hercules went East once more, to cement a closer relationship between his bankers in New York and those in Milwaukee, and to inquire into the sale of the Wisconsin land mortgages to eastern interests so that the Milwaukee & Mississippi might have the money it needed so badly to finish its line. In New York he saw that ships from abroad still brought thousands of immigrants to America; every train bound for the western lands was crowded with men, women, and children and their spare baggage, hopeful of a new life in this vital new country; people with eager, glowing faces; children wide-eyed with wonder at sight of their new country; old men taciturn and watchful; women resigned to whatever might come.

He turned homeward again filled with new confidence in the

ever-increasing prosperity of the Middle West, riding in an immigrant-crowded train, so that he might be among these people, talk with those whose language he could speak or who could speak even a rudimentary English or French. The immigrants rode with faces pressed to the windows of the cars, so that they might see all of the countryside, frosted with April green, their rapid passage permitted. Hercules was stirred by the happiness shining in their eyes.

He went to Chicago and up the lake to Milwaukee, where he went to a hotel. He had hardly settled himself before E. H. Brodhead and John Catlin, president of the Milwaukee & Mississippi, waited upon him.

Catlin, a short, wiry man, with keen dark eyes heavily bushed over by black brows and surmounted by a high forehead, was restrained in his manner, but Brodhead was bursting with eagerness.

"We tried to reach you in Prairie du Chien, Dousman," said Brodhead, "but you were already off to New York. We knew you were bound back by way of Milwaukee, so we kept track of arrivals. Here we are. We've got a little problem."

"Money again? Or is it something new and different?"

Catlin shook his head. "We thought you might be interested. You've done a good deal for the road already, put yourself out, arranged to buy land for us—we naturally thought of you when this came up."

"I'll listen," said Hercules.

Brodhead, who had brought rolls of maps with him, immediately unrolled one of them and spread it on the bed in the room. Hercules saw that it was a map of the proposed railroad from Milwaukee to Madison, although the rails still fell short of Madison.

"You see how far we are now, Dousman. We should reach Madison soon—very soon."

"At least by next year," put in Catlin dryly. "Let's not promise ourselves too much."

"Well, the point isn't when we reach Madison," Brodhead

went on. "The fact is, we've already got far enough along to think of moving passengers and goods all the way to the Mississippi as well as up the Wisconsin."

"How?" asked Hercules bluntly. "If at the present rate of construction you don't hope to be in Madison until next year? It'll take you three, four more years to reach Prairie du Chien."

"That's exactly the point, Dousman," said Brodhead, smiling. "That's where you come in. We're proposing to establish a daily line of coach wagons from the present terminus of the road to the Wisconsin River at Arena. These coaches will carry passengers and goods to the Wisconsin; once there, steamboats can be used to carry north to Fort Winnebago and south to Prairie du Chien. Can it be done?"

He unrolled another map, this time of the road from Madison to the Wisconsin River Valley. He put his finger on Arena.

"You see," he went on, "from here—it's an ideal location—we're right at the river. Coaches first, then later on the cars, as soon as we get the rails to this point. The Wisconsin River traffic north would have perhaps only the stop at Sac Prairie before the Portage—canoes could move up the Fox or steamboats—we could connect with the lake again at Green Bay at the one end."

Hercules pondered the plan. It was not unfeasible. Its motive was less obvious. Catlin watched him with narrowed eyes. He lit a cigar, offered another to Hercules; Brodhead declined one brusquely and fell silent, waiting for Hercules to speak.

"Well," said Hercules at last cautiously, "I believe the plan has some promise. If I understand you, you'll take care of the wagons from this end, and I'm to arrange the boats."

"That's it," said Brodhead.

"One boat every other day up the Wisconsin ought to be enough," speculated Hercules. "There wouldn't be much traffic that way—the Sac Prairie country's still small—five hundred people or so north of Pierneau's place, scattered all over the prairie between the Wisconsin and the hills north, west, and east—and Winnebago gets some of its goods from the Fox River traffic. Then two boats from Prairie du Chien to Fort Winnebago will have four days each to make the trip; that'll give them abundant time to do all their business on the route, and they'd connect here with the daily packets bound for Minnesota, and for traffic down the Mississippi, too, of course."

"Will you undertake it, Dousman?" asked Catlin.

"Let me think on it. Right now steamboating is at its height. George Catlin's rhapsodic account of the tour from the mouth of the Wisconsin to the Falls of St. Anthony above St. Paul has made the 'fashionable tour' the thing to take, and the upper Mississippi trade is incredible. So others may want to put in boats, too. It ought to pay well. Besides, I've been thinking of going into the business more actively. I had an interest in some of the Campbell boats—the *West Newton*, the *Nominee*, the *Dr. Franklin*—but late last January I wrote Campbell and gave him power of attorney for myself and Bernard Brisbois, who shared my interest, to transfer it to Daniel Harris and the Minnesota Packet Company, which we formed at the end of the season last autumn."

"That leaves you free to start fresh," said Brodhead.

"I want to think it over carefully, gentlemen. I believe in making haste slowly. The road is costing about twenty-five thousand a mile now—that's four thousand more than it took to reach Eagle. What will it be by the time you reach Arena, to say nothing of Prairie du Chien?"

"We do everything we can to hold expenses down, Dousman," said Catlin.

"I'm sure of it. But there must be awkward managing somewhere—costs shouldn't rise like that. Are we expanding too fast?"

"Without reaching the Mississippi, our primary purpose hasn't been fulfilled," protested Brodhead.

"Not that I'm losing faith in the enterprise," Hercules went on. "Far from it. I'm prepared to take another ten-thousand-dollar bond at eight per cent later this year—and I ought to be able to sell twice that much in bonds in Galena and the Fond du Lac region." He coughed and let the smile vanish from his face. "But now, gentlemen, let's face one another squarely. Isn't it a fact that you're proposing this boat line out of desperation? There just isn't enough money to get past Madison, is there?"

Brodhead gaped. Catlin simply shook his head.

"Nor is there a possibility of raising it?"

"Not as we're set up at present."

"I thought so. Well, we want the line at Prairie du Chien. We'll say nothing of this, and I'll see what I can do between Prairie du Chien and Madison."

"About the boats," reminded Brodhead gently.

"When I get home I'll get some figures on the probable costs. Perhaps it's time for me to run my own boats."

Brodhead smiled in relief. Turning to Catlin, he said, "I told you Dousman wouldn't hold it against us for choosing the lower town site for the station."

"Eventually it'll be in the upper town," said Hercules, unruffled. "I expect to put up a hotel near the station—but I'm dubious!"

Catlin got to his feet. "Well sir, we'll keep you informed of our progress—and we'll trust to your customary enterprise."

They shook hands. Catlin and Brodhead were plainly convinced that nothing would prevent Hercules from falling in with their plans; at the same time, they were relieved that Hercules had fathomed the reason for their anxiety to establish some sort of route to the Mississippi until money could be found to finish laying the rails.

On his return home, Hercules sat down immediately and wrote to the builders in Pittsburgh, Wheeling, and Elizabeth, Kentucky, asking for bids on steamboats capable of navigating the Wisconsin. They ought to be side-wheelers, which would be more maneuverable in the Wisconsin, with its many islands and its occasionally narrow channels, and perhaps less than two hundred fifty tons. He was filled with enthusiasm tempered with caution; despite the probable cost of the boats, he was already committed to this new project, because steamboating to Point Boss would open up more country along the Wisconsin. The furthering of the cause of the Milwaukee & Mississippi, however, would take more than a line of steamboats to ply the Wisconsin.

Next day he sent LeBrun around to Bernard Brisbois with a note asking Brisbois to come over at his convenience for a little talk. Brisbois returned with LeBrun, his tall, broad-shouldered figure towering above LeBrun, dwarfing the boy.

"I know you don't send for people without good reason, Dousman," he said, pulling up a chair to sit down.

"I've been to Milwaukee," said Hercules without preamble. He summarized his conversation with Catlin and Brodhead, while Brisbois listened attentively.

"So if we're to get the railroad into Prairie du Chien, we'll have to do it ourselves, is that it?" answered Brisbois. "Do you want help on the boats?"

"I think I can handle that, Bernard. I've got something else on my mind. I propose organizing a new railroad company to take the line from Madison to the Mississippi; we'll raise the capital among us—not just the two of us, but someone from Madison, too—and then consolidate with the Milwaukee & Mississippi. How does that sound to you?"

"We don't have much choice, do we?"

Hercules shrugged. "Only that of participating or not doing so. We're in deep enough already."

"Go on, Dousman. You've thought this thing out."

"I propose to send a letter to Colonel Bird, and suggest that he sound out opinion in Madison. Then we'll meet there this day week—at Bird's—and form our corporation. Will you come in?"

"You know I will. I've been as impatient as you with the Milwaukee & Mississippi. I only hope that our corporation won't be just another brick sunk into the mud of their roadbed."

"Good. I'll write Bird at once and dispatch the letter by hand."

"Make it next Thursday for Madison, Dousman."

"That will set the meeting for the following Saturday. We can be back home early the following week if all goes well."

"That's agreeable." He got up to go but lingered, bending above Hercules at his desk. "Tell me—how much do you think we'll have to go in for?"

"At least twenty thousand at the start. It all depends on how many we can get to go in with us and how much the lot of us can raise. There's no use setting our goal too low—it'll take money to come down the Wisconsin—a lot of trestles, a lot of fill—the ground's not firm for a lot of the way."

"Well, I'll match you, Dousman. I've never lost a penny on anything we went into."

"And we won't lose in this," promised Hercules. "Even if it may take a while." He turned to LeBrun. "Louis, some brandy." And to Brisbois, "We'll drink on it!"

Hercules and Bernard Brisbois reached the Madison Hotel in midmorning of Saturday the following week. They had taken two days to make the trip, by intent; instead of following the usual route over the Wisconsin and along the ridge, they chose to go up the Wisconsin River Valley, paralleling the proposed route of the railroad as closely as possible, although they made no attempt to make the two river crossings that would be necessary below Boscobel, and crossed well up, near Arena, then following the fertile black-earthed valley which led from that point at the Wisconsin all the way to the country of the Four Lakes.

Colonel Bird was spurred to immediate activity at sight of them. "I've sent out the word," he said. "And I'll send someone after the men. Our businessmen are naturally very much interested. We can already count on Burdick and Simeon Mills. There'll be others, but with a nucleus we can go forward. Excuse me—make yourselves at home—I'll send for Mills and Burdick."

Colonel Bird darted out of the room, but was soon back again, talking rapidly about events at the capital. Bird was in a position to overhear all the small talk and gossip that went on in the capital, and Hercules listened as Bird gave it as his opinion that, once Governor Farwell was out of office, the Whigs would have a devil of a time getting back into any major office; only the support of the Free-Soilers had put Farwell in, and even now a Democratic majority in both houses seemed to point to a Democrat as the next governor—and a non-temperance man, if the Democrats could find one, for the Free-Soilers and Whigs were largely temperance men. In response to a pointed question from Brisbois, Bird guessed that no governor who would be elected could afford to be anti-railroad, despite the difficulties which were beginning to arise as a result of the sale of farm mortgages.

The arrival of Elisha Burdick and Simeon Mills put an end to Bird's monologue. Both men were in early middle age. Mills was a slender, handsome man, with deep-set, somber eyes, a wide, expressive mouth, and a shock of brown hair. His manner was reserved and contemplative, against Burdick's geniality. Burdick was shorter than Mills, florid of countenance, and given to rotundity both of body and oratory. Bird made the introductions all around and brought something to drink from the barroom.

"We've been told something about your plans, Dousman," said Burdick. "Let's hear more."

"Mr. Brisbois will explain," said Hercules.

Brisbois immediately launched into an account of the difficulties besetting the Milwaukee & Mississippi. Eastern capital was chary of coming in; railroads were mushrooming up all over the country. The farm mortgage policy had exhausted itself; now it was up to the businessmen of the fast-growing communities to make the completion of the railroad possible.

As he talked, Hercules watched the expressions on the faces of the other men. Bird was keenly interested. Mills sat with his chin cupped in one hand, listening intently, computing costs behind his impassive face. Burdick nodded from time to time, fingering the knobbed head of his cane.

"What we propose," concluded Brisbois, "is the formation of a corporation to be known as the Madison and Prairie du Chien Rail Road Company, for the sole purpose ultimately of consolidating with the Milwaukee & Mississippi to bring the road to the Mississippi."

"Conservatively, how much do you estimate it will cost to complete the line from Madison?" asked Mills quietly.

Brisbois looked at Hercules.

"Let's not be conservative," said Hercules. "We might be disappointed—just as the gentlemen from Milwaukee were. Shall we say three million?"

Burdick's pale eyes rolled aloft. He gasped.

Mills only smiled. "Where do we begin?"

"Well, to start with, Brisbois and I propose to put in twenty thousand each."

"So will I," said Colonel Bird at once.

"Twenty thousand!" exclaimed Burdick. "Fifteen of us at that figure would be only ten per cent of the money we'll need."

"Don't forget—we're not alone in this," said Bird.

"At the moment we are," countered Burdick.

"We'll also want to remember that the men in Sac Prairie have been agitating for a railroad for some time—we can count on money from there," said Hercules. "The point to bear in mind is that we don't need three million to incorporate. We already have sixty thousand."

"Eighty," said Mills gently.

"Well, I'll go along, too," said Burdick, not to be outdone.

"We've made a good beginning," said Hercules. "Brisbois and I expect to spend the weekend in Madison. With your help, we'll raise as much money as we can. We'll carry on from there."

They shook hands all around and sat down together to work out details of the proposed corporation.

One day late in the following week, as Hercules came by the ferry landing south of the island on which the house on the mound stood, he saw on the ferry just pulling out a boy helping Jean Brunet. He stared after the departing craft. The boy was certainly George. He seemed absurdly slight of build to be working so hard. And young—barely thirteen.

For months Hercules had been able, in the press of business affairs, to keep the thought of George at bay. Now, suddenly, he was flooded with remorse. Was it Jean's idea that the boy do such grueling work? he wondered. Or Julia's? Might there not be friction over the boy between Jean and Julia? The boy would then be in the middle, unable to help himself, forced to divide his loyalties between his foster father and his foster mother.

There must be something I can do, he thought guiltily.

He looked away as the ferry drew out toward the channel, and walked on back up along the Marais de St. Feriole to the bridge. He was troubled, this time with the accumulated weight of his months-long disregard of George. The ferry required the utmost of a man; it would mean very hard work for the boy—hardening work. Perhaps it would not harm George, but it came at a time when he ought to be giving more of his time to study and the reading of books.

He brooded at the office, and at the dinner table he was unaccountably silent, giving but monosyllabic replies to Jane's chatter, until she, too, was silent, biting her lip and eying him suspiciously. He seemed oblivious of Miss McCleod—even of Dédé—and finally, of her. She was aware that it was not a matter of business which preoccupied him so, and she did not question him, remembering how he had said there were some things he must work out by himself.

But that night, after he had gone to bed and lay tossing from side to side, she could be still no longer. She sat up in bed and cried, "Mistaire Dousman—it is too much! Something bothair you. I know it. You toss and turn. You do not sleep. What have you do?"

"Nothing, Jane. Go to sleep."

"Nothing, indeed! I know my husban' bettair than that. Say to me what you have do!"

"I've done nothing." He could not help adding, "Perhaps that's the trouble."

"What is it, Mistaire Dousman?"

"Nothing—nothing. I'm all right."

"No, that is lie," she said forcefully. "You do not respec' me when you lie to me, Mistaire Dousman." She turned and moved closer to him, looking down at him as if she hoped to see in the darkness of the room some clue to what it was that troubled him. "If it is something you do to be ashame' of, say it to me so I can see whethair I, too, should be ashame' for you. If it is business, which is none of my affair, then say so to me, and I will be still, I will not bothair you."

"It's not business, Jane."

"Then say!"

He lay thinking how unfair it was to Jane that she should not know. He had made up his mind to go to Julia Brunet in the morning, to confront her with his knowledge of his son's identity, to demand that the boy be released to him, to be raised in the house on the mound, to take his place publicly as Hercules' son. Jane had a right to know this before he translated it into action.

"I wait, Mistaire Dousman."

He slid out of bed, went over to his desk, and lit the oil lamp there. He put on his robe while she watched, her eyes challenging him, daring him to speak. He did not know how to begin, and walked once across the room and back.

"Mistaire Dousman try to work up his courage. I know. It do not take courage to say to me what is on your min'."

"Yes, Jane, it does," he answered, still walking back and forth, gazing at her sideways, with his head bent a little. "It's something I ought to have known before we were married."

"Mistaire Dousman has foun' he do not love me!" she cried.

"Oh, don't talk foolishly," he said with a sigh. "It's not that at all. How could it be, when you have so much evidence to the contrary?"

She looked archly at him. "What do any woman know of any man? Especially when he is so much gone from her. But if it is not that, Mistaire Dousman, why, there is nothing worse to be afraid of."

"Isn't there?" He smiled grimly. "Tell me, Jane, do you remember Cecile Gardepi?"

"That little dark one," she answered. "But yes—Mistaire Dousman one time vair' fon' of that one. Do he not one time spen' a week with her?"

Hercules was thunderstruck. He stopped pacing and stood looking at her in his astonishment, his hands gripping the foot of the bedstead.

"How the devil do you know that?" he demanded.

"When a woman love a man, she make sure she know evair' thing she can about him. You do not think in such a little town as Prairie du Chien othairs do not see and talk about these things. They tell me, Madame Rolette—your partnair's wife—so I should know what Mistaire Dousman do."

"And what else have they told you?"

"Nothing. Mistaire Dousman so busy with his business mattairs he have time only for Margaret, whom he marry, and then, after she die, for Cecile—when all the time he say it is Jane who eat up his heart inside him."

She gave him a provocative smile; her eyes danced to belie the demureness with which she sat in the middle of the bed, her hands clasped before her.

He went around the bed, sat down beside her, took her into his arms. He kissed her long and hard. "You vixen, Jane, why didn't you ever say anything?"

"It was not my affair, Mistaire Dousman. She was vair' pretty—I remembair her. But she went away . . ." She looked at him with innocent inquiry. "Do Mistaire Dousman sen' her away?"

"No, Jane," he said flatly; "she went away to have a baby—my son."

Her lips made a round O of astonishment; she was too startled to speak. This, at least, she had not known, had never suspected, any more than he. He hastened to go on, before she could say anything.

"I didn't know it then—I found out only five years ago, one night when Souligne came to me."

"The night we had the party for Dédé!" she cried. "Evair since that time I have see Mistaire Dousman have something on his min'—deep in his min', to trouble him."

"Yes, that was the night."

She took a deep breath and shook her head a little, as in bewilderment. "So now, say to me, Mistaire Dousman, what has happen'? What have you do? Where is this boy? His mothair, I think, was drown'."

Hercules told her what had taken place since the night of Souligne's visit five years before. The words, pent up for so long, came out in a torrent. He overlooked nothing. When he had finished, he felt not only drained but also tremendously relieved.

"Five year!" she whispered. "An' you go see him from Souligne's house. How could Mistaire Dousman keep himself from go' there to take his son?"

"I didn't know what Julia intended—what she planned. I don't know yet, but I'm going over first thing in the morning. Besides, I had to think of you, of Dédé . . ."

"Mistaire Dousman know me well enough now to know I would not stan' between him and his son," she said gently and with faint indignation. "What shall he do now?"

"Jane, I want the boy."

"Of course Mistaire Dousman want the boy."

"I want to bring him here. I don't care what people might say—they *will* talk, you know—just as they talked about Margaret—and Julia will be the worst one."

"I'm not sure," said Jane thoughtfully. "Julia hate' you. She hate' me vair' much more. She hate' us for Joe's sake, she care not how wrong it is. I am not sure she talk. You may be surprise' by Julia, Mistaire Dousman."

He shook his head, as if to shake off Julia Brunet. "I'm not troubled about her. It's you—you don't care if he comes here—if everyone knows?"

"I do not care. I wish only that Mistaire Dousman do as he please. I wish only that Mistaire Dousman be happy. He should have his son here. I regret only that Mistaire Dousman did not take me into his confidence from the firs'. It would have save' me many uneasy times—and you, too."

"Yes, Jane, I know. But I had to think this thing through and I'm afraid I kept putting it off, looking the other way, looking, instead, to business to let me forget. I'm not sure I've thought it through yet, but I want the boy, I want him here, to let him grow up as he should, not working on the ferry at something in which he'll make no progress—even worse, perhaps, next in Jean's tavern."

"Not jus' because Mistaire Dousman think I am too gentle with Dédé?" she insinuated with a little smile.

He had to grin. "You think of everything, Jane."

"Mistaire Dousman teach me to do so."

"You really want George to come as much as I do?"

"If George come here, I will be mothair to him jus' as I am to Dédé. If this is what Mistaire Dousman want, this is what Madame Dousman want. Now put out this light, come to bed —you will need res' before you tell Julia what is in your min'."

He put out the light and crawled back into bed. Jane put her arms tenderly about him; he kissed her, and for a while they lay in each other's embrace; but presently he turned over on his back and lay there without sleeping.

A score of questions beset him. Jane's awareness of his intimacy with Cecile Gardepi surprised him, but it should not have done so, he reflected, since others must have known of it. Her complaisance in the face of learning of the existence of his son by Cecile surprised him even more. He had expected her to raise some protest. She had never seemed eager for Emily to come down to live with them, but, then, Emily had never particularly wanted to, and he had not insisted that she do so, and then, of course, Emily had married so soon. . . . But the boy was a different matter, not to be compared with Emily. He had not expected Jane to fall in with his plans so readily; he could not help thinking that Jane must have some reservations about George's coming; why had she not given voice to them? It would be only natural that she would have doubts about the wisdom of bringing him to the house on the mound—a boy of thirteen, one of whom, in reality, neither of them knew anything, for all that he was Hercules' son. Yet she had said absolutely nothing in the way of protest, and now she lay sleeping with the serene confidence of a child.

It was not only of Jane that he thought. What of Jean Brunet? Perhaps it was Jean, rather than Julia, to whom he should make application for the boy. It was not Hercules' custom to plunge unwittingly forward into anything, least of all a matter of such gravity. He had better see Jean first.

He rose with the rising sun, dressed, and went out without breakfast. He had no appetite. He went first to Brunet's tavern on the island, but he had already gone from there; then he crossed the bridge over the Marais de St. Feriole and went down along the Mississippi to the ferry landing. Even at this hour the ferry was out in the water, on its way to the Iowa shore. Hercules sat down on a sack of grain to wait.

It was a morning of clouds, not an overcast, for the sun shone at his back, but one nevertheless that presaged rain, for the clouds lying along the hills across the Mississippi were dark and leaden, and seemed to be waiting only an auspicious moment to push up the sky and move east to close upon the sun. The river was filled with life. Water birds flew crying up and down, settling on the water with infinite grace, and lumbering aloft with wild cries at each disturbance. Out on the broad current of midstream a side-wheeler, whose name Hercules could not make out, was moving down-river, obviously not intending to stop either on the Wisconsin or the Iowa side, loaded with grain, no doubt, and bound for some southern port. The boat saluted the ports, going by; its whistle was mellow and filled the morning with music.

Hercules was impatient. Now that he had come this far, he wanted to be done with the task before him. But there was no hastening it; he must wait upon Brunet's ferry, even as a trio of passengers who had come down silently behind Hercules and now stood talking in subdued voices must wait. He looked at them curiously. They were a family group—father, mother, son. The boy was twelve—about the same age as George. He stood looking eagerly into the west. Hercules thought they looked vaguely familiar. Probably one of the families recently come into the country near Prairie du Chien, giving up to move West.

He spoke to them and confirmed his guess. They were going West, deep into Iowa, perhaps beyond. He returned to contemplation of the river and the changing times. "West" had once meant Prairie du Chien, Dubuque, or the Iowa shore just across the Mississippi; then Fort Snelling, St. Peter's, Pembina. Now it had a far sound—the sound of a place inconceivably beyond Prairie du Chien, perhaps under those leaden clouds along the western rim, perhaps even past that, in a place where those clouds would show in the east, or perhaps be invisible under the turn of earth. Even the grain on which he sat—and the grain going down the Mississippi from St. Paul—these were signs of the change. He had foreseen them long ago; there was satisfaction in that. Still, the changes had come about before he had expected them to, almost before he was ready. . . . But then, he asked himself, what man is ready for any tomorrow?

After a while the ferry came back, nosing into its place. Brunet jumped off. He was a short, powerful man, dark-skinned, almost swarthy, with large black eyes and long black hair in which, as in his rough beard, the gray was beginning to show. Seeing Hercules, he raised an arm in greeting, and turned to give orders for the unloading. Then he waved his passengers forward and shouted that unloading and reloading would take some time. He looked toward Hercules once more; Hercules beckoned him.

As he came over, he said, "Hoh! Dousman—I do not t'ink to see you here. You go crosst to Iowa?"

"I wanted to talk to you, Brunet."

"Talk den," said Brunet, taking a stand before him with his legs spread and his thumbs hooked in his belt.

"I wanted to find out something about the boy."

"George?" Brunet was honestly incredulous. His eyebrows went up. "Has he do somet'ing?"

"No, no," said Hercules testily. "I wanted to find out where you got him."

Brunet was frankly baffled. He looked at Hercules askance, as if he had taken leave of his senses. "Julia," he said at last. "She fin' him in La Baye."

He said this with such an air of innocence that Hercules could not believe he had any knowledge of George's paternity.

"You go ask Julia. She know," Brunet went on. "I know not'ing. One tam she visit up dere—den she come back wit' de boy. She say she fin' him dere, his mothair gone, his fathair—" He shrugged. "Who know? I no say anyt'ing. We nevair have de children; *le bon Dieu* not wish it so—so we keep him. He is good boy, no trouble, vair' quiet—Julia, she keep him so."

"But didn't she ever tell you anything about his parents?"

Brunet spread his hands. "W'at she know? She say she fin' him wit' frien' in La Baye. Frien' no want dis baby. Julia want boy, so she take him. I no care."

Brunet turned and shouted at his men, pointing to the baggage behind his passengers. Then he turned back to Hercules once more, his eyes inquiring.

"You want maybe to see de boy? I lef' him home, but dis afternoon he work wit' me."

Hercules shook his head. He thanked Brunet. The Frenchman saluted him, then bounded back to his ferry, shouting orders in his native tongue. Hercules walked rapidly back into the village.

So Brunet knew nothing. Hercules did not believe he could have dissembled so well. Julia had not told him. If she had, he might have come to Hercules himself with the story. Perhaps he would have insisted that she take the boy to Hercules. Brunet was an honest man, but not above currying the favor of those who might be of assistance to him, men with money or influence. Now, of course, it was too late; Brunet had become accustomed to George, perhaps even attached to him; George was no longer an impersonal baby his wife had brought down the river from Green Bay.

Hercules walked rapidly around to the Brunet house. The clouds in the west were mounting the heavens, but the sun still shone out of the east, very bright, very warm. The air was still, as if settling in for a storm to come boiling out of the thunderheads. The Brunet house seemed to be waiting.

He knocked on the door.

The door was opened, but only a little way. Julia Brunet stood filling the opening.

"Mistaire Dousman come early in the morning," she said.

"Good morning, Julia. I wanted to see you."

She made no move to admit him, which irritated him. He pushed his way into the house.

Her lips tightened. "Mistaire Dousman force his way . . ."

He interrupted her brusquely. "I have something to say to you, Julia, and I don't mean to say it in the street." Since she made no move to shut the door, even though he was inside the house, he seized the doorknob and pushed it shut.

She shrugged, stepped ahead of him, and walked into her small sitting room, saying dryly, "I need not invite Mistaire Dousman to sit down. He need not be invite'."

"Julia, we have more serious things to discuss than your ruffled feelings. I have feelings, too. I've held off for a long time, but I've come at last and I mean to have it out with you."

"I know what you do to Joe," she said harshly.

"Oh, forget Joe," he almost shouted. "He's dead. Let him rest in peace."

Her lips tightened. She sat down, clasping her hands so tightly together over her knees that the skin whitened. "I do not forget my brothair," she said coldly.

"Julia, I've come about George," he said bluntly.

Apart from a slight narrowing of her eyes he could detect no emotion on her face. She did not move, save for her lips. "What is it with George?"

"I know all about him."

"Mistaire Dousman know more of him than I do," she replied.

"There's no need to bluff, Julia. George is my son by Cecile Gardepi. You know this, and I know it now, too. I didn't know it for a long time."

"Mistaire Dousman has the papairs to prove this?"

"Papers!" He shook his head brusquely. "You only have to look at him. He's the image of me as a boy. No one who knew me then could mistake it."

"Pairhaps it is fortunate for you—for Madame Dousman—that Mistaire Dousman was not small boy when he come to Prairie du Chien, *hein?* Pairhaps then evair'one would know what you claim to know. How is it you say this thing?" She smiled confidently. "Pairhaps Cecile, she tell you?"

"You know as well as I that Cecile died a year or so after the boy was born. You got him from her sister."

"Mistaire Dousman have lettair from her sistair to prove this?" She seemed to mock him with the beady intensity of her gaze; it was as if she played a game, every move of which she was informed of in advance; she waited only upon him to make the moves she knew he would make, knowing what her next move would be.

"Julia, I mean to have the boy. He can come to the house to live with us—I'll train him to step into the business . . ."

She held up a hand, suddenly imperious. A little smile played at her forbidding lips. It was as if she had looked forward to this scene for a long time, as if she had practiced it so long that she knew every word and gesture by heart. He was silent.

"Mistaire Dousman cannot have George," she said flatly.

"Julia, he's my son!" he cried, leaning above her.

She sat as straight as possible on the rocker's edge, closing her eyes against his intensity, making herself appear formidable, immovable.

"I know George is Mistaire Dousman's son," she said softly. "But he belong to me! And if Mistaire Dousman say to anybody I tell him George is his son, I will say he lie."

"But why, Julia? Why are you doing this?"

"Because we have raise' him—he is like our own son—because now you will know pairhaps how Joe suffair . . ."

He flung himself angrily away from her. "Always Joe! Joe has nothing to do with this! Joe's last years would have been miserable if it hadn't been for me. You never raised a finger to help your brother when he needed help. You never even called on him when he was ill. You did nothing, nothing—do you hear? I had to do it—I, his partner—not you, his sister. The only pain Joe had was from the disease that killed him."

"And what was that disease?" she cried out. "But the watching how all that was his became yours, Mistaire Dousman?—his business, his land, his home—even his wife, that woman who could not wait to marry you . . ."

"She waited a year!"

"I tol' Joe he mus' not marry a girl so much youngair than he—but he did."

"Stop your foolish tongue, Julia," he said sharply. "Jane was the most devoted of wives, and she went through a great deal with Joe, not only his illness, but his drinking, his frequent absences from home without explanation—but these are things you don't want to know; so why talk of them? I didn't come here to talk about Joe—or Jane—or you. I came to talk about my son."

"I have say what there is to be say about George."

"Julia," he said again, "I mean to have the boy."

"Mistaire Dousman will jus' have to resign himself to do without George," she answered serenely.

"I don't intend to."

She opened her eyes and regarded him curiously. "Mistaire Dousman can do nothing. George bear our name. George was with us evair since he was a baby. He is out of Mistaire Dousman's reach, because Mistaire Dousman cannot prove . . ."

"There must be proof somewhere. If there is, I'll find it."

She continued to look at him thoughtfully; her eyes held not only triumph and challenge, but also a certain wariness. Then she sighed. "Pairhaps Mistaire Dousman would like to hear it from George himself." Without waiting for his assent, she turned and called to the boy.

George came from an adjoining room—perhaps the kitchen, thought Hercules. He might even have overheard part of what had been said. He betrayed nothing, however; his face was bland, expressionless; he returned Hercules' eager glance with a hard-eyed gaze that disconcerted Hercules. He tried in vain to find any warmth in the boy's face, but there was none; his unwavering eyes matched the firmness of his mouth, the pale tautness of his features, the sensitive quivering of his nostrils. Cecile's nose, thought Hercules fleetingly.

"George," said Julie, "Mistaire Dousman want you should go to work at his house . . ."

"Office," put in Hercules with a dry throat.

George only shook his head.

"Mistaire Dousman is vair' important man," said Julia. She glanced toward Hercules with slyly mocking eyes. "Pairhaps he make big man of you, George."

"No," said George curtly. He added accusingly, "You saw me on the ferry. That's where I work."

"Yes, I did," answered Hercules. "I think you might like it better with me." He resisted the sudden impulse to beg the boy to come, to say to him that he was his father, that he had only recently found it out, that he wished now to make it up to him.

George shook his head again, a pronounced sullenness on his face. His eyes seemed to smoulder.

"George," said Julia with cajoling softness, "this man—Mistaire Dousman—he is your fathair, your real fathair. What have you to say to him?"

For an instant the boy's eyes sprang to life in a blaze of hatred—it was unmistakable. He gathered himself together tensely, as if he were about to spring at Hercules. Then he spat in Hercules' direction and ran from the room.

Hercules flashed a quick glance toward Julia.

"You see, Mistaire Dousman," she said, spreading her hands in mock helplessness.

"I see," he said quietly. "You'll hear from me again, Julia."

He turned and strode toward the door. As he closed it behind him, he heard her strident laughter ring out. Peal after peal of laughter rose in the house behind him. He stood for a moment, listening; he was appalled at the intensity of her hatred. Then her laughter subsided suddenly, and the door opened.

"Mistaire Dousman was in hurry to come in—and in hurry to go out," said Julia, looking at him from the open doorway with a scornful smile. "Good-by, Mistaire Dousman."

"I'll be back," he promised, turning away.

"Do you still want George, Mistaire Dousman—jus' as he is?" she taunted his retreating back.

A cold anger possessed him; his mood was as dark as the louring clouds pressing down upon the village, making the day gray and the air sultry and menacing. He knew now that Julia Brunet had waited for this scene; she had known that ultimately he must come to her, either of his own free will or because of her provocation. But if she had anticipated this so much, why had she not precipitated it? A word from her would have brought it about years ago. She had nursed her hatred a long time—even before Joe had died; she had had the boy more than a year, almost two years or over, when Joe died. She had hated him then. Why had she not brought George forward after Joe's death, when it was apparent that Jane and he would be married? She might then have hoped to interrupt that marriage she affected to despise so much. Even now, no act, no word of Julia's had brought about this scene she had clearly enjoyed so much. Why?

There was but one reason, he felt sure, and in this lay her own weakness: she had grown fond of the boy herself, even though she had gone to great pains to poison George's mind against his father, subtly, never too much at a time—for that would have defeated her purpose—a little now, a little more later. He could imagine what she had told him—how his father had cast him out, unwanted, spurned. The hatred in George's eyes was too manifest to be misunderstood. Hercules was convinced that this was the explanation for her silence—she had grown so fond of George that she would fight now to keep him.

He went straight back to the house on the mound.

Jane was in the conservatory, feeding her paroquets. Dédé and Miss McCleod were also there. The boy came running up to Hercules as he came in.

"Papa, Mother's going to let me have her paroquets," he cried. "I can take care of them, she says."

"That's good. It will give you some responsibility—teach you how to do such little chores." Just the same, he thought, as he hoisted the boy to his shoulders, it was another of Jane's ways of coddling the boy. He was irritated, but this irritation was subordinated to his cold fury at Julia Brunet, a fury, strangely enough, not unmixed with a certain sympathy.

Jane, searching his face, said to Miss McCleod, "Take Dédé outside, Miss Penelope."

Hercules bent; his son slid off his shoulders to the floor, landing lightly on his feet: a gay, happy boy. How unlike George! Hercules could not help thinking. Dédé ran to Miss McCleod and gave her his hand trustingly.

When they had left the conservatory, Jane turned to Hercules. "You have seen Julia, Mistaire Dousman."

"Yes." He told her what had taken place.

She came to him, put her arms around him, and stood there with her sympathetic face turned up to his. "My poor Mistaire Dousman," she murmured. "I fear' it would be so. I have know' Julia a long time. She have been much alone, much turn' in. She was devote' to Joe, but from a distance only; she always say she do not want to interfere. So now she has her revenge —on us both, on your direc', on me because she know I suffair when Mistaire Dousman do."

He kissed her gratefully.

"What will Mistaire Dousman do now?" she asked.

"There's only one thing to do. I'll get proof he's my son. She knew it; she didn't deny it when I put it to her; so if she knew, I, too, can find out. First thing, I'll go to Green Bay—

I've got to go up that way anyway in June to look at some land around Fond du Lac; I can go on over to Green Bay and stay with your sister—and look around for the proof I need."

She turned her face and put her cheek against his chest. "Mistaire Dousman do not wish any advice from me," she said quietly, as if she were eager to give it.

"You know I always listen to you, Jane."

"Oh, yes, Mistaire Dousman *listen.*"

"Say it, then."

"I say to Mistaire Dousman—leave the boy where he is. She has made him hate you. How can Mistaire Dousman be sure he can change that—aftair thirteen years?"

"I can't. But I'm not going to sit back and do nothing. I'll do what I can to win him over."

Outside, the wind rose and the sky blackened.

"Dédé should come in. It's going to storm," Hercules said.

"Miss Penelope will take care of him. Say to me—do Mistaire Dousman wish me to speak to Julia?"

"Of course not. This is between Julia and me. She'd like nothing better than to have you come to her. We'll not give her that satisfaction—besides, there's no need for it."

Rain began to fall suddenly in a torrent, pelting against the windows. Dédé and Miss McCleod came running up the lawn from the little pond beyond the conservatory, the boy screaming in excitement.

"Mistaire Dousman mus' do as he wish," said Jane quietly.

She turned to meet Dédé, who came bursting into the conservatory, raindrops pearled on his gay face.

Late that night Hercules closed and locked the office. He had spent the evening making plans for the steamboat line to run up the Wisconsin from Prairie du Chien, having ordered a boat of two hundred thirty-five tons from the yards in Elizabeth, Kentucky. He walked across the yard, past the icehouse, to the kitchen steps. He still smoked a cigar he had lit in the office, and he paused at the foot of the steps to finish it.

The night was overpoweringly fragrant with post-rain smells. The morning's shower had lasted two hours; its warmth had brought out all the musks of the earth, the perfumes of newly-opened leaves and blossoms, the pungences of old wood and last years leaves lying under snow most of the time since November. He stood drinking in the night air, listening for nocturnal sounds, of which there were only duck voices on the river, for it was too early in the month for whippoorwills to have come back, and the owls were still.

The sky was clear; stars glittered among the branches of the tree growing next the steps; over in the west, just touching the rim of the highest hill there, the waxing moon, past the first quarter, was slipping down the slopes of heaven. The south wind blew softly, bearing as from a distance the thin, twittering sounds of woodcocks making their mating dances. From high over suddenly came the honking of wild geese flying north.

He stood thinking about Julia and George. His anger had passed. He was filled with regret—the kind of regret a man feels when he has left something undone too long and believes that if he had not done so, events might have been altered. To this regret was added sympathy for Julia; his anger had not permitted him to see her in perspective earlier in the day—besides, a good part of his ire had been directed against himself; but he understood now what her dilemma must be; however mean her motives might originally have been, however vindictive she felt, she doubtless was attached to George in her own way, and even her confidence that Hercules would not be able to turn up proof of George's parentage only covered the fear that he might. Against that contingency, she had already prepared by poisoning George against him. What could she have told him—except to point to him as his father, who did not want him, who spurned him, playing upon his sensitivity, his pride, developing resentment and hatred? It was a cruel thing to have done, but Hercules understood it, however much he drew back in disgust from what Julia had done. He had been shocked when George spat at him; it had been so spontaneous; it had not been prompted by anything Julia had said or done at that moment—just a natural expression of contempt and hatred, one that rose from the deepest kind of conviction; it was an act that could not have been premeditated.

He threw his cigar away and went quietly into the house. He walked up the back stairs in the dark and into the hall there. At the door to Dédé's room he paused; it stood open, and after a brief hesitation he went in. He lit a candle in the candelabrum that stood on a little table not far from the bed and carried it over to the bedside.

Dédé lay on his back, his left arm folded on his breast, his right flung out toward the edge of the bed. His left hand was clenched about the blanket; his right lay open. How small his hands were! The fair face looked pale, the dark, touseled hair made a crown of ringlets on the pillow. He lay without moving; his even breathing was the only sound in the room; it made a gentle susurrus that sounded louder than it was because of the stillness of the night.

As he stood there, Hercules wondered whether George's coming would affect Dédé's future. Would what he was about to do turn the course of Dédé's life? He had thought of this before; it had given him pause as long as five years ago; now he thought of it anew. But Jane would protect her son from the very shadow of harm, he thought, and George—if he came—would be with Hercules, to be trained for the business. Seeing Dédé now, he thought again of how Jane coddled and shielded him; the boy was ever in her aura, never far from her or Eugenie or Miss McCleod, a boy surrounded by women who must mould his earliest world upon a world of women. True, LeBrun continued to give Dédé hours of riding; once in a while Hercules found time to ride with him, as he had taught him to swim in the Mississippi, and had taken him once, to hunt, over Jane's violent protest. But all this was not enough; Dédé grew in her image; Dédé's world was Jane's, a far cry from his father's.

But nothing would be permitted to touch him, no matter what took place. George was not yet here. George was not even within reach as yet, Hercules reminded himself. There was no good in worrying about an eventuality until it was at the threshold. He had an uneasy conviction that he was further now from George than he had been five years ago.

He put out the candle and went quietly from the room.

Late in May Thunder Walker made his appearance. He came walking into the office one windy evening just after LeBrun had gone to the house. His catlike entrance was so noiseless that Hercules was not aware of his presence until his scant clothing whispered as the Winnebago lowered himself to the floor behind him.

Hercules turned. He recognized Thunder Walker in the dusk of the room. "Where've you been? Almost two years! I thought you were dead."

"Me tough," said the Winnebago disdainfully.

"Here." Hercules reached into his desk and brought out a cigar. He thrust it at Thunder Walker, who bit off a piece of it and sat chewing it lustily. "Now, then, where do you come from?"

Thunder Walker explained, with many gestures, as usual, that his people had moved to the Crow Wing country of Minnesota. They had joined other Winnebago there, and Thunder Walker had gone to visit them. He had also visited their cousins, the Sioux. Now he bore a message for Hercules from the Sioux chief, Brown Elk. Brown Elk wished to thank Hercules for the return of his greatnephew.

"I'm glad he got him back," answered Hercules, "but it wasn't my doing. The Commissioner of Indian Affairs took care of the matter. All I did was write him a letter."

Nevertheless, Thunder Walker went on, others had written letters: they had done no good. It was not until Hercules had written that anything happened, so he laid his success at last to Hercules.

Hercules shrugged. "Let him believe as he likes."

The Winnebago continued. The Sioux treaty had at last been

signed, and the Sioux were moving West. Many of them were dissatisfied because the half-breeds had been paid so much by the Great White Father for the lands at Lake Pepin. Many others who were not moving far from the Crow Wing country made loud talk of revenge; there was much bitterness; it would be well, thought Thunder Walker, if Hercules would notify the Indian agents along the Mississippi and the Red River that there was discontent. There were strange, light-haired white men coming into the Sioux country across the Mississippi.

"Norwegians and Swedes," said Hercules; he explained briefly where they came from.

The Sioux did not like to see these white men come, even though the Indians had sold their lands, said Thunder Walker.

Hercules shook his head impatiently. "This always happens. There's nothing to be done. The Sioux should have done as the Menominee did—they didn't sell their lands around Lake Poygan; they're still on them, despite all the government can do. Only this winter I sent them another load of provisions when they let me know they were in need."

Thunder Walker continued with his recital of complaints. The old Winnebago was a bottomless container for every scrap of gossip and small talk he had encountered; he enjoyed relaying everything to Hercules, for it was beyond him to tell what any white man might consider of importance, so he told it all.

Hercules hardly listened. For more than a quarter of a century he had heard similar recitals. All the Indians, regardless of tribe or nation, seemed to be convinced that all the fault lay with the white men. It was true that much fault did lie with perfidious whites, but the Indians were very difficult to deal with, they were all too much like whimsical boys, with their hearts set on one thing one day and on another the day after. The treaty they signed with much self-congratulation on Monday they were ready to repudiate on Tuesday in favor of something other they conceived to be better, although it was quite as likely to be worse.

"You not hear what Thunder Walker say," said the Winnebago suddenly.

"Oh, I heard it, all right," answered Hercules. "Trouble is, I always have the feeling I've heard it so often before."

The Winnebago's eyes glinted with merriment. "Much," he agreed, nodding vehemently. "White men do not change. Red men do not change either."

Then he fell silent, waiting on Hercules.

"Where do you go from here, Thunder Walker?"

The Indian pointed into the northeast. He had come down the Mississippi by canoe with his friend, Red Gopher. They intended now to go up the Wisconsin and down the Fox.

"To Green Bay?"

Perhaps all the way to Mackinac.

"Well, if you're going to Green Bay, you might be able to do something for me."

Thunder Walker immediately said fervently that he would be glad to serve Hercules.

"You remember that boy you watched for me five years ago?"

The Winnebago nodded. No doubt, he said, Hercules had now taken the boy.

Hercules shook his head.

The amazement on Thunder Walker's face was almost ludicrous to see. Plainly, he could not fathom Hercules' inability or reluctance to act; he did not know how to explain the deviousness of white men. He waited in silence for some explanation.

"I've got to go to Green Bay next month to set on foot some inquiries about the boy's mother," Hercules went on, refusing to satisfy the Indian's curiosity—how could he explain his attitude to Thunder Walker, or indeed to any Indian?—"and I want someone I can trust to carry a letter to my brother-in-law, Henry Baird. I'd rather not entrust it to the mail service. Will you take it?"

Thunder Walker answered with a curt nod.

"You won't have any trouble finding Henry. Everybody

knows him in Green Bay. Right now he's president of the village board up there. I want the letter given to him personally—into his hands—not to anyone else."

The Winnebago nodded again.

"Tell Henry I'm going up to Fond du Lac to look over some land between that place and the lake. I'll make my headquarters at the inn of Sylvanus Wade east of Fond du Lac—and I'll hope to see him in Green Bay toward the end of the month."

Thunder Walker got to his feet. He was ready to go at once. Red Gopher would be waiting, and he did not want his companion to wait too long, especially if there were any firewater to be had. He waited patiently while Hercules wrote to Baird, setting down in his letter all the particulars he knew and guessed about Cecile Gardepi's visit to Green Bay, as well as those inquiries he wished Baird to undertake.

The Indian took the letter, pushed it down along his skin at one hip, gravely raised his arm in farewell, and was gone.

"Is the horse ready, Louis?" asked Hercules as LeBrun appeared at the door of the kitchen where Hercules sat by candlelight eating a hasty breakfast before dawn.

"Yes, Mr. Dousman."

"And you, too?"

"Yes, Mr. Dousman."

"Go to the office and fill that blue keg with water. Put some ice into it. We'll need it. The day feels hot already and we'll be on the road a long time."

LeBrun vanished into the thinning darkness of the early morning.

Hercules could hear the horses outside. LeBrun had brought them to the kitchen porch steps. There he had packed them for the journey into the North. Now, as soon as he came with the water keg, they could set out.

Hercules had not yet finished breakfast when LeBrun stuck his head in to say, "All ready, Mr. Dousman."

Hercules pushed away from the table at once.

They rode northeast out of Prairie du Chien, Hercules on Major, LeBrun on a young bay mare recently added to the stable. A third horse carried supplies for the journey, as well as blankets to sleep in, and netting to cover their faces by night to protect them from the onslaught of the mosquitoes, which were thick in many places.

The warmth of the June morning before sunrise presaged a hot day. No wind stirred. A few stars still shone in the sky, but the dawn light was beginning to spread over the heavens, and the morning air was filled with the songs and cries of many birds. Not far out of Prairie du Chien they rode past the Barrette farm, where the new house Hercules had built for Emily and her husband stood glowing white in the dusk; from it came the thin crying of Emily's second little daughter, now half a year old. But the house was still dark.

The road northeast of Prairie du Chien was well traveled to that place where it divided into two roads—one to cross the Wisconsin on the way to Madison, the other to follow along the Wisconsin's meandering course northeastward. This road wound over knolls and ridgeland, down through low country, avoiding marshland; it was not well worn, for it was used only by a few horsemen and some wagons at wide intervals. Yet only a few years ago no road at all had existed in this place; all the traffic between Green Bay and Prairie du Chien had been by canoe. Even today Hercules would have gone by canoe had it not been for the necessity of examining land he owned and other land he wished to buy between Fond du Lac and Sheboygan, on the east side of Lake Winnebago, and the demands of freedom of travel in that area.

They rode steadily all day, though from time to time Hercules consulted a map he carried with him and rode back from the river to look over land areas he had marked on it. At dusk they halted along the river, where Hercules stripped off his clothes, motioning LeBrun to do likewise. Both of them washed the day's heat off in the cool Wisconsin. Then they dressed again, mounted their horses, and climbed to the top of a hill not far back from the river's edge, selecting this high place to be as free as possible of the mosquitoes along the bottoms.

LeBrun built a fire to heat water for tea to drink with their supper. The horses were turned out to graze while the two of them sat eating.

"Tired, Louis?" asked Hercules.

"Yes, Mr. Dousman."

"Sore?"

"A little."

"Quite a change from the canoe or the steamboat, eh? Well, if we make good time, we'll sleep in beds tomorrow night."

LeBrun volunteered nothing. He waited for Hercules to speak. He was naturally taciturn, but despite his tiredness and soreness, he seemed eagerly aware of all the country. The alertness and agility which had been obvious at his coming to stay at the house on the mound had only been intensified; he had grown observant and was unusually perceptive in anticipating either Hercules' or Jane's wishes.

After they had eaten, they sat for a little while watching the evening come in. Over in the west shone Jupiter and Venus, not far above the horizon; high over lay the moon in first quarter. From the river below the hill rose the fresh smell of the water mingled with the cloying sweetness of locust blossoms. Nighthawks flew spiraling aloft, crying harshly, and coasted down the heavens, dropping like stones only to vault upward with a booming sound as the wind tore through their stiffened wing feathers. Whippoorwills and owls called out of the woods, filling the night with sound augmented by the stridulation of crickets all around, and the occasional scream of a lynx.

They wrapped themselves in light coverings, having taken off as much of their clothing as Hercules thought wise, and, having made little frames for their heads and necks to support the mosquito netting, they slept.

On the second night, as Hercules had calculated, they reached the hilltop home of Baron Chalfonte Pierneau—a proud house of yellow stone that dominated the beautiful Sac Prairie rolling away into the north to the ancient bluffs that cut it off. They reached the house past the supper hour; already lights flickered and gleamed in the little village along the river north of the Pierneau place, and the house on the hill was soft with yellow lamplight shining in every room, even in the turret facing east above the roof. Aristide Clement, one of Pierneau's men, had seen them approaching as he rode up the hill from the west, and reported their coming to Pierneau.

Pierneau was on the veranda to greet them when they broke out of the tree-arbored trail up the slope. "Dousman! I never thought I'd live to the day you rode up to my house on a horse."

Hercules explained why he was riding.

"You'll have supper at once," said Pierneau. "The women began to set the table the moment Aristide reported your arrival." He brushed aside Hercules' protests, pointing out that Clement had not yet had supper, and the woman had to get something ready for him, in any case, so they might as well set three places.

Hercules sent LeBrun around to the stables with the horses. He himself followed Pierneau inside. The old house had not changed much since last Hercules had seen it—he could not remember when that was—or since first he had laid eyes on it twenty years before; perhaps it had mellowed a little, but when first Hercules had visited it, it was already almost half a century old, and the old baron, Chalfonte's father, had lain for years in the family cemetery on the hilltop just northeast of the house.

Past the low veranda and the entranceway Pierneau led the way straight to the dining room, which was the near room to the west. Candles lit the table, and at it sat Madeleine, Chalfonte's wife, a fair-skinned woman with lustrous dark hair in which, as yet, there was no hint of gray to match her husband's gray lines in beard and hair. She greeted Hercules quietly.

As they talked, Aristide Clement came in from the kitchen: a hearty, big-boned man whose heavy-featured face was crowned by a long mane of ashen hair. He, too, greeted Hercules like an old friend, his blue eyes flashing with pleasure; he had often been to the Company office in Prairie du Chien with furs collected here at Pierneau's. After him came LeBrun, somewhat diffidently, and hard on his heels, with a tray of food, Molly Fonda, who had been in charge of the Pierneau kitchens since Hercules had known Chalfonte.

Hercules had had little opportunity to speak since he entered the house, apart from making monosyllabic replies, for Chalfonte had kept up a steady stream of talk—of his mother, making her excuses for not joining them, since she was unwell and kept to her room much of the time; of the conditions of travel now that roads and trails were being opened up in all directions; of the wet spring just past; of the fading away of the fur trade and the concomitant rise in agricultural pursuits; but at last he heard Pierneau mention his cousin.

"By the way, Dousman," Pierneau was saying, "we had a message from Augustin to pass on to you next time we met. Let me see—his letter came in last month—the first word we've had from California since winter set in. He said to tell you he ran into your man, Sark, in Sacramento, and that he seems to have done well for himself."

"I'm happy to hear it. We've had no word from him, but there was good reason for it."

Pierneau next asked about the progress of the Milwaukee & Mississippi. "We'd hoped the line would come closer to Sac Prairie. But then, down the valley straight to the Wisconsin at Arena does seem the more logical choice. We can hope for an extension up the river—perhaps to go on north over the bluffs—but at at least a spur line."

"They'll have to reach the Mississippi first—and that'll take several years yet, at the present rate of progress."

"Well, it won't be so long. Now that Chicago and New York are connected by railroad, we're bound to the East. To tell the truth, I don't know whether I'm sorry or glad."

Hercules laughed. "You were always an unreconstructed idealist, Pierneau."

While they talked, night closed down upon the house. Hercules, who sat facing windows that opened out to the west, saw the outlines of the trees gradually fade and darkness sweep in over the tawny prairie; along the western rim lay a great flaming band of saffron and magenta, which deepened to copper and mother-of-pearl, and gave way at last to a lemon glow surmounted by a wash of emerald and aquamarine, out of which shone with supernal beauty the evening stars.

He ate slowly, listening, interjecting a few words now and then, answering Madeleine Pierneau's inquiries about Jane and Dédé, thinking of what an aura of peace and contentment reigned here in this house, now more than sixty years old. But already, he reminded himself, the house on the mound had stood for more than a decade.

"I suppose, Mr. Dousman," said Madeleine suddenly in her quiet voice, "you're no longer used to sleeping on the ground."

He smiled. "I assure you, Mrs. Pierneau, my bones have never ached so much as they did this morning. Even ten years ago I thought nothing of spending nights outside—but at my age now, well"—he shrugged—"you see how carefully I planned the trip—the second night here; the third at the Agency House at the Portage; and only two or three nights under heaven. And I may beg your indulgence again and repeat my visit on my return trip."

"Please do!"

"And now I see Louis is already nodding . . ."

Madeleine rose. "Please come with me, Mr. LeBrun."

Hercules got to his feet, too, and excused himself. "We'll be off to an early start—before breakfast."

Pierneau was up to see them start away in the morning. The day was overcast, and a cooling wind blew out of the west, making a waving sea of the long grass among the oak openings of the prairie beyond the boundaries of Pierneau's fields.

"Better stay, Dousman," he urged. "It looks like rain."

"No, no, thanks—I must go."

"Well, if you're bound to set out, weather notwithstanding, I can't stop you. But I'd advise you to take the ferry in Sac Prairie and cross to the other side. The road from Madison to Portage is more traveled—you can cut across country and intersect it, or just follow the river up on the other side."

Hercules thanked him, and they rode off down the north slope of the Pierneau hill toward the prairie and the settlement on it, beginning the longer lap of their journey.

Hercules and LeBrun reached Wade House in eight days. The hostelry stood almost halfway between Fond du Lac and Sheboygan, and on the way there Hercules had examined several areas of land, arranging to sell some which he already owned, taking claim to others; he had visited land agents in Fond du Lac, as well as old friends along the way. Tired as he was when he reached Wade House along the plank road leading east from Fond du Lac, he was still fired with anticipation as he neared Green Bay, hopeful of learning there something which would permit him to bring George Brunet into his home.

Wade House had been built on the banks of a small stream known as the Mullet River. It was of three stories, with wide, pillared porches all along its front, on both ground floor and second story. A stagecoach was just loading for Fond du Lac when Hercules and LeBrun arrived; the unharnessed horses were being led to the blacksmith shop across the stream, and Sylvanus Wade himself was bidding the coach driver good-by. He was a sturdy man of middle height, approaching sixty, with a thin-lipped mouth and keen eyes overshadowed by thick black eyebrows. His face was framed in a Quaker beard, beginning to grow white. Hercules had known him when he had lived for a while in Fort Atkinson.

The stage pulled out, but Sylvanus Wade continued to stand there, watching Hercules ride up.

"Greetings, Mr. Dousman," he called out. "I've got rooms ready for you—heard you were coming."

"Is that so, Mr. Wade?" answered Hercules, curious. "I don't recall sending word ahead."

Wade shrugged. He turned and walked across the veranda

into the taproom. Hercules followed, while LeBrun tied up the horses. "Now you're here," Wade went on, "you'll have company in a short time, I'll be bound. The Indians know you're coming."

Hercules guessed that Thunder Walker had made his coming known. "What Indians?" he asked.

"The Menominees." Wade crossed to the bar and went around behind it. "What'll you have, Mr. Dousman?"

"Some brandy, please."

"And the young fellow?"

"A little of the same."

Hercules sat down in the hand-hewn captain's chair beside the one table in the room. LeBrun came in and joined him. Wade edged out from behind the bar with their brandy. He stood to talk with them while they drank.

"The Indians'll have seen you come—you know how they are, Mr. Dousman. So you'll have company come to call. D'you want to see 'em, or not?"

"You know how Indians are, Mr. Wade," said Hercules humorlessly. "If I don't see them when they come, they'll continue to come until I do."

"There's a chief with 'em, too. They're camped not far away, I believe. They've been around for the last four days. You're planning to stay more than the night, Mr. Dousman?"

"Two or three days."

"You've come at a good time; there's a ball in the hall tonight."

Hercules groaned. "I want sleep, not dancing, Mr. Wade. Right now, though, both Mr. LeBrun and I will want to bathe. Can that be arranged?"

"I reckon it can, Mr. Dousman. Just come along with me."

When Hercules came back into the taproom after he had bathed, Wade gestured wordlessly toward the front porch. Hercules was startled to see there a deputation of Menominee. He crossed to the door and went out.

The Menominee immediately raised their hands in greeting

and one of them stepped out from among the others. Hercules would have recognized anywhere that almost pathetically short, squat man—it was Chief Oshkosh, and his wrinkled face was wreathed in smiles.

"Dousman, our friend," he said, and held his hand out stiffly, so that Hercules might shake it in the manner of white men.

Hercules clasped his hand.

"We come thank Dousman," said Oshkosh. Thereupon he launched into one of those interminable speeches so dear to the Indians. He thanked Hercules in the name of his people, and for himself especially, because on many occasions when the Menominee were desperately in need of food, Hercules had provided it; because Hercules had always taken their part in their dealings with the Great White Father; because Hercules had upheld their right to reject the Crow Wing country of Minnesota as their future home.

"I told the representatives of the Great White Father," Oshkosh said in his own language, "that I would sooner take the poorest land in Wisconsin than the richest land anywhere else."

"The Crow Wing country was rich, good earth," Hercules pointed out.

"But it had no rice." And, having said so much, Oshkosh had said all that needed to be said for a Menominee. He went on to point out that he was an old man, he would soon be gathered to his ancestors, he had come personally to thank Dousman.

Hercules was certain that, despite the genuineness of Oshkosh's gratitude, there was something more to this insistent visit. He waited, bemused, through all the chief's incessant speech, and presently it came.

The Menominee, said Oshkosh, had a request to make. He, Oshkosh, and many other chiefs had been to Washington to see the Great White Father, who had sent them to New York. They had even been to see a white singer named Jenny Lind, who made a very big noise and then a little noise, which was proof that white men had more money than they needed, when they could pay so much to hear this lady sing. Now the Menominee would move, said Oshkosh, to the Wolf River, which was north of their present lands. This was to be their home forever; the Great White Father had promised it. But for the first season on this new land, which was more barren than their ancestral acres, the Menominee would need help.

"Very well," said Hercules, "I'll send your people some supplies. I know most of them have already gone to this place, during the time of the hunter's moon last year and the moon of falling leaves. When do you go?"

"Soon. We have yet to treat with the government for terms, but if Keshena and I sign, it will be as we have said."

"The government is more patient with your people, Oshkosh, than it was with the Winnebago, the Sauk, the Fox—even the Sioux. It would be better to sign when you reach common ground."

This Oshkosh did not want to hear. He shook his head, even stamped one foot in sudden anger. Hercules held back his laughter; it was comic to see Oshkosh angry and petulant over so small a thing as advice that went counter to his notion. Oshkosh stepped back among his braves—there were seven of them in all—and once more raised his hand.

"Farewell, Dousman. We are friends of many moons. When I go to the Wolf River country, I go as an old man. I will not see you again; Manitou does not wish it to be. If all white men were as you, Dousman, the red man could live in peace with white men as his brothers. Farewell." For a moment he made a picture of moving dignity.

All the Menominee raised their arms in the gesture of parting; then they filed off the porch and around the inn to walk to where they had encamped before beginning their journey back to their own land. None had spoken but Oshkosh; he spoke for them, as they wished.

Hercules watched them move away, knowing that it would be as Oshkosh said: they would not meet again. Then he turned and went back into the taproom where LeBrun waited.

That evening he ventured into the ballroom for half an hour

to enjoy the gay music and watch the couples dance the cotillion. The ballroom was on the third floor of Wade House; it could be reached only by a narrow, winding stair, so narrow, indeed, that many of the ladies must have felt cramped going up in their wide skirts. Off its far side opened rooms for travelers, but they were so small and, because of their proximity to the dance floor, so noisy, that half the night would be gone ere the travelers stopping in them could get to sleep. Fortunately, Hercules had a room on the second floor, but poor LeBrun lay in one of these small cubicles trying to sleep.

Hercules did not stay long, for he was tired. He passed a few words with Sylvanus Wade—the old man, flushed of face and merry of eye, enjoyed the ball as much as the youngest dancer—then descended and went to bed.

For three days Hercules rode out from Wade House, examining land for the purpose of investing in it, visiting prospective buyers who had written him at Prairie du Chien, and signing papers for the transfer of some of his property to a friend of former Governor Tallmadge. The inn made an excellent base of operations; the food prepared in its spacious kitchen was of the best; the company in the taproom was always congenial; and although the inn was usually filled to capacity, there were no more dances during his stay, and little, therefore—save the incessant traffic moving along the plank road—to interrupt his sleep.

He left Wade House at last with reluctance, and rode to Sheboygan. From there he went up along the lake to Green Bay, where he made his way straight to the home of his brother-in-law.

Henry Baird was not at home. His wife, Elizabeth, Jane's sister, assured him that her husband would be back by suppertime. Since it was midafternoon when Hercules arrived, that time was not too far away.

"Then I'll rest a little, if you don't mind," said Hercules.

"You can rest tonight, Mr. Dousman," said Elizabeth. "Here

I haven't seen you for evair so long, and I must know how Jane and Dédé are."

Jane's younger sister was fairer than Jane. Her eyes, which had the same quality as Jane's, were set a little more widely apart, and her nose was broad in contrast to the aquilinity of Jane's. Their mouths were similarly shaped; they wore their hair alike, parted in the middle and drawn tight to their heads; and they were in many ways exactly akin, except that Elizabeth was heavier.

"Everybody's fine at home," said Hercules. "I know Jane writes to you in detail so you'll know as much as I do."

"You men nevair know anything," cried Elizabeth, raising her long, dark brows in mock despair.

"I must say, Elizabeth, now I get a good look at you and see how broad you're getting, you're beginning to resemble a squaw. Are you sure there isn't some Indian blood in you?"

Elizabeth flashed a glance of surprise at him. "Didn't Jane evair tell you? Our grandmother Marcot, who was Madame Schindler, was the granddaughter of the Ottawa chief, Returning Cloud, and of Clear Day Woman. It's good blood."

Hercules was astonished. He was also amused. It was not something Jane would have thought of telling him because it would not have occurred to her to do so. Yet she must have known, for Captain Henry Fisher, her father, would have been as proud of it as Elizabeth manifestly was.

"I'm sure it is, Elizabeth. Jane just didn't happen to tell me."

"She forgot it, then."

LeBrun came in to say that the horses had been fed and tied up, and added that he was tired.

"Come, follow me," said Elizabeth. "I'll show you where you can rest."

Hercules looked longingly after LeBrun, but Elizabeth had no intention of freeing him.

"Once Henry comes home, he'll talk, and I won't," she said. She resumed her questions, prodding Hercules to replies. She talked principally about the steady growth of Green Bay, and was proud that Henry had been chosen president of the village board, although she admitted that now everyone with a complaint came to him, and he scarcely had time for his law practice.

She was still talking when Henry Baird came. He was a man of close to six feet in height, with clear, penetrating eyes and a square look to his face which Hercules searched in vain for any clue to what news Henry might have for him. His mouth was uncompromising, and his glance was emotionless. His hair, worn short, was ruffled, as if he had passed his hands through it many times.

He greeted Hercules with some restraint, explaining that he had had a trying day, and foresaw no end to such days. "I tell you, Hercules, avoid public office like the plague," he finished vehemently.

"In my field, I certainly will. But in yours—I should think the law and public office go hand in hand. They're complementary callings, aren't they?"

He wanted to bring up the subject of Cecile Gardepi at once, but it was plain from the time he had spent alone with Elizabeth that Henry had told her nothing of Hercules' request, nor had Jane evidently written anything to her about George. He sat through supper talking about the larger events of the day—the progress of road and railroad building in Wisconsin, the inadequacy of President Fillmore, the amazing Abolitionist excitement fanned everywhere by a colorful romance titled *Uncle Tom's Cabin*, published a year ago.

After supper, Baird got up, beckoning to Hercules. "Come and walk with me, Hercules."

They went outside and began to walk into the village, despite the threat of rain from low, dark clouds.

"That was a surprising assignment you passed on to me, Hercules," said Henry, a troubled note in his voice. "I hardly knew what to make of it."

"There's nothing to make of it," answered Hercules in a flat voice. "The boy is mine; he's a picture of me when young." He outlined the circumstances of his affair with Cecile Gardepi. "So you see, I had no suspicion that she was pregnant by me, or even that she was pregnant. You know, I married Margaret—I'd probably have married Cecile, but evidently that wasn't what she wanted, although what she might have wanted no one ever got to know. She was rather a strange girl. She died not long after—within a year, I think." He shrugged. "But that doesn't matter. It's the proof I need to have."

"I'm not sure I approve of what you want to do, Hercules."

"Let me be the judge of that, Henry. As my son, he has a right to be with me. I want to teach him the business—it may be he'll be harder, tougher than Dédé—Jane babies him, and I'm afraid she'll leave him too soft. I may be wrong, but dare I take the chance as long as George is my son?"

"What does Jane say?"

"She's at one with me in wanting him to come."

"Because you want it, probably. I don't know that you've fully considered everything. How does the boy feel about it?"

"He hates me."

"Hates you?" Henry was amazed. "But why should he?"

"Because Julia has poisoned him against me. That was part of her revenge."

"Then he won't want to come?"

"Perhaps not—at first."

Baird shook his head. "I don't like it. I don't like a bit of it. What has this woman to gain by such an act? By now she's fond of him, too."

"I find myself attracted to him also, Henry. A strange, wild boy—a solitary, in a sense, although he plays with other boys. He's taciturn, he seldom speaks, although he answers when he's spoken to—but above all else, my son."

"Nevertheless . . ."

"Don't lecture me, Henry," interrupted Hercules impatiently. "I've struggled with myself for years—ever since I found out. At first I wanted to deny it; I tried to find other explanations, but the boy's resemblance was too great to support any denial.

Then I held off because of Jane and Dédé, but this was no fairer to George than my attempt to deny him. Even so, it was five years before I finally confronted Julia, while I had waited all that time for her to tell me what she obviously knew—she admitted she knew, though she'll deny it if anyone puts it to her. Now, tell me, what have you learned about the boy's birth?"

"Nothing—except that he was born in the house of Elise Antaya—Cecile's married sister. About six years older than Cecile, I'm told."

"Where can I find Mrs. Antaya?"

"I can't tell you, Hercules. They left Green Bay about ten years ago. Her husband appears to have been an indifferent workman—he worked at all kinds of jobs but never held one very long."

"The point is, then, where did they go?"

"No one seems to know."

"There must be someone who could guess where they might have gone."

"So far I've not found anyone."

"Then there must be somebody—a midwife, perhaps a doctor—who attended the birth. She might have said something . . ."

"Hercules, Hercules," protested Baird. "No one's doubting that the birth took place, only that it's your son. Only Elise Antaya could say that, and then only if Cecile told her as much. We don't know that she did."

"I want to find out."

"The whole question is one that may be incapable of proof, now that Cecile's dead. Elise may be dead, too. Tell me, how do you propose to go about persuading the boy to come to you?"

"I mean to win him by kindness."

"He may reject that, coached by Julia."

"Then, at the last, I can have recourse to law."

"Without proof?"

"Henry, they'd only have to look at the two of us, side by side—compare early likenesses of me with the child today—no one could doubt it."

"Except a court of law," replied Baird dryly. "You don't have anything but circumstantial proof, Hercules. If you had a statement from the mother—even a statement from her sister, who attended her . . ." He shrugged. "But either one seems out of the realm of possibility."

"Henry, I won't give up now."

They walked for a while in silence. Mosquitoes annoyed them, and a light, drizzling rain began to fall.

Presently Baird spoke again. "I'll tell you—there's one thing. If you mean to go into court with such a circumstantial case—if you could find out—mind you, it might not help at all, but it's a point . . ."

"Say it."

"If you could show that the boy wasn't legally adopted. My guess would be that he wasn't, that he was just taken because his mother didn't want to be troubled with him—or, who knows, because Julia might have promised to give him to you."

"Henry, if Julia found out about the boy's parentage, someone else must know."

"Yes, that follows. But it won't do any good if that someone else is dead."

"Promise me, at least you'll make further inquiries."

"Very well. I will. But you keep out of it here, Hercules. Let me do the prying."

"As you like."

Hercules was disappointed, but he concealed his feelings. They turned back toward the house, walking rapidly, because rain was coming down heavily now.

Rain fell for two days. Immediately after the sky cleared and the wind's direction changed, Hercules and LeBrun set out for Prairie du Chien.

6. Currents Turn Awry

Winter-Summer, 1854

The months passed, the year turned; no word came from Henry Baird. Frustrated in his eagerness to act after so long a delay, Hercules threw himself into the affairs of his various enterprises with new energy. He invested large sums of money in wheat, oats, and pork. He bought land covered with pine trees in the river valleys along the Chippewa, St. Croix, and upper Wisconsin rivers. He increased his holdings in bonds of the Milwaukee and Prairie du Chien, and vented some of his ire in irritation at the slowness of construction in a letter to President Catlin— "Are the officers of the Company not sensible that, while delays in construction are constant and very leniently dealt with, land values in the right of way of the road have increased to twenty-five dollars an acre? By contrast, I have just sold one of my Green Bay farms at eight dollars an acre, and derived a very good profit therefrom. Yet here we are being forced to pay twenty-five, and all because there is nothing but delay and more delay."

Jane recognized in this almost frenzied devotion to business an effort to compensate himself for his helplessness about George; it was an attempt to keep his thoughts from the boy. But while in the past, waiting on Julia Brunet's move, Hercules had found himself able to go about his work without thinking of George for long periods at a time, now, since his declaration to her and his rebuff by the boy, he found it quite impossible not to think of George, to plan how he might persuade him to come to the house on the mound. He sent gifts; they were returned. He offered to send the boy East to school; his offer was not even answered. The Brunets and George might as well have lived in New Orleans, for all that Hercules saw of his son.

In midwinter Hercules and Bernard Brisbois drove to Madison by sleigh to meet at Bird's hotel with other members of the Madison and Prairie du Chien Rail Road Company, which had been consolidated with the Milwaukee & Mississippi. The weather was mild; a good snow cover lay on the ground, and the journey, broken but once over night, was not difficult. Yet it seemed long to Hercules, who traveled most of the way in silence unusual for him.

"He has something on his mind," said Brisbois to Bird on their arrival. "He acts caged."

"The money he sank in the road, most likely," guessed Bird.

Hercules only smiled.

"Now we'll have a little something to eat, while I send word out to the others that you're here," continued Bird. "Come along. We'll go into my own quarters. My wife and family aren't home."

He showed Hercules and Brisbois into his rooms and then went into the kitchen to order food and dispatch a boy for Simeon Mills and Elisha Burdick. When he came back, Hercules and Brisbois were warming themselves at the fireplace.

"I'm surprised to see you at this time of the year," said Bird.

"We felt something ought to be done to prod the men in Milwaukee," said Brisbois.

"At this rate," added Hercules, "our Chicago rivals will be at the Rockies before we've reached the Mississippi."

One of the kitchenmaids came in with a tray of food.

"Ah, well, eat something—we'll talk about it later when the others get here. If you'll excuse me, I'll fetch something to drink."

Both Mills and Burdick joined them within a quarter of an hour. They sat in a half-circle around the fireplace, greetings having been exchanged, and listened as Hercules talked.

"Gentlemen, I regret to say that the Chicago lines have beaten us to the Mississippi. They've been pushing steadily west; they'll be at the river by March. Indeed, they boast they'll be at Rock Island before that."

"Well, they're not there yet," said Burdick doggedly. "A lot of things can happen to prevent it."

"It's no use taking any comfort in such an eventuality. They've beaten us, and that's all there is to it. Nothing can prevent their getting there before us when they're only a month from the river. How far are we? Years!" He shook his head grimly and went on. "When we formed the Madison and Prairie du Chien Company and consolidated with the Milwaukee & Mississippi, we had every reason to believe that the road would at least be in Madison by this time."

Burdick groaned aloud. "Yes, and here it's stuck in Stoughton."

Colonel Bird was optimistic. "The last word I have, gentlemen, is May—May of this year for the rails to reach Madison."

"I want to see it before I believe it," said Brisbois.

"The thing is, we ought to do something," Hercules went on. "As it looks now, the road can't reach Prairie du Chien in less than two years—and it might take longer."

"But what is there to do?" put in Mills mildly. "It seems to me they're doing everything they can, and without much help from people owning the right of way, what can we do?"

"We could memorialize the members of the board," suggested Burdick.

Brisbois shook his head. "Mr. Dousman and I have both written them at length—we've both put more money into the Company. So that won't do it. It seems to us, frankly, that there's been a lot of wasteful extravagance. We have nothing to show for it."

"Then let one of us go to Milwaukee in person and see what

more can be done," suggested Mills sensibly. "You, Dousman?"

Hercules shook his head. "I've been at meetings of the board. It ought to be someone else. How about you, Bird?"

"Yes, Bird! I approve of Bird," said Burdick.

"Well, I could go, I suppose," said Bird reluctantly. "I still think, since Dousman has put more money into the road than any of us, he'll bring more weight to bear. I wish you'd reconsider, Dousman."

Hercules shook his head. "No, gentlemen. That's precisely the reason I shouldn't be the one to put spurs to the board. I dislike anything that smacks of money pressure. Colonel Bird seems to me a very good choice. Besides, I have many other pressing matters to wait upon."

They sat far into the night, studying maps of the proposed route of the railroad, pondering the replacement of Byron Kilbourn and Kilbourn's interest in the new LaCrosse and Milwaukee Road, but in all this Hercules took ever less part—he had all along had some doubt about Kilbourn's impulsive ambition, and he did not doubt that some of the mismanagement of the Company's affairs would ultimately be traced to Kilbourn—because he was unable to take his thoughts for very long at a time from George, who grew daily more important to him and his plans for the future. Why had Henry not written? Could it be that he was so much out of sympathy with Hercules' goal that he could not bring himself to push the inquiry? He wished it were possible to reach Henry and prod him, but the mails in winter were haphazard and subject to frequent delays. If someone were traveling in that direction . . .

"Are there travelers from the Green Bay region in town, Colonel?" he asked suddenly.

"Why, Judge Doty is staying here. He's down from his island and going back tomorrow."

"Where is he?"

"He's in number nine. Not far from your room, Dousman. I've put you in five."

Hercules excused himself. He went to his room, sat down to paper, and let what was in him pour out in a note to Baird.

"In the absence of any further information from you about the subject of my inquiry last fall, I suppose I will have no alternative but to inquire elsewhere. Will you let me know whether the lady had any other relatives either in that vicinity or somewhere else, or perhaps whether her husband had any? We had an Antaya family in Prairie du Chien, but there seems to have been no relationship with the Antaya of Green Bay.

"I chafe at this delay."

Then he carried the letter down the hall to number nine. Seeing that a light still burned in the room, he knocked on the door.

"Come in," called Doty.

Hercules opened the door and stepped into the room.

James Duane Doty, onetime judge, former governor of Wisconsin Territory, and until recently a congressman from the new state, sat on the floor in the midst of opened newspapers. His bright, earnest eyes looked out of a friendly foxlike face surmounted by tousled graying hair.

"Dousman! What brings you out of Prairie du Chien?"

"A railroad meeting."

"I might have known. The richest man in the Middle West must be about making more money. Sit down. Pray overlook my occupation—I'm trying to make some sense out of Douglas's Nebraska bill. The thing seems to be a nullification of the promise of the Missouri Compromise, and it's hurting the Democrats—and me. I'd hoped to be the candidate of the party for the senate when Isaac Walker's term expires. But now this . . ."

Hercules sat down. "I don't know that it'll affect your chances, Judge."

Doty shrugged resignedly. "I'm afraid you're no politician. I hope you're right, but I don't think you are. You ought to live in the northern part of the state. They're agitating there for a new party—in fact, they're planning a gathering in Ripon this coming March to make a beginning. Both Whigs and Democrats who claim to be disillusioned with their parties are behind it." He smiled grimly. "I sometimes wish I'd kept out of politics, but I'm in it now to stay. Can I count on your support, Dousman?"

"Over Walker? Of course."

"Walker won't be a candidate again, I understand. So I don't know at the moment who'll oppose me. Kilbourn's after the nomination, I know, and he has a lot of support down Milwaukee way. So has Tweedy. Charlie Durkee seems to be the favorite of the radicals up North." He got to his feet, stepping out of the opened newspapers, and stood with his hands clasped behind him, his waistcoat swinging open. "You didn't come here to talk politics, Dousman."

"I came to ask a favor of you."

"What is it?"

"I want to send a letter to my brother-in-law in Green Bay—Henry Baird. The mails are so uncertain, and since Bird tells me you're heading back to Menasha in the morning, I wondered whether you'd take the letter as far as that place. I leave it to your discretion to send it on by hand, if possible, from there."

"Glad to."

Hercules thanked him and gave him the letter. Then, wishing him success in his hope for the nomination as the senatorial candidate, he withdrew. He stood at the head of the stairs listening to sounds from below, intending to return to the meeting; but since it was clearly breaking up, he retraced his steps to his room. He was satisfied at having done something—even so slight as this—to relieve his frustration about George and the silence from Green Bay. The letter would bring a reaction of some kind from Baird.

LeBrun raised his head attentively and shot a glance toward Hercules, who was bent over his desk. "Do you hear that, Mr. Dousman?"

Hercules raised up and listened.

From outside several voices rose and fell, as from someone

running through the streets beyond the grounds. "A boat! A boat!"

"It's the first boat, Mr. Dousman," said LeBrun.

Hercules went to the door. He looked south, across the island and the south end of the Marais de St. Feriole, toward the docks. The Mississippi shone brown with silt. In the village excitement rose like a wave—people shouted the news to one another, villagers came running down toward the landing, as always, every spring, when the first boat came. It was the fifth of April, and the sun shone warmly out of a cloudless heaven; bees hummed in the soft maple blossoms, and bluebottle flies buzzed at the panes. Hercules could just see the stacks rising along the docks, and the black smoke thinning in the south wind.

"It is," said Dousman, "and I hope she's got some of our goods on board."

As he stood watching, Hercules saw the stacks of a second steamboat move in toward the landing. By this time people were streaming toward the docks from all sides. Now, at last, the long winter siege was over—sleighs could be put away once more, the boats would bring news of the outside world until snow and ice locked Prairie du Chien away for another season, and the villagers gave vent to their release from the winter's imprisonment with shouts, gay laughter, even songs. A new spirit pervaded the town and the people with the coming of the first boat each spring.

Hercules stood bemused for some time, lulled by the somnolence of the sunny morning air. Then, as he was about to return to his desk, he caught sight of a little Negro boy coming on the run, half-skipping along, from the lane into the grounds, where he came to a stop and looked uncertainly toward the house on the mound. He held a folded white paper in one hand.

"Over here, boy," called Hercules.

The boy saw Hercules, who had stepped forward out of the doorway. He came skipping over.

"Mist' Dousman, sah?" he asked.

"I'm Mr. Dousman."

"Here dis," said the boy, handing him the message. "I'm Petah," he added.

"Thank you, Peter."

Hercules opened it and read. "Captain Gleim presents his compliments to Mr. Dousman. I have brought your new boat, the *Ocean Wave,* up from Elizabeth. Would you like to try her out? We'll be unloaded by noon, and will be free for the afternoon."

"Wait here," Hercules instructed the boy.

Peter sat down on the step, pulling his wide-brimmed straw hat forward to shield his face from the sun.

Hercules crossed to the house. He went from room to room, looking for Jane. He found her, with Dédé and Miss McCleod, in the great long attic over the second story.

"Whatever are you doing here?" he asked.

Jane smiled at his surprise. "Mistaire Dousman do not see what wondairful place to play this will be for Dédé when it rain outside." Her voice sounded hollow in the attic space, dimly lit by gable windows.

"But he has the entire house to play in!"

"He will want place all his own, you'll see."

Hercules glanced at his son. "Do you, Dédé?"

"Yes, Papa."

"Well, then, it will be yours. We'll put into it whatever you like." He turned to Jane. "The new steamboat's in from Kentucky, Jane. Would you like to take a little trip in her this afternoon?" He included Miss McCleod in a sweep of his hand. "We could all go."

"I would love to go," cried Jane, clasping her hands ecstatically. "All wintair we have sit here—now and then a party or a dinnair—but we go nowhere."

"Have lunch a little early, then. I'll send word to Captain Gleim to bring the boat up to our wharf."

Hercules returned to the office, gave Peter ten cents, and told him to tell Captain Gleim to expect them at twelve-thirty at the dock behind the house, and to be prepared to run down to Cassville.

They boarded the *Ocean Wave* promptly at the hour set. She was a side-wheeler, as Hercules had indicated she should be. Although it was obvious that she was new, she already bore the marks of her long passage down the Ohio and up the Mississippi. The lower deck had evidently been crowded and all but two of the cabins had been occupied.

Captain Gleim, a fat man with a grave face out of which shone laughing eyes, explained that he had brought up a full cargo, with twenty-one passengers on the lower deck, discharging into Iowa and Illinois, and a few for Cassville and Prairie du Chien. He praised the *Ocean Wave*. He reminded Hercules, while Jane and Miss McCleod went about inspecting the staterooms and the handsome central cabin, that he had been a river-boat captain for close to twenty years; in all that time he had never captained a better boat. True, he had taken larger boats up and down the river, but the *Ocean Wave* was the trimmest.

Hercules estimated her cost: twenty thousand—perhaps a shade less. In one season, if the trade held, she could pay for herself; thereafter, she would make good money even in a relatively poor season, but with immigrants flocking upriver to St. Paul, and with furs, wheat, and lead going down the river, the *Ocean Wave* would be kept busy, despite all the revenue the independent captains could take away from the packet boats. But of course there were the Wisconsin River runs to be added. The thought of the railroad at Rock Island, and its carrying the produce of the upper Mississippi Valley all the way by rail to New York, gave him but a momentary uneasiness; one rail line could not carry it all.

Captain Gleim excused himself. He gave the signal to loosen the hawsers; two sharp blasts of the whistle exploded into the drowsy noon, and with measured slowness the *Ocean Wave* drew away from the landing west of the house, went down around the curve of the island through the east channel, past the docks, and into the west channel, bound down-river for Cassville, thirty miles away.

Hercules rejoined his family. Dédé ran all about the upper deck, stopping now and then to point excitedly to something that caught his eye. Miss McCleod followed him primly about, as if her very presence were enough to prevent any accident to him. Perhaps it was, thought Hercules, who had been impressed more than once with her quiet efficiency.

"Do you like her, Jane?"

"Mistaire Dousman—the cabins, they are so small."

"Oh, yes, they must be. If we had very large staterooms, we'd have to charge more than the traveling trade would pay. They'd rather be cramped and pay less than have plenty of room at more cost."

"An' down below—on the lowair deck, it mus' be vair' crowded. No wondair the cholera is always so bad, an' so many die."

He gave her a bemused glance. "Jane, Jane, you always think of the unfortunate . . ."

"Who do so? Not vair' many people! You, too, Mistaire Dousman—you think of them. You sen' food to the Indian. You are kin' to the poor. You do many things you nevair tell me, but I fin' out. An' now you wish to bring this boy, George, to our house, to raise him."

"Ah, but he won't come."

"But you pairsis'—Elizabeth have write to tell me so."

So Henry Baird had had his letter! He had talked the matter over with Elizabeth. Hercules smiled. He had not known heretofore that Baird had received the letter, for he could hardly expect Doty to let him know he had sent it on. All these months—but it was scarcely two; it only seemed longer.

"Yes, Henry's helping me devise means of persuading George to come to live with us," he said slowly.

"You do not say this to me, Mistaire Dousman," reproached Jane.

"I didn't think of it. Besides, you know I seldom talk of any matters until they're concluded one way or another. We have to find Mrs. Antaya, Cecile's sister. We have to learn whether George was adopted by the Brunets, or simply taken to live with them."

"Would it not be bettair jus' to talk to George?"

"My God, Jane, I've tried! I've tried everything—I've sent gifts, even a horse; I wanted to send him East to school. He won't have anything, he won't take a thing . . ."

"But if we could talk to him!"

"He won't listen. God knows I've tried. She's turned him against me."

"Me, too. I know Julia."

"I expect to hear from Henry any day now. When I do, I'll try to find Mrs. Antaya."

"I still think, Mistaire Dousman, you should go straight to the boy—make him listen to you, say to him you are his fathair, say to him . . ."

But now she was still. Miss McCleod and Dédé were coming near, and she stood watching expectantly. Her eyes shone with affection for her son, her entire face seemed to become vibrant, to glow. She doted on the boy.

Seeing her so, Hercules could not help thinking uneasily of how it would be when George came to live in the house, when it became apparent that George was being made ready to go into the business. Would she continue to be so complacent? She, too, like Henry Baird, strongly suggested that he was in error to bring George to the house against his will. Admittedly, George's willingness to come was to be preferred; but Hercules was cut off from the attempt to reach him; he would keep on trying, but in the meantime, was it not folly to stop arming himself, if possible, against the time when all else but legal means failed?

As always, Dédé ran to his mother; he seemed not to see Hercules, although in a moment he looked around Jane and made a face, followed by a wide grin for his father. More and more, every day, Hercules thought, he has Jane's looks; he'll be a handsome fellow. Already Dédé rode very well, and he had a genuine fondness for the horses. This was gratifying, but this was virtually all; the boy cared nothing for ball games, and while he swam well, he did not seem much interested in canoeing or in any form of boating. Perhaps Hercules was wrong to expect of him—growing up in a world of steamboats and railroads—that he be master of the paddle as his father had been. And, worst of all, Dédé seemed little inclined for the woods, save on occasion to hunt at Hercules' insistence.

The thought of George tormented him. He looked away from Jane and Dédé. The *Ocean Wave* was riding the water smoothly, passing McGregor, terraced along the hill slopes of its valley stretching westward from the Mississippi's shore, passing the high hills beyond, flung up against the blue heaven, the hills brown still with autumn's sereness, upon which blossomed a haze of green and occasional patches of flowers—bloodroots, hepaticas, rock cress—and over which sunlight and new leaf color commingled in the air in a shimmering that lent the hills a singularly unreal beauty, an enchantment.

Across, on the east shore of the Mississippi, the broad mouth of the Wisconsin opened out, its waters losing themselves in countless sloughs and at last becoming one with the surging Mississippi, high now with the thaw water rushing down from the far North, from beyond St. Paul, the country of the lakes and little rivers, from its source, the jeweled Lake Itasca discovered a quarter of a century ago by Schoolcraft. The *Ocean Wave* rode the churning water like a leaf, moving with unusual speed, which was half the work of her paddle wheels, half the force of the water. The rich musk of thaw smell rose from the brown water.

Captain Gleim came around the deck. "You like her, Mr. Dousman?"

"A fine boat, Captain."

"I told you."

"How long to Cassville?"

"Less than two hours at this speed."

"Excellent time."

"The high water does it. It'll be that much slower going back. She's eating wood, too. We'll have to take on wood at Cassville, so we'll tie up there awhile."

"We'll have a chance to stretch our legs on shore then," said Hercules.

At a quarter after two the *Ocean Wave* edged in toward the dock at Cassville. The little village lay clustered in a valley in the hills and stretched out up and down the shore of the river. Red-brick stores and houses of brick and white siding shone among the trees and their frost of green. A crowd of people came running down to the dock, and eager hands reached for the hawsers as the roustabouts threw them over the side.

Dédé was first off the boat. From somewhere, as if by magic, the little Negro boy, Peter, made his appearance, running down the gangplank at Dédé's heels. Miss McCleod hurried after them, while Jane came down on Hercules' arm.

As suddenly as it had come, the crowd faded. They had seen that the *Ocean Wave* carried neither goods nor passengers, that she had stopped only to load wood, at which the roustabouts were already busy. But among them Hercules saw a familiar face—that of a man who stood his ground, spread-legged, his hands clasped behind him, his handsome face with its dark, pointed beard, its wide-set blue eyes, its thick, carelessly kept hair swept back in an unruly pompadour, turned toward Dousman with a little smile of recognition.

"Governor Dewey!" cried Hercules, advancing upon him.

"You forget, Dousman, I'm not governor any longer. I've gone back to representing Grant County in the senate. How are you?"

They shook hands, while Hercules said to Jane, "You must remember our first governor, Nelson Dewey, Jane."

"Of course. We are happy to see you." She gave him her hand.

"What brings you here, Dewey?" asked Hercules.

"As a matter of fact, I'm thinking of moving back to Cassville. You know, I lived here first—in 1836, when I came into

Wisconsin Territory from Cooperstown. I don't think I'll stand for re-election, and I'm planning to come back here—build a house—not like yours—what is it you call it?—Château Brilliante?—but a substantial place, just the same, somewhere not too far from the river."

"Have you a place in mind?"

Dewey nodded. "General Dennison is selling out, and I'm down today inspecting the land. It looks good to me—hill property, but I'd like a place with a view. I'll have a higher mound than you, Dousman." He laughed. "As for being here, on the dock—I confess, steamboats have always fascinated me."

They laughed together. Jane turned nervously to look to where Dédé and Peter raced along the dock, but she was reassured by the sight of Miss McCleod managing to stay not too far behind them.

"I should have thought you'd stay in Lancaster," said Hercules.

"If nothing else—I can see the boats here. But come, need we stand here?"

Hercules explained that the *Ocean Wave* was his new boat, that it had been run down to Cassville only on a brief excursion, and must return to Prairie du Chien before evening. "Perhaps some day you'll own a boat yourself. We'll expect you up for dinner some evening."

"Don't be surprised if I do follow your example, Dousman." He turned to Jane. "But dinner invitations, I think, properly come from the ladies."

"We should be delight' to have Mistaire Dewey an' his family without the steamboat," said Jane.

Dewey bowed graciously.

At this moment the *Ocean Wave*'s whistle blew two short blasts; its departure bell began to ring.

"Captain Gleim's ready," said Hercules. "Our excuses, Dewey."

"We'll be neighbors soon," promised Dewey.

Dédé, followed by Peter, came running toward the gangplank, the faithful Miss McCleod coming after—noticeably laggard, however.

"Winded, Miss Penelope?" Hercules asked as they came up to her.

"I thank heaven for that whistle, Mr. Dousman."

The roustabouts began to unwind the hawsers, the gangplanks were raised, and with more ringing of the bell and blowing of the whistle the *Ocean Wave* swung out into the current once more and began the stiff journey up the Mississippi.

They came in toward the docks at Prairie du Chien at six o'clock, just as Jean Brunet's ferry was starting out from shore. As the boat passed, Hercules saw watching him from the ferry his son, George, gazing at him as across a wide and deep gulf, with a kind of proud, defiant insolence in his eyes. For a moment Hercules gazed back, repressing the impulse to call to him, then he turned away.

The boy's face hung before him all night long. He felt his pride, his defiance, his challenge of him, his hatred—everything unsaid had been in that fixed gaze—not alone the antipathy, but the blind wishing to know why Hercules had waited so long to acknowledge him, the angry, proud refusal to accept his father now over the Brunets who had raised and cared for him.

In the morning Hercules rose early and made his way down to the ferry before it began its first crossing.

George was there, as he had known he would be.

Jean was there, too, watching him approach with an expressionless face. He stood picking at his teeth with a long splinter of wood he had cut off a board.

"You cross dis morning, *hein?*" he asked as Hercules came up.

Hercules shook his head brusquely. "I want to talk to the boy."

George backed away.

Jean turned with deliberate slowness and looked at him. "You talk," he said stolidly. The boy's wish made no difference to him; he did not wish to be a party to giving offence to Hercules. He walked away with a careless wave of his hand.

George backed against a crate of furniture, his hands flat against the boards, his face sullen. He offered not a word, only waited.

"I want to talk to you, George," said Hercules, suddenly diffident, feeling guilty because it was Brunet who had made this possible, it was not by George's wish. He hesitated. A baffling silence fell, invaded by sounds from around them—the water's voices, the crying of birds, the shouting of men.

"Talk, then," growled George.

"George, I want to ask you again to come live at my house—it's as much yours as mine. After all, I *am* your father, even if I didn't find it out until long after you were born—no one told me, your mother had gone away, died . . ."

George made no reply. Hercules felt futile. He hardly knew what to say. He scarcely knew what he said. The boy listened because he had been bidden to do so, for no other reason. His ears might hear the words, nothing more. Still, Hercules went on.

"I hope to fit you for the business, so that when I die you can step in."

The boy made a sudden, angry gesture, pointing toward Brunet. "You take me away from them!" he said with suppressed fury. "You want I should go to you now?"

"No, I don't want to take you away, I want rather to share you. Try to see that . . ."

George's burst of furious words ended. He returned to his former stolidity. He stood as if he feared that Hercules would hurl himself upon him, drag him bodily from the ferry across the landing, up along the Marais de St. Feriole, across the bridge to the house on the mound.

"I ask it as your father," Hercules said again.

"*He* is my papa!" said the boy, stabbing his finger again in the direction of Brunet.

What was there to say? It was true, Jean Brunet was the only father the boy had known. It would be folly to deny it. Brunet had not mistreated him. Neither had Julia—unless one could look upon the way she had poisoned George's mind against his real father as mistreatment. But fostering hatred in one so young was subtler.

"I see there's little use to speak to you," he said then. "If you weren't so young—perhaps you'll learn this some day—you'd know better than to accept anything at the value others give it."

"Even you?" asked George mockingly.

"Even me," replied Hercules without hesitation. "Learn to come to your own decisions. Make up your own mind with such evidence as you can find for yourself. Don't take the word of others."

He stopped. The boy was simply deaf to anything he might say. Perhaps another time might come. He stood looking at him. Yes, he was certainly a Dousman. No question about it. The boy's face gave back scorn, hatred. Was there something more? A question, perhaps? A doubt? Hercules saw it in his eyes, fleetingly, uncertainly. If there were but so much, his visit would not have been in vain.

He bade the boy good-by and walked away.

Behind him, George began to whistle as he went to join Brunet at his work.

Perhaps Jane was right, Hercules thought, as he walked along. Perhaps he should leave well enough alone. Perhaps he could do no more than provide for the boy in his will, let him go his own way, just as he liked. But, then, what of the business it had taken so many years to build up? If only he could be sure that Jane's absorption in Dédé would not soften him!

Jane was still at breakfast when Hercules came in and sat down.

"Where have Mistaire Dousman go before he eat?" she asked, giving him a perplexed glance.

He looked around for Miss McCleod, but, hearing Dédé's voice outside, guessed that she was with him. "I had a talk with George," he said shortly. His expression told Jane all she needed to know.

"My poor Mistaire Dousman!" she cried, reaching a hand out

to cover his. "I know what he say—he do not wish to come."

He nodded.

"Why do not Mistaire Dousman leave him be? Pairhaps he is happy as he is? Aftair all, it is not as if we did not have Dédé." She paused momentarily, then, withdrawing her hand, asked, "Or is not Mistaire Dousman satisfy' with our son?"

"No, it's not that. I only wish he could be more of a boy."

"Do he not ride?" she asked indignantly. "Do he not swim?"

"Jane, it's more than that. He needs the companionship of other boys. He's six. He has a tutor, he has a governess, he has Louis, and, of course, us. But what he needs is boys his age. A party now and then."

"But I do not wish him to be with rough boys."

"That's just it," said Hercules shortly. "By God! he's never as much as been with another boy his age except his cousin Kirby! He's growing up in a world of women. I don't want him feminized. I need this boy—and you do, too, after I'm gone."

"We mus' not quarrel over Dédé," protested Jane gently.

"I'm not quarreling, Madame," answered Hercules. But immediately he added, "I'm sorry," for his voice was rising. He got up, went around the table, and kissed Jane. "We'll see," he went on, standing beside her chair, "perhaps George can be persuaded to come. But, then, perhaps you wouldn't want Dédé to be with him, either. I suppose you'd call George a rough boy."

"No rougher than my Joe," she answered, which was true. "And Joe is now representative in the legislature, and vair' well known. Do he not keep the capital of Minnesota Territory for St. Paul, when they wish to remove it to St. Petair?"

Hercules laughed, because Jane did not know just how her son had effected this—not by any oratorical magic or even by persuading influential people to stay the change, but by the simple expedient of vanishing from the session with both his person and the bill that had passed both houses, and remaining absent, hidden away, until the session had been adjourned and the bill prevented from becoming law. He said no more. There was nothing else to be said because it was plain that Jane did not intend to relinquish for an instant her domination of Dédé. He could only hope for the best—and, to be sure, he would implement that hope whenever he could; he would do all in his power to make a man out of this child. But, at the same time, he would not forget George.

In May, finally, came word from Henry Baird.

"If you are still of one mind about this matter, we have reason to believe that Mrs. Antaya left here for Mackinac, to stay at that place with an aunt, named Gentile . . ."

The arrival of the letter plunged Hercules at once into feverish activity. He sent word to Lapiage, asking him to find Benoit; he wished the two of them to stand ready to go with him as far as Green Bay. They would take one of his steamboats, bought for the Wisconsin River trade, as far as the Portage, then go by canoe down the Fox to Green Bay, from which place he would go on alone by lake boat to Mackinac.

Benoit, however, was not in the vicinity. He was somewhere up the Mississippi, Lapiage reported, but he had sent word by various steamboats for Benoit to come back to Prairie du Chien with his canoe. It might take weeks, it might take but a few days; no one could tell just where Benoit would be found.

Hercules resigned himself to waiting.

He had not shown Jane the letter from Baird, nor had he as yet told her he was about to go to Mackinac. What reason would he give? He could say he was off to see his father, and he did intend to visit him when he reached the island. But while he waited, he was given reason—a letter from Marthe Dousman, his sister-in-law, was brought down from Mackinac, saying that his old father lay mortally ill.

He showed it at once to Jane.

"Mistaire Dousman mus' go," she decided.

"I am going. I've sent for Benoit and Lapiage. I'll go the old way—up the rivers. It'll be like a pilgrimage into the past." Then, because he could not practice any deceit, he showed her Baird's letter, too.

She read it quietly. "Mistaire Dousman go see this woman, too, no?"

"I expect to see her."

"An' if you fin' her there, an' she tell you yes, this boy, this George, is Mistaire Dousman's son—what then?"

"Then I must find out whether the Brunets adopted the boy —or just took him."

"And so then?"

"Then I'll ask Julia once more to give him up."

"An' if she do not?"

"I can have the law in."

Jane looked at him thoughtfully for a moment; her eyes fell. She shook her head. "I do not think that Mistaire Dousman is wise to go to the law. The law will make no difference to George. You cannot say in a law you mus' like this man or hate that one, Mistaire Dousman. An' if the law say to you that you may have this boy, what then?"

"I'll take him. Kindness softens the hardest heart in the long run."

"He may not give Mistaire Dousman the long run."

Hercules sighed. "Tell me, Jane, are you opposed absolutely to my trying to bring George here?"

"No, Mistaire Dousman, I do not oppose you. If it is your wish, it is mine, also. But I do not think it wise."

"I must do as I think best, Jane."

"I expec' Mistaire Dousman to."

Three days later Benoit made his appearance. Lapiage had already communicated Hercules' wish to him, and he came bursting into the office filled with enthusiasm.

"Lak old tam, eh, M'sieu' Dousman? You, me, Lapiage—togethair once more!"

Hercules looked at him critically. He knew Benoit was growing older, but there seemed to be an agelessness about the big *voyageur*. "You brought your canoe, Benoit? I remembered yours as stronger and larger than most. If not, we can take one from here."

"I bring eet, M'sieu' Dousman."

"Well then, if you have anything you want to be doing, get about it. We'll start just as soon as the *Alhambra* can get up steam. Load your canoe and take it over to the boat. Get hold of Lapiage to lay in supplies enough to last us down the Fox—and for the entire route back by river."

Benoit grinned and was gone. Hercules saw him cross the grounds in great running leaps.

They left Prairie du Chien in early afternoon. The *Alhambra* was one of Hercules' own steamboats on the regular Wisconsin River run, traveling from Prairie du Chien sometimes as far north as Point Boss, and her captain knew the river bed as well as the shifting sand bars and the frequency of uprooted trees lying off the river's many islands would permit.

Once out of the Mississippi, their passage was slow. Stops were scheduled for English Prairie, Helena, and Sac Prairie before the Fort Winnebago stop, which was the place of the portage to the Fox, although the portage was no longer necessary, since a canal had been dug to connect the upper reaches of the Fox with the Wisconsin.

It was late in the day before they reached English Prairie, a distance of fifty miles above Prairie du Chien, and nightfall when the *Alhambra* put in at Helena. The boat traveled at a snail's pace by night, although now and then the nearly full moon shone brightly from among scudding clouds, spreading a ghostlike illumination over the river, where the shadows of trees pressed in darkly from the islands and both shores. Night birds kept Hercules awake—owls, even a loon in one place, herons, ducks—their cries mingling with the occasional screams of lynx and the yawping bark of foxes.

At dawn the *Alhambra* moved past the Pierneau house, glinting and gleaming in the first sunlight touching the top of the high hill. In the morning the boat docked at Sac Prairie. Three hours from Sac Prairie the *Alhambra* reached Fort Winnebago.

The canoe was rapidly unloaded. Lapiage, Benoit, Hercules—all carried off the supplies; then Benoit and Lapiage brought off the canoe and put it into the water of the canal, where it was reloaded at once. Hercules got into the middle, the *voyageurs* took the paddles, and they started along the canal toward the narrow channel of the Fox.

"This makes me feel young again," said Lapiage. "So many times I came this way—only then, we made the portage."

"De muscle will tell you differen', eh, M'sieu' Dousman. You no feel so young."

Hercules agreed. The *voyaguers* shouted back and forth, exhilarated at being once more at the paddles along the old Fox-Wisconsin route, refreshed and renewed by this journey. For that matter, Hercules felt the same sense of freedom that animated the men. Being out under the sky in a canoe once more, actually on the way to Mackinac, with the song of the paddles in his ears, and the voices of the countryside rising, made him wonder how long it had been since last he had gone on a journey by canoe. He did not dare to think of it. A long time ago. Although it seemed but around some corner just turned, almost yet within reach, years had gone by. He had been driven by business affairs, harried by the events of life, which came so thickly now as the frontier pushed west of Prairie du Chien, and preoccupied with his family to such an extent that he had not even written to his father oftener than once in six weeks, if then.

What Benoit had said was only too true. Hercules doubted if he could paddle very long before his muscles cried out in protest. The old days of the long journey by canoe from Mackinac to Prairie du Chien were gone. Yet only twenty years ago the Fox-Wisconsin waterway was a highway for *voyageurs*, *engagés*, traders, even the travelers and adventurers who dared the unknown country beyond the lakes and returned to Europe to write books about it—such men as Captain Marryat, or Count Brogmar, who was drawn back to the wild country he had first seen two decades ago, to live on the Sac Prairie for almost a decade before moving west to California. Now it was a byway for steamboats, it was becoming a stream that was haunted by casual fishermen who replaced the once-intrepid trappers who had known every twist and turn of every tributary.

And was not this quest on which he traveled—this search for means to bring George to the house on the mound—was not this itself like a search for renewal of a kind, an inquiry into the past in an effort to bring back to life the youth which had become legend? In a sense, he was in flight from the house of his present to the home of his past—the Mackinac where he had lived as a child, without care or responsibility, without trial or grief, looking forward to challenge and manhood, knowing no restraint except for that brief time of the British occupation. Now he looked back from manhood with longing he need not suppress, since he was not ashamed of it, as every man regards his childhood and youth with the nostalgia of one who wants to return to that time of tranquillity but knows he cannot, he is irrevocably lost to it as it is lost to him. It seemed to Hercules significant that events should have brought together his quest for George with this pilgrimage to his father's bedside.

On the ninth day out of Prairie du Chien, Hercules saw with mingled emotions the hump of land that was Mackinac rising out of the blue water of the straits. A sense of guilt at being so long away from what had been his home for so many years, joy at sight of this familiar scene once more, anticipation at seeing his father again coupled with the hope that the old man might still be alive—all these emotions took possession of him. He waited upon that moment when the white walls of the fort shone in the sun; it came—and now the houses of the town clustered below the fort began to stand out individually. But he sought in vain for many he had once known; they were gone; others stood in their places; time had left its mark upon Mackinac as upon all the frontier.

From the boat Hercules went up out of the town, past the fort, to the rolling country beyond. The old farm, at least, had not changed. How many times he had gone this way! He remembered the night he had gone for Lieutenant Hanks, to bring him at Papa's request, so that Papa might tell him that Mackinac was besieged by the British and their Indian allies. More than forty years ago! The past crowded in upon him, invisible yet tangible; it seemed to rush at him through the grasses where he walked, it shouted at him from the old trees beside the road. He could still see in his mind's eye the sharp clash of the Americans and the redcoats—it had taken place almost directly before the house toward which he now hurried.

The house was but little altered. The trees before it had almost doubled in size, it seemed to Hercules. Some had been cut down. Others were new, still saplings, not long planted. That would have been like Papa, he thought—he would be about at something as long as he could move.

Marthe met him at the door. His brother George's wife had come up from Milwaukee to help care for her father-in-law. She was a strong-featured woman, with dark graying hair and a mouth small in proportion to her size.

She greeted him quietly in a hushed voice. "He's sleeping, Hercules." As she stepped aside for him, she asked, "Would you like me to get you something to eat?"

"I've no appetite for food just now. How is he?"

"Much the same. Every day a little weaker. That's the way the doctor said it would be. He can't recover." She gave him a curious glance. "I never dreamed my letter would bring you here, Hercules; I know how busy you are."

He shrugged. "I had some business to attend to, anyway. How long have you been here, Marthe?"

"A month. When Susan left, she sent word to us. I came up by the first boat."

He inclined his head toward the bedroom. "Is he in any pain?"

"He doesn't seem to be."

"He's asked for us?"

She gave him a look which said he had not. "You're so far away—you, George, Talbot, and John. Sometimes his mind wanders; he talks about Nancy and Presley—he forgets they've been dead these eleven years. But he doesn't ask for anyone; he knows, even now, it's hard for his sons to come. He'll be surprised to see you. He should wake soon now."

"I'll go in to him."

He got up and walked quietly into the familiar bedroom where his parents had always slept. He went over to the bed, pulled up a chair, and sat down.

Michael Dousman lay breathing shallowly on a hard, firm bed, his head sunk into the pillow. He was gaunt with age. A thin scraggling of beard covered his firm chin. His lips were bloodless, and his cheeks, with the bones showing high through the thin skin, were pale, too. His brows had grown more shaggy, but at the same time the hair of his head had thinned almost to vanishing, and the scalp shone through, gleaming in the wan light of the room.

Hercules sat there looking at him. This was but the worn shell of his father. It was hard to believe that this dying man had once, almost single-handed, arranged for the surrender of the American fort to the besieging British in order to spare the inhabitants the ravages of the Indians fighting with the redcoats—that he had, later, connived with the Americans to bring them back to the island when the war went against the British in the lower lakes. He had been captain of the militia, leader among the agents of the Astor Company at Mackinac, with such strong right hands as the traders Drew and Aiken. All save Dousman were dead now, and the trade gone—even the time vanished into the past.

Marthe came to the threshold on tiptoe, looked in, and withdrew. But her shadow crossing the old man's face woke him. His lids opened slowly, and for a few moments he lay without motion, his eyes fixed on the ceiling, low and intimate above him, built long ago by his own hands. Then he grew conscious of someone sitting beside the bed; he turned his head with infinite slowness and stared at Hercules.

"Hercules! My boy!" he murmured incredulously.

"Yes, Father. I came up."

"I'd have looked to see any of the others before you." The old man spoke slowly and with effort. "You've always been . . ." He stopped and would not finish.

"Too busy," Hercules finished for him. "I know. I still am. But Marthe wrote you were ill, and I came."

The old man gazed at him for a long minute without saying anything, as if he could not yet believe that he sat there, filling Hercules with guilt and shame that he had not been home before this.

"You're all well?" asked the old man anxiously.

"All, Father. Jane sends her love—and Dédé—he's six now."

The old man turned his head and closed his eyes. "Jane," he whispered. "Your mother's name, too—Jane Aiken McDonald. I remember Fisher's daughter as a little girl." He was silent, husbanding his strength. Then he started to talk again. "Do you find the island changed?"

"Very much."

"I scarcely noticed it. But then—you haven't been here . . . It's a long time. If you see it day after day, the change comes a little at a time, you hardly see it." He strove to rise on his elbow, but the effort was too much for him; he sank back, breathing fast. Then in an altered voice he said, "Hercules, I've made my will. It's good you're here—I wanted to speak to you about it. I mentioned you—hardly more. A hundred dollars. Out of probably fifty thousand. I left it to the others—they need it, but you—you're rich—they tell me you're a millionaire."

Hercules nodded. "The others need it more than I do; it suits me."

A feeble smile touched the colorless lips. "I knew you'd understand, Hercules."

He sighed and seemed to sink deeper into the pillow. There he lay, quiet, as if the effort of talking had been so great that he needed to relax now and gather new strength to go on.

"I knew you'd succeed, Hercules. I remember—old Drew said you'd have a bright journey through life," he said in a whisper, and was silent once more.

"Succeed?" echoed Hercules, startled. "Are you measuring me by my money, Father?"

"No, no—but money goes with some kinds of success. You've known how to put your skill and wits to good use. I hear of you from many quarters, and I know how well you learned the value of compromise during the War of 1812, when we were occupied here—how well you learned it!"

Hercules did not know what to say. For one thing, he did not know what his father implied. For another, he did not want to tax the old man's fading strength. Just the same, he could not help wondering whether he had accepted any compromise about George. But the old man could not know of this; his father could not have meant to criticize him; he was as proud of Hercules now as he had been over the small part he had played in the war. A little smile clung to the old man's lips—it was one of satisfaction—and the open eyes dwelt fondly upon Hercules, lit by happiness at sight of one of his children.

"Tell me—what are you doing now?" asked the old man.

Hercules told him. He spoke of everything but the thing uppermost in his mind—of railroading, of the people flowing into the upper Middle West, of his steamboating interests, of the growth of the towns along the Fox-Wisconsin waterway, even of the Indians—but he said not a word about George Brunet. He went on talking for some time before he realized that the old man was asleep.

He got up noiselessly and walked out of the room.

"I'm going into the village," he told Marthe. "He's sleeping."

"He sleeps most of the time, Hercules."

It took Hercules less than half an hour to find Yvonne Gentile. He knocked on her door, excitement mounting within him, together with apprehension that now, having come this far, he might, after all, fail to find the corroboration he sought.

The woman who answered his knock was most certainly Cecile Gardepi's sister—older, perhaps, but with such a marked resemblance to Cecile that for a moment Hercules could not speak.

"Yes, M'sieur?" she asked, her black eyes flickering over him.

"You are Yvonne Gardepi Gentile, Madame?" he asked, as suddenly embarrassed as a schoolboy.

She nodded suspiciously. The question in her eyes grew larger.

"I'm looking for Elise Antaya. I understood she came here ten years ago, perhaps longer than that."

"What do you wish of her?"

"Forgive me—that's between us, Madame."

"I'm sorry, M'sieur—she isn't here."

"Not here!" he cried, dismayed. "But I was told in Green Bay she had come . . ."

She broke in suddenly. "I know you. You're Michael Dousman's son. But which one?"

He offered his name.

"Hercules, yes, that's it. Please to come in."

She stood aside.

As he walked past her, he asked, "Do you know my father?"

"Everybody here knows Mr. Dousman. There aren't many left from the old days, you see, and we know them all." Now that she had established a point of contact with him, she was disarmingly friendly; talk flowed from her as water from a fountain; all her suspicion of him and his motives had vanished. He sat down and listened to her talk of what his father had done, what he had said last time she had spoken with him, and then at last heard her ask, "Now what is it about Elise?"

"It's really about Cecile," he stammered. "I wanted to ask about her."

"Poor Cecile!" She crossed herself. "You know she's dead? Drowned?"

He nodded.

"Well, of course, I can't tell M'sieur Dousman anything about her—she lived for a while in Prairie du Chien, then in Green Bay. Then she went to St. Louis, and it was near there she died."

"Why St. Louis?"

"Our brother Antoine lives there."

Suddenly, intuitively, he knew that Elise Antaya had gone to St. Louis, too.

"But Elise was with you here?" he pressed her.

"Yes. Three years. But the isolation of Mackinac in winter depressed her. She wanted life. She was much like Cecile. Her husband wasn't with her here, but they're together again."

"Where?"

"In St. Louis, M'sieur Dousman. With Antoine."

Now that he knew where Elise Antaya was, Hercules was anxious to get away. But Yvonne Gentile held him with her talk; it was an hour before he could escape. The sun was already going down.

He hurried back to the farm, fearful that his father might have died in his absence. But nothing had changed; all was as before. The old man still slept, and Marthe was waiting in the kitchen for Hercules to join her at supper.

Hercules settled himself at the farm. He could not leave until he knew what was to happen. If his father was dying, he wanted to be there to the end. He wrote letters to Jane and LeBrun, as well as to Benoit and Lapiage, who waited at Green Bay upon his return, advising them that he might be at Mackinac perhaps a fortnight, perhaps even a month, depending upon his father's condition. As the days passed, he sat for many hours at his father's bedside, in an aura of past time, living again with the old man so many of those precious hours vanished like the sunlight of those days. They talked about many things; indeed, they reached the point where they had little more to say because the old man insisted upon retracing the same subjects again and again, and he had exhausted them. But Hercules did not mind; the old man's voice, the circumstances of Hercules' being at the farm once more, the persistence of memory combined to give him a sense of well-being, as were he briefly drawn away from the always impending present.

Two weeks slipped by. Then one morning Marthe found Michael Dousman dead in bed. She called Hercules, and they set about making the funeral arrangements.

As soon as possible after the funeral, Hercules set out by steamboat for Green Bay. There he paused only long enough to call on Henry and Elizabeth Baird, to acquaint them with what he had learned at Mackinac; then he started up the Fox with Benoit and Lapiage, bound for home.

They reached Prairie du Chien at the end of the month in a cloud of mosquitoes, brought to life by a week of unseasonably hot, wet weather lying over the Mississippi Valley.

Jane was shocked at Hercules' appearance. "Mistaire Dousman look sunburn' an' bit up—he look unhappy!" she cried, as she ran to embrace him when he appeared in her morning room.

He laughed heartily. "Dear Jane, it's only that I've got soft. I'm not used to what was once a daily occurrence in the season. I could do with a bath later on. Where's Dédé?"

"He ride with Louis."

She said this disapprovingly, but he exclaimed "Good!" and kissed away the protest he gave her no chance to put into words.

"Do Mistaire Dousman fin' what it is he look for in Mackinac?"

"No, Jane. Later on, I'll have to go to St. Louis. Mrs. Antaya's there. Now that Father's dead, I'll have to see to the estate."

"Oh, he die!"

"I wrote you."

"I am sorry, I do not get the lettair. But of this othair—promise me, Mistaire Dousman, if you do not fin' it in St. Louis, you will give up."

"Why should I make such a promise?"

"Because I wish it."

"I'll think of it. But come—I want something to eat. So do Lapiage and Benoit; they'll be coming to the house in a few minutes. We can talk afterward. Have Giselle get something ready. We'll eat in the kitchen—it's more convenient. I want to get at the mail. Come along and tell me what's happened while I was up North—everything."

"Nothing happen'," she replied.

"I thought I saw a new man working among the grape arbors."

"Oh, that is Jake Schafer. He is jus' a boy. I employ him. I give him money, too, so he can sen' for his sweetheart from Germany. He is the mos' wondairful gardenair!" She looked at him anxiously. "You do not min'?"

"Of course not."

Suddenly tears misted her eyes. "And then, Mistaire Dousman—my pet deer! You remembair my pet deer? He die. The Mississippi come up too high—the poor thing drown in his paddock!"

"We'll find you another," he promised.

"An' mos' of all—we miss the railroad when it come into Madison. All those people! And such a celebration! Mistaire Bernard Brisbois was there—he can tell you all about it."

Abruptly Hercules was brought back to the reality his quest had blinded him to—the affairs of the railroad, which had made a steady levy against his funds, the road which now more than ever must be brought through to Prairie du Chien. He must learn at the soonest moment how things went with the road, what the chances were of proceeding west of Madison now. With any luck at all, the Milwaukee and Mississippi ought to reach Arena before the end of the year, and from there the line would be in direct touch with Prairie du Chien by boat.

Lapiage and Benoit came in, diffidently. They never came into the house on the mound without apology in word or manner; the free-and-easy manner which had been theirs when they came to the old office or to Hercules' old quarters in town was lost before the splendor of the house. This always troubled Hercules. Surely he himself had not changed!

The *voyageurs* sat down, and Jane turned from Hercules to them, striving to make them feel at home. From outside rose Dédé's happy shouting, and for a moment Hercules was transfixed between three worlds—that left behind in Mackinac, the world of his early years; the time of now; and that shadowy, nebulous world toward which he reached, that of George Brunet and the tenuous ties that bound Hercules to him and to his mother, the amour of a week in a life crowded by time and events, and suspended between the wild wilfulness of Rolette and the love for Jane which had given no promise then of fulfillment.

As Hercules rode back into the grounds from the north, his son riding at his side, Dédé pointed excitedly to three strange horses at the stable.

"Company, Papa," he said. "Or did you order more horses?"

"No."

LeBrun came out of the office as they came riding up. He took the horses. "Three men from the railroad company, Mr. Dousman. They went to the house."

Miss McCleod was at the west door for Dédé.

Hercules surrendered the boy to her and went on into the house, down the hall to the drawing room, from which came the sound of voices. Jane stood there, the three men grouped around her.

Hercules recognized the short, compact form of John Catlin, still president of the Milwaukee and Mississippi, and beyond him the large-framed figure of the chief engineer, Brodhead, but the third man, likewise taller than Catlin, with a broad Irish face, and, under jutting brows, twinkling eyes which were not without an edging of frost, he did not know.

"Good afternoon, gentlemen," he said, and walked into the room.

Jane excused herself at once.

"We missed you at Madison, Dousman," said Brodhead.

"I'd like to have been there, but my father died at Mackinac; I had to go up."

"Of course," said Catlin, pressing forward. "We want you to meet the man we've chosen to be our agent at Prairie du Chien —John Lawler."

Lawler put out a large, capable hand and grasped Hercules'

hand firmly. "I expect we'll see a lot of each other, sir," he said. "I'm coming in a little later with my family—just as soon as we can start the erection of the station here."

"And when will that be?" asked Hercules. "You know how impatient I am."

"I can't blame you, Dousman," said Brodhead. "But it's a plain fact that you can't push the work without money. That's been our problem. At least, we've reached Madison. We're not wasting time. We're pushing west to Arena right away. We should be there soon."

"This year?"

"Next for certain."

Hercules smiled tightly. "Gentlemen, if the fur trade had made such progress, you'd see a pauper before you now."

"I can understand your impatience, Dousman," said Catlin soothingly, "but the fact is we've gone ahead as fast as we could. You know all the trouble we've had—that new law passed last April requiring us to make out for the state treasurer a report of our earnings for tax purposes—one per cent of the gross, mind you!—the defaulting of the mortgages—you know all that. Now we've decided to adhere to strictly moderate dividends, so that we can build up a reserve fund; it's senseless to distribute all the earnings of the road."

"Seems to me I pointed that out at least three years ago."

"I believe you did," said Brodhead dryly. "What we came here today for, however, was to introduce Lawler. We've chosen him because he's had experience, and we're looking forward to crossing the Mississippi."

Hercules chuckled. "The entire assets of the Company so far would be needed to bridge the Mississippi here."

"We don't propose a bridge."

"No, sir," put in Lawler crisply. "We can produce barges to carry four cars at a time, with a steamboat fore and one aft, and thus make connections with rails on the other side."

"Of course, that's a look into the future, but we're prepared for it," Brodhead went on. "We've even got hold of a young

Bavarian—Mike Spettel—who's very handy at inventing things. He's talking about a bridge on pontoons for the deep part of the river."

"Right now, though," said Hercules, "bringing the rails to Prairie du Chien is the first order of business, and I'm interested in anything definite you can tell me about your plans. You have a good many investors in this region. They're all anxious to know when they can begin to ship by rail."

"We've brought maps and charts showing projections and progress," said Catlin.

"I propose we look them over. How about it? Will you gentlemen stay for dinner?" He did not wait for a reply. "Good! I'll tell Jane. Let's go to the office."

In July Hercules went to St. Louis on board the *Itasca,* one of the fastest boats on the Mississippi. Reaching the city early in the morning, he went directly to Stambaugh's store, hoping that his old friend would be there. In most places the blinds were still up, and, once away from the jostling roustabouts at the docks, Hercules walked through an almost sleeping city.

Stambaugh's store was open. At the moment of Hercules' entrance, Stambugh himself was alone behind the counter, busy with a sallow-faced man, neither young nor yet quite middle-aged. Stambugh looked up as Hercules came in; his saturnine face lit up.

"Mr. Dousman—an unexpected pleasure! It's been a while since you were down."

"Good morning, Stambaugh. I almost feared you'd still be closed."

Stambaugh's customer turned and looked at Hercules through the blue smoke from the long black cigar clamped between his teeth.

"Here's a man, Grant, you might get to know if you don't know him already," Stambaugh told him. "He's the wealthiest man in the upper Mississippi Valley. Mr. Hercules Dousman—

Captain Ulysses Grant." To Dousman, Stambaugh added, "Grant's selling real estate."

Grant stepped forward and held out his hand. "If you're interested, sir," he began, his lively eyes narrowing in an assessment of Hercules as a potential client.

Hercules cut him off. "Not now, Captain Grant. But if you ever have anything in the way of a good investment, I'd be delighted to learn of it. You can always find me through Stambaugh."

"Thank you, sir. I'm hardly ready for it yet. I'm just back from the West. I resigned my commission and hope to do better in real estate. Just finished a little cabin outside St. Louis and hope to open an office downtown." He turned to Stambaugh once more. "Good day, Stambaugh."

He shook hands again with Hercules, and left the store.

"Captain of what?" asked Hercules then. "He doesn't look like a riverman."

"No, Colonel. He's an ex-army man. Didn't make a go of it, they tell me. Inclined to like his liquor a little too much, for one thing. Now he's trying his hand at real estate. Well, every man to his measure, I always say. What can I do for you today?"

"I'll order later. Just now I'm looking for an address." Hercules showed him the paper on which Yvonne Gentile had written her brother's address.

"Oh, that's not too far from here, Colonel. Could I send for my carriage to take you there?"

"Is it within walking distance?"

"Yes."

"Then I'll walk. It's still early. By the time I get there, it'll be late enough to call. If you'll just show me which way to go . . . ?"

Stambaugh came around the counter and walked to the door with Hercules, apologizing because he could not personally escort him to Antoine Gardepi's house, since none of his clerks had come in as yet. Hercules was relieved; he wanted no company.

He listened carefully to Stambaugh's directions, then he set out.

He reached the house in forty minutes, walking leisurely.

He mounted the steps and knocked.

A voice screamed from behind the door: "Go away! Antoine has gone to the office. Antaya isn't here."

Hercules knocked again, louder this time.

The door was jerked open. An angry-faced woman stood there. One look at her was enough for Hercules; she, too, was a Gardepi; her dark skin, her snapping eyes, her working mouth —all spoke of her paternity.

"I wanted to see you, Elise," he said.

Her anger gave way to astonishment. "I don't know you. How is it you know me?"

"You're Elise Antaya, sister of Yvonne Gentile and Antoine Gardepi, sister, too, of Cecile Gardepi . . ."

She looked at him, open-mouthed. He pushed her gently to one side and walked into the house, which she had evidently been cleaning. She made no protest. She closed the door and came walking after him.

"Who are you, then?" she demanded.

"Say I am an old friend of Cecile's."

"I never saw you before."

"Nor I you," said Hercules, sitting down.

His self-possession upset Mrs. Antaya. She set up against the wall the broom she carried, wiped her hands nervously on her apron, and came back to where Hercules sat.

"I must say, you're a one! Walk right in—make yourself at home. What is it you want?" she asked.

"Please sit down. You needn't stand." As she sat down, he went on. "I want you to remember something, Mrs. Antaya. It goes back a way—fourteen years."

"There's nothing I've done I need to be ashame' of," she cried. "Fourteen years ago! I wasn't even here that time—I was living . . ."

"In Green Bay."

"You know all about me?"

"Not all. But enough. You lived in Green Bay then. Later you went to Mackinac without Antaya; then, after three years, you came here. But it's in Green Bay I want you to put your memory. You were living there when Cecile came to you."

Her eyes grew suddenly dark with suspicion. "How do you know that?" she cried. "Mrs. Brunet promise' never to say it to anybody."

"Mrs. Brunet has never said a word—until she knew what she kept hidden was known."

"Who are you then?" she demanded.

"Let me ask—you answer," he said persuasively. "First, tell me this—did Cecile ever tell you who the father of her boy was?"

Elise Antaya nodded, half-fearfully.

"Who?"

She shook her head. "I promise' my sister I would never tell it."

"But you did tell it, didn't you?"

"I swear, on my honor!"

"To Mrs. Brunet?"

"No, before God, I did not!"

So, then, Julia Brunet had known about his brief week with Cecile. Perhaps she had had Cecile watched. She had guessed well. It would have been easy to do, given the suspicion, for Cecile had gone from Prairie du Chien soon after that halcyon week and been away for so long. He tried to remember whether Julia Brunet had gone to Green Bay that year, but he could not; so many people had gone up and down the waterway, it was impossible to recall them all.

"But now Cecile has been dead a long time, and the boy has a real father somewhere. Did you ever think of that, Elise?" he asked.

"Are they unkind to him?"

He shook his head. "What was his name—the father's?"

"I cannot tell you."

"Elise, I have reason to believe that I am his father," he said gently. "Will you give me his first initial?"

She looked at him hesitantly. "It is 'H'."

"It is 'H'," he repeated. "And the second one?"

"You tell me that," she challenged him.

"D," he said. He saw by her eyes that he had given her the correct initial. "The name is Hercules Dousman. I am he."

She only stared at him. "To think," she half-whispered, "after so long a time—fourteen years!"

"Will you tell me now about Cecile?"

"I will." She clasped her hands together and bent forward earnestly. "She came to me. She say to me that she is to have a baby. I ask her then who the father is, and why she do not marry him. She say he would not want to marry her, he is in love with another woman."

"I'd have married her. She never told me. I never guessed."

Elise Antaya went on. "I ask' her to say many times who he is. But she would not. The baby came, and that time, while she was in labor, she mention your name. I ask' her then, afterward, and she confess' it is you who are the boy's father. At firs' the boy make her very happy, but then . . ." She shrugged. "Well, there is a wildness in us all, it come and it go like the wind. She grow dissatisfied, she want' to go away . . ."

"How old was the boy then?"

"Two, three months—maybe five. I don't remember. She went to St. Louis. She came to be with Antoine. The baby she left with me. She did not want him. Then this Mrs. Brunet came and ask' to take him, to care for him."

"How did she know?"

"She did not say. But others knew in Green Bay; she could have learn' there. She know it was Cecile's baby. She beg to take him. She come back day after day. She say she have no children, the good Lord have not bless' her, and at last I say to her if Cecile return and want her boy, I will tell her, and she mus' give him up. She say she will."

Perhaps Julia Brunet envisioned Cecile's dramatic return to Prairie du Chien and counted on the revelation that the boy was Hercules' child from her at such a time—before his marriage to Jane. Could she have planned such an eventuality? Hardly, he thought. It might have occurred to her momentarily, but she could hardly have believed Cecile would turn up in search of the boy. Or that she would lend herself to any scheme of Julia's, had she come back.

"Tell me, Elise, did Mrs. Brunet adopt the boy?"

Mrs. Antaya looked puzzled.

Hercules explained. Had Julia Brunet made a court record of her adoption? Or had she just taken the baby and gone?

"She jus' take him."

He smiled with satisfaction. "Now, Elise—there's something I must ask you to do. Will you write down these facts—I'll tell you what to write—and sign the paper in the presence of witnesses?"

She looked suddenly frightened. "I don't wish to get into trouble."

"There'll be no trouble. The paper is all I want. I must have such proof that he wasn't legally adopted. That's all."

Still she was undecided. "Is the boy well?" she wanted to know. "Do you see him?" And, at his nod, "But why is this, Mr. Dousman?"

Hercules tried to explain. But his words seemed to him twisted and meaningless. He ended by saying only, "What it comes down to is this—I can offer him much more than the Brunets. It wouldn't be as if he were being taken from them—they live not far from where I live. He could spend as much time with them as he likes."

She gave in at last. "I will do this thing you ask."

She found paper and pen, and sat down with an air of guilty resignation, waiting upon him.

"I, Elise Antaya," he began, "being the sister of Cecile Gardepi, formerly of Prairie du Chien, now dead, do hereby declare that she came to me in the year 1840, when I was then living in Green Bay."

"Not so fast, Mr. Dousman."

He waited. When she looked up, he went on: ". . . She was at that time pregnant. She remained with me until she bore a son, whom she named George. She admitted to me that his father was Hercules L. Dousman, of Prairie du Chien; that he did not know of her pregnancy by him; and that he was not to be told of this event. Later, after she had gone away . . ." He paused again, waiting for her to catch up. ". . . Mrs. Julia Brunet of Prairie du Chien, who was visiting in Green Bay, came and wished to take the boy into her care. I permitted her to do so with the understanding that if his mother returned and wished to resume his custody, she would give him up. To the best of my knowledge, Mrs. Brunet did not legally adopt the boy now known as George Brunet."

She finished putting down his words and looked up expectantly.

"That's all," he said. "Now if you can call in two neighbors, we'll have them sign as witnesses."

"I hope this is the right thing I've done, Mr. Dousman."

"I believe it is, or I wouldn't have asked you to do it."

Half an hour later he walked back toward Stambaugh's with the signed document in his pocket, confident that he had in it the power he needed to force Julia to compromise about George. Not for a long time had a morning seemed so bright.

Hercules felt now that he could bide his time. He was, in any case, extremely reluctant to force the issue of George. Better by far to win him to some kind of voluntary acceptance than to resort to law. His confidence did not fade. He felt secure in the possession of Elise Antaya's statement, which he locked in the office safe as soon as he reached Prairie du Chien.

When they were alone together on the evening of his return home, he told Jane what he had learned.

"An' now what do Mistaire Dousman do?" she asked anxiously.

"I'll try to talk to George and Julia again."

"That is good. It is nevair wise to ac' in haste."

The very next morning Hercules made his way early to the landing below the island. He met the boy on the path not very far from the edge of the river.

George saw him, hesitated, and came to a stop.

"I thought by this time you might feel a little kinder toward me, George," said Hercules.

The boy watched him warily. Almost as if he were afraid, thought Hercules. He made no move toward him, but stood where he was. The breadth of the path separated them, and Hercules knew intuitively that if he advanced any closer, the boy would turn and run.

"I've been hoping," Hercules went on, "that you might change your mind—let me send you off to school, come back into the business . . ."

George said nothing. He stood looking at Hercules with that same hostile uncertainty, as if he knew he must hate him but did not entirely understand why, yet was unwilling to relinquish the hatred he had been taught. Perhaps he feared that any concession to Hercules might be an act of disloyalty to his foster parents.

"Are you afraid to speak, George?" Hercules asked gently.

The boy shook his head.

In the interval since Hercules had last seen him, George had grown more stalwart. He now had quite broad shoulders; he no longer looked but fourteen—he might have been sixteen, even seventeen. His work on the ferry had made him muscular. But his face was sensitive, and his eyes were soft, belying the set hardness of his mouth at this moment. The illusion of looking at a specter of his youth persisted for Hercules.

Abruptly George turned and began to walk rapidly toward the river.

Hercules made no move to stop him.

Almost to the river the boy turned and looked back—a searching glance. Then he went on.

Hercules knew beyond doubt that the boy was lost to him, unless he could soften Julia Brunet. He could not otherwise reach George.

7. *The Lance of Justice*

Winter-Summer, 1855

THE FIRMNESS OF HERCULES' DETERMINATION TO FACE JULIA again was thinned insidiously by doubt. He had gone impulsively from his fruitless meeting with George to the Brunet house, but all there was silent; Julia was not at home. Thereafter he had been assailed by second thoughts, aided not a little by Jane's reproachful silence. Perhaps, he reasoned, he was being unfair to Jane and Dédé; perhaps her coddling of the boy would not impair his heritage and leave him unfit to follow in his father's footsteps.

He put off going to see Julia from day to day, from week to week. The year faded into winter. Prairie du Chien lay white under snow early in the season, but the weather, after a fortnight of bitter cold, grew mellow.

One morning Hercules announced at breakfast that he meant to go hunting. "Louis and I and Dédé," he said.

"Not our boy!" cried Jane in dismay. "He's too young."

"He'll be seven in two months, Jane. He likes to ride, and he's as skilled as any man three times his age."

"Where do Mistaire Dousman expec' to go?"

"Over across the Mississippi. The ice is as solid as a drum."

"But those hills, Mistaire Dousman—they are so high!"

"And well wooded. The men have reported deer in some numbers over there. I want to see how well he can shoot. He's been practicing with that gun I gave him for Christmas."

"I did not wish Mistaire Dousman to give him a gun."

Miss McCleod spoke up suddenly. "A gun tends to be a hardening influence."

"Exactly," replied Hercules. "Don't you think it's time we began to harden him a little? After all, the world's no tender place—and once we're gone, who'll protect him?"

"Mistaire Dousman expec' his son to be a big man when he is but a little boy," protested Jane. "But here he come now—ask him if he wish to go."

Dédé came skipping into the room. He shouted "Good morning!" and crossed to his mother, presenting his cheek to be kissed. Then he sat down next to Miss McCleod.

"Would you like to go hunting today, Dédé?" asked Hercules.

"Yes, Father," answered the boy without hesitation.

"You wish to go out and kill the animals?" asked Jane.

The boy looked at her, wide-eyed, as if this possibility had not occured to him. He glanced back toward Hercules. A little frown grew on his forehead.

"Jane, you're weighting the question and confusing him," said Hercules. "Have a lunch packed for us; we'll go before noon."

They set out at ten o'clock, riding down past the now barren arbors where grapevines lay securely covered against winter, and going directly to the river, which lay beneath ice that ranged from eight to twelve inches in thickness. They crossed the east channel to the islands, made their way among them, and then found themselves on the west channel of the Mississippi.

The morning was clear but not very cold. In sheltered places, where sunlight gathered, a little thawing took place. The clear air rang with crow calls and the phoebelike song of chickadees, beautiful fluting notes that carried far in the mellow air. Snow underfoot was dry and powdery; in some places, where the wind had drifted it, it was as much as four feet deep. The horses prudently went around such drifts, keeping to the level, where snow lay only a little more than a foot in depth.

On the west shore of the Mississippi the hills rose dark and challenging, flung formidably upon the cobalt heaven. South along the river lay McGregor; north rose only an endless ridge of hills, all heavily wooded. In three places thin trails of smoke drifted up from maple-syrup camps. Leaving the river, Hercules led the way diagonally up the slope into the hills. Dédé came after; LeBrun brought up the rear. They moved single file up the face of the ridge.

In one place they passed a syrup camp. The maple sap cooked slowly in a long, low pan set on a frame of stones between which a bed of coals and flames kept the sap hot. A lone Winnebago tended the sap; beyond him, two men from the Frenchtown part of Prairie du Chien unloaded pails of freshly gathered sap from a little cart. Hercules waved and shouted as they rode by.

"Seen any deer?" called Hercules.

"Up ahead," answered one of the men. "Up over the hill, M'sieu' Dousman." He pointed in the direction they traveled.

They reached the top of the ridge. The fragrant smoke from the syrup camp still lingered there, borne aloft by the south wind. Hercules paused in an open place and looked down. Below lay the Mississippi, most of it solidly frozen over; in all its length sweeping from north to south only a few patches of water were visible. Beyond the unbroken west channel lay the dark, tree-girt islands, the east channel, the island of the mound; on the prairie the village seemed scarcely more than a cluster of houses, so small did it seem in contrast to the magnificent sweep of prairie reaching to the eastern bluffs. It was a pattern of black and white, crowned by the high, cloudless blue dome of heaven—dark roofs of houses, groves of trees on the prairie, the islands, and athwart the hills.

Hercules gazed out over this scene so much like an etching. For almost thirty years this had been home to him. Five thousand acres of it—more or less—belonged to him: prairie, fields, woods, level land, and hills, improved and unimproved, all around the village, even to the mouth of the Wisconsin emptying into the Mississippi not far south of Prairie du Chien. He wanted to turn to Dédé, who sat alertly astride his horse beside him, to say to him that some day this would be his, but he held back the words; he did not know that the boy would choose to remain here, he did not even know what division would have to be made between him and George. Instead, he turned and looked to LeBrun.

"Louis, we'll have to be down wind."

"I know, Mr. Dousman." LeBrun waited on Hercules' decision.

Hercules looked reflectively ahead.

"Just the same," said LeBrun suddenly, "the wind's hardly noticeable. It's been dying away, turning a little west." He licked a finger and held it up into the air. "Southwest by west, sir."

"Good. We'll ride up to the Indian mound ahead—it's not too far away. Dédé can take his position there. You and I'll drive the deer toward him."

He started away at once and rode until he came to a dense grove of trees. There he stopped and dismounted, motioning the others to do likewise.

"We'll tether the horses here. The mound's not far off. We'll want to keep the horses out of the way—the deer can smell them, too."

Once the horses were tethered, they went ahead on foot. Dédé, who had ridden his horse most of the way in silence, was delighted to be making his way through the snow under his own power, trying in vain to step into the prints Hercules left. He went laughing and shouting, until Hercules had to warn him to be less noisy, for he might frighten the deer away. Deer tracks lay everywhere among the trails scribbled in the snow by foxes and rabbits. In one place there was the track of a bear.

The site of the ancient Indian mound was semi-open. Big trees grew back from it; saplings grew on and about the mound, which was a manifest effigy even under its snow cover. Hercules stationed Dédé at the edge of the woods, opposite a deer run, where he would be hidden and could yet command the run and the space around the mound.

"Be very careful, Dédé," he cautioned. "Shoot only at the deer—when you see him plainly."

The boy nodded impatiently. "I know how to shoot, Papa. I can hit any target."

LeBrun nodded eagerly, to corroborate his boast.

"All right, Louis. We'll push into the woods and try to find some deer. God knows there are plenty of tracks."

"They're quite fresh, too," said LeBrun, who had bent to examine them.

"You go this way—I'll go that," directed Hercules.

They set off down the slope to the west and began to make a wide loop into the woods, at first walking against the wind, then gradually working around so that their scent might help to stir any deer before them and move the animals up the slope toward the Indian mound.

They had not gone far before deer tracks became more numerous. Hercules lost sight of LeBrun, and stood for a moment to look sharply around him. The woods hemmed him in; despite the blue looking down through the intertwined branches of the trees towering above him, Hercules felt enclosed in a kind of semi-darkness. He pushed on. Suddenly three deer started up on his left.

He began to circle them, running. Of the three, one was a handsome buck. This was the deer Dédé ought to get, he thought. But if he did not hurry, they would be off in another direction.

LeBrun, too, had set up deer. No less than seven of them flashed past Hercules, with LeBrun coming along behind them. The three Hercules had flushed turned and bounded off the other way, just as he had foreseen. Hercules abandoned them; he set off after LeBrun's deer, shouting to alert Dédé. LeBrun came bearing in from the southwest. Because he could move faster than Hercules, he passed and was soon lost among the trees on the slope ahead.

They were a hill and a little swale from the place of the Indian mound. The deer were moving straight toward the mound, diagonally through the woods, following the run that would take them directly past the place where Dédé stood.

Hercules slowed up. He could not run; it was too hard on him; the rigor of stumbling through the snow caused a sharp pain to needle through his upper chest. He stood against a tree to rest and catch his breath, while the pain in his chest subsided. The deer must be almost at the mound by now, he estimated. LeBrun could not be too far behind.

He started forward again, climbing slowly. He paused now and then to listen. At any moment he should hear the crashing shot of Dédé's gun.

He heard nothing.

He reached the top of the slope, descended, and began to mount the hillside that reached to the place of the Indian mound. Up ahead, high on the ridge, he could see LeBrun standing. The deer must have gone over the ridge by this time. Yet he had heard no shot. He climbed steadily.

At last he reached LeBrun's side. "What happened?" he asked breathlessly.

LeBrun pointed silently.

Dédé stood as they had left him, save that now he was more in the open. His gun lay cradled in his arm; it had evidently not been moved. His hands were in his pockets, and he was staring raptly in the direction the deer had gone.

"He didn't shoot," said LeBrun laconically.

"Buck fever?"

LeBrun shook his head. "No, it wasn't that. You know, Mr. Dousman, Madame had for so long that pet deer in the paddock north of the house. The boy used to feed it before it was drowned that time—you know how it would be."

Hercules walked out of the woods and over to his son.

"Why didn't you shoot, Dédé?" he asked.

"Oh, Papa—they were so pretty!" he cried. "I couldn't."

Hercules bit his lip in vexation. He wanted to reprimand

Dédé, but he could not. What could he say? This was more of Jane's work, however unwitting; it softened the boy. She would say he was too young—only seven!—what could he say in answer? Could he tell her that time was growing ever shorter, that it was never too early for Dédé to learn? Dédé did not seem to have any of that iron so necessary to his future.

"Come," he said brusquely, "we'll go back."

"Are you angry with me, Papa?" asked Dédé anxiously.

"No, son."

The boy was not quite reassured; his blue eyes turned from Hercules to LeBrun, questioningly. LeBrun smiled. Hercules smiled, too, and patted Dédé's head affectionately.

"It will come to you—later, perhaps. Eh, Louis?"

LeBrun ducked his head. The boy, reassured, started ahead down the trail they had made coming up the hill.

"You expect too much, Mr. Dousman," said LeBrun softly, coming up to Hercules.

Hercules did not reply, only pushed forward.

The clarity of the day had given way to a cloudy haze. A low, rolling bank of cumulus clouds had pushed up out of the west; wisps and tatters of clouds were crossing the face of the sun. The sky reflected Hercules' mood, and the cloud shadows on the white prairie were symbols of his troubled thoughts. Dédé chattered happily with LeBrun, who had gone ahead to lead the way down; Hercules was satisfied to bring up the rear. He felt impotent against the shell of protection Jane had woven about their son; he could not bring himself to break it, to disturb the harmony of life in the house on the mound, for everything there went with a serenity he had not dreamed was possible in those dark days when Jane had fought through the years of her first husband's decline and death.

Yet the very clouds and the shadows on the landscape invested the day with the promise of events to come, gave life to what before had been but a beautiful but static landscape; now it was no less beautiful, but it was charged with a disturbing animation which was the very heart of that change which was the prime integer of all life. So it must be also with the clouds upon his personal landscape, thought Hercules.

They crossed the Mississippi north of their first crossing and came down to the house from above. Jane already stood at the back door watching for their coming; Hercules divined at once that she had had everyone looking for them. Her face betrayed nothing of what she thought; but it did not matter to Hercules; he knew she was pleased to see no game on the horses.

She came out, shawled, to embrace Dédé. "Did not my little traisir' see a deer?"

"Oh, Mama—there were seven—one for each year I am old!" He turned brightly to Hercules. "Weren't there, Papa?"

"Yes, son."

Jane flashed a smile to Hercules.

"Mama, they were so pretty! Just like your deer used to be!"

"Mistaire Dousman no doubt think them pretty, too?"

He recognized the taunt in her voice but would not rise to it. "A wild animal in its native haunts is always a thing of beauty," he said tranquilly.

Miss McCleod appeared at the steps and held out her hand for Dédé. "Come now, young man—in to get warm!"

Jane relinquished him, and the boy ran into the house shouting over his shoulder, "Thank you, Papa! Thank you!"

"You see now, Mistaire Dousman?" asked Jane gently.

He smiled. "I see now, Madame."

She leaned forward to present her cheek. He kissed it, then caught her to him and pressed his mouth with almost bruising force to hers.

She gasped and pulled away, but her eyes danced. "Mistaire Dousman will see," she said. "Dédé will not disappoint him—I promise it."

What he conceived to be Dédé's failure troubled Hercules despite Jane's promise. Could she know just how far to bend the tree before its direction became permanent? Despite his affection and respect for her, he doubted her judgment in this. He spoke no word of his disappointment; he felt they were all against him—Jane, Miss McCleod, Eugenie, even LeBrun, but it disturbed him, he brooded about it, and his thoughts turned again and again to George, notwithstanding George's coldness toward him, which, after all, was the product of his foster mother.

One warming morning in the middle of March Hercules left the office and walked to the Brunet house. It was a day of thaw; the earth showed through the diminishing snow in many places; paths and lanes were puddled, and the air was sweet with the fragrance of thawing snow. Already killdeers cried along the river, and the feel of spring was in the warm sunlight.

The Brunet house looked deserted, but someone was at home, for the door stood ajar, and smoke came lazily out of the chimney. He knocked—at first gently, then more peremptorily. Undoubtedly Julia had marked his approach and chosen deliberately to make him wait. He stood in growing impatience.

The door was pulled open abruptly. Julia stood there.

"Oh, it's you," she said insolently. She did not invite him in.

"Julia, I must talk with you," he said humbly. "May I come in?"

"I think Mistaire Dousman and I have talk' ourselves out last time he was here."

"I think not. I now have legal proof that George is my son."

She looked uncertain for but a moment; then she smiled in superior fashion and stepped aside, motioning him in. "What do it matter, Mistaire Dousman—this proof?" she asked, after she had closed the door. "You have talk' to George. You know how he feel. He have told me."

"And I know he reflects your own hatred of me, Julia. That must be changed."

"Mistaire Dousman give no orders here. Sit down, if you like."

"I'll stand, thanks."

"If Mistaire Dousman do not min', I will sit to listen to

him," she said. Her attitude was so scornful, so provocative, that Hercules had to fight the impulse to give way to angry recriminations. "What is this proof you have?"

Hercules explained. He traced his course to Elise Antaya and told her he had a statement from Elise to say that Cecile Gardepi had confessed that Hercules was the father of her son. Several times he caught himself pacing the floor; he had to exert effort to stop, to stand quietly before Julia Brunet and speak in a controlled voice. "I have this in her writing, witnessed, Julia," he finished. "It will stand up in any court."

"But George is mine, Mistaire Dousman," she replied, unruffled. "No court can change it—even if you wish it. Besides, Mistaire Dousman would nevair go to court with this—this paper," she sneered. "For would not evairyone then know?"

"It never seems to have occurred to you that I've never been troubled by gossip. The higher a man rises, the more he is slandered. The mountain on the plain always stands as a target for the stones of the plain-dwellers."

"But your wife, your son—do not they mean anything to Mistaire Dousman?" she taunted him. "Or have you become such a big man you think nobody and nothing can touch you?"

He sighed. "You have a picture of me in your mind, Julia, and you don't want anything to change it. I beg you to try to look at George differently—let him come to me, let me send him to school, let me train him in the business—it's to his advantage. I expect to put him into my will. I don't want to take him away from you, only to share him. After all, he's my son."

"But he do not belong to you, Mistaire Dousman," she said in a low, intense voice, "and he will not. Just as you have take' evairything that was Joe's—his land, his business, even his wife—so I have for Joe's sake take' this boy."

"Julia, I don't want to go to court . . ."

"Mistaire Dousman will not go. No judge can undo what I have done." She laughed mockingly.

He held back his anger with visible effort. He waited a few moments before he trusted himself to speak, lest his voice betray his fury, and paced across the little room and back before he replied.

"Julia, I found out one more thing—you never took the trouble to adopt the boy. So there are no legal barriers to my claim on him. I hope you understand that means I can take the boy."

"Law!" she answered defiantly. "What do I care about the law? It is true, I have not adopt' George—but he is mine, he is not yours, for all that you are his father, and the law can do nothing about it. You think because you have so much money, you own so much land, you have so much influence, you think because of this you can have what you want. You had your way with Joe, but you won't have it with me. I'm not old, and sick, and dying, like Joe was—so you could take advantage of him when he couldn't help himself . . ."

"Julia! I beg you—for the boy's sake—get over your prejudices. You don't want to know the truth—you'll ruin George's life because you think you're getting even for a wrong which was never done. You must know better than this."

She sprang to her feet, her eyes flashing. "You come here to lie to me—to threaten me," she cried. "I know you think too much of your wife—Joe's wife—to do anything foolish."

His anger boiled over. He flung himself toward the door, kicking aside a chair in his way. He pushed out of the house, slamming the outer door so hard that the house shook. He did not look back to see whether Julia had followed him to the threshold.

He went straight back to the office. Brushing aside a query from LeBrun, he sat down to his desk and did not rise again until he had drafted a petition to the probate judge to force the Brunets to give his son George up to him out of their illegal custody.

He dispatched it by LeBrun's hand before he could change his mind.

LeBrun had hardly vanished from the grounds, before Hercules began to feel remorseful. He resisted regret; he had tried every other way before resorting to the courts; perhaps now Julia would agree to some kind of mutually satisfactory compromise. Moreover, he told himself, regret was folly; it would have come to this later, in any event; it might as well come now.

Presently he left the office for the house. Dédé was busy with his tutor, and Miss McCleod was in the kitchen, giving instructions to Giselle. Jane would then be alone elsewhere in the house.

He found her in the morning room, contemplating some new music. She looked up, smiling, at his entrance.

"Oh, Mistaire Dousman—Madame Rice has sen' me some new piano pieces by that man who write *Old Folks at Home*. See?" She held up two folded sheets titled *Old Dog Tray* and *My Old Kentucky Home,* but even as she held them aloft, she saw by the set of his mouth that something had taken place. She dropped them. "What has happen'?" she asked in a quiet voice.

"Jane—I thought you should know—I've petitioned the probate judge to take George."

For a moment her gaze did not waver; then she lowered her eyes; a cloud crossed her face. "If Mistaire Dousman has do' so, it is too late for me to objec'. But I do not think it wise."

"Jane, I tried every other course."

"I know. We shall hope now it will turn out for the bes'. I do not care for Julia. I do not even worry how Mistaire Dousman feel. I think only of this boy. It will be vair' hard on him to divide his loyalty."

"I want him only to come here with an open mind and heart."

"But Julia has close' his heart." She put her music away, got up, and came to his side. She embraced him, saying, "I hope he will come. I know how much he mean to Mistaire Dousman. I know how much it will help him to come. But, Mistaire Dousman, I fear for him."

"It will come out all right, never fear."

But an insidious apprehension began to grow in him, despite the confidence he felt in the rightness of his decision.

A fortnight passed.

Then, early one April morning, Julia Brunet appeared without warning at the office. There was an angry wildness in her eyes, and her mouth was grim.

Hercules turned at once to LeBrun. "Leave us, Louis." To her he said, "Come in, Julia."

She waited until LeBrun had passed her on his way out, then she came halfway into the office and stood there, ignoring Hercules' gesture toward the chair LeBrun had quitted.

"I have been serve' with a papair by the court—about George," she began. "Mistaire Dousman, you cannot do this."

"You told me that before," he answered coldly. "But you see, I can. I tried to tell you that, Julia."

"You cannot take George away from me."

"I told you before I didn't want to take him away—only to share him."

"And when he come here—when he see all this great house, all the fine things in it—the way Mistaire Dousman live—then he will not want to come back to us."

"Is that all the faith you have in him?" He could not help adding, "Were you so busy teaching him to hate me you forgot to teach him to love you?"

Her aging face flushed.

"Sit down, Julia," he invited her. He got up and pushed LeBrun's chair up to her. "Perhaps now we can talk sensibly about George."

She sat down. "I do not wish to talk. I wish only that this papair be call' back."

"It's too late for that, Julia. If you hadn't been so busy enjoying what you thought was your triumph and revenge, we might have talked this thing over sensibly before you drove me to court—where you were so sure I wouldn't go. You've been wrong in everything you did, Julia. As many times as I came to you, you rebuffed me every time. Now you're here and all you know is to say what you wish. Nothing at all about what I wish."

"What is it Mistaire Dousman want?" she asked warily.

"You know what I want. We must make some workable arrangement so that George can come here to live—at least part of the time; that I may send him to school."

She shook her head. "It cannot be."

"Then there's no alternative but to let the petition to the judge go through. I need hardly tell you—though you'll probably not want to believe me—that the court will take George from you and give him to me as his father."

"No! No!" she cried out, her face twisting with pain and anger.

"Then let's be sensible and approach the matter another way," said Hercules gently. "I no more than you wish to go into court about this; perhaps we can work together to prevent it. The solution lies with you, Julia."

Instantly her eyes narrowed with suspicion. "There's nothing I can do," she said. "I have already do' . . ." But here she stopped.

"Yes, I know. You boasted to me not long ago that no judge could undo what you have done to George. Now it's up to you to undo it, Julia—if you can."

"I do not know," she said weakly.

"I'll hold the petition in abeyance by asking the court to take no further action pending word from me—let's say, for a month. Will that give you time enough?"

"I do not know," she said again in a tired voice, as if she contemplated with dread the task before her. "George is firm in his min'—he will be hard to change."

"But not more than a month. If by that time the boy hasn't come to me, then I'll have to instruct the court to proceed with the action."

"Come to you?" she repeated.

"Yes. He, too, has rebuffed every effort I made to speak with him. Now I expect him to come to me here. I don't think that's asking too much." He shrugged. "You've taunted me so often with the fact that I couldn't buy his affection; so I suppose at first we can enter into no more than a business arrangement—at least until he learns that I bear him only affection and concern for his well-being."

"You wait' so long to show it, Mistaire Dousman."

He was stung. "I've known beyond doubt that George was my son only for a year," he retorted angrily. "I suspected it before, but I had no proof. I've gone to you repeatedly—you know with what result. Yet you have the temerity to reprove me now for not doing what you did everything possible to prevent me from doing. I'm a patient man, Julia—I've endured your insults, your unfounded slanders, and possibly your mistreatment of my son—all without violence, but I won't tolerate reproof of this kind from you. If you persist in that attitude, is there any use trying to keep this out of the court? I don't think so."

"I will try, Mistaire Dousman," said Mrs. Brunet in a flat voice. "I will talk to George—I do not know how it will come out—but I'll try."

"Make it clear to him what the alternative is, Julia. You owe it to him—and don't deceive him any more about me either as his father or as a man."

"I will try. But why do you do this, Mistaire Dousman?"

"Do you have to ask why a father wants his son? More than that, I need him to help me here, maybe even take my place when I'm gone—he seems sturdy and strong. I'm sure he has a mind of his own; he'll know how to make decisions, once he's free of the poison you've pumped into him."

Her face flushed angrily. "And if he do not believe me now?"

Hercules shrugged.

She got to her feet. "I will try, Mistaire Dousman," she said again, uncertainly.

He almost felt sorry for her. He was annoyed with himself for having spoken as bluntly as he had, but he had been honest; he had felt what he said, and he had given words to his feelings. He got up, too, and crossed to hold the door open for her.

She did not bid him good day. She did not even look at him,

but passed with head averted, cradling her hatred still, and with it now a sense of defeat that would only sharpen her hatred. How much this hatred must have meant to her all these years! he thought. It must have become firmly allied to her loyalty to her dead brother, and it would therefore have been enhanced in her eyes.

After she had gone, LeBrun came quietly back into the office and sat down at his desk.

"Don't begin work, Louis," said Hercules, who had returned to his own desk and was writing a note. "I want you to take this letter to the judge."

Whatever Julia Brunet did now, he was determined to keep his part of the bargain: the court would not press her to relinquish the boy for the period of a month.

The Mississippi opened late that spring. Cold weather held on. Birds that came up from the South sought sunny places out of the cold winds that blew; animals from the surrounding hills ventured close to the village at night in search of food, rousing the dogs to furious barking. The wind held to the north until a day in April, when, suddenly, it died away and sprang up from the south. Thereafter it blew steadily, with increasing warmth, and at last the ice in the river went out, and the floodwaters began to pour down the valley, joined by thaw water from every tributary.

Within a week steamboats began to move up the river; the valley sprang into renewed life. The Indians came in with their winter's bag of furs and the squaws with their mocucks of maple sugar. Benoit, Lapiage, and other traders came in laden with furs. LeBrun spent days at the warehouse getting the furs ready for shipment down-river by steamboat, Benoit coming in from time to time to lend a hand. Food came to the landing at the house on the mound and had to be unloaded by the roustabouts, who made processions of singing workers from the river to the cellars, the office, and the icehouse, bearing flour, corn, dried fruit, liquor, powder, a chest of tea, bags of peas, barrels of sugar, boxes of soap, linseed oil, nails, and the countless items needed for the trade.

Day after day went by so filled with work that Hercules was scarcely aware of the passage of time as April began to fade. The boats brought more than food. Land speculators moved up the river; settlers came in greater numbers, some to disembark at Prairie du Chien and move into the country around the village. John Lawler came in, paid his respects to Hercules, and began to recruit men to build the Milwaukee and Mississippi station in the lower town. And one of the early boats down the Wisconsin brought Elizabeth Baird to visit.

Hercules did not know of her arrival until he came in for dinner that evening and saw her sitting at the table.

"Elizabeth!" he cried out in astonishment. "I thought I saw a ghost—you're a stranger here."

"I'm busy, too, you know." She offered her cheek to be kissed.

"Is Henry with you?"

"No—he can't believe Green Bay could get along without him." She laughed. "Is he not like all men? They nevair think the world moves without them!" She turned to Jane. "You remembair that time Joe think you cannot do without him—and you drew up those article' of separation?"

Jane nodded. Her eyes danced at the memory of it.

Hercules looked from one to the other of them. "What was this? I don't remember anything of that sort. They were separated for a while . . ."

"Perhaps Jane do not tell you, no?" asked Mrs. Baird.

"No, I never did," answered Jane. "Poor Mistaire Dousman! He have so many thing' on his min' that time, I did not have the heart to tell him. But I did indeed put down article' of separation aftair Joe talk about liv' apart—but then M'sieu' Rolette was not near' so anxious. Jus' the same, we do live apart a while."

Hercules was amused. Perhaps Joe had told something of this to his sister, adding this, too, to her hatred of him, for, if Julia had suspected a liaison between him and Jane, she would naturally blame such a proposal on Hercules.

"How long will you be with us, Elizabeth?" asked Hercules.

"But one week."

"Only a week!" cried Jane in dismay. "Why, Elizabet', if you call jus' on your frien's here, it will leave you no time for us! You mus' stay longair!"

"One week I tell Henry," said Mrs. Baird firmly. "One week it will be."

"Then I know what I shall do," said Jane. "I will save you trouble to call on your frien's—we will have a party an' invite them all to this house to see you." She glanced at Hercules. "Do Mistaire Dousman agree?"

"Whatever you like, Jane."

"Then it is settle'." To Miss McCleod she added, "We shall make up the lis' right aftair dinnair."

The party took place on the fourth night of Elizabeth Baird's visit. Jane had found a little group of four people who could play musical instruments well enough so that the guests could dance after dinner, and she had invited not only all the friends Elizabeth wanted to see, but also everyone else of whom she could think. The house was gay with lights, and the library and drawing room were soon crowded with guests. Among them was John Lawler, who sought out Hercules, after paying his respects to Mrs. Baird.

"Thought I'd tell you Brodhead's coming in tomorrow or next day," he said, drawing Hercules over toward the library fireplace. "Had word from him two days ago. We're just about at the river with the line, and Brodhead's beginning to think about Prairie du Chien now."

"Not this year or next, the way the line's been going," said Hercules. "How's the station coming?"

"We're making good progress. It's time to start thinking about that hotel you were planning to build there."

Jane appeared in the hall and beckoned Hercules toward the drawing room, walking back the way she had come.

Hercules crossed the library, Lawler at his side, still talking fast, as if he feared Hercules would escape him. They had just reached the hallway, when the front door was flung wide with a crash.

Hercules started and turned.

Julia Brunet stood there, disheveled and distraught. Her face was a mask of fury and grief. For a moment no one moved. Julia stood on the threshold, one arm clinging to the door; those guests who had seen her looked on in astonishment. In the middle of the drawing room Jane stirred and began to walk toward the hall.

Then Julia saw Hercules. "You, Mistaire Dousman!" she shouted. "You—you . . . !"

Hercules excused himself calmly and walked toward Julia. He seized her firmly by the arm, turned her around, and drew her outside to the veranda, closing the doors behind them. Inside, the musicians burst into a gay waltz.

"Now, Julia—what is it?"

"He's gone. An' you are the fault of it—you, Mistaire Dousman," she cried, while tears of rage and grief started afresh down her cheeks. And, almost before he realized what she was about to do, she flung herself upon him and began to beat him with her fists.

He caught her wrists and held her away from him. Tears ran unheeded down her cheeks; she bowed her head; her tears fell hotly on Hercules' hands. He released her. She stood quietly sobbing.

"Calm yourself, Julia. Tell me what's happened."

"George is gone," she said, and sobbed anew.

"Gone where?"

"I do not know. He has run away."

For a moment Hercules stood in doubt. But Julia Brunet's grief was too genuine for simulation. George must indeed have run away, just as she said.

"Come," he said gently. "We'll go to the office where we can talk. There's too much noise here."

She went docilely, as if all the fire in her had gone out. The music from the house receded, diminishing in volume; the laughter and hum of conversation were lost to the night. In the office even the music sounded farther away than the choir of the frogs along the river.

Hercules pushed forward a chair for Julia, then he went over to his desk and waited for her to speak.

"I do as you say I should do, Mistaire Dousman," she said. "I tell George he mus' go to you. He say nothing. He only look at me. He do not believe me. An' when I tell him you have go' to court, he say he understan'—he think you force me to say this to him."

"I see." Of course, that was to be expected. If Julia had put it that way, what else would the boy think? And Julia would have put it as spitefully as her nature demanded.

"I talk to him many time'. Jean also talk to him. Jean say to him more than I say."

By this, Hercules concluded that Jean had told the boy bluntly that his foster mother had misled him in regard to Hercules.

"He do not believe Jean, either. He say we are scared of you an' your money. He say if you go to court the court will do as you say, no mattair what is true."

"And did you tell him what was true, Julia?"

"Before God, Mistaire Dousman, I do tell him. But he will not believe me. I try—I try . . ."

"You did your work too well, Julia."

"I tell him day after day. I say he must go to you. I say he will not be take' away. An' evair' day he say less. At last he say nothing at all, jus' look at me. He will not sleep. It bothair him vair' much."

A boy of fifteen, thought Hercules. Julia's change of face would trouble him, perhaps deeply. With all her vindictiveness, her hatred, her desire for vengeance so long given to the boy as a background, small wonder that he should be torn by conflict at her reversal, and believe that only fear of his power could have brought this about. How could he resolve such a conflict, except in flight, if he were unwilling to face Hercules and come to his own conclusions?

"When did you find out he had gone?"

"Jus' a little while ago."

"So he has been gone, then, how long?"

She looked at him guiltily. "Mistaire Dousman, he has been gone three, maybe four days."

"Four days!" he cried. "Why didn't you come to me right away?"

"I think perhaps he come to you an' do not wish to say so to me. I expec' him back evair' day, but he do not come. So tonight I go to his room, an' for the firs' time I see he has take' his things, an' I know he would not do so to come to you." She bit back more tears, then added, "An' I find a little note he write for me." She reached into the pocket of the apron she wore and handed it to him.

It was badly crumpled. Hercules smoothed it out.

"I have gone away. Do not look for me."

It was not even signed. It was addressed to no one. It was as if the conflict within him prevented any term of endearment from being written, not even so much as a word of affection for the Brunets who had raised him.

"It was on the chair by his bed," she went on. "I have not see' it when I look into the room before. But tonight, when I see his things are gone, then I see it, I read it."

Four days. Even three days would be enough to give the boy a good start.

"Mistaire Dousman—all this—it was you who did this," she cried with sudden vehemence.

"I'm sorry about it, Julia," answered Hercules. "But I can't take all the blame, or even any great part of it. If you hadn't deliberately poisoned him—if you could have been a little bigger than your foolish hatred of me . . ."

She began to weep again, convulsively. He made no effort to stop her. She had plainly been very fond of George. It was unfortunate that her craving for vengeance against Hercules should have taken precedence over her affection for the boy. Now, at last, it had fallen back upon her. If she had not inculcated George so with hatred for his father, he would have been able to accept her suggestion that he go to see Hercules in the hope of effecting some compromise.

Actually, in a way, Hercules was proud of the boy. He had struck out on his own; he had made his decision, bolting free of both his foster parents and his father. The change in Julia must have seemed to him as alien as Hercules had been painted for him; at that point he could neither go forward nor retreat, for his foster parents had become as unknown as Hercules had been made to seem. So he had cut away from them both.

"I know, I know," murmured Julia, as her sobs subsided, "if I had not tol' him—if I had not make him hate you, it would not have happen'—it is my punishment. Oh, if only he were here, I would willingly have him come live with you, Mistaire Dousman! Now he is lost—he is gone . . ."

"I'll have a search made for him. We'll see."

"Do you think he can be foun'?"

"We'll try to find him. If and when we do, I think we'd all better sit down together and plan something for him that he will find acceptable, if only on condition."

She looked at him hopefully. Her arrogance, her insolence, her evident hatred—all were gone. She seemed now a pathetic old woman; it pricked his conscience to see her so; he would have preferred her scorn; it seemed to him that if he had not pressed his wish for George, if he had not insisted on discovering her purpose in keeping George away from his father without disclosing him to Hercules, all would still be well, George would be happy with his foster parents—he had never known any other; he need not have known any other . . . But this was vain speculation. Could Hercules himself have done anything other? The boy was his son—ultimately, his responsibility. He had braved the clack of hostile tongues to set in motion a petition to bring the boy to his side, where he belonged.

Recriminations now were idle. The problem was to find

George, and, having found him, to fetch him back or persuade him to come voluntarily.

"I'll do all I can to find him, Julia," he said, getting up.

She came to her feet, too. She stood for a few moments more, looking at him, her eyes troubled, reproachful, as if she could not relinquish the conviction that his was the fault.

"I wish this did not happen, Mistaire Dousman. I'm sorry."

"I, too. But it's done—and we'll have to see what we can do now."

She walked to the door. "Good night, Mistaire Dousman."

"Good night, Julia."

As she stepped out into the night, she began to sob again. She ran, sobbing, down the lawn and across to the gate.

Music from the party drifted down to Hercules from the house, mingling with the hyla song from the river and the sloughs. He stood contemplating the party; he was in no mood for more of it. He went back into the office, locking the door behind him. He sat down, lit a cigar, and went to work.

There were dozens of letters to write, even without trying to guess which way George might have gone. He could have struck out in any direction, no matter to what point he could be traced. He would have taken a boat; someone would remember that. He could have gone north to St. Paul, or south to St. Louis. From either of those river ports he could have vanished in any direction. In his place, Hercules thought, I'd have gone west.

He wrote letters to friends, enlisting their help, and to private inquiry agents, not only in St. Paul and St. Louis, but also in New Orleans, Cincinnati, Pittsburgh, even New York. He wrote rapidly, setting forth a brief description of George, which was not hard to do; he had only to describe himself as a youth, as he had been in that final year of British occupation of Mackinac. He also wrote to every steamboat captain in the Minnesota Packet Company, as well as a general letter to the steamboat captains on the Mississippi and Ohio.

When he finished, the hour was late. He had not been aware

of the passage of time, and was astonished to see that the house on the mound was all but dark. A solitary light burned in the library—all else was locked in sleep. The guests had gone, the musicians had departed, the party was over; the sounds of laughter and music had been supplanted by the songs of the hylidae and the crying of whippoorwills, together with the shouts and chants of roustabouts at the steamboat landing, where the blacks were crouched around a fire to keep warm in the April night.

He hurried to the house.

Jane sat alone in the library. She gazed at him reproachfully as he came in, and shook her head.

"Mistaire Dousman! To leave me so to make the excuse for my husban' who has gone off into the night with anothair woman!"

"I'm sorry, Jane—I couldn't get back. It was Julia."

"I saw her. What has happen'?"

"George has run away. I've been at the office writing letters of inquiry in the hope of finding him."

"What has Julia do?"

He explained.

"My poor Mistaire Dousman!" she cried, when he had finished. "Did I not say I was worry' about this boy? Now see what you and Julia have do' to him. That poor boy! Pairhaps I should have talk' to him before you—he might have listen' to me."

"Not if Julia could help it. He wouldn't have listened to you any more than to me. She realizes now, I think—but it's too late for remorse at this point."

She rose and linked her arm with his. "Come to bed now, Mistaire Dousman, and sleep on it. In the morning you will know bettair what to do."

Next morning Hercules haunted the landing, until he learned from one of George's young friends, who had seen him, that George had boarded the *Itasca* bound for St. Louis. Beyond this point Hercules could not go; not until he could see the captain of the *Itasca* could he learn whether the boy had been remembered. Even so, if George had got off at St. Louis, the chance of anyone's remembering him was remote. Finding George, he knew, was not a matter of a week or a month or two—but far more, perhaps a year. He was not sanguine.

LeBrun turned to Hercules, who was bent over his desk. "Company coming, Mr. Dousman—to the office."

Hercules straightened up and walked to where he could see. An elegantly dressed gentleman was striding up the walk toward the office. A fine beaver hat shadowed his face in the June afternoon sun. His firm, determined step was familiar.

"By heaven!" exclaimed Hercules. "It's Sark!"

He pushed open the door and shouted a welcome.

Jonas Sark raised his hand in greeting. In a few moments he was at the office steps, shaking Hercules' hand.

"Man, you look like a different person," said Hercules, drawing him into the office. "Louis, get us something to drink. What will you have, Jonas?"

"Brandy—as usual."

LeBrun went out and around the office into the cellar below.

"Tell me what's happened to you, Jonas."

"Well, for one thing—I've gone back to my own name. Even though it doesn't seem to fit me as well as Sark. But keep on calling me Sark—it belongs to me here in this place."

"You've done well? Married?"

"Two children." He grinned. "They're over visiting their grandparents with my wife. We've been East. We're on our way back to Sacramento now."

He went on to give Hercules a brief account of his life—how he had discovered gold— "I'm not as rich as you, but I don't complain!"—how he had invested in real estate in California, following the example Hercules had set him. He was now in the land business in Sacramento; he meant to stay in it. "I could retire, but, like you, I was never made to sit idle."

LeBrun came in with brandy and poured two glasses of it.

"Tell me, Mr. Dousman—was there ever any inquiry for those fellows?"

"None. Thunder Walker's turned up some time later, below McGregor—the authorities concluded he had fallen into the water. Of the other, nothing was heard from again."

"And from—New York?"

"Well, from what talk I had with Ferrier when I visited him afterward, I gathered that the Astors themselves knew nothing of the matter; it was Ferrier's game, alone."

"That surprises me."

"It didn't particularly surprise me. The old man was ruthless in his way, but some of his employees identified their welfare with that of the Company and went ahead without instructions from above. Ferrier was one of them."

" 'Was'?"

"He died last winter. When I talked with him three years ago, he asked whether I knew what had become of you. I simply told him you'd left Prairie du Chien. He wanted to be informed if ever I heard from you, but I gather that apart from that he wasn't pressing any search. I suppose he concluded that as long as you were out of the way—out of the general region where your father was killed—no one in the Company had anything further to fear from any disclosure you might make."

Sark nodded. He was satisfied. He drank his brandy ruminatively. He asked about the fur trade, and seemed surprised when Hercules told him that furs were still being shipped from Prairie du Chien and St. Paul, although other posts on the upper Mississippi were no longer doing so.

Presently he rose to go. "Is there anything I can do for you in Sacramento, Mr. Dousman?"

Hercules laughed. "I don't need gold. I think not, but thanks for asking." A thought struck him suddenly. "Still, perhaps there *is* something. You must have made quite a few contacts in that part of the West, Jonas?"

Sark grinned and said he had.

"There's someone I'm anxious to locate. I don't know where he is—don't even know that he's gone west of the river. But he should be less hard than some to locate—he's only a boy, fifteen, big for his age, and looks older. I've a description of him set down here, one I've sent out to inquiry agents in various cities. I'll let you take that. I don't impose on you?"

"Not at all, Mr. Dousman. I'm glad to do anything I can. I always figure you put up with a good deal from me."

Hercules took from his desk the description of George he had written some time ago. "Here it is. The boy may answer to the name of George Brunet; he may have changed his name. I'd be inclined to think he has. But come, I'll walk to the gate with you."

As they walked across the lawn, Hercules told him the story of George Brunet, so that Sark might know why his interest in him was so strong.

"I remember the boy," said Sark. "He'll be older now, though."

"Only three years. He's grown sturdier, his shoulders have broadened—and he looks a good deal like me."

"He should be easy to see and recognize—if he's about to be seen. Well, I'll do what I can. I have friends in many places around Sacramento—even as far away as Los Angeles—though I'd hardly expect him to be there."

"Jonas, he may be anywhere."

They shook hands.

"Come in again if you find time before you leave town," invited Hercules.

He watched his one-time employee stride down the lane toward the house along the Marais de St. Feriole, where the Gauchers still lived, and where his family now visited. Sark was as self-reliant as ever. Destiny had been kind to him; if he had not gone West, he might never have grown wealthy and never won free from his deep-rooted desire for revenge upon his father's murderers and the vast, impersonal Company which employed them.

The summer faded.

Slowly, one by one, the friends and inquiry agents to whom Hercules had written about George reported on their initial inquiries. There was no word of the boy. From the moment he had left the *Itasca,* at St. Louis, all trace of him was lost.

Then, early one morning in August, while Hercules and Jane were at breakfast, Giselle came diffidently out of the kitchen to say that someone was at the back door, asking for Mr. Dousman.

Hercules excused himself and went to the kitchen porch.

Jean Brunet stood there, hands in his pockets, chewing at a straw.

"Good morning, Jean."

Brunet touched his cap in response. "My wife she say to tell you she have lettair from George."

"Where is he?"

"He do not say. My wife say for you to come look at it. I tell her I stop see you on my way to de ferry."

He touched his cap again and started away.

Immediately after breakfast Hercules walked over to the Brunet house. Julia expected him; seeing him come, she opened the door to him before his knock fell upon it, and stood aside to let him pass.

Her face was resigned. She had been crying again, but she was now composed. As soon as he had stepped inside the house, she handed him the note she had been holding in her hand. She said nothing.

He took it eagerly, unfolded it, and read it at a glance:

Dear Mama & Papa, I write to say I am sorry I had to go away. But I am not coming back. Do not worry about me. I will be all right. I am going far away. I could not go to him. But if it was true what you told me first, then it was a lie what you told me last. If it was true what you told me last, it was a lie when you said it was not that way before. If you lied to me, then I lied to him the way I talked to him and acted to him. I could not go there this way because I might never know what was a lie and what was not, and besides he was forcing you to say it, wasn't he?

Love from George.

Hercules bit his lip. A slow pain spread through him. He gave the letter back to Julia and held out his hand.

"The envelope, Julia?"

She gave it to him.

He studied it. Mailed at St. Louis in May. So she had had the letter for some time, hoping further word would come from George, hesitating to disclose it to Hercules. He was too weary to feel aggrieved; he was positive that the boy would have been gone from St. Louis long before the letter reached Prairie du Chien. Besides, the most searching inquiry in that city had revealed no trace of George beyond the docks.

"This is all, Julia?"

"Yes, Mistaire Dousman."

"No further word since this?"

"No, Mistaire Dousman." Tears appeared suddenly in her eyes. "He is gone for good—and you see, he says it, it is my fault, my fault . . ."

He wanted to say something comforting, but he could find no words to speak. What she said was the truth, however unpleasant it must be for her to accept it.

"Right and wrong have many faces and many shadings, Julia," he said as he handed the envelope back to her.

She was sobbing now. She took it with trembling fingers and put the letter back into it.

How old she is! he thought. He had never regarded her as old before, but even if she were younger than Joe—and she was—she must now be well into her sixties, almost seventy.

"What about you, Mistaire Dousman?" she cried. "You have make many searches. Have you hear' nothing?"

"Nothing. I've had many reports come in to me from all over. No one saw George after he left the boat at St. Louis."

She put one hand up over her eyes, pressing it against her face. She shook her head slowly from side to side. "He is gone. I will nevair see him again, nevair."

"Don't be so sure, Julia. He may learn that the world can be a harsh, cruel place. He may be back."

But even as he spoke, he was convinced that she was more right than he.

He thanked her gravely, bade her good-by, and went out of the house to walk back to the office, deeply dejected.

8. Heart's Wilderness

Spring, 1857

WITH THE FIRST FLOODS OF SPRING THAT MARCH, THUNDER Walker paid one of his increasingly rare visits to the meeting place of the rivers. He came down from La Crosse, and drew his canoe well up the bank away from the landing west of the house on the mound. Then he came walking stolidly up toward the office just as Hercules and Dédé were preparing to mount their horses to ride out of Prairie du Chien to where the rails of the Milwaukee and Mississippi were approaching their terminus.

Hercules mounted and waited until the Winnebago came up. Thunder Walker raised his arm aloft in greeting. Hercules responded.

"We're just riding out a little way, Thunder Walker," he said. "Want to ride along?"

The Winnebago grunted and nodded.

Hercules looked to LeBrun. "Bring out the bay, Louis." To the Indian he said, "Louis will saddle him."

Thunder Walker shook his head vehemently. "No saddle," he said, and patted his rump.

LeBrun brought the horse out of the stable. Thunder Walker caught her by the neck and swung himself on her broad back, much to the delight of Dédé.

"Papa! Papa!" he cried. "Did you see him?"

Hercules nodded and started away.

"Your boy?" asked Thunder Walker.

"He'll be nine next month," answered Hercules.

Had Hercules ever brought home his other son? Thunder Walker wanted to know.

"No. He ran off, Thunder Walker. Two years ago."

If the Winnebago was surprised, he did not show it. He had long ago got over being surprised at anything white men did. Besides, Indian boys sometimes ran away, as he pointed out to Hercules, but they always came back, they were punished, and sometimes they were better braves because they had run away. It might be so of this boy, too. He pointed to the sun, which shone with unusual warmth for March, and said that as it passed from east to west day after day, all things were resolved.

Hercules made no reply, and the Indian was silent.

They rode first to the railroad station in lower town. Some of the workmen were still busy finishing off the building. Lawler, seeing the three riders outside, came out of the station office.

"Good morning, Dousman. Leaving town?"

"Just taking my son for a little ride. We thought we'd ride out to the work crew."

Lawler's naturally down-turned mouth turned up in a grin. "That's not nearly as far as it was a year ago, eh?" He flashed a glance at Thunder Walker. "Got a bodyguard with you, I see."

"An old friend," said Hercules curtly.

"Well, Dousman, you'll be glad we've got a date for our entry into Prairie du Chien with our first train. April fifteenth."

Hercules turned and looked pointedly up the right of way for sight of the rails.

"I know what you're thinking, Dousman, but it won't be later than that day; it might be earlier. You'll hear from Milwaukee—they'll want you and perhaps Brisbois to have a hand in the celebration."

"I'll wait to hear. I've waited so long—a month or more won't make much difference. By the way, Jane says to tell you she'd like you and Mrs. Lawler to come to dinner some evening. And you're to bring that young fellow, Spettel."

"Just let us know when."

They rode on out of Prairie du Chien to the east.

"Who is the man with the fox face?" asked Thunder Walker in his own tongue.

Hercules replied in the same language that Lawler represented the railroad company.

Thunder Walker opined that Lawler had sharp eyes and a smooth tongue. He was a shrewd, cunning man, in the Winnebago's opinion. Since this reflected Hercules' own judgment, he was surprised; he never ceased to marvel at Thunder Walker's ability to sum up character. It was a trait common to many Indians he had known.

"Boy good rider," said Thunder Walker then.

Hercules glanced toward Dédé. The boy rode with the ease of one who had ridden a long time. He was superbly self-confident. He trusted his mount to follow the road, and his eyes darted alertly here and there, missing nothing. He sat astride his horse as straight as a stick.

Suddenly, without warning, Thunder Walker dug his heels into his horse and rode her sharply against Dédé's mount. The boy's horse shied and reared up; Dédé leaned forward, coolly, held to his mount, and brought him under control, as the Indian watched approvingly and Hercules' hands tightened on his reins.

Thunder Walker turned to Hercules, his eyes showing his pleasure; he ignored Dédé's angry, "What'd you do that for?" "He's like his father," the Indian said. "He has good iron in him. You have made a good son, friend Dousman."

"Just the same, I'd be obliged if you didn't test him again like that. He might have been thrown."

"He ride too well," answered Thunder Walker.

"I wish he could shoot as well as he rides," Hercules said, keeping to the Winnebago tongue so that Dédé would not understand. "The fact is, the boy refuses to hunt."

The Winnebago grunted. The white man, he said scornfully, thought only of killing. He takes his gun, goes out to kill some animal, and then is able to say to himself how great he is—like a god, with his gun holding the power of life or death over lesser creatures. The Indian killed only for food, not for the pleasure of flattering his vanity. It was good that the boy would not hunt. It was not necessary that he should do so, for now the food came to him on the big boats and soon it would come on the iron horse. Why should he go forth into the woods to kill and maim when he had no need to do so?

Hercules suffered the rebuke in good-natured silence.

They were now passing the Barrette farm, and Hercules turned into the yard around the house he had built for Emily and her husband. Two dogs ran out, barking. Hercules rode around to the back door, knowing that at this hour Emily would be in the kitchen.

The dogs' antics brought her to the door. She had grown somewhat heavier, but her serenity was unchanged.

"Well, Papa, what brings you?" she asked tranquilly.

"We're just riding by."

She turned and pulled her second daughter out from behind her ample skirts. "Theresa—say 'good morning' to your grandpapa."

"Good morning, Gran'papa," said the little girl in a piping voice.

Hercules smiled.

"And your Uncle Dédé."

"An' my Uncle Dédé." She added, wide-eyed, "Oh, Mama, there's an Indian!"

"You're all well, Emily?" said Hercules.

"Yes, thank you. Virginie's in school. Charlie's in town somewhere."

"You seldom come to see us."

"Papa, you have your own problems."

"Come whenever you like, Emily—all of you."

They talked for a little while. Then Emily and her daughter

went back into the house and the three of them rode on, bearing away from the farm toward the river.

Presently they reached the place where the main body of men working on the railroad were. The road bed had been laid down all the way into Prairie du Chien; the ties had been set in for most of the way; but here the rails were being connected to that part of the line already in place. The air rang with the blows of the sledges pounding spikes into place, the shouting of the men, one to another, the cursing of foremen. Far back up the tracks men still worked at leveling the embankment.

Hercules watched meditatively. It had taken almost ten years to come to this point from Milwaukee. In the beginning he had counted on perhaps two years, three at most. Ten years! Even now, if they did not hurry, no one knew that they would reach the Mississippi. The year's first reports from the East counseled against ominous signs on the financial horizon; market trouble seemed to impend.

Dédé was impatient. Having had his fill of watching the crew at work, he looked anxiously at Hercules. "Can we go back, Papa?"

"Would you like to ride a little more?"

"Oh, not here. Into the hills."

"All right, Dédé. Take the lead."

The boy swung away toward the hills rising almost sheer in the east. Their challenge gave Hercules pause. Not so Dédé. He rode forward without faltering. Hercules looked at Thunder Walker, whose face was bland, unmoving; but he was convinced that the Winnebago laughed behind his eyes. He pointed to the hills; the Indian only nodded and gave his heels to the horse.

The Winnebago lamented as they rode. He bemoaned the coming of the iron horse. Now there was nothing left for him and others of his kind but to go into the northwest, where this great black monster and its train of cars could not come. All was changed. All the days when a man moved about free under heaven were gone. Nothing was left of the old way of life.

Hercules listened without replying. What Thunder Walker said was true. It had been true centuries ago; it would be true centuries hence. Change was the order of life; it could never be otherwise. For him, too, much had altered since he had left Mackinac. For him, the rivers, the lake, the wilderness had been the challenge to bring out his best. Perhaps for the boy beside him the sunlit hills ahead were the first challenge.

Dédé reached the slope ahead of them. With unerring intuition, he began to go diagonally up the steep face of the hill. Hercules flashed a glance at Thunder Walker. The Indian rode with his eyes fixed curiously on the boy, nodding complacently.

Watching Dédé's sureness and manifest skill, Hercules' doubts began to thin and wash away.

Early in April came a long report from Sark. Hercules seized upon it eagerly; herein lay his last hope of discovering some trace of George. All other inquiries had ceased.

"I have come to the reluctant conclusion," Sark wrote, "that to pursue this search any further would be useless. I have had a constant inquiry afoot for almost two years; I have tracked down personally half-a-dozen young boys who have come West on their own; but none is your boy, George. I have been in San Francisco, and both north and south of that city. I have enlisted the good offices of Count Brogmar and his family, who have been my friends since you sent me to them, and they have put their resources into the search. Spanish friends all the way to Mexico have also made inquiries. It has all been in vain.

"It is possible that the boy may have gone to some obscure mining camp in the southwest, or even in California; but if so, I have no means of discovering him. I am bound to say also that many such boys—and even many men—coming into this country, where a good deal of lawlessness exists, have the misfortune to find gold, and are done to death by those who want to possess themselves of their gold or their claims, and, however painful it might be to consider it, this possibility cannot be dismissed as far as the boy is concerned.

"If it is your wish that I pursue the inquiry, I will do so, but I am of the opinion that nothing would be gained by it. The boy has now been gone two years, and by this time he will have found a place for himself, or he would have returned home."

Sark had appended a detailed list of the places to which he had gone in search of George, but Hercules scarcely glanced at it. He had feared from the first what the outcome of the search for George would be; now his fears were realized. George had fled, a sadly confused boy—fled into freedom from his perplexing doubts, away from the hatred he had been taught and that which might have come to him had he learned beyond doubt that his foster mother had deliberately kept him from his father to achieve an unreasoning vengeance of her own for a wrong which had never been done.

He turned Sark's letter over and wrote:

In the event of the reappearance of the boy known as George Brunet, raised by Jean and Julia Rolette Brunet in Prairie du Chien, and vanished therefrom in April, 1855, at my death or within a reasonable time thereafter, I give and bequeath to him subject to no condition whatsoever the sum of $25,000, together with all interest in the farm known as the Sieuchile Farm north of Prairie du Chien, of which he may dispose as he sees fit.

He signed and dated it, marking it as a codicil to his will. The date, he saw with a gently ironic smile, was Dédé's birthday.

Jane appeared suddenly at the door of the office, carrying her parasol. She was radiant in a new dress that shimmered and shone in the morning sun.

"Dédé is already in the carriage, and Louis at the reins. Do Mistaire Dousman come? Or would he prefair to go in his canoe?"

Hercules laughed. "I'm ready for the great day." He glanced at the clock.

"We have plenty time. Bettair for us to be early than late. Would it not be a shame if after the train come so late to Prairie du Chien we should be late to board it on its firs' trip down from Boscobel?"

Jane had spent half the early hours of the day looking over Miss McCleod's plans for tonight's party to celebrate the arrival of the first train from Milwaukee and the joining of Lake Michigan traffic to that of the Mississippi. Hercules had been ready before anyone else, and Miss McCleod had prepared Dédé, after Hercules had gone to the office. So Jane had been the last to get ready, and here she was pretending to be waiting on Hercules. He got up.

She took his arm. They walked out to the carriage, which had been brought around to the gate. Dédé was leaning out, calling anxiously.

"Hurry up, hurry up—we'll be late."

"He is so excite'," said Jane.

"They wouldn't leave without us," said Hercules tranquilly. "They wouldn't dare. Aftair all, it will be like riding to Prairie du Chien over Mistaire Dousman's money—that is what built this part of the line."

He handed Jane into the carriage and got in after her. Louis flicked the reins, and the horses started away. They rode over the Marais de St. Feriole and out of Prairie du Chien into the northeast.

The day was uncommonly warm for the fifteenth of April. A soft breeze blew out of the south, and for some distance out of Prairie du Chien the air was fragrant with the musk of thaw water that still filled the Mississippi. Meadow larks and bluebirds started up from the roadside, and killdeers flew crying low over the fields.

"It will be a long ride, Jane," said Hercules. "Three hours at the best, if the roads were good. There are still muddy places; so we'll likely be on the road a good four. Perhaps you shouldn't have come; you'll be exhausted for the party tonight—and God knows how long the dinner at French's will take!"

"Mistaire Dousman undairrate me." She scrutinized his face

anxiously with narrowed eyes. "Has Mistaire Dousman's pain gone from his ches'?"

"Yes," he said easily. But it was not quite true; a kind of stabbing pain, lodged deep under his skin, was still to be felt in the upper part of his chest, not far below his neck, not a sharp or unbearable pain, but something that came and ebbed, and was gone sometimes for days at a time before returning again.

"One thing," said LeBrun over his shoulder, "if we do run into muck and get stuck, we're never far from the tracks."

"We can hitch a ride," said Dédé, looking at his parents with mischievous eyes, as if already contemplating some plan to make it necessary to do so.

"We'll get there all right, and the train will reach the terminus. President Brodhead came in last night so as to be on hand to welcome it at the station with Brisbois and the others."

They reached Boscobel in midafternoon. Louis drove directly to the long platform that served in place of a railroad station, for the town consisted of but a few buildings, and the platform was used primarily as a wooding station. They got out of the carriage.

"Take the carriage back, Louis," said Hercules.

"I'd better wait, Mr. Dousman," said LeBrun anxiously. "Just in case the train doesn't come."

Jane laughed. "I think Louis do not have much faith."

"One must admit there's some basis for it," said Hercules, remembering the years of delay in bringing the railroad to Prairie du Chien.

"Papa, I see smoke!" cried Dédé excitedly.

Even as the boy spoke, the whistle of the locomotive rang down the valley. A hush fell on the platform as the train came into sight, and a few people came running from the houses clustered near. Flags and bunting decorated the engine, almost concealing its outlines; one huge banner bore the image of a badger and the legend, "Wisconsin, the Badger." The whistle's blasts grew more frequent as the train of cars slowed down for the platform, and a great cloud of black smoke belched out of the high, wide-mouthed conical stack rising behind the square headlight. The locomotive's bell rang steadily.

"It's named *Prairie du Chien,*" cried Dédé. "See, Papa—right there on the front of the engine."

"Yes, Dédé," answered Hercules as he scanned the windows of the three new passenger cars attached to the baggage car. He caught sight of Colonel Bird, now mayor of Madison, who had boarded the train at that station. Then he took Dédé by one hand and Jane by the arm. "This way," he said.

They mounted the steps and entered the last of the three cars. Bird greeted them joyously.

"We've waited for this day a long time, eh, Dousman?" he cried, shaking hands with Hercules and bowing to Jane. Turning, he swept the other occupants of the car with one arm. "I think you know all these gentlemen, Dousman. And I believe Madame Dousman has made the acquaintance of the Company officers. There are guests of the line from New York, Chicago, and other points in the other cars; you can meet them in Prairie du Chien."

"I hardly counted on an entirely new train," said Hercules.

"The locomotive was built in Jersey City. Two of the cars came out of Buffalo, but this one was put together under John Bailey's direction in our own shop in Milwaukee. Holton says it stands up well against anything on rails in the United States. But come—sit down. We're only stopping here long enough to take on wood and water."

"You'll find our townspeople turned out," said Hercules.

"They wait already when we begin our journey," put in Jane.

Three sharp blasts of the locomotive's whistle signaled the beginning of the last part of the run. The bell began to ring once more. The car lurched forward and started to move. Dédé crowded to a window, chattering excitedly. Jane grew a little pale, and for a moment she closed her eyes to shut out the sight of the Boscobel houses moving past at an ever-increasing speed. When she opened them again, the train was out of the village, moving among the woods in the bottoms of the Wisconsin River.

"Madame is not well?" asked Bird solicitously.

"Pairfec'ly," answered Jane. "Mistaire Bird do not know this is the firs' time I have ever ride' on the train."

Bird turned to Hercules again and began to regale him with a recital of costs and income, to which Hercules listened with only one ear; he sat watching the landscape passing and thought of the change the coming of the train would make in the life of Prairie du Chien. Would it mean the decline of steamboating even as the arrival of the first steamboat had signaled the end of canoe and keelboat traffic?

Just before five o'clock in the afternoon the train pulled into the station at Prairie du Chien, heralding its arrival with prolonged blasts of its whistle, which were answered by steamboat whistles at the landing not far away. Outside, milling about the station on both sides of the tracks, hundreds of people shouted and cheered, and the Prairie du Chien Artillery Company met the train with a salute of two hundred guns. President Brodhead, flanked by Bernard Brisbois and John Lawler, stood at the forefront of the crowd.

As the train stopped, Brodhead mounted to the rear platform and held up his arms for silence. "Ladies and gentlemen—before we make any speeches, we have an important ceremony to perform. Attend us, please."

As he spoke, a brakeman came from the baggage car bearing on his shoulders an eight-gallon keg. Brodhead pointed to it, then he leaped from the coach platform, beckoning to Hercules, and took the keg himself.

Hercules descended to walk at his side. Jane, Dédé, the officers of the Company and their guests formed a phalanx behind them. The crowd pressed after, shouting and laughing.

"What's in the keg? . . . Brandy?"

"Give us a drop!"

"What'll you take for it?—I'll bid five dollars!"

Each cry was greeted with good-natured laughter.

Brodhead did not slacken his pace, though he smiled at every sally. At the shore of the Mississippi Brodhead put the keg down. A brakeman came up with a sledge hammer. Brodhead took it and handed it to Hercules.

"As you've fought harder for this terminus than anyone else, Dousman, yours ought to be the honor."

Hercules took the sledge. With one blow he broke in the top of the keg. Water splashed out.

"Now, then," said Brodhead, bending with Hercules to empty the water into the river. "Let the waters of Lake Michigan be joined with those of the Mississippi!"

A great cheer rang out. Although only those at the front knew what the cheer was for, those at the rear took it up spontaneously.

"Now for the speeches," said Brodhead. "You'll say a few words, I trust, Dousman?"

Hercules nodded.

They made their way back through the mellow amber sunlight of late afternoon to the train.

It was past midnight when Hercules, tired after the dinner for the officials and their guests at French's hotel, and the party that followed at the house on the mound, made his way to the office before going to bed, to glance at the mail he had not yet had opportunity to see. The waning moon was just up over the hills east of the village, and the night was soft with the fragrances and musks of spring. A solitary screech owl made its soft, bell-like sounds down along the river, and presently subsided into a keening wail. From here and there in the village sounds of revelry still rose, subdued against the frog choir rising from the bottoms.

He let himself into the office and crossed in the darkness to his desk, where LeBrun had placed his mail, as always. He lit the lamp, found a cigar, and lit that. He sat for a moment, enjoying the flavor of the tobacco, washing his thoughts clear of the events of the day. A little pain nagged at his chest. For a while after dinner he had felt bilious, but this had passed. He supposed he would have to see Dr. Foote one of these days. He eyed the mail with distaste, but he was not given to putting off tasks, however unpleasant they might be or however unlike work he might feel.

He began to go through the letters one by one.

A letter from the irresponsible Du Baye of Portage City, trying to explain why he had not paid Hercules his share of the money received for goods sold to the Chippewa. All excuses and lies, thought Hercules, irritably, for he had trusted Du Baye far too long against his own better judgment.

A letter from Ramsay Crooks, concerning details of the American Fur Company account. This he put aside for further study in the morning.

A letter from his brother John in Milwaukee, to say that the Scotch rat terrier and the Polander hens with one cock he had ordered would be sent by train as soon as service was begun.

A letter from C. P. Hanscom about someone to publish a paper in Prairie du Chien.

A letter from Sibley about the danger of the suspension of William Bell & Company in New York, and the money Bell & Company owed Hercules. This letter, too, he put aside for study tomorrow.

He came suddenly to one without a return address, written in a hasty scrawl. Mailed in St. Paul, Hercules saw, but showing so much wear that he was positive it had been carried a long way overland by hand before it had been deposited for mailing. He studied the envelope under the lamp. Yes, the stamp had been put on over wrinkled and smudged paper. A trader's letter, sent from an outpost in the Northwest. He opened it.

He saw first its date: "December 17, 1856." Then his eyes dropped to the superscription: "Dear Father," and went at once to the signature: "George."

His pulse came with sudden quickening; for a moment pain arrowed through his chest. He flattened the letter under the lamp and read its carefully written words:

Dear Father—I am sorry if I have done you wrong. Each time I look in the glass, I see your face in mine. I know now that you are indeed my father, if ever I had doubt of it. But I could not come to stay with you. I would not have been happy there. I would not have been satisfied to stay with Brunets any more, either, as things were. I am well. I have a place to work. I am not in want. I have learned that you were searching for me. Please, there is no use to do this. I am all right where I am. I do not want to come back, ever. I will not come back. I do not know who to believe. I do not want to know. I have friends here where I am. Please, forget about me.

Nothing more.

Hercules read it again. He studied the envelope anew for some clue to where George might be. Somewhere in the vast wilderness of the Northwest. He might be anywhere between St. Paul and Winnipeg—even to the far coast of Canada. It would be hopeless to attempt to find him. Even if he were found, the letter made it clear that he would not come back.

He leaned back and closed his eyes. He felt ineffably weary, drained of all desire. Perhaps he had counted too much on George, on finding him again, on achieving his goal for the boy. He knew now beyond doubt that this could not be. If only Souligne had not come to him! If only he had waited upon Julia to approach him! If only . . . But it was too late for regret.

He put out the light. Still carrying George's letter, he walked to the door, threw out his cigar, and locked the office. He crossed in the wine moonlight to the house. The night pulsed with the voices of the frogs—peepers, tree frogs, spring cricket frogs sent their voices aloft in a triumphant paean. The screech owls had moved closer now; they were conducting a clacking colloquy near the stable, where he saw three ghostlike fluffs of white, and knew them for young birds—sitting all in a row on the branch of a tree.

The house was dark. He let himself in by the back door and stood for a moment in the kitchen to accustom his eyes to the blackness. Then he went purposefully to Dédé's room.

By the glow of a small lamp he stood looking down on his son.

His only son—there was no other he could reach. Dédé lay on his side, his body curved, his curly head dark on the pillow. He looked so fragile that it was hard to believe he had maneuvered a high-spirited horse up the eastern hills all the way to old Michel Brisbois's grave—a triumph that had given even Thunder Walker pause.

He felt rather than saw Jane come in. She walked to his side and slipped her hand into his.

Without a word he handed her George's letter.

She took it over to the night lamp and read it.

She came back. "My poor Mistaire Dousman!" she whispered.

He put his arm around her and drew her close. He kissed her. Dédé stirred and moaned a little, turning in his dream. The moonlight made a spectral parallelogram upon the floor near his bed.

"Do not grieve," Jane said quietly. "I promise you—you will be proud of Dédé. He will not disappoint Mistaire Dousman. Only believe in me."

He only held her tightly to him. He ought never to have allowed his faith in her to be shaken. Dédé would be the man he hoped he would be. What had Thunder Walker said? *He has good iron in him.* Jane had known all along what he had but found out.

He turned and said gruffly, "We'd better get to bed."

Jane followed him obediently, darkness concealing her tender, tolerant smile.

Afterword: Come Like Shadows, So Depart 1868

THE PAIN AT HIS HEART GNAWED INSISTENTLY. HERCULES raised his head and looked from the office window, across the sweep of lawn before the house to where the maple planted by his hand years ago now yielded a gracious shade coolly at the southeast corner. He was tired, tired of all these old records—the papers of the old Fur Company sold four years ago—what was left of it. The maple's shade invited him.

He got up and walked slowly out of the building, turning his labored steps toward the tree, beneath which his armchair waited for him. The summer sun was hot, but a refreshing west wind rustled among the trees, making a silver magic of turned poplar and oak leaves. Phlox and sweet rocket bloomed in almost wild profusion in the flower beds between the house and the ponds in the south. He paused a moment before the house to allay the nagging pain at his heart, his eyes turned to the wide veranda, to the great doors of the house standing open now to the afternoon, and the sun-shot dusk of the hall beyond. He wondered where Jane was.

He reached the maple's shade and sat down gratefully. Behind him footsteps came quickly, anxiously. Hercules waited for the dark, troubled face of LeBrun to appear above him. There it was suddenly; Hercules did not at first hear what

LeBrun said, thinking with dispassionate intensity that Louis, too, was aging, although he could not be much more than thirty-five. Presently he gave his attention to LeBrun's words.

"Mr. Dousman should not exert himself so much; he knows what the doctor has said."

Hercules waved this away, increasing the anxiety pressing upward behind LeBrun's eyes, evident in the taut lines of his mouth. "I'm at rest now, in any case, Louis. Where's Madame Dousman?"

"I don't know, sir."

"Send Miss Penelope to me."

LeBrun had a moment of indecision, but presently he nodded and began to walk rapidly toward the house. Hercules leaned back, fixing his eyes upon the blue, cloudless sky above the Mississippi. So he still sat when he heard Miss McCleod coming, her approach, as always, heralded by her song: *Arouse ye, Arouse ye, my brave mountain boy* . . . He turned his head a little so that the bright green-blue of her dress with the white apron precise upon it came into his sight. He waited.

Miss McCleod's song stopped ominously. In a second her narrowed eyes gazed stonily down at him, her firm mouth disapproving, and she clasped her wrists across her bosom. "Does Mr. Dousman think he knows better than his doctor?" she demanded. She gave him no time to answer, but went on upbraiding him, growing gentler with every sentence. He smiled and half-closed his eyes; he felt better; the tugging at his heart was gone, the arrow of pain in his chest had faded, and he took delight not alone in the wind's softness but even in Miss McCleod's earnest vehemence.

When she had finished and stood daring him to defend himself, he grinned and asked, "Where's Madame Dousman? I haven't seen her in the past hour."

"Young Mr. Dousman has come home from Racine College. Madame has gone to ride with him."

"I want to see her when she comes. Send her to me."

Miss McCleod had a moment of indecision. "Very well," she

said finally. She half-turned, but could not resist hoping that Hercules would rest here until someone came for him. Then she strode purposefully back to the house.

Hercules held his smile. He thought with a warm glow inside him of how devoted his servants were. Looking around him now, seeing on all sides of him his tangible dream of a home second to none in Wisconsin, he was satisfied. West of the ponds stood the greenhouse, and beyond it the flowers Jane had had planted; even now, despite the hot sun, Jake and Lena Schafer were at work among them, pausing from time to time to exchange words with Peter Fernette, who was trimming grass away from the trunks of trees. The perfume of beebalm drifted on the wind, and the fresh fragrance of water rose from the ponds. Down on the Mississippi a steamboat went whistling by. High overhead swallows dipped and soared, and over the hills beyond the Mississippi a great bald eagle was suspended darkly upon the blue, riding the air currents.

Slowly, insidiously, his satisfaction was invaded by a subtle discontent, the old gnawing he had known for more than two decades, the caged futility of a man bound by countless factors beyond his control. His pleasure in his possessions was fleeting always; now it took on a touch of bitterness. Somewhere out in the world beyond this place was his lost son, George, forever out of reach, but never out of heart and mind. All his possessions had not won George for him, any more than they had been able to improve the lot of thousands of people for whose welfare he had worked, even as he had once worked for the Winnebago, the Menominee, the Sioux. Wealth, possessions—all were meaningless. There was only Jane—nothing touched her, not even the years of their marriage, and he felt flowering within him anew the incredible happiness which he had always known with her, that happiness which for a decade and a half, before Joe's early death, he had thought lost to him. And after Jane, there was Dédé . . .

Sitting there with his earth underfoot and under eye, with the village just beyond his grounds, and the hills edging the prairie east and west, as always, eternally they would, and the Mississippi flowing toward its meeting with the Wisconsin, and, past it, far down, the sea, he dredged up from the channels of his memory the words of the trader, Drew. *That boy'll have a bright journey through his life. Ye mark my words!* He smiled with affection for his father's old companion, and with bitterness at the emptiness of his prophecy. Yet he had been right in part—Hercules had never known want, he had almost always known moderate wealth, he had been able to buy the things he wanted; it was to the unseeing eye a bright journey, indeed; but the place behind was dark, save for the light that Jane and Dédé made in it. He wondered whether man's hopes inevitably came to this end: warping futility and despair. He had compromised with life more often than life had compromised with him.

A long, melancholy whistle broke the afternoon's quiet. One of the locomotives of the Milwaukee & St. Paul was edging on to the barges run by Lawler to cross to the McGregor side of the river; the hills of the Iowa side threw back the sound, and, as always, a steamboat on the river mocked the locomotive's whistle. He remembered how Thunder Walker had scorned the iron horse, foreseeing that all his people and those of the Sioux and the other nations would be pushed still farther into the West by the spreading rails—even as it had happened after the bloody Sioux uprising at New Ulm six years before. Thunder Walker, too, was gone, vanished into the West, perhaps dead.

He was dozing when he heard one of the outer gates swing shut. He opened his eyes and looked down the walk. Jane was walking in on Dédé's arm; her laughter rang joyously into the hot afternoon. They had seen him and were coming across the lawn to where he sat. He could not help thinking how handsome they looked: Dédé with his soft, thick, wavy hair, his clear, unwavering blue eyes, his sensitive mouth, with a symmetry of features which could have come only from his mother; and Jane, with little of age about her, standing somewhat below their son's six feet, and the same pert, slight figure as always. It might have been yesterday that he had first stepped across the threshold of Rolette's home and confronted this vision! Beyond them, in the roadway, LeBrun was leading away Jane's white horse and the low phaeton in which they had been riding.

Jane bent and kissed him.

"Did you have a good ride?" he asked.

"Vair' nice," she assured him. "And I have such a good drivair!"

Dédé smiled indulgently.

Hercules looked at him soberly. "My boy, you have a responsibility in your mother, but don't let her seeming weakness deceive you. Your mother is a woman who knows what she wants, no matter how helpless she may seem."

Jane said, "All my life it seem' Mistaire Dousman has make such handsome speeches!"

"If you don't mind," said Dédé, "I'll go on to the house. I'll have to dress, you know." He set out at once.

Hercules shook his head. "Dress, dress—in my day . . ."

He was hushed gently by Jane. "In Mistaire Dousman's day he was dress' more than anyone else. He was dress' all the time. I know. It was always the firs' thing I thought about you. Why, Mistaire Dousman were dress' even when he go to see the Indians!"

Together they watched their son make his leisurely way across the veranda into the house. When he had gone, Hercules tightened his hold on Jane's hand and held her eyes with his own. There flowed between them now a deep current of affection and understanding, shadowed over by Hercules' illness.

"Are you satisfy' with him, Mistaire Dousman?"

"Need you ask?"

"I promise' Mistaire Dousman he will not be disappoint'. I am happy he is not." Then she added, more critically, "Mistaire Dousman know when the doctair was las' here, he forbade any exercise at all. We mus' be vair' careful."

He shook his head. "Jane, I couldn't be still. I wasn't made to sit quietly. I wasn't made just to enjoy wealth, as if it were an end in itself. It never is; it couldn't be. I must do as I must, and take the consequences."

A momentary paleness touched her cheeks. "The doctair have nevair been able to do anything with Mistaire Dousman. Pairhaps I mus' try again. I shall come and sit with you and stay with you and nevair let you out of my sight until you are bettair again."

He smiled at her, looking uneasily away. "We've been very happy, Jane. I don't think anyone could have been happier. Do you remember that first time I saw you?"

For a brittle moment they were lost in memory, the old years flowering between them. He thought suddenly of Emily, and said abruptly that he meant Emily and her husband to have another farm. "With seven children, they may need it. That one down past the French Cemetery. You know it, Jane."

"Yes. M'sieu' Rolette once own' that land."

"That's the place. Remind me in the morning to make out the papers."

She nodded. "Now I go to change my clothes. I will come right back and do what I say. Togethair we will see that you obey the doctair."

She kissed him. He held her to him a little while. Then he watched her walk away with a feeling of tranquillity, such as it seemed to him he had never known before. Perhaps he was, however incredible it might seem, getting better. With her going, the day's warmth made itself felt again. He turned his eyes to the wind-troubled water of the ponds.

He sat there in soothing quiet until he was sharply aware once more of the arrow of pain in his chest. He adjusted himself to ease his muscles, and leaned back his head so that he might look down the river to the western hills, where the sunlight lay hot and pale yellow.

LeBrun was there abruptly. "Mr. Dousman?"

"What is it?" he asked tiredly.

Behind LeBrun stood someone else, a stranger to Hercules. LeBrun turned to him, making an all-embracing gesture. "Mr.

Cowper would like to know the way to pronounce an Indian word he has."

"Ah," said Hercules, brightening, "let me see it."

Cowper handed him a paper upon which the word had been underlined. Hercules looked at it: an old treaty, he thought. "Accent on the third syllable," he murmured. "So: Pee-kee-*tol*-a-ka. Of course, you know the name of that river is now Pecatonica."

He did not hear Cowper's answer. Suddenly, fiercely, the pain inside him mushroomed up, spreading. Mechanically he repeated the Indian name. His mind transcended pain, flashing back to that time he had served on the council that had taken this land from the Winnebago; from there his instant thought became kaleidoscopic, embracing all his time, from Mackinac to the house on the mound, with so great a clarity that it might have lain there before him as grass and trees and ponds lay. He was conscious of a thousand memories.

He half-rose and began to fall forward. LeBrun was there, holding him in his arms, calling anxiously. In the moment before his eyes closed, he saw Jane running swiftly toward them from the house, and he thought peacefully, It will be all right now—Jane's coming. He took a deep, gasping breath; he smiled for Jane, and fell back into his chair.

He was dead.

So short had been the moment that only now the eagle above the western hills went swiftly down wind, screaming his challenge above the meeting place of the rivers, driving away from the mound, with the westerning sun red on his breast and no cloud in the sky.

Epilogue: The House

The house remained, changed a little here and there, but ever less than the country around the mound, the prairie of the Dog, where great locomotives came crying through the land, and winged armadas made by man passed high overhead through the domain of hawk and eagle, and houses spread east and north over the prairie.

Years diminished the acres, but not the place of the mound. The voracious river ate away a little of its earth, the grape arbors grew old, died, were leveled. Madame Jane followed Hercules. Dédé came with his lovely Nina to live in the house. Dédé died, leaving Nina with their children in the house. In time, Nina, too, died, and the children lived elsewhere.

The house was abandoned.

But the house, like the mound, endured. It withstood desertion, it defied neglect, it continued to stand, stanch and proud, beside the broad Mississippi, and, in the turning of the wheel, it was refurbished, took on new splendor, new life . . .

It became one with the mound. The mound took it unto itself, and the house became the mound . . .

A Note to the Reader

Essentially, the events—even to the minor details—of this narrative are historically accurate; but, in the interests of accuracy, it should be pointed out that while Hercules Dousman did indeed have a son named George, who was in the custody of Jean and Julia Brunet, while he did try to persuade the boy to come to live with him and even went to court to compel the Brunets to give him up, while the boy did run away and was never thereafter heard from, he was Hercules' son not by Cecile Gardepi, who is the creation of the writer, but of Margaret Campbell, who was, unhappily—or perhaps felicitously for the purpose of this narrative—disposed of too rapidly in this novel's predecessor, *Bright Journey*, to allow her time enough to have George. The author's first duty being to his fiction, Cecile Gardepi had to be invented.

Acknowledgments

This novel could not have been written without recourse to such books as: *Prairie du Chien,* by Peter Lawrence Scanlan; *Steamboating on the Upper Mississippi,* by William J. Petersen; *Old Times on the Upper Mississippi,* by George Byron Merrick; *Red Men Calling on the Great White Father,* by Katharine C. Turner; *James Duane Doty: Frontier Promoter,* by Alice E. Smith; *The Milwaukee Road,* by August Derleth; and the *Wisconsin Historical Collections;* and such papers as the letters of Hercules L. Dousman in the State Historical Library, and pertinent letters from Mrs. Virginia Dousman Bigelow. I want to acknowledge also, with gratitude, the able assistance of Miss Alice Conger, Mrs. Martha Grelle, Mr. and Mrs. Martin J. Dryud, Mrs. Florence Bittner, Benton Wilcox, and Paul Vanderbilt.

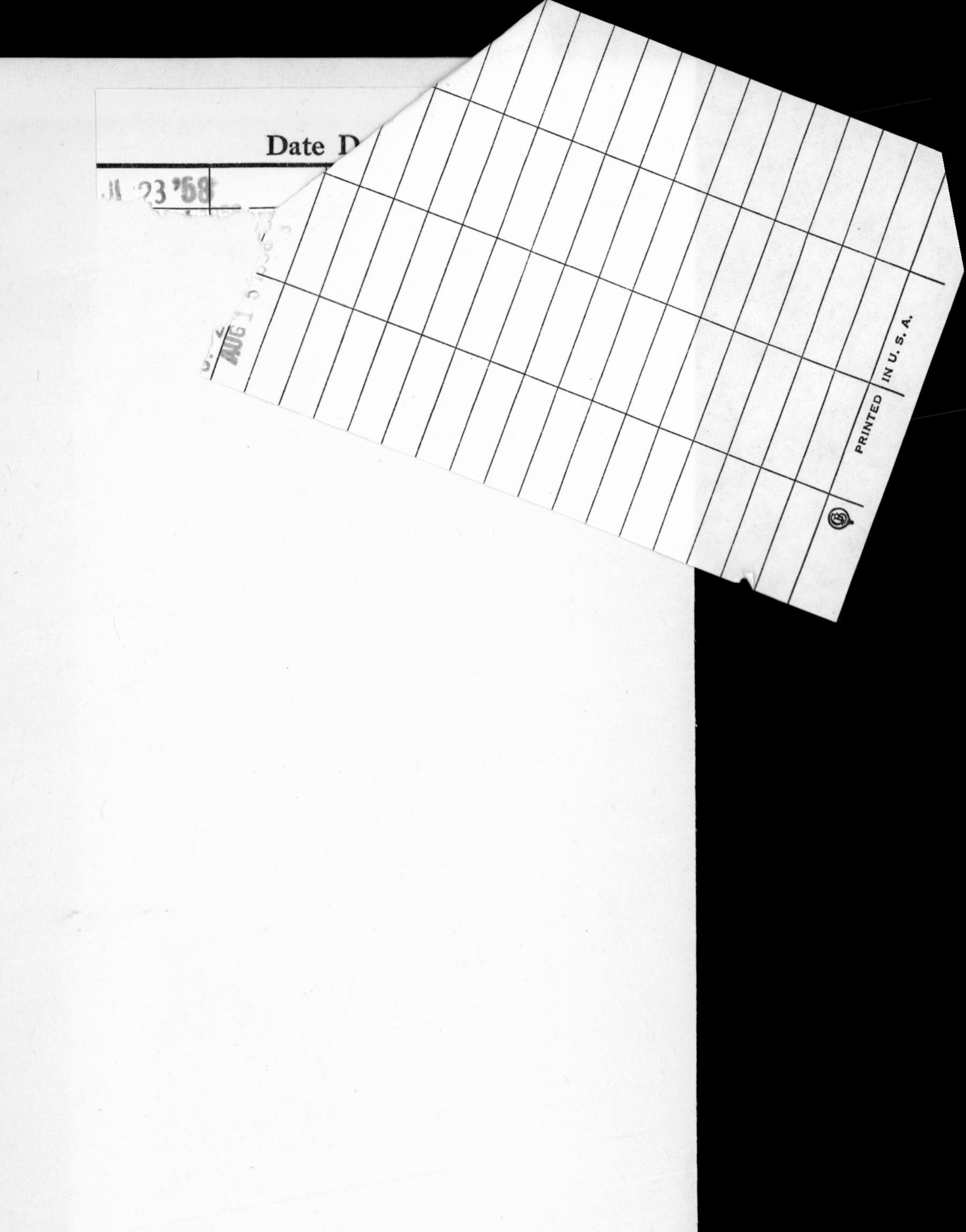
Date D
JL 23 '58
AUG 1 5
PRINTED IN U. S. A.